Let the games begin . . .

Over forty years ago, Robert Sheckley's "The Prize of Peril" was perhaps the first story to predict reality TV, as a man on a television show must try to stay alive for one week—while eluding hunters out to kill him.

Kate Wilhelm's brilliant, amazingly prescient "Ladies and Gentlemen, This Is Your Crisis!" depicts a "Survivor"-type reality-based TV show and its obsessed audience.

Allen Steele's "Her Own Private Sitcom" shows that everyone can become a star on reality TV—and what happens when their fans become disgusted with their narcissistic ways.

Alastair Reynolds's taut, fast-paced "Stroboscopic" merges computer games and daredevil exhibitions to produce a sport in which everything can change in the blink of an eye—sometimes with fatal results.

Jonathan Lethem's "How We Got in Town and Out Again" looks at an impoverished future America desperate for entertainment—and the down-and-outers desperate enough to provide it for them.

Vernor Vinge's "Synthetic Serendipity" shows us a rapidly approaching future in which the older generation is obsolete against tech-savvy Whiz Kids, who prove that boys will still be boys—especially when there are dangerous games to be played . . .

Edited by Jack Dann & Gardner Dozois

UNICORNS!
MAGICATS!
BESTIARY!
MERMAIDS!
SORCERERS!
DEMONS!
DOGTALES!
SEASERPENTS!
DINOSAURS!
LITTLE PEOPLE!
MAGICATS II
UNICORNS II
DRAGONS!
INVADERS!
HORSES!
ANGELS!

HACKERS
TIMEGATES
CLONES
IMMORTALS
NANOTECH
FUTURE WAR
GENOMETRY
SPACE SOLDIERS
FUTURE SPORTS
BEYOND FLESH
FUTURE CRIMES
A.I.S
ROBOTS
FUTURES PAST
DANGEROUS GAMES

DANGEROUS GAMES

EDITED BY

Jack Dann and Gardner Dozois

ACE BOOKS, NEW YORK

THE BERKLEY PUBLISHING GROUP
Published by the Penguin Group
Penguin Group (USA) Inc.
375 Hudson Street, New York, New York 10014, USA
Penguin Group (Canada), 90 Eglinton Avenue East, Suite 700, Toronto, Ontario M4P 2Y3, Canada
(a division of Pearson Penguin Canada Inc.)
Penguin Books Ltd., 80 Strand, London WC2R 0RL, England
Penguin Group Ireland, 25 St. Stephen's Green, Dublin 2, Ireland (a division of Penguin Books Ltd.)
Penguin Group (Australia), 250 Camberwell Road, Camberwell, Victoria 3124, Australia
(a division of Pearson Australia Group Pty. Ltd.)
Penguin Books India Pvt. Ltd., 11 Community Centre, Panchsheel Park, New Delhi—110 017, India
Penguin Group (NZ), 67 Apollo Drive, Mairangi Bay, Auckland 1311, New Zealand
(a division of Pearson New Zealand Ltd.)
Penguin Books (South Africa) (Pty.) Ltd., 24 Sturdee Avenue, Rosebank, Johannesburg 2196,
South Africa

Penguin Books Ltd., Registered Offices: 80 Strand, London WC2R 0RL, England

DANGEROUS GAMES

An Ace Book / published by arrangement with the authors

PRINTING HISTORY
Ace mass-market edition / April 2007

Cover art by axb group. Cover design by Rita Frangie.
Art for "The Ichneumon and the Dormeuse" © 1995 by Terry Dowling.
Interior text design by Tiffany Estreicher.

ISBN: 978-0-441-01490-3

ACE
Ace Books are published by The Berkley Publishing Group,
a division of Penguin Group (USA) Inc.,
375 Hudson Street, New York, New York 10014.
ACE and the "A" design are trademarks belonging to Penguin Group (USA) Inc.

PRINTED IN THE UNITED STATES OF AMERICA

10 9 8 7 6 5 4 3 2 1

ACKNOWLEDGMENT IS MADE FOR PERMISSION TO REPRINT THE FOLLOWING MATERIAL:

"The Prize of Peril," by Robert Sheckley. Copyright © 1958 by Mercury Press, Inc. First published in *The Magazine of Fantasy & Science Fiction,* May 1958. Reprinted by permission of the author's estate.

"Anda's Game," by Cory Doctorow. Copyright © 2004 by Cory Doctorow. First published electronically in *Salon,* November 15, 2004. Reprinted by permission of the author.

"Ladies and Gentlemen, This Is Your Crisis!," by Kate Wilhelm. Copyright © 1976 by Damon Knight. First published in *Orbit 18* (Putnam), edited by Damon Knight. Reprinted by permission of the author.

"Stroboscopic," by Alastair Reynolds. Copyright © 1998 by *Interzone.* First published in *Interzone,* August 1998. Reprinted by permission of the author.

"Synthetic Serendipity," by Vernor Vinge. Copyright © 2004 by Vernor Vinge. First published electronically on *IEEESpectrum-online,* July 31, 2005. Reprinted by permission of the author.

"How We Got in Town and Out Again," by Jonathan Lethem. Copyright © 1996 by Dell Magazines. First published in *Asimov's Science Fiction,* September 1996. Reprinted by permission of the author.

"Red Sonja and Lessingham in Dreamland," by Gwyneth Jones. Copyright © 1996 by Gwyneth Jones. First published in *Off Limits* (St. Martin's Press), edited by Ellen Datlow. Reprinted by permission of the author.

"The Halfway House at the Heart of Darkness," by William Browning Spencer. Copyright © 1998 by William Browning Spencer. First published in *Lord of the Fantastic* (Avon Eos), edited by Martin H. Greenberg. Reprinted by permission of the author.

"Her Own Private Sitcom," by Allen Steele. Copyright © 1999 by Dell Magazines. First published in *Analog Science Fiction and Fact,* January 1999. Reprinted by permission of the author.

"The Ichneumon and the Dormeuse," by Terry Dowling. Copyright © 1996 by *Interzone*. First published in *Interzone,* April 1996. Reprinted by permission of the author.

"Winning Mars," by Jason Stoddard. Copyright © 2005 by *Interzone*. First published in *Interzone,* January/February 2005. Reprinted by permission of the author.

CONTENTS

PREFACE

Playing games is one of the things that makes us human, and goes back thousands of thousands of years into the blurry depths of prehistory; games resembling chess and checkers and Go or "Chinese checkers" have been found in the ruins of vanished civilizations from Egypt to China to Sumer, and crude dice made from animal bones have been found in caves lived in by Ice Age hunters. Who knows what games were played that left no trace behind in the archeological record? My guess is that some sort of chase-and-catch games, the ancestors of soccer and football, were played wherever there were the combination of good summer weather, an empty meadow, and restless hunters still charged up from the hunt, and those long nights huddled around an Ice Age fire had to be filled *somehow,* if not with dice, then with cards (which probably would leave no trace behind, but which likely have a heritage almost as old as dice), or word-games, or the kinds of finger-games such as "Paper, Scissors, Stone" or "Thumb War" that may well go back to a time before there were such things as paper or scissors ("Mammoth, Spear, Stone," perhaps?).

All games are *competitions,* though, which implies a

winner and a loser. And the best games are those that have an element of *risk* involved in them. The more dangerous they are, in fact, the more the loser has at stake, the better we like them. And the ultimate stake is life itself.

Even today, in spite of living in a safety-obsessed culture where every jar and bottle has a warning label on it and every car comes equipped with air-bags and seat-belts—or maybe *because* we live in such a culture—people like dangerous games, as witness the development and sudden popularity of "Extreme Sports," and the more dangerous they are, the more popular they are as well. It only takes a slight heightening of conditions to imagine a game where there's not just risk, but a certainty of death for one competitor or another, like the Roman gladiatorial games, and science fiction writers have been coming up with just such scenarios, like Frederic Pohl and C.M. Kornbluth's *Gladiator-At-Law,* for decades now.

Another parallel social development predicted long ago by SF writers is the "Reality Show," and stories such as Robert Sheckley's "The Prize of Peril" and "The Seventh Victim" and Kate Wilhelm's "Ladies and Gentlemen, This Is Your Crisis!" that strongly resemble shows such as *Survivor*, were around long before "reality television" was even a gleam in a TV producer's eye. As was the idea that *every moment* of your life would not only be observed but would become fodder for entertainment television. This is a version of *1984* that never occurred to Orwell—that people would not only *want* Big Brother to watch them, but that *other people* would find it fascinating to watch too, so that today you not only are watched by security cameras every time you go into a bank or a store or a gas station or even walk down the street—with nobody objecting to this—but people willingly take web-cams into their *bedrooms* as well and record themselves having sex to broadcast to wide audiences on the internet. Some of the most popular shows on television involve "ordinary people" under 24-hour-a-day scrutiny by the cameras.

All this seems weird enough to old dinosaurs like your

editors who grew up in the '50s, but where is it going to go and what's going to happen *next*, in the future? Our intuition is that you ain't seen *nothing* yet.

So open up this book and let some of SF's most expert dreamers show you eleven extreme and radical games that people in the future will play. Dangerous games. Games more addictive than heroin, and just as deadly. Games that will take you completely out of this world and into fantastical and fabulous realms of your own creation, where the dangers are still as real as a knife in the dark. Games that will become the hit TV shows of the future and will boil couch potatoes everywhere in their skins. Games that affect reality itself, where your success or failure in life depends on your gaming skills. Games that will take you to Mars and to the icy darkness of the outer Solar System. Games that you *can't* stop playing, even if you want to.

Dangerous games. Games to die for—quite literally.

Enjoy! The game is afoot!

THE PRIZE OF PERIL

Robert Sheckley

The late Robert Sheckley was one of science fiction's premiere satirists and humorists, rivaled for that title only by Kurt Vonnegut and Douglas Adams (who was himself clearly influenced by Sheckley), and he was more prolific than either of them, particularly at shorter lengths, turning out hundreds of short stories over the course of his fifty-three year career. Sheckley sold his first novel, Immortality, Inc., *in 1958, and followed it up over the years with other novels such as* Dimension of Miracles, Mindswap, The Status Civilization, Journey Beyond Tomorrow, Watchbird, Journey of Joenes, The 10th Victim, Hunter/Victim, Victim Prime, *and* Godshome. *He has also written five mystery novels as Stephen Dain, three "Hob Draconian" mysteries under his own name, a* Babylon 5 *novel, and three novels in collaboration with Roger Zelazny,* Bring Me the Head of Prince Charming, A Farce to Be Reckoned With, *and* If at Faust You Don't Succeed. *His many short stories have been collected in* Can You Feel Anything When I Do This?, Citizen in Space, Notions: Unlimited, The People Trap and Other Pitfalls, Pilgrimage to Earth, Shards of Space, The Robot Who Looked Like Me, Untouched by Human Hands, *and others. His last book was a massive retrospective collection,* The Masque of Manana. *He was named Author Emeritus by the Science Fiction Writers of America in 2001. He died in 2005.*

Two of his most famous stories, "The Seventh Victim" and the story that follows, "The Prize of Peril," predicted the twin crazes of reality TV and Adventure Gaming more than forty years before they actually came into existence—and still bear palpable stings in their sleek and shiny tails even to this very day.

RAEDER lifted his head cautiously above the windowsill. He saw the fire-escape, and below it a narrow alley. There was a weather-beaten baby carriage in the alley and three garbage cans. As he watched, a black-sleeved arm moved from behind the furthest can, with something shiny in its fist. Raeder ducked down. A bullet smashed through the window above his head and punctured the ceiling, showering him with plaster.

Now he knew about the alley. It was guarded, just like the door.

He lay at full length on the cracked linoleum, staring at the bullet hole in the ceiling, listening to the sounds outside the door. He was a tall man with bloodshot eyes and a two-day stubble. Grime and fatigue had etched lines into his face. Fear had touched his features, tightening a muscle here and twitching a nerve there. The results were startling. His face had character now, for it was reshaped by the expectation of death.

There was a gunman in the alley and two on the stairs. He was trapped. He was dead.

Sure, Raeder thought, he still moved and breathed, but that was only because of death's inefficiency. Death would take care of him in a few minutes. Death would poke holes in his face and body, artistically dab his clothes with blood, arrange his limbs in some grotesque position of the graveyard ballet . . .

Raeder bit his lip sharply. He wanted to live. There had to be a way.

He rolled onto his stomach and surveyed the dingy cold-water apartment into which the killers had driven him. It was a perfect little one-room coffin. It had a door, which was watched, and a fire escape, which was watched. And it had a tiny windowless bathroom.

He crawled to the bathroom and stood up. There was a ragged hole in the ceiling, almost four inches wide. If he could enlarge it, crawl through into the apartment above . . .

He heard a muffled thud. The killers were impatient. They were beginning to break down the door.

He studied the hole in the ceiling. No use even considering it. He could never enlarge it in time.

They were smashing against the door, grunting each time they struck. Soon the lock would tear out, or the hinges would pull out of the rotting wood. The door would go down, and the two blank-faced men would enter, dusting off their jackets . . .

But surely someone would help him! He took the tiny television set from his pocket. The picture was blurred, and he didn't bother to adjust it. The audio was clear and precise.

He listened to the well-modulated voice of Mike Terry addressing his vast audience.

". . . terrible spot," Terry was saying. "Yes, folks, Jim Raeder is in a truly terrible predicament. He had been hiding, you'll remember, in a third-rate Broadway hotel under an assumed name. It seemed safe enough. But the bellhop recognized him, and gave that information to the Thompson gang."

The door creaked under repeated blows. Raeder clutched the little television set and listened.

"Jim Raeder just managed to escape from the hotel! Closely pursued, he entered a brownstone at one fifty-six West End Avenue. His intention was to go over the roofs. And it might have worked, folks, it just might have worked. But the roof door was locked. It looked like the end . . . But Raeder found that apartment seven was unoccupied and unlocked. He entered . . ."

Terry paused for emphasis, then cried—*"and now he's trapped there, trapped like a rat in a cage! The Thompson gang is breaking down the door! The fire escape is guarded! Our camera crew, situated in a nearby building, is giving you a close-up now. Look, folks, just look! Is there no hope for Jim Raeder?"*

Is there no hope? Raeder silently echoed, perspiration pouring from him as he stood in the dark, stifling little bathroom, listening to the steady thud against the door.

"Wait a minute!" Mike Terry cried. *"Hang on, Jim Raeder, hang on a little longer. Perhaps there is hope! I have an urgent call from one of our viewers, a call on the Good Samaritan Line! Here's someone who thinks he can help you, Jim. Are you listening, Jim Raeder?"*

Raeder waited, and heard the hinges tearing out of rotten wood.

"Go right ahead, sir," said Mike Terry. *"What is your name, sir?"*

"Er—Felix Bartholemew."

"Don't be nervous, Mr. Bartholemew. Go right ahead."

"Well, okay. Mr. Raeder," said an old man's shaking voice, *"I used to live at one five six West End Avenue. Same apartment you're trapped in, Mr. Raeder—fact! Look, that bathroom has got a window, Mr. Raeder. It's been painted over, but it has got a—"*

Raeder pushed the television set into his pocket. He located the outlines of the window and kicked. Glass shattered, and daylight poured startlingly in. He cleared the jagged sill and quickly peered down.

Below was a long drop to a concrete courtyard.

The hinges tore free. He heard the door opening. Quickly Raeder climbed through the window, hung by his fingertips for a moment, and dropped.

The shock was stunning. Groggily he stood up. A face appeared at the bathroom window.

"Tough luck," said the man, leaning out and taking careful aim with a snub-nosed .38.

At that moment a smoke bomb exploded inside the bathroom.

The killer's shot went wide. He turned, cursing. More

smoke bombs burst in the courtyard, obscuring Raeder's figure.

He could hear Mike Terry's frenzied voice over the TV set in his pocket. *"Now run for it!"* Terry was screaming. *"Run, Jim Raeder, run for your life. Run now, while the killers' eyes are filled with smoke. And thank Good Samaritan Sarah Winters, of three four one two Edgar Street, Brockton, Mass., for donating five smoke bombs and employing the services of a man to throw them!"* In a quieter voice, Terry continued. *"You've saved a man's life today, Mrs. Winters. Would you tell our audience how it—"* Raeder wasn't able to hear any more. He was running through the smoke-filled courtyard, past clotheslines, into the open street.

* * *

HE walked down 63rd Street, slouching to minimize his height, staggering slightly from exertion, dizzy from lack of food and sleep.

"Hey, you!"

Raeder turned. A middle-aged woman was sitting on the steps of a brownstone, frowning at him.

"You're Raeder, aren't you? The one they're trying to kill?"

Raeder started to walk away.

"Come inside here, Raeder," the woman said.

Perhaps it was a trap. But Raeder knew that he had to depend upon the generosity and good-heartedness of the people. He was their representative, a projection of themselves, an average guy in trouble. Without them, he was lost. With them, nothing could harm him.

Trust in the people, Mike Terry had told him. They'll never let you down.

He followed the woman into her parlor. She told him to sit down and left the room, returning almost immediately with a plate of stew. She stood watching him while he ate, as one would watch an ape in the zoo eat peanuts.

Two children came out of the kitchen and stared at him.

Three overalled men came out of the bedroom and focused a television camera on him. There was a big television set in the parlor. As he gulped his food, Raeder watched the image of Mike Terry and listened to the man's strong, sincere, worried voice.

"There he is, folks," Terry was saying. *"There's Jim Raeder now, eating his first square meal in two days. Our camera crews have really been working to cover this for you! Thanks, boys . . . Folks, Jim Raeder has been given a brief sanctuary by Mrs. Velma O'Dell, of three forty-three Sixty-Third Street. Thank you, Good Samaritan O'Dell! It's really wonderful how people from all walks of life have taken Jim Raeder to their hearts!"*

"You better hurry," Mrs. O'Dell said.

"Yes, ma'am," Raeder said.

"I don't want no gunplay in my apartment."

"I'm almost finished, ma'am."

One of the children asked, "Aren't they going to kill him?"

"Shut up," said Mrs. O'Dell.

"Yes, Jim," chanted Mike Terry. *"You'd better hurry. Your killers aren't far behind. They aren't stupid men, Jim. Vicious, warped, insane—yes! But not stupid. They're following a trail of blood—blood from your torn hand, Jim!"*

Raeder hadn't realized until now that he'd cut his hand on the windowsill.

"Here, I'll bandage that," Mrs. O'Dell said. Raeder stood up and let her bandage his hand. Then she gave him a brown jacket and a gray slouch hat.

"My husband's stuff," she said.

"He has a disguise, folks!" Mike Terry cried delightedly. *"This is something new! A disguise! With seven hours to go until he's safe!"*

"Now get out of here," Mrs. O'Dell said.

"I'm going, ma'am," Raeder said. "Thanks."

"I think you're stupid," she said. "I think you're stupid to be involved in this."

"Yes, ma'am."

"It just isn't worth it."

Raeder thanked her and left. He walked to Broadway, caught a subway to 59th Street, then an uptown local to 86th. There he bought a newspaper and changed for the Manhasset through-express.

He glanced at his watch. He had six and a half hours to go.

* * *

THE subway roared under Manhattan. Raeder dozed, his bandaged hand concealed under the newspaper, the hat pulled over his face. Had he been recognized yet? Had he shaken the Thompson gang? Or was someone telephoning them now?

Dreamily he wondered if he had escaped death, or was he still a cleverly animated corpse, moving around because of death's inefficiency? (My dear, death is so *laggard* these days! Jim Raeder walked about for hours after he died and actually answered people's *questions* before he could be decently buried!)

Raeder's eyes snapped open. He had dreamed something . . . unpleasant. He couldn't remember what.

He closed his eyes again and remembered, with mild astonishment, a time when he had been in no trouble.

That was two years ago. He had been a big, pleasant young man working as a truck driver's helper. He had no talents. He was too modest to have dreams.

The tight-faced little truck driver had the dreams for him. "Why not try for a television show, Jim? I would if I had your looks. They like nice, average guys with nothing much on the ball. As contestants. Everybody likes guys like that. Why not look into it?"

So he had looked into it. The owner of the local television store had explained it further.

"You see, Jim, the public is sick of highly trained athletes with their trick reflexes and their professional courage. Who can feel for guys like that? Who can identify? People want to watch exciting things, sure, but not when some joker is making it his business for fifty thousand a year. That's why organized sports are in a slump. That's why the thrill shows are booming."

"I see," said Raeder.

"Six years ago, Jim, Congress passed the Voluntary Suicide Act. Those old senators talked a lot about free will and self-determinism at the time. But that's all crap. You know what the Act really means? It means the amateurs can risk their lives for the big loot, not just professionals. In the old days you had to be a professional boxer or footballer or hockey player if you wanted your brains beaten out legally for money. But now that opportunity is open to ordinary people like you, Jim."

"I see," Raeder said again.

"It's a marvelous opportunity. Take you. You're no better than anyone, Jim. Anything you can do, anyone can do. You're *average*. I think the thrill shows would go for you."

Raeder permitted himself to dream. Television shows looked like a sure road to riches for a pleasant young fellow with no particular talent or training. He wrote a letter to a show called *Hazard* and enclosed a photograph of himself.

Hazard was interested in him. The JBC network investigated, and found that he was average enough to satisfy the wariest viewer. His parentage and affiliations were checked. At last he was summoned to New York and interviewed by Mr. Moulain.

Moulain was dark and intense, and chewed gum as he talked. "You'll do," he snapped. "But not for *Hazard*. You'll appear on *Spills*. It's a half-hour daytime show on Channel Three."

"Gee," said Raeder.

"Don't thank me. There's a thousand dollars if you win or place second, and a consolation prize of a hundred dollars if you lose. But that's not important."

"No, sir."

"*Spills* is a little show. The JBC network uses it as a testing ground. First and second-place winners on *Spills* move on to *Emergency*. The prizes are much bigger on *Emergency*."

"I know they are, sir."

"And if you do well on *Emergency,* there are the first-class thrill shows, like *Hazard* and *Underwater Perils,* with their nationwide coverage and enormous prizes. And then comes the really big time. How far you go is up to you."

"I'll do my best, sir," Raeder said.

Moulain stopped chewing gum for a moment and said, almost reverently, "You can do it, Jim. Just remember. You're *the people*, and *the people* can do anything."

The way he said it made Raeder feel momentarily sorry for Mr. Moulain, who was dark and frizzy-haired and pop-eyed, and was obviously not *the people*.

They shook hands. Then Raeder signed a paper absolving the JBC of all responsibility should he lose his life, limbs, or reason during the contest. And he signed another paper exercising his rights under the Voluntary Suicide Act. The law required this, and it was a mere formality.

In three weeks, he appeared on *Spills*.

The program followed the classic form of the automobile race. Untrained drivers climbed into powerful American and European competition cars and raced over a murderous twenty-mile course. Raeder was shaking with fear as he slid his big Maserati into the wrong gear and took off.

The race was a screaming, tire-burning nightmare. Raeder stayed back, letting the early leaders smash themselves up on the counterbanked hairpin turns. He crept into third place when a Jaguar in front of him swerved against an Alfa-Romeo and the two cars roared into a plowed field. Raeder gunned for second place on the last three miles, but couldn't find passing room. An S-curve almost took him, but he fought the car back on the road, still holding third. Then the lead driver broke a crankshaft in the final fifty yards, and Jim ended in second place.

He was now a thousand dollars ahead. He received four fan letters, and a lady in Oshkosh sent him a pair of argyles. He was invited to appear on *Emergency*.

Unlike the others, *Emergency* was not a competition-type program. It stressed individual initiative. For the show, Raeder was knocked out with a nonhabit-forming narcotic. He awoke in the cockpit of a small airplane, cruising on autopilot at ten thousand feet. His fuel gauge showed nearly empty. He had no parachute. He was supposed to land the plane.

Of course, he had never flown before.

He experimented gingerly with the controls, remembering that last week's participant had recovered consciousness in a submarine, had opened the wrong valve, and had drowned.

Thousands of viewers watched spellbound as this average man, a man just like themselves, struggled with the situation just as they would do. Jim Raeder was *them*. Anything he could do, they could do. He was representative of *the people*.

Raeder managed to bring the ship down in some semblance of a landing. He flipped over a few times, but his seat belt held. And the engine, contrary to expectation, did not burst into flames.

He staggered out with two broken ribs, three thousand dollars, and a chance, when he healed, to appear on *Torero*.

At last, a first-class thrill show! *Torero* paid ten thousand dollars. All you had to do was kill a black Miura bull with a sword, just like a real, trained matador.

The fight was held in Madrid, since bullfighting was still illegal in the United States. It was nationally televised.

Raeder had a good cuadrilla. They liked the big, slow-moving American. The picadors really leaned into their lances, trying to slow the bull for him. The banderilleros tried to run the beast off his feet before driving in their banderillas. And the second matador, a mournful man from Algiceras, almost broke the bull's neck with fancy cape-work.

But when all was said and done, it was Jim Raeder on the sand, a red muleta clumsily gripped in his left hand, a sword in his right, facing a ton of black, blood-streaked, wide-horned bull.

Someone was shouting, "Try for the lung, *hombre.* Don't be a hero, stick him in the lung." But Jim only knew what the technical advisor in New York had told him: Aim with the sword and go in over the horns.

Over he went. The sword bounced off bone, and the bull tossed him over its back. He stood up, miraculously un-gouged, took another sword and went over the horns again with his eyes closed. The god who protects children and fools must have been watching, for the sword slid in like a needle through butter, and the bull looked startled, stared at him unbelievingly, and dropped like a deflated balloon.

They paid him ten thousand dollars, and his broken collarbone healed in practically no time. He received twenty-three fan letters, including a passionate invitation from a girl in Atlantic City, which he ignored. And they asked him if he wanted to appear on another show.

He had lost some of his innocence. He was now fully aware that he had been almost killed for pocket money. The big loot lay ahead. Now he wanted to be almost killed for something worthwhile.

So he appeared on *Underwater Perils,* sponsored by Fairlady's Soap. In face mask, respirator, weighted belt, flippers and knife, he slipped into the warm waters of the Caribbean with four other contestants, followed by a cage-protected camera crew. The idea was to locate and bring up a treasure which the sponsor had hidden there.

Mask diving isn't especially hazardous. But the sponsor had added some frills for public interest. The area was sown with giant clams, moray eels, sharks of several species, giant octopuses, poison coral, and other dangers of the deep.

It was a stirring contest. A man from Florida found the treasure in a deep crevice, but a moray eel found him. Another diver took the treasure, and a shark took him. The brilliant blue-green water became cloudy with blood, which photographed well on color TV. The treasure slipped to the bottom, and Raeder plunged after it, popping an eardrum in the process. He plucked it from the coral, jettisoned his weighted belt and made for the surface. Thirty feet from the top he had to fight another diver for the treasure.

They feinted back and forth with their knives. The man struck, slashing Raeder across the chest. But Raeder, with the self-possession of an old contestant, dropped his knife and tore the man's respirator out of his mouth.

That did it. Raeder surfaced and presented the treasure at the standby boat. It turned out to be a package of Fairlady's Soap—"The Greatest Treasure of All."

That netted him twenty-two thousand dollars in cash and prizes, and three hundred and eight fan letters, and an interesting proposition from a girl in Macon, which he seriously considered. He received free hospitalization for his knife slash and burst eardrum, and injections for coral infection.

But best of all, he was invited to appear on the biggest of the thrill shows. *The Prize of Peril.*

And that was when the real trouble began . . .

The subway came to a stop, jolting him out of his reverie. Raeder pushed back his hat and observed, across the aisle, a man staring at him and whispering to a stout woman. Had they recognized him?

He stood up as soon as the doors opened, and glanced at his watch. He had five hours to go.

* * *

AT the Manhasset station, he stepped into a taxi and told the driver to take him to New Salem.

"New Salem?" the driver asked, looking at him in the rear-vision mirror.

"That's right."

The driver snapped on his radio. "Fare to New Salem. Yep, that's right. *New Salem.*" They drove off. Raeder frowned, wondering if it had been a signal. It was perfectly usual for taxi drivers to report to their dispatchers, of course. But something about the man's voice . . .

"Let me off here," Raeder said.

He paid the driver and began walking down a narrow

country road that curved through sparse woods. The trees were too small and too widely separated for shelter. Raeder walked on, looking for a place to hide.

There was a heavy truck approaching. He kept on walking, pulling his hat low on his forehead. But as the truck drew near, he heard a voice from the television set in his pocket. It cried, *"Watch out!"*

He flung himself into the ditch. The truck careened past, narrowly missing him, and screeched to a stop. The driver was shouting, "There he goes! Shoot, Harry, shoot!"

Bullets clipped leaves from the trees as Raeder sprinted into the woods.

"It's happened again!" Mike Terry was saying, his voice high-pitched with excitement. *"I'm afraid Jim Raeder let himself be lulled into a false sense of security. You can't do that, Jim! Not with your life at stake! Not with killers pursuing you! Be careful, Jim, you still have four and a half hours to go!"*

The driver was saying, "Claude, Harry, go around with the truck. We got him boxed."

"They've got you boxed, Jim Raeder!" Mike Terry cried. *"But they haven't got you yet! And you can thank Good Samaritan Susy Peters of twelve Elm Street, South Orange, New Jersey, for that warning shout just when the truck was bearing down on you. We'll have little Susy on stage in just a moment . . . Look, folks, our studio helicopter has arrived on the scene. Now you can see Jim Raeder running, and the killers pursuing, surrounding him . . ."*

Raeder ran through a hundred yards of woods and found himself on a concrete highway, with open woods beyond. One of the killers was trotting through the woods behind him. The truck had driven to a connecting road and was now a mile away, coming toward him.

A car was approaching from the other direction. Raeder ran into the highway, waving frantically. The car came to a stop.

"Hurry!" cried the blond young woman driving it.

Raeder dived in. The woman made a U-turn on the

highway. A bullet smashed through the windshield. She stamped on the accelerator, almost running down the lone killer who stood in the way.

The car surged away before the truck was within firing range.

Raeder leaned back and shut his eyes tightly. The woman concentrated on her driving, watching for the truck in her rear-vision mirror.

"*It's happened again!*" cried Mike Terry, his voice ecstatic. "*Jim Raeder has been plucked again from the jaws of death, thanks to Good Samaritan Janice Morrow of four three three Lexington Avenue, New York City. Did you ever see anything like it, folks? The way Miss Morrow drove through a fusillade of bullets and plucked Jim Raeder from the mouth of doom! Later we'll interview Miss Morrow and get her reactions. Now, while Jim Raeder speeds away—perhaps to safety, perhaps to further peril—we'll have a short announcement from our sponsor. Don't go away! Jim's got four hours and ten minutes until he's safe: Anything can happen!*"

"Okay," the girl said. "We're off the air now. Raeder, what in the hell is the matter with you?"

"Eh?" Raeder asked. The girl was in her early twenties. She looked efficient, attractive, untouchable. Raeder noticed that she had good features, a trim figure. And he noticed that she seemed angry.

"Miss," he said, "I don't know how to thank you for—"

"Talk straight," Janice Morrow said. "I'm no Good Samaritan. I'm employed by the JBC network."

"So the program had me rescued!"

"Cleverly reasoned," she said.

"But why?"

"Look, this is an expensive show, Raeder. We have to turn in a good performance. If our rating slips, we'll all be in the street selling candy apples. And you aren't cooperating."

"What? Why?"

"Because you're terrible," the girl said bitterly. "You're

a flop, a fiasco. Are you trying to commit suicide? Haven't you learned *anything* about survival?"

"I'm doing the best I can."

"The Thompsons could have had you a dozen times by now. We told them to take it easy, stretch it out. But it's like shooting a clay pigeon six feet tall. The Thompsons are co-operating, but they can only fake so far. If I hadn't come along, they'd have had to kill you—air-time or not."

Raeder stared at her, wondering how such a pretty girl could talk that way. She glanced at him, then quickly looked back to the road.

"Don't give me that look!" she said. "You chose to risk your life for money, buster. And plenty of money! You knew the score. Don't act like some innocent little grocer who finds the nasty hoods are after him. That's a different plot."

"I know," Raeder said.

"If you can't live well, at least try to die well."

"You don't mean that," Raeder said.

"Don't be too sure . . . You've got three hours and forty minutes until the end of the show. If you can stay alive, fine. The boodle's yours. But if you can't, at least try to give them a run for the money."

Raeder nodded, staring intently at her.

"In a few moments we're back on the air. I develop engine trouble, let you off. The Thompsons go all out now. They kill you when and if they can, as soon as they can. Understand?"

"Yes," Raeder said. "If I make it, can I see you some time?"

She bit her lip angrily. "Are you trying to kid me?"

"No. I'd like to see you again. May I?"

She looked at him curiously. "I don't know. Forget it. We're almost on. I think your best bet is the woods to the right. Ready?"

"Yes. Where can I get in touch with you? Afterward, I mean."

"Oh, Raeder, you aren't paying attention. Go through

the woods until you find a washed-out ravine. It isn't much, but it'll give you some cover."

"Where can I get in touch with you?" Raeder asked again.

"I'm in the Manhattan telephone book." She stopped the car. "Okay, Raeder, start running."

He opened the door.

"Wait." She leaned over and kissed him on the lips. "Good luck, you idiot. Call me if you make it."

And then he was on foot, running into the woods.

* * *

HE ran through birch and pine, past an occasional split-level house with staring faces at the big picture windows. Some occupant of those houses must have called the gang, for they were close behind him when he reached the washed-out little ravine. Those quiet, mannerly, law-abiding people didn't want him to escape, Raeder thought sadly. They wanted to see a killing. Or perhaps they wanted to see him *narrowly escape* a killing.

It came to the same thing, really.

He entered the ravine, burrowed into the thick underbrush and lay still. The Thompsons appeared on both ridges, moving slowly, watching for any movement. Raeder held his breath as they came parallel to him.

He heard the quick explosion of a revolver. But the killer had only shot a squirrel. It squirmed for a moment, then lay still.

Lying in the underbrush, Raeder heard the studio helicopter overhead. He wondered if any cameras were focused on him. It was possible. And if someone were watching, perhaps some Good Samaritan would help.

So looking upward, toward the helicopter, Raeder arranged his face in a reverent expression, clasped his hands and prayed. He prayed silently, for the audience didn't like religious ostentation. But his lips moved. That was every man's privilege.

And a real prayer was on his lips. Once, a lipreader in

the audience had detected a fugitive *pretending* to pray, but actually just reciting multiplication tables. No help for that man!

Raeder finished his prayer. Glancing at his watch, he saw that he had nearly two hours to go.

And he didn't want to die. It wasn't worth it, no matter how much they paid! He must have been crazy, absolutely insane to agree to such a thing . . .

But he knew that wasn't true. And he remembered just how sane he had been.

* * *

ONE week ago, he had been on *The Prize of Peril* stage, blinking in the spotlight, and Mike Terry had shaken his hand.

"Now, Mr. Raeder," Terry had said solemnly, "do you understand the rules of the game you are about to play?"

Raeder nodded.

"If you accept, Jim Raeder, you will be a *hunted man* for a week. *Killers* will follow you, Jim. *Trained* killers, men wanted by the law for other crimes, granted immunity for this single killing under the Voluntary Suicide Act. They will be trying to kill *you,* Jim. Do you understand?"

"I understand," Raeder said. He also understood the two hundred thousand dollars he would receive if he could live out the week.

"I ask you again, Jim Raeder. We force no man to play for stakes of death."

"I want to play," Raeder said.

Mike Terry turned to the audience. "Ladies and gentlemen, I have here a copy of an exhaustive psychological test which an impartial psychological testing firm made on Jim Raeder at our request. Copies will be sent to anyone who desires them for twenty-five cents to cover the cost of mailing. The test shows that Jim Raeder is sane, well-balanced and fully responsible in every way." He turned to Raeder.

"Do you still want to enter the contest, Jim?"

"Yes, I do."

"Very well!" cried Mike Terry. "Jim Raeder, meet your would-be killers!"

The Thompson gang moved onstage, booed by the audience.

"Look at them, folks," said Mike Terry, with undisguised contempt. "Just look at them! Antisocial, thoroughly vicious, completely amoral. These men have no code but the criminal's warped code, no honor but the honor of the cowardly hired killer. They are doomed men, doomed by our society, which will not sanction their activities for long, fated to an early and unglamorous death."

The audience shouted enthusiastically.

"What have you to say, Claude Thompson?" Terry asked.

Claude, the spokesman of the Thompsons, stepped up to the microphone. He was a thin, clean-shaved man, conservatively dressed.

"I figure," Claude Thompson said hoarsely, "I figure we're no worse than anybody. I mean, like soldiers in a war: *They* kill. And look at the graft in government, and the unions. Everybody's got their graft."

That was Thompson's tenuous code. But how quickly, with what precision, Mike Terry destroyed the killer's rationalizations! Terry's questions pierced straight to the filthy soul of the man.

At the end of the interview, Claude Thompson was perspiring, mopping his face with a silk handkerchief and casting quick glances at his men.

Mike Terry put a hand on Raeder's shoulder. "Here is the man who has agreed to become your victim—if you can catch him."

"We'll catch him," Thompson said, his confidence returning.

"Don't be too sure," said Terry. "Jim Raeder has fought wild bulls—now he battles jackals. He's an average man. He's *the people*—who mean ultimate doom to you and your kind."

"We'll get him," Thompson said.

"And one thing more," Terry said, very softly. "Jim Raeder does not stand alone. The folks of America are for him. Good Samaritans from all corners of our great nation stand ready to assist him. Unarmed, defenseless, Jim Raeder can count on the aid and goodheartedness of *the people,* whose representative he is. So don't be too sure, Claude Thompson! The average men are for Jim Raeder—and there are a lot of average men!"

* * *

RAEDER thought about it, lying motionless in the underbrush. Yes, *the people* had helped him. But they had helped the killers, too.

A tremor ran through him. He had chosen, he reminded himself. He alone was responsible. The psychological test had proved that.

And yet, how responsible were the psychologists who had given him the test? How responsible was Mike Terry for offering a poor man so much money? Society had woven the noose and put it around his neck, and he was hanging himself with it and calling it free will.

Whose fault?

"Aha!" someone cried.

Raeder looked up and saw a portly man standing near him.

The man wore a loud tweed jacket. He had binoculars around his neck and a cane in his hand.

"Mister," Raeder whispered, "please don't tell!"

"Hi!" shouted the portly man, pointing at Raeder with his cane. "Here he is!"

A madman, thought Raeder. The damned fool must think he's playing Hare and Hounds.

"Right over here!" the man screamed.

Cursing, Raeder sprang to his feet and began running. He came out of the ravine and saw a white building in the distance. He turned toward it. Behind him he could still hear the man.

"That way, over there. Look, you fools, can't you see him yet?"

The killers were shooting again. Raeder ran, stumbling over uneven ground, past three children playing in a tree house.

"Here he is!" the children screamed. "Here he is!"

Raeder groaned and ran on. He reached the steps of the building and saw that it was a church.

As he opened the door, a bullet struck him behind the right kneecap.

He fell, and crawled inside the church.

The television set in his pocket was saying, *"What a finish, folks, what a finish! Raeder's been hit! He's been hit, folks, he's crawling now, he's in pain, but he hasn't given up! NOT Jim Raeder!"*

Raeder lay in the aisle near the altar. He could hear a child's eager voice saying, "He went in there, Mr. Thompson. Hurry, you can still catch him!"

Wasn't a church considered a sanctuary? Raeder wondered.

Then the door was flung open, and Raeder realized that the custom was no longer observed. He gathered himself together and crawled past the altar, out of the back door of the church.

He was in an old graveyard. He crawled past crosses and stars, past slabs of marble and granite, past stone tombs and rude wooden markers. A bullet exploded on a tombstone near his head, showering him with fragments. He crawled to the edge of an open grave.

They had deceived him, he thought. All of those nice, average, normal people. Hadn't they said he was their representative? Hadn't they sworn to protect their own? But no, they loathed him. Why hadn't he seen it? Their hero was the cold, blank-eyed gunman: Thompson, Capone, Billy the Kid, Young Lochinvar, El Cid, Cuchulain, the man without human hopes or fears. They worshipped him, that dead, implacable robot gunman, and lusted to feel his foot in their face.

Raeder tried to move, and slid helplessly into the open grave.

He lay on his back, looking at the blue sky. Presently a black silhouette loomed above him, blotting out the sky. Metal twinkled. The silhouette slowly took aim.

And Raeder gave up all hope forever.

"*Wait, Thompson!*" roared the amplified voice of Mike Terry. The revolver wavered.

"*It is one second past five o'clock! The week is up! JIM RAEDER HAS WON!*"

There was pandemonium of cheering from the studio audience.

The Thompson gang, gathered around the grave, looked sullen.

"*He's won, friends, he's won!*" Mike Terry cried. "*Look, look on your screen! The police have arrived, they're taking the Thompsons away from their victim—the victim they could not kill. And all this is thanks to you, Good Samaritans of America. Look folks, tender hands are lifting Jim Raeder from the open grave that was his final refuge. Good Samaritan Janice Morrow is there. Could this be the beginning of a romance? Jim seems to have fainted, friends; they're giving him a stimulant. He's won two hundred thousand dollars! Now we'll have a few words from Jim Raeder!*"

There was a short silence.

"*That's odd,*" said Mike Terry. "*Folks, I'm afraid we can't hear from Jim just now. The doctors are examining him. Just one moment . . .*"

There was a silence. Mike Terry wiped his forehead and smiled.

"*It's the strain, folks, the terrible strain. The doctor tells me . . . Well, folks, Jim Raeder is temporarily not himself. But it's only temporary! JBC is hiring the best psychiatrists and psychoanalysts in the country. We're going to do everything humanly possible for this gallant boy. And entirely at our own expense.*"

Mike Terry glanced at the studio clock. "*Well, it's about*

time to sign off, folks. Watch for the announcement of our next great thrill show. And don't worry, I'm sure that very soon we'll have Jim Raeder back with us."

Mike Terry smiled, and winked at the audience. *"He's bound to get well, friends. After all, we're all pulling for him!"*

ANDA'S GAME

Cory Doctorow

Here's a fast-paced tale that takes us inside a very dangerous game, one with real-world implications—and demonstrates that even in a game, there are sometimes things more important than hit-points and treasure.

Cory Doctorow is the co-editor of the popular Boing Boing *website (boingboing.net), a co-founder of the internet search-engine company OpenCola.com, and until recently was the outreach coordinator for the Electronic Frontier Foundation (www.eff.org). In 2001, he also won the John W. Campbell Award as the year's Best New Writer. His stories have appeared in* Asimov's Science Fiction, Science Fiction Age, The Infinite Matrix, On Spec, Salon, *and elsewhere, and were recently collected in* A Place So Foreign and Eight More. *His well-received first novel,* Down and Out in the Magic Kingdom, *won the Locus Award as Best First Novel, and was followed shortly by a second novel,* Eastern Standard Tribe. *Doctorow's other books include* The Complete Idiot's Guide to Publishing Science Fiction, *written with Karl Schroeder, and a guide to* Essential Blogging, *written with Shelley Powers. His most recent book is a new novel,* Someone Comes to Town, Someone Leaves Town. *He has a website at www.craphound.com.*

ANDA didn't really start to play the game until she got herself a girl-shaped avatar. She was twelve, and up until then, she'd played a boy-elf, because if you played a girl you were an instant perv-magnet, and none of the girls at Ada Lovelace Comprehensive would have been caught dead playing a girl character. In fact, the only girls she'd ever seen in-game were being played by boys. You could tell, cos they were shaped like a boy's idea of what a girl looked like: hooge buzwabs and long legs all barely contained in tiny, pointless leather bikini-armour. Bintware, she called it.

But when Anda was twelve, she met Liza the Organiza, whose avatar was female, but had sensible tits and sensible armour and a bloody great sword that she was clearly very good with. Liza came to school after PE, when Anda was sitting and massaging her abused podge and hating her entire life from stupid sunrise to rotten sunset. Her PE kit was at the bottom of her school-bag and her face was that stupid red colour that she *hated* and now it was stinking maths which were hardly better than PE but at least she didn't have to sweat.

But instead of maths, all the girls were called to assembly, and Liza the Organiza stood on the stage in front of Miss Cruickshanks the principal and Mrs. Danzig, the useless counsellor. "Hullo, chickens," Liza said. She had an Australian accent. "Well, aren't you lot just precious and bright and expectant with your pink upturned faces like a load of flowers staring up at the sky?

"Warms me fecking heart it does."

That made her laugh, and she wasn't the only one. Miss Cruickshanks and Mrs. Danzig didn't look amused, but they tried to hide it.

"I am Liza the Organiza, and I kick arse. Seriously." She tapped a key on her laptop and the screen behind her lit up. It was a game—not the one that Anda played, but something space-themed, a space-station with a rocketship in the background. "This is my avatar." Sensible boobs, sensible armour, and a sword the size of the world. "In-game, they call me the Lizanator, Queen of the Spacelanes, El Presidente of the Clan Fahrenheit." The Fahrenheits had chapters in every game. They were amazing and deadly and cool, and to her knowledge, Anda had never met one in the flesh. They had their own *island* in her game. Crikey.

On screen, The Lizanator was fighting an army of wookiemen, sword in one hand, laser-blaster in the other, rocket-jumping, spinning, strafing, making impossible kills and long shots, diving for power-ups and ruthlessly running her enemies to ground.

"The *whole* Clan Fahrenheit. I won that title through popular election, but they voted me in cos of my prowess in *combat*. I'm a world-champion in six different games, from first-person shooters to strategy games. I've commanded armies and I've sent armies to their respawn gates by the thousands. Thousands, chickens: my battle record is 3,522 kills in a single battle. I have taken home cash prizes from competitions totalling more than 400,000 pounds. I game for four to six hours nearly every day, and the rest of the time, I do what I like.

"One of the things I like to do is come to girls' schools like yours and let you in on a secret: girls kick arse. We're faster, smarter and better than boys. We play harder. We spend too much time thinking that we're freaks for gaming and when we do game, we never play as girls because we catch so much shite for it. Time to turn that around. I am the best gamer in the world and I'm a girl. I started playing at ten, and there were no women in games—you couldn't even buy a game in any of the shops I went to. It's different now, but it's still not perfect. We're going to change that, chickens, you lot and me.

"How many of you game?"

Anda put her hand up. So did about half the girls in the room.

"And how many of you play girls?"

All the hands went down.

"See, that's a tragedy. Practically makes me weep. Gamespace is full of *cock*. It's time we girled it up a little.

So here's my offer to you: if you will play as a girl, you will be given probationary memberships in the Clan Fahrenheit, and if you measure up, in six months you'll be full-fledged members."

In real life, Liza the Organiza was a little podgy, like Anda herself, but she wore it with confidence. She was solid, like a brick wall, her hair bobbed bluntly at her shoulders, dressed in a black jumper over loose dungarees with giant goth boots with steel toes that looked like something you'd see in an in-game shop, though Anda was pretty sure they'd come from a real-world goth shop in Camden Town.

She stomped her boots, one-two, thump-thump, like thunder on the stage. "Who's in, chickens? Who wants to be a girl out-game and in?"

Anda jumped to her feet. A Fahrenheit, with her own island! Her head was so full of it that she didn't notice that she was the only one standing. The other girls stared at her, a few giggling and whispering.

"That's all right, love," Liza called, "I like enthusiasm. Don't let those staring faces rattle yer: they're just flowers turning to look at the sky. Pink-scrubbed, shining, expectant faces. They're looking at you because *you* had the sense to get to your feet when opportunity came—and that means that someday, girl, you are going to be a leader of women, and men, and you will kick arse. Welcome to the Clan Fahrenheit."

She began to clap, and the other girls clapped too, and even though Anda's face was the colour of a lollipop-lady's sign, she felt like she might burst with pride and good feeling and she smiled until her face hurt.

> Anda,

her sergeant said to her,

> how would you like to make some money?
> Money, Sarge?

Ever since she'd risen to platoon leader, she'd been getting more missions, but they paid *gold*—money wasn't really something you talked about in-game.

The Sarge—sensible boobs, gigantic sword, longbow, gloriously orcish ugly phiz—moved her avatar impatiently. "Something wrong with my typing, Anda?"

> No, Sarge

she typed.

> You mean gold?
> If I meant gold, I would have said gold. Can you go voice?

Anda looked around. Her door was shut and she could hear her parents in the sitting-room watching something loud on the telly. She turned up her music just to be safe and then slipped on her headset. They said it could noise-cancel a Blackhawk helicopter—it had better be able to overcome the little inductive speakers suction-cupped to the underside of her desk. She switched to voice.

"Hey, Lucy," she said.

"Call me Sarge." Lucy's accent was American, like an old TV show, and she lived somewhere in the middle of the country where it was all vowels, Iowa or Ohio. She was Anda's best friend in-game, but she was so hardcore it was boring sometimes.

"Hi, Sarge," she said, trying to keep the irritation out of her voice. She'd never smart off to a superior in-game, but v2v it was harder to remember to keep to the game norms.

"I have a mission that pays real cash. Whichever paypal you're using, they'll deposit money into it. Looks fun, too."

"That's a bit weird, Sarge. Is that against Clan rules?" There were a lot of Clan rules about what kind of mission you could accept and they were always changing. There were kerb-crawlers in gamespace and the way that the Clan leadership kept all the mummies and daddies from going ape-poo about it was by enforcing a long, boring code of conduct that was meant to ensure that none of the Fahrenheit girlies ended up being virtual prozzies for hairy old men in raincoats on the other side of the world.

"What?" Anda loved how Lucy quacked *What?* It sounded especially American. She had to force herself from parroting it back. "No, geez. All the executives in the Clan pay the rent doing missions for money. Some of them are even rich from it, I hear! You can make a lot of money gaming, you know."

"Is it really true?" She'd heard about this but she'd assumed it was just stories, like the kids who gamed so much that they couldn't tell reality from fantasy. Or the ones who gamed so much that they stopped eating and got all anorexic. She wouldn't mind getting a little anorexic, to be honest. Bloody podge.

"Yup! And this is our chance to get in on the ground floor. Are you in?"

"It's not—you know, *pervy*, is it?"

"Gag me. No. Jeez, Anda! Are you nuts? No—they want us to go kill some guys."

"Oh, we're good at that!"

* * *

THE mission took them far from Fahrenheit Island, to a cottage on the far side of the largest continent on the gameworld, which was called "Dandelionwine." The travel was tedious, and twice they were ambushed on the trail, something that had hardly happened to Anda since she joined the Fahrenheits: attacking a Fahrenheit was bad for your health, because even if you won the battle, they'd bring a war to you.

But now they were far from the Fahrenheits' powerbase, and two different packs of brigands waylaid them on the road. Lucy spotted the first group before they got into sword-range and killed four of the six with her bow before they closed for hand-to-hand. Anda's sword—gigantic and fast—was out then, and her fingers danced over the keyboard as she fought off the player who was attacking her,

her body jerking from side to side as she hammered on the multibutton controller beside her. She won—of course! She was a Fahrenheit! Lucy had already slaughtered her attacker. They desultorily searched the bodies and came up with some gold and a couple scrolls, but nothing to write home about. Even the gold didn't seem like much, given the cash waiting at the end of the mission.

The second group of brigands was even less daunting, though there were twenty of them. They were total noobs, and fought like statues. They'd clearly clubbed together to protect themselves from harder players, but they were no match for Anda and Lucy. One of them even begged for his life before she ran him through,

> **> please sorry u cn have my gold sorry!!!11!**

Anda laughed and sent him to the respawn gate.

> **> You're a nasty person, Anda**

Lucy typed.

> **> I'm a Fahrenheit!!!!!!!!!!**

she typed back.

* * *

THE brigands on the road were punters, but the cottage that was their target was guarded by an altogether more sophisticated sort. They were spotted by sentries long before they got within sight of the cottage, and they saw the warning spell travel up from the sentries' hilltop like a puff of smoke, speeding away toward the cottage. Anda raced up the hill while Lucy covered her with her bow, but that didn't stop the sentries from subjecting Anda to a hail of flaming spears from their fortified position. Anda set up her standard dodge-and-weave pattern, assuming that the sentries were non-player characters—who wanted to *pay* to sit around in gamespace watching a boring road all day?—and to her surprise, the spears followed her. She took one in the chest and only some fast work with her shield and all her healing scrolls saved her. As it was, her constitution was knocked down by half, and she had to retreat back down the hillside.

"Get down," Lucy said in her headset. "I'm gonna use the BFG."

Every game had one—the Big Friendly Gun, the generic term for the baddest-arse weapon in the world. Lucy had rented this one from the Clan armoury for a small fortune in gold and Anda had laughed and called her paranoid, but now she helped her set it up and thanked the gamegods for her foresight. It was a huge, demented flaming crossbow that fired five-metre bolts that exploded on impact. It was a beast to arm and a beast to aim, but they had a nice, dug-in position of their own at the bottom of the hill and it was there that they got the BFG set up, deployed, armed and ranged.

"Fire!" Lucy called, and the game did this amazing and cool animation that it rewarded you with whenever you loosed a bolt from the BFG, making the gamelight dim towards the sizzling bolt as though it were sucking the illumination out of the world as it arced up the hillside, trailing a comet-tail of sparks. The game played them a groan of dismay from their enemies, and then the bolt hit home with a crash that made her point-of-view vibrate like an earthquake. The roar in her headphones was deafening, and behind it she could hear Lucy on the voice-chat, cheering it on.

"Nuke 'em till they glow and shoot 'em in the dark! Yee-haw!" Lucy called, and Anda laughed and pounded her fist on the desk. Gobbets of former enemy sailed over the tree-line dramatically, dripping hyper-red blood and ichor.

In her bedroom, Anda caressed the controller-pad and her avatar punched the air and did a little rugby victory dance that the All-Blacks had released as a limited edition promo after they won the World Cup.

Now they had to move fast, for their enemies at the

cottage would be alerted to their presence and waiting for them. They spread out into a wide flanking manoeuvre around the cottage's sides, staying just outside of bow-range, using scrying scrolls to magnify the cottage and make the foliage around them fade to translucency.

There were four guards around the cottage, two with nocked arrows and two with whirling slings. One had a scroll out and was surrounded by the concentration marks that indicated spellcasting.

"GO GO GO!" Lucy called.

Anda went! She had two scrolls left in her inventory, and one was a shield spell. They cost a fortune and burned out fast, but whatever that guard was cooking up, it had to be bad news. She cast the spell as she charged for the cottage, and lucky thing, because there was a fifth guard up a tree who dumped a pot of boiling oil on her that would have cooked her down to her bones in ten seconds, if not for the spell.

She power-climbed the tree and nearly lost her grip when whatever the nasty spell was bounced off her shield. She reached the fifth man as he was trying to draw his dirk and dagger and lopped his bloody head off in one motion, then backflipped off the high branch, trusting to her shield to stay intact for her impact on the cottage roof.

The strategy worked—now she had the drop (literally!) on the remaining guards, having successfully taken the high ground. In her headphones, the sound of Lucy making mayhem, the grunts as she pounded her keyboard mingling with the in-game shrieks as her arrows found homes in the chests of two more of the guards.

Shrieking a berzerker wail, Anda jumped down off of the roof and landed on one of the two remaining guards, plunging her sword into his chest and pinning him in the dirt. Her sword stuck in the ground, and she hammered on her keys, trying to free it, while the remaining guard ran for her on-screen. Anda pounded her keyboard, but it was useless: the sword was good and stuck. Poo. She'd blown a small fortune on spells and rations for this project with the expectation of getting some real cash out of it, and now it was all lost.

She moved her hands to the part of the keypad that controlled motion and began to run, waiting for the guard's sword to find her avatar's back and knock her into the dirt.

"Got 'im?" It was Lucy, in her headphones. She wheeled her avatar about so quickly it was nauseating and saw that Lucy was on her erstwhile attacker, grunting as she engaged him close-in. Something was wrong, though: despite Lucy's avatar's awesome stats and despite Lucy's own skill at the keyboard, she was being taken to the cleaners. The guard was kicking her ass. Anda went back to her stuck sword and recommenced whanging on it, watching helplessly as Lucy lost her left arm, then took a cut on her belly, then another to her knee.

"Shit!" Lucy said in her headphones as her avatar began to keel over. Anda yanked her sword free—finally—and charged at the guard, screaming a ululating war cry. He managed to get his avatar swung around and his sword up before she reached him, but it didn't matter: she got in a lucky swing that took off one leg, then danced back before he could counterstrike. Now she closed carefully, nicking at his sword-hand until he dropped his weapon, then moving in for a fast kill.

"Lucy?"

"Call me Sarge!"

"Sorry, Sarge. Where'd you respawn?"

"I'm all the way over at Body Electric—it'll take me hours to get there. Do you think you can complete the mission on your own?"

"Uh, sure." Thinking, *Crikey, if that's what the guards* outside *were like, how'm I gonna get past the* inside *guards?*

"You're the best, girl. OK, enter the cottage and kill everyone there."

"Uh, sure."

She wished she had another scrying scroll in inventory so she could get a look inside the cottage before she beat its door in, but she was fresh out of scrolls and just about everything else.

She kicked the door in and her fingers danced. She'd killed four of her adversaries before she even noticed that they weren't fighting back.

In fact, they were generic avatars, maybe even non-player characters. They moved like total noobs, milling around in the little cottage. Around them were heaps of shirts, thousands and thousands of them. A couple of the noobs were sitting in the back, incredibly, still crafting more shirts, ignoring the swordswoman who'd just butchered four of their companions.

She took a careful look at all the avatars in the room. None of them were armed. Tentatively, she walked up to one of the players and cut his head off. The player next to him moved clumsily to one side and she followed him.

> Are you a player or a bot?

she typed.

The avatar did nothing. She killed it.

"Lucy, they're not fighting back."

"Good, kill them all."

"Really?"

"Yeah—that's the orders. Kill them all and then I'll make a phone call and some guys will come by and verify it and then you haul ass back to the island. I'm coming out there to meet you, but it's a long haul from the respawn gate. Keep an eye on my stuff, OK?"

"Sure," Anda said, and killed two more. That left ten. *One two one two and through and through,* she thought, lopping their heads off. *Her vorpal blade went snicker-snack.* One left. He stood off in the back.

> no porfa quiero mi plata

Italian? No, Spanish. She'd had a term of it in Third Form, though she couldn't understand what this twit was saying. She could always paste the text into a translation bot on one of the chat channels, but who cared? She cut his head off.

"They're all dead," she said into her headset.

"Good job!" Lucy said. "OK, I'm gonna make a call. Sit tight."

Bo-ring. The cottage was filled with corpses and shirts. She picked some of them up. They were totally generic: the shirts you crafted when you were down at Level 0 and trying to get enough skillz to actually make something of yourself. Each one would fetch just a few coppers. Add it all together and you barely had two thousand gold.

Just to pass the time, she pasted the Spanish into the chatbot.

> no [colloq] please, I want my [colloquial] [money|silver]

Pathetic. A few thousand golds—he could make that much by playing a couple of the beginner missions. More fun. More rewarding. Crafting shirts!

She left the cottage and patrolled around it. Twenty minutes later, two more avatars showed up. More generics.

> are you players or bots?

she typed, though she had an idea they were players. Bots moved better.

> any trouble?

Well all right then.

> no trouble
> good

One player entered the cottage and came back out again. The other player spoke.

> you can go now

"Lucy?"

"What's up?"

"Two blokes just showed up and told me to piss off. They're noobs, though. Should I kill them?"

"No! Jeez, Anda, those are the contacts. They're just making sure the job was done. Get my stuff and meet me at Marionettes Tavern, OK?"

Anda went over to Lucy's corpse and looted it, then set out down the road, dragging the BFG behind her. She stopped at the bend in the road and snuck a peek back at the cottage. It was in flames, the two noobs standing amid them, burning slowly along with the cottage and a few thousand golds' worth of badly crafted shirts.

* * *

THAT was the first of Anda and Lucy's missions, but it wasn't the last. That month, she fought her way through six more, and the paypal she used filled with real, honest-to-goodness cash, Pounds Sterling that she could withdraw from the cashpoint situated exactly 501 metres away from the schoolgate, next to the candy shop that was likewise 501 metres away.

"Anda, I don't think it's healthy for you to spend so much time with your game," her Da said, prodding her bulging podge with a finger. "It's not healthy."

"Daaaa!" she said, pushing his finger aside. "I go to PE every stinking day. It's good enough for the Ministry of Education."

"I don't like it," he said. He was no movie star himself, with a little pot belly that he wore his belted trousers high upon, a wobbly extra chin and two bat wings of flab hanging off his upper arms. She pinched his chin and wiggled it.

"I get loads more exercise than you, Mr Kettle."

"But I pay the bills around here, little Miss Pot."

"You're not seriously complaining about the cost of the game?" she said, infusing her voice with as much incredulity and disgust as she could muster. "Ten quid a week and I get unlimited calls, texts and messages! Plus play of course, and the in-game encyclopedia and spellchecker and translator bots!" (This was all from rote—every member of the Fahrenheits memorised this or something very like it for dealing with recalcitrant, ignorant parental units.) "Fine then. If the game is too dear for you, Da, let's set it aside and I'll just start using a normal phone. Is that what you want?"

Her Da held up his hands. "I surrender, Miss Pot. But *do* try to get a little more exercise, please? Fresh air? Sport? Games?"

"Getting my head trodden on in the hockey pitch, more like," she said, darkly.

"Zackly!" he said, prodding her podge anew. "That's the stuff! Getting my head trodden on was what made me the man I are today!"

Her Da could bluster all he liked about paying the bills, but she had pocket-money for the first time in her life: not book-tokens and fruit-tokens and milk-tokens that could be exchanged for "healthy" snacks and literature. She had real money, cash money that she could spend outside of the 500 meter sugar-free zone that surrounded her school.

She wasn't just kicking arse in the game, now—she was the richest kid she knew, and suddenly she was everybody's best pal, with handsful of Curlie Wurlies and Dairy Milks and Mars Bars that she could selectively distribute to her schoolmates.

* * *

"**GO** get a BFG," Lucy said. "We're going on a mission."

Lucy's voice in her ear was a constant companion in her life now. When she wasn't on Fahrenheit Island, she and Lucy were running missions into the wee hours of the night. The Fahrenheit armourers, non-player-characters, had learned to recognise her and they had the Clan's BFGs oiled and ready for her when she showed up.

Today's mission was close to home, which was good: the road-trips were getting tedious. Sometimes, non-player-characters or Game Masters would try to get them involved in an official in-game mission, impressed by their stats and weapons, and it sometimes broke her heart to pass them up, but cash always beat gold and experience beat experience points: *Money talks and bullshit walks,* as Lucy liked to say.

They caught the first round of sniper/lookouts before they had a chance to attack or send off a message. Anda used the scrying spell to spot them. Lucy had kept both BFGs armed and she loosed rounds at the hilltops flanking the roadway as soon as Anda gave her the signal, long before they got into bowrange.

As they picked their way through the ruined gobbets of the dead player-character snipers, Anda still on the lookout, she broke the silence over their voicelink.

"Hey, Lucy?"

"Anda, if you're not going to call me Sarge, at least don't call me 'Hey, Lucy!' My dad loved that old TV show and he makes that joke every visitation day."

"Sorry, Sarge. Sarge?"

"Yes, Anda?"

"I just can't understand why anyone would pay us cash for these missions."

"You complaining?"

"No, but—"

"Anyone asking you to cyber some old pervert?"

"No!"

"OK then. I don't know either. But the money's good. I don't care. Hell, probably it's two rich gamers who pay their butlers to craft for them all day. One's fucking with the other one and paying us."

"You really think that?"

Lucy sighed a put-upon, sophisticated, American sigh. "Look at it this way. Most of the world is living on like a dollar a day. I spend five dollars every day on a frappuccino. Some days, I get two! Dad sends Mom three thousand a month in child-support—that's a hundred bucks a day. So if a day's money here is a hundred dollars, then to a African or whatever my frappuccino is worth like *five hundred dollars.* And I buy two or three every day.

"And we're not rich! There's craploads of rich people who wouldn't think twice about spending five hundred bucks on a coffee—how much do you think a hotdog and a Coke go for on the space station? A thousand bucks!

"So that's what I think is going on. There's someone out there, some Saudi or Japanese guy or Russian mafia kid who's so rich that this is just chump change for him, and he's paying us to mess around with some other rich person. To them, we're like the Africans making a dollar a day to craft—I mean, sew—T-shirts. What's a couple hundred bucks to them? A cup of coffee."

Anda thought about it. It made a kind of sense. She'd been on hols in Bratislava where they got a posh hotel room for ten quid—less than she was spending every day on sweeties and fizzy drinks.

"Three o'clock," she said, and aimed the BFG again. More snipers pat-patted in bits around the forest floor.

"Nice one, Anda."

"Thanks, Sarge."

* * *

THEY smashed half a dozen more sniper outposts and fought their way through a couple packs of suspiciously bad-ass brigands before coming upon the cottage.

"Bloody hell," Anda breathed. The cottage was ringed with guards, forty or fifty of them, with bows and spells and spears, in entrenched positions.

"This is nuts," Lucy agreed. "I'm calling them. This is nuts."

There was a muting click as Lucy rang off and Anda used up a scrying scroll to examine the inventories of the guards around the corner. The more she looked, the more scared she got. They were loaded down with spells; a couple of them were guarding BFGs and what looked like an even *bigger* BFG, maybe the fabled BFG10K, something that was removed from the game economy not long after gameday one, as too disruptive to the balance of power. Supposedly, one or two existed, but that was just a rumour. Wasn't it?

"OK," Lucy said. "OK, this is how this goes. We've got to do this. I just called in three squads of Fahrenheit veterans and their noob prentices for backup." Anda summed that up in her head to four hundred player characters and maybe three hundred nonplayer characters: familiars, servants, demons . . .

"That's a lot of shares to split the pay into," Anda said.

"Oh ye of little tits," Lucy said. "I've negotiated a bonus for us if we make it—a million gold and three missions' worth of cash. The Fahrenheits are taking payment in gold—they'll be here in an hour."

This wasn't a mission anymore, Anda realised. It was war. Gamewar. Hundreds of players converging on this shard, squaring off against the ranked mercenaries guarding the huge cottage over the hill.

* * *

LUCY wasn't the ranking Fahrenheit on the scene, but she was the designated general. One of the gamers up from Fahrenheit Island brought a team flag for her to carry, a long spear with the magical standard snapping proudly from it as the troops formed up behind her.

"On my signal," Lucy said. The voice chat was like a windtunnel from all the unmuted breathing voices, hundreds of girls in hundreds of bedrooms like Anda's, all over the world, some sitting down before breakfast, some just coming home from school, some roused from sleep by their ringing game-sponsored mobiles. "GO GO GO!"

They went, roaring, and Anda roared too, heedless of her parents downstairs in front of the blaring telly, heedless of her throat-lining, a Fahrenheit in berzerker rage, sword swinging. She made straight for the BFG10K—a siege engine that could level a town wall, and it would be hers, captured by her for the Fahrenheits if she could do it. She spelled the merc who was cranking it into insensibility, rolled and rolled again to dodge arrows and spells, healed herself when an arrow found her leg and sent her tumbling, springing to her feet before another arrow could strike home, watching her hit points and experience points move in opposite directions.

HERS! She vaulted the BFG10K and snicker-snacked her sword through two mercs' heads. Two more appeared—they had the thing primed and aimed at the main body of Fahrenheit fighters, and they could turn the battle's tide just by firing it—and she killed them, slamming her keypad, howling, barely conscious of the answering howls in her headset.

Now *she* had the BFG10K, though more mercs were closing on her. She disarmed it quickly and spelled at the nearest bunch of mercs, then had to take evasive action against the hail of incoming arrows and spells. It was all she could do to cast healing spells fast enough to avoid losing consciousness.

"LUCY!" she called into her headset. "LUCY, OVER BY THE BFG10K!"

Lucy snapped out orders and the opposition before Anda began to thin as Fahrenheits fell on them from behind. The flood was stemmed, and now the Fahrenheits' greater numbers and discipline showed. In short order, every merc was butchered or run off.

Anda waited by the BFG10K while Lucy paid off the Fahrenheits and saw them on their way. "Now we take the cottage," Lucy said.

"Right," Anda said. She set her character off for the doorway. Lucy brushed past her.

"I'll be glad when we're done with this—that was bugfuck nutso." She opened the door and her character disappeared in a fireball that erupted from directly overhead. A door-curse, a serious one, one that cooked her in her armour in seconds.

"SHIT!" Lucy said in her headset.

Anda giggled. "Teach *you* to go rushing into things," she said. She used up a couple scrying scrolls making sure that there was nothing else in the cottage save for millions of shirts and thousands of unarmed noob avatars that she'd have to mow down like grass to finish out the mission.

She descended upon them like a reaper, swinging her sword heedlessly, taking five or six out with each swing. When she'd been a noob in the game, she'd had to endure endless fighting practice, "grappling" with piles of leaves and other nonlethal targets, just to get enough experience points to have a chance of hitting anything. This was every bit as dull.

Her wrists were getting tired, and her chest heaved and her hated podge wobbled as she worked the keypad.

> Wait, please, don't—I'd like to speak with you

It was a noob avatar, just like the others, but not just like it after all, for it moved with purpose, backing away from her sword. And it spoke English.

> nothing personal

she typed

> just a job
> There are many here to kill—take me last at least. I need to talk to you.
> talk, then

she typed. Meeting players who moved well and spoke English was hardly unusual in gamespace, but here in the cleanup phase, it felt out of place. It felt *wrong*.

> My name is Raymond, and I live in Tijuana. I am a labour organiser in the factories here. What is your name?
> i don't give out my name in-game
> What can I call you?
> kali

It was a name she liked to use in-game: Kali, Destroyer of Worlds, like the Hindu goddess.

> Are you in India?
> london
> You are Indian?
> naw im a whitey

She was halfway through the room, mowing down the noobs in twos and threes. She was hungry and bored and this Raymond was weirding her out.

> Do you know who these people are that you're killing?

She didn't answer, but she had an idea. She killed four more and shook out her wrists.

> They're working for less than a dollar a day. The shirts they make are traded for gold and the gold is sold on eBay. Once their avatars have leveled up, they too are sold off on eBay. They're mostly young girls supporting their families. They're the lucky ones: the unlucky ones work as prostitutes.

Her wrists *really* ached. She slaughtered half a dozen more.

> I've been trying to unionise them because they've got a very high rate of injury. They have to play for 18-hour shifts with only one short toilet break. Some of them can't hold it in and they soil themselves where they sit.
> look

she typed, exasperated.

> it's none of my lookout, is it. the world's like that. lots of people with no money. im just a kid, theres nothing i can do about it.
> When you kill them, they don't get paid.

no porfa quiero mi plata

> When you kill them, they lose their day's wages. Do you know who is paying you to do these killings?

She thought of Saudis, rich Japanese, Russian mobsters.

> not a clue
> I've been trying to find that out myself, Kali.

They were all dead now. Raymond stood alone amongst the piled corpses.

> Go ahead

he typed

> I will see you again, I'm sure.

She cut his head off. Her wrists hurt. She was hungry. She was alone there in the enormous woodland cottage, and she still had to haul the BFG10K back to Fahrenheit Island.

"Lucy?"

"Yeah, yeah, I'm almost back there, hang on. I respawned in the ass end of nowhere."

"Lucy, do you know who's in the cottage? Those noobs that we kill?"

"What? Hell no. Noobs. Someone's butler. I dunno. Jesus, that spawn gate—"

"Girls. Little girls in Mexico. Getting paid a dollar a day to craft shirts. Except they don't get their dollar when we kill them. They don't get anything."

"Oh, for chrissakes, is that what one of them told you? Do you believe everything someone tells you in-game? Christ. English girls are so naive."

"You don't think it's true?"

"Naw, I don't."

"Why not?"

"I just don't, OK? I'm almost there, keep your panties on."

"I've got to go, Lucy," she said. Her wrists hurt, and her podge overlapped the waistband of her trousers, making her feel a bit like she was drowning.

"What, now? Shit, just hang on."

"My mom's calling me to supper. You're almost here, right?"

"Yeah, but—"

She reached down and shut off her PC.

* * *

ANDA'S Da and Mum were watching the telly again with a bowl of crisps between them. She walked past them like she was dreaming and stepped out the door onto the terrace. It was nighttime, eleven o'clock, and the chavs in front of the council flats across the square were kicking a football around and swilling lager and making rude noises. They were skinny and rawboned, wearing shorts and string vests, with strong, muscular limbs flashing in the streetlights.

"Anda?"

"Yes, Mum?"

"Are you all right?" Her mum's fat fingers caressed the back of her neck.

"Yes, Mum. Just needed some air is all."

"You're very clammy," her mum said. She licked a finger and scrubbed it across Anda's neck. "Gosh, you're dirty—how did you get to be such a mucky puppy?"

"Owww!" she said. Her mum was scrubbing so hard it felt like she'd take her skin off.

"No whingeing," her mum said sternly. "Behind your ears, too! You are *filthy*."

"Mum, *owwww*!"

Her mum dragged her up to the bathroom and went at her with a flannel and a bar of soap and hot water until she felt boiled and raw.

"What *is* this mess?" her mum said.

"Lilian, leave off," her dad said, quietly. "Come out into the hall for a moment, please."

The conversation was too quiet to hear and Anda didn't want to, anyway: she was concentrating too hard on not crying—her ears *hurt*.

Her mum enfolded her shoulders in her soft hands again. "Oh, darling, I'm sorry. It's a skin condition, your father tells me, Acanthosis Nigricans—he saw it in a TV special. We'll see the doctor about it tomorrow after school. Are you all right?"

"I'm fine," she said, twisting to see if she could see the "dirt" on the back of her neck in the mirror. It was hard because it was an awkward placement—but also because she didn't like to look at her face and her soft extra chin, and she kept catching sight of it.

She went back to her room to google Acanthosis Nigricans.

> A condition involving darkened,
> thickened skin. Found in the folds of
> skin at the base of the back of the
> neck, under the arms, inside the elbow
> and at the waistline. Often precedes a
> diagnosis of type-2 diabetes, especially
> in children. If found in children,
> immediate steps must be taken to prevent
> diabetes, including exercise and
> nutrition as a means of lowering insulin
> levels and increasing
> insulin-sensitivity.

Obesity-related diabetes. They had lectures on this every term in health class—the fastest-growing ailment among British teens, accompanied by photos of orca-fat sacks of lard sat up in bed surrounded by an ocean of rubbery, flowing podge. Anda prodded her belly and watched it jiggle.

It jiggled. Her thighs jiggled. Her chins wobbled. Her arms sagged.

She grabbed a handful of her belly and *squeezed it,* pinched it hard as she could, until she had to let go or cry out. She'd left livid red fingerprints in the rolls of fat and she was crying now, from the pain and the shame and oh, God, she was a fat girl with diabetes—

* * *

"JESUS, Anda, where the hell have you been?"

"Sorry, Sarge," she said. "My PC's been broken—" Well, out of service, anyway. Under lock-and-key in her dad's study. Almost a month now of medications and no telly and no gaming and double PE periods at school with the other whales. She was miserable all day, every day now, with nothing to look forward to except the trips after school to the newsagents at the 501-meter mark and the fistsful of sweeties and bottles of fizzy drink she ate in the park while she watched the chavs play footy.

"Well, you should have found a way to let me know. I was getting worried about you, girl."

"Sorry, Sarge," she said again. The PC Baang was filled with stinky spotty boys—literally stinky, it smelt like goats, like a train-station toilet—being loud and obnoxious. The dinky headphones provided were greasy as a slice of pizza, and the mouthpiece was sticky with excited boy-saliva from games gone past.

But it didn't matter. Anda was back in the game, and just in time, too: her money was running short.

"Well, I've got a backlog of missions here. I tried going out with a couple other of the girls—" A pang of regret shot through Anda at the thought that her position might have been usurped while she was locked off the game, "—but you're too good to replace, OK? I've got four missions we can do today if you're game."

"Four missions! How on earth will we do four missions? That'll take days!"

"We'll take the BFG10K." Anda could hear the savage grin in her voice.

* * *

THE BFG10K simplified things quite a lot. Find the cottage, aim the BFG10K, fire it, whim-wham, no more cottage. They started with five bolts for it—one BFG10K bolt was made up of twenty regular BFG bolts, each costing a small fortune in gold—and used them all up on the first three targets. After returning it to the armoury and grabbing a couple of BFGs (amazing how puny the BFG seemed after just a couple hours' campaigning with a really *big* gun!) they set out for number four.

"I met a guy after the last campaign," Anda said. "One of the noobs in the cottage. He said he was a union organiser."

"Oh, you met Raymond, huh?"

"You knew about him?"

"I met him too. He's been turning up everywhere. What a creep."

"So you knew about the noobs in the cottages?"

"Um. Well, yeah, I figured it out mostly on my own and then Raymond told me a little more."

"And you're fine with depriving little kids of their wages?"

"Anda," Lucy said, her voice brittle. "You like gaming, right, it's important to you?"

"Yeah, 'course it is."

"How important? Is it something you do for fun, just a hobby you waste a little time on? Are you just into it casually, or are you *committed* to it?"

"I'm committed to it, Lucy, you know that." God, without the game, what was there? PE class? Stupid Acanthosis Nigricans and, someday, insulin jabs every morning? "I love the game, Lucy. It's where my friends are."

"I know that. That's why you're my right-hand woman, why I want you at my side when I go on a mission. We're bad-ass, you and me, as bad-ass as they come, and we got that way through discipline and hard work and really *caring* about the game, right?"

"Yes, right, but—"

"You've met Liza the Organiza, right?"

"Yes, she came by my school."

"Mine too. She asked me to look out for you because of what she saw in you that day."

"Liza the Organiza goes to Ohio?"

"Idaho. Yes—all across the US. They put her on the tube and everything. She's amazing, and she cares about the game, too—that's what makes us all Fahrenheits: we're committed to each other, to teamwork, and to fair play."

Anda had heard these words—lifted from the Fahrenheit mission statement—many times, but now they made her swell a little with pride.

"So these people in Mexico or wherever, what are they doing? They're earning their living by exploiting the game. You and me, we would never trade cash for gold, or buy a character or a weapon on eBay—it's cheating. You get gold and weapons through hard work and hard play. But those Mexicans spend all day, every day, crafting stuff to turn into gold to sell off on the exchange. *That's where it comes from*—that's where the crappy players get their gold from! That's how rich noobs can buy their way into the game that we had to play hard to get into.

"So we burn them out. If we keep burning the factories down, they'll shut them down and they'll find something else to do for a living and the game will be better. If no one does that, our work will just get cheaper and cheaper: the game will get less and less fun, too.

"These people *don't* care about the game. To them, it's just a place to suck a buck out of. They're not players, they're leeches, here to suck all the fun out."

They had come upon the cottage now, the fourth one, having exterminated four different sniper-nests on the way.

"Are you in, Anda? Are you here to play, or are you so

worried about these leeches on the other side of the world that you want out?"

"I'm in, Sarge," Anda said. She armed the BFGs and pointed them at the cottage.

"Boo-yah!" Lucy said. Her character notched an arrow.

> Hello, Kali

"Oh, Christ, he's back," Lucy said. Raymond's avatar had snuck up behind them.

> Look at these

he said, and his character set something down on the ground and backed away. Anda edged up on them.

"Come on, it's probably a booby-trap, we've got work to do," Lucy said.

They were photo-objects. She picked them up and then examined them. The first showed ranked little girls, fifty or more, in clean and simple T-shirts, skinny as anything, sitting at generic white-box PCs, hands on the keyboards. They were hollow-eyed and grim, and none of them older than her.

The next showed a shantytown, shacks made of corrugated aluminium and trash, muddy trails between them, spraypainted graffiti, rude boys loitering, rubbish and carrier bags blowing.

The next showed the inside of a shanty, three little girls and a little boy sitting together on a battered sofa, their mother serving them something white and indistinct on plastic plates. Their smiles were heartbreaking and brave.

> That's who you're about to deprive of a day's wages

"Oh, hell, *no*," Lucy said. "Not again. I killed him last time and I said I'd do it again if he ever tried to show me photos. That's it, he's dead." Her character turned towards him, putting away her bow and drawing a short sword. Raymond's character backed away quickly.

"Lucy, don't," Anda said. She interposed her avatar between Lucy's and Raymond. "Don't do it. He deserves to have a say." She thought of old American TV shows, the kinds you saw between the Bollywood movies on telly. "It's a free country, right?"

"God *damn* it, Anda, what is *wrong* with you? Did you come here to play the game, or to screw around with this pervert dork?"

> what do you want from me raymond?

> Don't kill them—let them have their wages. Go play somewhere else

> They're leeches

Lucy typed,

> they're wrecking the game economy and they're providing a gold-for-cash supply that lets rich assholes buy their way in. They don't care about the game and neither do you

> If they don't play the game, they don't eat. I think that means that they care about the game as much as you do. You're being paid cash to kill them, yes? So you need to play for your money, too. I think that makes you and them the same, a little the same.

> go screw yourself

Lucy typed. Anda edged her character away from Lucy's. Raymond's character was so far away now that his texting came out in tiny type, almost too small to read. Lucy drew her bow again and nocked an arrow.

"Lucy, DON'T!" Anda cried. Her hands moved on their own volition and her character followed, clobbering Lucy barehanded so that her avatar reeled and dropped its bow.

"You BITCH!" Lucy said. She drew her sword.

"I'm sorry, Lucy," Anda said, stepping back out of range. "But I don't want you to hurt him. I want to hear him out."

Lucy's avatar came on fast, and there was a click as the voicelink dropped. Anda typed onehanded while she drew her own sword.

> dont lucy come on talk2me

Lucy slashed at her twice and she needed both hands to defend herself or she would have been beheaded. Anda blew out through her nose and counterattacked, fingers pounding the keyboard. Lucy had more experience points than her, but she was a better player, and she knew it. She hacked away at Lucy, driving her back and back, back down the road they'd marched together.

Abruptly, Lucy broke and ran, and Anda thought she was going away and decided to let her go, no harm no foul, but then she saw that Lucy wasn't running away, she was running *towards* the BFGs, armed and primed.

"Bloody hell," she breathed, as a BFG swung around to point at her. Her fingers flew. She cast the fireball at Lucy in the same instant that she cast her shield spell. Lucy loosed the bolt at her a moment before the fireball engulfed her, cooking her down to ash, and the bolt collided with the shield and drove Anda back, high into the air, and the shield spell wore off before she hit ground, costing her half her health and inventory, which scattered around her. She tested her voicelink.

"Lucy?"

There was no reply.

> I'm very sorry you and your friend quarrelled.

She felt numb and unreal. There were rules for Fahrenheits, lots of rules, and the penalties for breaking them varied, but the penalty for attacking a fellow Fahrenheit was—she couldn't think the word; she closed her eyes, but there it was in big glowing letters: EXPULSION.

But Lucy had started it, right? It wasn't her fault.

But who would believe her?

She opened her eyes. Her vision swam through incipient tears. Her heart was thudding in her ears.

> The enemy isn't your fellow player. It's not the players guarding the fabrica, it's not the girls working there. The people who are working to destroy the game are the people who pay you and the people who pay the girls in the fabrica, who are the same people. You're being paid by rival factory owners, you know that? THEY are the ones who care nothing for the game. My girls care about the game. You care about the game. Your common enemy is the people who want to destroy the game and who destroy the lives of these girls.

"Whassamatter, you fat little cow? Is your game making you cwy?" She jerked as if slapped. The chav who was speaking to her hadn't been in the Baang when she arrived, and he had mean, close-set eyes and a football jersey and though he wasn't any older than her, he looked mean, and angry, and his smile was sadistic and crazy.

"Piss off," she said, mustering her braveness.

"You wobbling tub of guts, don't you DARE speak to me that way," he said, shouting right in her ear. The Baang fell silent and everyone looked at her. The Pakistani who ran the Baang was on his phone, no doubt calling the coppers, and that meant that her parents would discover where she'd been and then—

"I'm talking to you, girl," he said. "You disgusting lump of suet—Christ, it makes me wanta puke to look at you. You ever had a boyfriend? How'd he shag you—did he roll yer in flour and look for the wet spot?"

She reeled back, then stood. She drew her arm back and slapped him, as hard as she could. The boys in the Baang laughed and went whoooooo! He purpled and balled his fists and she backed away from him. The imprint of her fingers stood out on his cheek.

He bridged the distance between them with a quick step and *punched her,* in the belly, and the air whooshed out of her and she fell into another player, who pushed her away, so she ended up slumped against the wall, crying.

The mean boy was there, right in front of her, and she could smell the chili crisps on his breath. "You disgusting whore—" he began and she kneed him square in the nadgers, hard as she could, and he screamed like a little girl and fell backwards. She picked up her schoolbag and ran for the door, her chest heaving, her face streaked with tears.

* * *

"**ANDA**, dear, there's a phone call for you."

Her eyes stung. She'd been lying in her darkened bedroom for hours now, snuffling and trying not to cry, trying not to look at the empty desk where her PC used to live.

Her da's voice was soft and caring, but after the silence of her room, it sounded like a rusting hinge.

"Anda?"

She opened her eyes. He was holding a cordless phone, sillhouetted against the open doorway.

"Who is it?"

"Someone from your game, I think," he said. He handed her the phone.

"Hullo?"

"Hullo, chicken." It had been a year since she'd heard that voice, but she recognized it instantly.

"Liza?"

"Yes."

Anda's skin seemed to shrink over her bones. This was it: expelled. Her heart felt like it was beating once per second, time slowed to a crawl.

"Hullo, Liza."

"Can you tell me what happened today?"

She did, stumbling over the details, back-tracking and stuttering. She couldn't remember, exactly—did Lucy move on Raymond and Anda asked her to stop and then Lucy attacked her? Had Anda attacked Lucy first? It was all a jumble. She should have saved a screenmovie and taken it with her, but she couldn't have taken anything with her, she'd run out—

"I see. Well it sounds like you've gotten yourself into quite a pile of poo, haven't you, my girl?"

"I guess so," Anda said. Then, because she knew that she was as good as expelled, she said, "I don't think it's right to kill them, those girls. All right?"

"Ah," Liza said. "Well, funny you should mention that. I happen to agree. Those girls need our help more than any of the girls anywhere in the game. I'm glad you took a stand when you did—glad I found out about this business."

"You're not going to expel me?"

"No, chicken, I'm not going to expel you. I think you did the right thing—"

That meant that Lucy would be expelled. Fahrenheit had killed Fahrenheit—something had to be done. The rules had to be enforced. Anda swallowed hard.

"If you expel Lucy, I'll quit," she said quickly, before she lost her nerve.

Liza laughed. "Oh, chicken, you're a brave thing, aren't you? No one's being expelled, fear not. But I wanna talk to this Raymond of yours."

* * *

ANDA came home from remedial hockey sweaty and exhausted, but not as exhausted as the last time, nor the time before that. She could run the whole length of the pitch twice now without collapsing—when she'd started out, she could barely make it halfway without having to stop and hold her side, kneading her loathsome podge to make it stop aching. Now there was noticeably less podge, and she found that with the ability to run the pitch came the freedom to actually pay attention to the game, to aim her shots, to build up a degree of accuracy that was nearly as satisfying as being really good in-game.

Her dad knocked at the door of her bedroom after she'd showered and changed. "How's my girl?"

"Revising," she said, and hefted her maths book at him.

"Did you have a fun afternoon on the pitch?"

"You mean 'did my head get trod on'?"

"Did it?"

"Yes," she said. "But I did more treading than getting trodden on." The other girls were *really* fat, and they didn't have a lot of team skills. Anda had been to war: she knew how to depend on someone and how to be depended upon.

"That's my girl." He pretended to inspect the paint-work around the light switch. "Been on the scales this week?"

She had, of course: the school nutritionist saw to that, a morning humiliation undertaken in full sight of all the other fatties.

"Yes, Dad."

"And—?"

"I've lost a stone," she said. A little more than a stone, actually. She had been able to fit into last year's jeans the other day.

He beamed at her. "I've lost three pounds myself," he said, holding his tum. "I've been trying to follow your diet, you know."

"I know, Da," she said. It embarrassed her to discuss it with him.

"Well, I just wanted to say that I'm proud of you. We both are, your Mum and me. And I wanted to let you know that I'll be moving your PC back into your room tomorrow. You've earned it."

Anda blushed pink. She hadn't really expected this. Her fingers twitched over a phantom game-controller.

"Oh, Da," she said. He held up his hand.

"It's all right, girl. We're just proud of you."

* * *

SHE didn't touch the PC the first day, nor the second. On the third, after hockey, she showered and changed and sat down and slipped the headset on.

"Hello, Anda."

"Hi, Sarge."

Lucy had known the minute she entered the game, which meant that she was still on Lucy's buddy-list. Well, that was a hopeful sign.

"You don't have to call me that. We're the same rank now, after all."

Anda pulled down a menu and confirmed it: she'd been promoted to Sargeant during her absence. She smiled.

"Gosh," she said.

"Yes, well, you earned it," Lucy said. "I've been talking to Raymond a lot about the working conditions in the factory, and, well—" She broke off. "I'm sorry, Anda."

"Me too, Lucy."

"You don't have anything to be sorry about," she said.

They went adventuring, running some of the game's standard missions together. It was fun, but after the kind of campaigning they'd done before, it was also kind of pale and flat.

"It's horrible, I know," Anda said. "But I miss it."

"Oh, thank God," Lucy said. "I thought I was the only one. It was fun, wasn't it? Big fights, big stakes."

"Well, poo," Anda said. "I don't wanna be bored for the rest of my life. What're we gonna do?"

"I was hoping you knew."

She thought about it. The part she'd loved had been going up against grownups who were not playing the game, but *gaming* it, breaking it for money. They'd been worthy adversaries, and there was no guilt in beating them, either.

"We'll ask Raymond how we can help," she said.

* * *

"**I WANT** them to walk out—to go on strike," he said. "It's the only way to get results: band together and withdraw your labour." Raymond's voice had a thick Mexican accent that took some getting used to, but his English was very good—better, in fact, than Lucy's.

"Walk out in-game?" Lucy said.

"No," Raymond said. "That wouldn't be very effective. I want them to walk out in Ciudad Juarez and Tijuana. I'll call the press in, we'll make a big deal out of it. We can win—I know we can."

"So what's the problem?" Anda said.

"The same problem as always. Getting them organised. I thought that the game would make it easier: we've been trying to get these girls organised for years: in the sewing shops, and the toy factories, but they lock the doors and keep us out and the girls go home and their parents won't let us talk to them. But in the game, I thought I'd be able to reach them—"

"But the bosses keep you away?"

"I keep getting killed. I've been practicing my sword-fighting, but it's so hard—"

"This will be fun," Anda said. "Let's go."

"Where?" Lucy said.

"To an in-game factory. We're your new bodyguards." The bosses hired some pretty mean mercs, Anda knew. She'd been one. They'd be *fun* to wipe out.

Raymond's character spun around on the screen, then planted a kiss on Anda's cheek. Anda made her character give him a playful shove that sent him sprawling.

"Hey, Lucy, go get us a couple BFGs, OK?"

LADIES AND GENTLEMEN, THIS IS YOUR CRISIS!

Kate Wilhelm

Here's another prescient—and chilling—piece that appeared decades before Survivor *was even a gleam in some TV executive's eye, but which is all-too-relevant even today . . .*

Kate Wilhelm began publishing in 1956, but in retrospect, she can more usefully be thought of as belonging to the New Wave era of the mid-'60s instead, because that's when her writing would take a quantum jump in power and sophistication, and she would begin to produce major work. By 1968, she won a Nebula Award for her short story, "The Planners," and her work continued to grow in complexity, ambition, depth of characterization, and maturity of expression, until she was producing some of the best work of the early '70s, particularly at novella length: the famous novella "Where Late the Sweet Birds Sang," "Somerset Dreams," "April Fool's Day Forever," "The Infinity Box," "The Encounter," "The Fusion Bomb," "The Plastic Abyss," and many others. She won a Hugo in 1976 for the novel version of "Where Late the Sweet Birds Sang," added another Nebula to her collection in 1986 with a win for her story "The Girl Who Fell Into the Sky," and yet another Nebula in 1987 for her story "Forever Yours, Anna."

Wilhelm's other books include the novels The Killer Thing, Let the Fire Fall, Margaret and I, The Winter Beach, Fault Lines, The

Clewisten Test, Juniper Time, Welcome, Chaos, Oh, Susannah!, Huysman's Pets, *and* Cambio Bay, *as well as the collections* The Downstairs Room, Somerset Dreams, The Infinity Box, Listen, Listen, Children of the Wind, *and* And the Angels Sing. *In recent years, she's become as well known as a mystery writer as an SF writer, publishing eight Constance and Charlie novels and eight Barbara Holloway novels. Her most recent books include* Skeletons: A Novel of Suspense, The Good Children, The Deepest Water, The Price of Silence, *and the nonfiction book* Storyteller: 30 Years of the Clarion Writers' Workshop. *With her late husband, writer Damon Knight, she ran the Milford Writer's Conference for many years, and both were deeply involved in the creation and operation of the Clarion workshop for new young writers. She lives in Eugene, Oregon.*

4 P.M. FRIDAY

Lottie's factory closed early on Friday, as most of them did now. It was four when she got home, after stopping for frozen dinners, bread, sandwich meats, beer. She switched on the wall TV screen before she put her bag down. In the kitchen she turned on another set, a portable, and watched it as she put the food away. She had missed four hours.

They were in the mountains. That was good. Lottie liked it when they chose mountains. A stocky man was sliding down a slope, feet out before him, legs stiff—too conscious of the camera, though. Lottie couldn't tell if he had meant to slide, but he did not look happy. She turned her attention to the others.

A young woman was walking slowly, waist high in ferns, so apparently unconscious of the camera that it could only be a pose this early in the game. She looked vaguely familiar. Her blond hair was loose, like a girl in a shampoo commercial, Lottie decided. She narrowed her eyes, trying to remember where she had seen the girl. A model, probably, wanting to be a star. She would wander aimlessly, not even trying for the prize, content with the publicity she was getting.

The other woman was another sort altogether. A bit overweight, her thighs bulged in the heavy trousers the contestants wore; her hair was dyed black and fastened with a rubber band in a no-nonsense manner. She was examining a tree intently. Lottie nodded at her. Everything about her spoke of purpose, of concentration, of planning. She'd do.

The final contestant was a tall black man, in his forties probably. He wore old-fashioned eyeglasses—a mistake. He'd lose them and be seriously handicapped. He kept glancing about with a lopsided grin.

Lottie had finished putting the groceries away; she returned to the living room to sit before the large unit that gave her a better view of the map, above the sectioned screen. The Andes, she had decided, and was surprised and pleased to find she was wrong. Alaska! There were bears and wolves in Alaska still, and elk and moose.

The picture shifted, and a thrill of anticipation raised the hairs on Lottie's arms and scalp. Now the main screen was evenly divided; one half showed the man who had been sliding. He was huddled against the cliff, breathing very hard. On the other half of the screen was an enlarged aerial view. Lottie gasped. Needle-like snow-capped peaks, cliffs, precipices, a raging stream . . . The yellow dot of light that represented the man was on the edge of a steep hill covered with boulders and loose gravel. If he got on that, Lottie thought, he'd be lost. From where he was, there was no way he could know what lay ahead. She leaned forward, examining him for signs that he understood, that he was afraid, anything. His face was empty; all he needed now was more air than he could get with his labored breathing.

Andy Stevens stepped in front of the aerial map; it was three feet taller than he. "As you can see, ladies and gentlemen, there is only this scrub growth to Dr. Burnside's left. Those roots might be strong enough to hold, but I'd guess they are shallowly rooted, wouldn't you? And if he chooses this direction, he'll need something to grasp, won't he?"

Andy had his tape measure and a pointer. He looked worried. He touched the yellow dot of light. "Here he is. As you can see, he is resting, for the moment, on a narrow ledge after his slide down sixty-five feet of loose dirt and gravel. He doesn't appear to be hurt. Our own Dr. Lederman is watching him along with the rest of us, and he assures me that Dr. Burnside is not injured."

Andy pointed out the hazards of Dr. Burnside's precarious position, and the dangers involved in moving. Lottie nodded, her lips tight and grim. It was off to a good start.

6 P.M. FRIDAY

Butcher got home, as usual, at six. Lottie heard him at the door but didn't get up to open it for him. Dr. Burnside was still sitting there. He had to move. Move, you bastard! Do something!

"Whyn't you unlock the door?" Butcher yelled, yanking off his jacket.

Lottie paid no attention. Butcher always came home mad, resentful because she had got off early, mad at his boss because the warehouse didn't close down early, mad at traffic, mad at everything.

"They say anything about them yet?" Butcher asked, sitting in his recliner.

Lottie shook her head. Move, you bastard! Move!

The man began to inch his way to the left and Lottie's heart thumped, her hands clenched.

"What's the deal?" Butcher asked hoarsely, already responding to Lottie's tension.

"Dead end that way," Lottie muttered, her gaze on the screen. "Slide with boulders and junk if he tries to go down. He's gotta go right."

The man moved cautiously, never lifting his feet from the ground but sliding them along, testing each step. He paused again, this time with less room than before. He looked desperate. He was perspiring heavily. Now he could see the way he had chosen offered little hope of getting down. More slowly than before, he began to back up; dirt and gravel shifted constantly.

The amplifiers picked up the noise of the stuff rushing downward, like a waterfall heard from a distance, and now and then a muttered unintelligible word from the man. The volume came up: he was cursing. Again and again he stopped. He was pale and sweat ran down his face. He didn't move his hands from the cliff to wipe it away.

Lottie was sweating too. Her lips moved occasionally with a faint curse or prayer. Her hands gripped the sofa.

7:30 P.M. FRIDAY

Lottie fell back onto the sofa with a grunt, weak from sustained tension. They were safe. It had taken over an hour to work his way to this place where the cliff and steep slope gave way to a gentle hill. The man was sprawled out face down, his back heaving.

Butcher abruptly got up and went to the bathroom. Lottie couldn't move yet. The screen shifted and the aerial view filled the larger part. Andy pointed out the contestants' lights and finally began the recap.

Lottie watched on the portable set as she got out their frozen dinners and heated the oven. Dr. Lederman was talking about Angie Dawes, the young aspiring actress whose problem was that of having been overprotected all her life. He said she was a potential suicide, and the panel of examining physicians had agreed Crisis Therapy would be helpful.

The next contestant was Mildred Ormsby, a chemist, divorced, no children. She had started on a self-destructive course through drugs, said Dr. Lederman, and would be benefited by Crisis Therapy.

The tall black man, Clyde Williams, was an economist; he taught at Harvard and had tried to murder his wife and their three children by burning down their house with them in it. Crisis Therapy had been indicated.

Finally Dr. Edward Burnside, the man who had started

the show with such drama, was shown being interviewed. Forty-one, unmarried, living with a woman, he was a statistician for a major firm. Recently he had started to feed the wrong data into the computer, aware but unable to stop himself.

Dr. Lederman's desk was superimposed on the aerial view and he started his taped explanation of what Crisis Therapy was. Lottie made coffee. When she looked again Eddie was still lying on the ground, exhausted, maybe even crying. She wished he would roll over so she could see if he was crying.

Andy returned to explain how the game was played: the winner received one million dollars, after taxes, and all the contestants were undergoing Crisis Therapy that would enrich their lives beyond measure. Andy explained the automatic, air-cushioned, five-day cameras focused electronically on the contestants, the orbiting satellite that made it possible to keep them under observation at all times, the light amplification, infrared system that would keep them visible all night. This part made Lottie's head ache.

Next came the full-screen commercial for the wall units. Only those who had them could see the entire show. Down the left side of the screen were the four contestants, each in a separate panel, and over them a topographical map that showed the entire region, where the exit points were, the nearest roads, towns. Center screen could be divided any way the director chose. Above this picture was the show's slogan: "This Is Your Crisis!" and a constantly running commercial. In the far right corner there was an aerial view of the selected site, with the colored dots of light. Mildred's was red, Angie's was green. Eddie's yellow, Clyde's blue. Anything else larger than a rabbit or squirrel that moved into the viewing area would be white.

The contestants were shown being taken to the site, first by airplane, then helicopter. They were left there on noon Friday and had until midnight Sunday to reach one of the dozen trucks that ringed the area. The first one to report in at one of the trucks was the winner.

10 P.M. FRIDAY

Lottie made up her bed on the couch while Butcher opened his recliner full length and brought out a blanket and pillow from the bedroom. He had another beer and Lottie drank milk and ate cookies, and presently they turned off the light and there was only the glow from the screen in the room.

The contestants were settled down for the night, each in a sleeping bag, campfires burning low, the long northern twilight still not faded. Andy began to explain the contents of the backpacks.

Lottie closed her eyes, opened them several times, just to check, and finally fell asleep.

1 A.M. SATURDAY

Lottie sat up suddenly, wide awake, her heart thumping. The red beeper had come on. On center screen the girl was sitting up, staring into darkness, obviously frightened. She must have heard something. Only her dot showed on her screen, but there was no way for her to know that. Lottie lay down again, watching, and became aware of Butcher's heavy snoring. She shook his leg and he shifted and for a few moments breathed deeply, without the snore, then began again.

Francine Dumont was the night M.C.; now she stepped to one side of the screen. "If she panics," Francine said in a hushed voice, "it could be the end of the game for her." She pointed out the hazards in the area—boulders, a steep drop-off, the thickening trees on two sides. "Let's watch," she whispered and stepped back out of the way.

The volume was turned up; there were rustlings in the undergrowth. Lottie closed her eyes and tried to hear them through the girl's ears, and felt only contempt for her. The girl was stiff with fear. She began to build up her campfire. Lottie nodded. She'd stay awake all night, and by late tomorrow she'd be finished. She would be lifted out, the end of Miss Smarty Pants Dawes.

Lottie sniffed and closed her eyes, but now Butcher's snores were louder. If only he didn't sound like a dying man, she thought—sucking in air, holding it, holding it, then suddenly erupting into a loud snort that turned into a gurgle. She pressed her hands over her ears and finally slept again.

2 P.M. SATURDAY

There were beer cans on the table, on the floor around it. There was half a loaf of bread and a knife with dried mustard and the mustard jar without a top. The salami was drying out, hard, and there were onion skins and bits of brown lettuce and an open jar of pickles. The butter had melted in its dish, and the butter knife was on the floor, spreading a dark stain on the rug.

Nothing was happening on the screen now. Angie Dawes hadn't left the fern patch. She was brushing her hair.

Mildred was following the stream, but it became a waterfall ahead and she would have to think of something else.

The stout man was still making his way downward as directly as possible, obviously convinced it was the fastest way and no more dangerous than any other.

The black man was being logical, like Mildred, Lottie admitted. He watched the shadows and continued in a southeasterly direction, tackling the hurdles as he came to them, methodically, without haste. Ahead of him, invisible to him, but clearly visible to the floating cameras and the audience, were a mother bear and two cubs in a field of blueberries.

Things would pick up again in an hour or so, Lottie knew. Butcher came back. "You have time for a quick shower," Lottie said. He was beginning to smell.

"Shut up." Butcher sprawled in the recliner, his feet bare.

Lottie tried not to see his thick toes, grimy with warehouse dust. She got up and went to the kitchen for a bag, and started to throw the garbage into it. The cans clattered.

"Knock it off, will ya!" Butcher yelled. He stretched to see around her. He was watching the blond braid her hair. Lottie threw another can into the bag.

9 P.M. SATURDAY

Butcher sat on the edge of the chair, biting a fingernail. "See that?" he breathed. "You see it?" He was shiny with perspiration.

Lottie nodded, watching the white dots move on the aerial map, watching the blue dot moving, stopping for a long time, moving again. Clyde and the bears were approaching each other minute by minute, and Clyde knew now that there was something ahead of him.

"You see that?" Butcher cried out hoarsely.

"Just be still, will you?" Lottie said through her teeth. The black man was sniffing the air.

"You can smell a goddam lousy bear a country mile!" Butcher said. "He knows."

"For God's sake, shut up!"

"Yeah, he knows all right," Butcher said softly. "Mother bear, cubs . . . she'll tear him apart."

"Shut up! Shut up!"

Clyde began to back away. He took half a dozen steps, then turned and ran. The bear stood up; behind her the cubs tumbled in play. She turned her head in a listening attitude. She growled and dropped to four feet and began to amble in the direction Clyde had taken. They were about an eighth of a mile apart. Any second she would be able to see him.

Clyde ran faster, heading for thick trees. Past the trees was a cliff he had skirted earlier.

"Saw a cave or something up there," Butcher muttered. "Betcha. Heading for a cave."

Lottie pressed her hands hard over her ears. The bear

was closing the gap; the cubs followed erratically, and now and again the mother bear paused to glance at them and growl softly. Clyde began to climb the face of the cliff. The bear came into view and saw him. She ran. Clyde was out of her reach; she began to climb, and rocks were loosened by her great body. When one of the cubs bawled, she let go and half slid, half fell back to the bottom. Standing on her hind legs, she growled at the man above her. She was nine feet tall. She shook her great head from side to side another moment, then turned and waddled back toward the blueberries, trailed by her two cubs.

"Smart bastard," Butcher muttered. "Good thinking. Knew he couldn't outrun a bear. Good thinking."

Lottie went to the bathroom. She had smelled the bear, she thought. If he had only shut up a minute! She was certain she had smelled the bear. Her hands were trembling.

The phone was ringing when she returned to the living room. She answered, watching the screen. Clyde looked shaken, the first time he had been rattled since the beginning.

"Yeah," she said into the phone. "He's here." She put the receiver down. "Your sister."

"She can't come over," Butcher said ominously. "Not unless she's drowned that brat."

"Funny," Lottie said, scowling. Corinne should have enough consideration not to make an issue of it week after week.

"Yeah," Butcher was saying into the phone. "I know it's tough on a floor set, but what the hell, get the old man to buy a wall unit. What's he planning to do, take it with him?" He listened. "Like I said, you know how it is. I say okay, then Lottie gives me hell. Know what I mean? I mean, it ain't worth it. You know?" Presently he banged the receiver down.

"Frank's out of town?"

He didn't answer, settled himself down into his chair and reached for his beer.

"He's in a fancy hotel lobby where they got a unit screen the size of a barn and she's got that lousy little portable . . ."

"Just drop it, will ya? She's the one that wanted the kid, remember. She's bawling her head off but she's not coming over. So drop it!"

"Yeah, and she'll be mad at me for a week, and it takes two to make a kid."

"Jesus Christ!" Butcher got up and went into the kitchen. The refrigerator door banged. "Where's the beer?"

"Under the sink."

"Jesus! Whyn't you put it in the refrigerator?"

"There wasn't enough room for it all. If you've gone through all the cold beers, you don't need any more!"

He slammed the refrigerator door again and came back with a can of beer. When he pulled it open, warm beer spewed halfway across the room. Lottie knew he had done it to make her mad. She ignored him and watched Mildred worm her way down into her sleeping bag. Mildred had the best chance of winning, she thought. She checked her position on the aerial map. All the lights were closer to the trucks now, but there wasn't anything of real importance between Mildred and the goal. She had chosen right every time.

"Ten bucks on yellow," Butcher said suddenly.

"You gotta be kidding! He's going to break his fat neck before he gets out of there!"

"Okay, ten bucks." He slapped ten dollars down on the table, between the TV dinner trays and the coffee pot.

"Throw it away," Lottie said, matching it. "Red."

"The fat lady?"

"Anybody who smells like you better not go around insulting someone who at least takes time out to have a shower now and then!" Lottie cried and swept past him to the kitchen. She and Mildred were about the same size. "And why don't you get off your butt and clean up some of that mess! All I do every weekend is clear away garbage!"

"I don't give a shit if it reaches the ceiling!"

Lottie brought a bag and swept trash into it. When she got near Butcher, she held her nose.

6 A.M. SUNDAY

Lottie sat up. "What happened?" she cried. The red beeper was on. "How long's it been on?"

"Half an hour. Hell, I don't know."

Butcher was sitting tensely on the side of the recliner, gripping it with both hands. Eddie was in a tree, clutching the trunk. Below him, dogs were tearing apart his backpack, and another dog was leaping repeatedly at him.

"Idiot!" Lottie cried. "Why didn't he hang up his stuff like the others?"

Butcher made a noise at her, and she shook her head, watching. The dogs had smelled food, and they would search for it, tearing up everything they found. She smiled grimly. They might keep Mr. Fat Neck up there all day, and even if he got down, he'd have nothing to eat.

That's what did them in, she thought. Week after week it was the same. They forgot the little things and lost. She leaned back and ran her hand through her hair. It was standing out all over her head.

Two of the dogs began to fight over a scrap of something and the leaping dog jumped into the battle with them. Presently they all ran away, three of them chasing the fourth.

"Throw away your money," Lottie said gaily, and started around Butcher. He swept out his hand and pushed her down again and left the room without a backward look. It didn't matter who won, she thought, shaken by the push. That twenty and twenty more would have to go to the finance company to pay off the loan for the wall unit. Butcher knew that; he shouldn't get so hot about a little joke.

1 P.M. SUNDAY

"This place looks like a pigpen," Butcher growled. "You going to clear some of this junk away?" He was carrying a sandwich in one hand, beer in the other; the table was littered with breakfast remains, leftover snacks from the morning and the night before.

Lottie didn't look at him. "Clear it yourself."

"I'll clear it." He put his sandwich down on the arm of his chair and swept a spot clean, knocking over glasses and cups.

"Pick that up!" Lottie screamed. "I'm sick and tired of cleaning up after you every damn weekend! All you do is stuff and guzzle and expect me to pick up and clean up."

"Damn right."

Lottie snatched up the beer can he had put on the table and threw it at him. The beer streamed out over the table, chair, over his legs. Butcher threw down the sandwich and grabbed at her. She dodged and backed away from the table into the center of the room. Butcher followed, his hands clenched.

"You touch me again, I'll break your arm!"

"Bitch!" He dived for her and she caught his arm, twisted it savagely and threw him to one side.

He hauled himself up to a crouch and glared at her with hatred. "I'll fix you," he muttered. "I'll fix you!"

Lottie laughed. He charged again, this time knocked her backward and they crashed to the floor together and rolled, pummeling each other.

The red beeper sounded and they pulled apart, not looking at each other, and took their seats before the screen.

"It's the fat lady," Butcher said malevolently. "I hope the bitch kills herself."

Mildred had fallen into the stream and was struggling in waist-high water to regain her footing. The current was very swift, all white water here. She slipped and went under. Lottie held her breath until she appeared again, downstream, retching, clutching at a boulder. Inch by inch she drew herself to it and clung there trying to get her breath back. She looked about desperately; she was very white. Abruptly she launched herself into the current, swimming strongly, fighting to get to the shore as she was swept down the river.

Andy's voice was soft as he said, "That water is forty-eight degrees, ladies and gentlemen! Forty-eight! Dr. Lederman, how long can a person be immersed in water that cold?"

"Not long, Andy. Not long at all." The doctor looked worried too. "Ten minutes at the most, I'd say."

"That water is reducing her body heat second by second," Andy said solemnly. "When it is low enough to produce unconsciousness . . ."

Mildred was pulled under again; when she appeared this time, she was much closer to shore. She caught a rock and held on. Now she could stand up, and presently she dragged herself rock by rock, boulder by boulder, to the shore. She was shaking hard, her teeth chattering. She began to build a fire. She could hardly open her waterproof matchbox. Finally she had a blaze and she began to strip. Her backpack, Andy reminded the audience, had been lost when she fell into the water. She had only what she had on her back, and if she wanted to continue after the sun set and the cold evening began, she had to dry her things thoroughly.

"She's got nerve," Butcher said grudgingly.

Lottie nodded. She was weak. She got up, skirted Butcher, and went to the kitchen for a bag. As she cleaned the table, every now and then she glanced at the naked woman by her fire. Steam was rising off her wet clothes.

10 P.M. SUNDAY

Lottie had moved Butcher's chair to the far side of the table the last time he had left it. His beard was thick and coarse, and he still wore the clothes he had put on to go to work Friday morning. Lottie's stomach hurt. Every weekend she got constipated.

The game was between Mildred and Clyde now. He was in good shape, still had his glasses and his backpack. He was farther from his truck than Mildred was from hers, but she had eaten nothing that afternoon and was limping badly.

Her boots must have shrunk, or else she had not waited for them to get completely dry. Her face twisted with pain when she moved.

The girl was still posing in the high meadow, now against a tall tree, now among the wild flowers. Often a frown crossed her face and surreptitiously she scratched. Ticks, Butcher said. Probably full of them.

Eddie was wandering in a daze. He looked empty, and was walking in great aimless circles. Some of them cracked like that, Lottie knew. It had happened before, sometimes to the strongest one of all. They'd slap him right in a hospital and no one would hear anything about him again for a long time, if ever. She didn't waste pity on him.

She would win, Lottie knew. She had studied every kind of wilderness they used and she'd know what to do and how to do it. She was strong, and not afraid of noises. She found herself nodding and stopped, glanced quickly at Butcher to see if he had noticed. He was watching Clyde.

"Smart," Butcher said, his eyes narrowed. "That sonabitch's been saving himself for the home stretch. Look at him." Clyde started to lope, easily, as if aware the TV truck was dead ahead.

Now the screen was divided into three parts, the two finalists, Mildred and Clyde, side by side, and above them a large aerial view that showed their red and blue dots as they approached the trucks.

"It's fixed!" Lottie cried, outraged when Clyde pulled ahead of Mildred. "I hope he falls down and breaks his back!"

"Smart," Butcher said over and over, nodding, and Lottie knew he was imagining himself there, just as she had done. She felt a chill. He glanced at her and for a moment their eyes held—naked, scheming. They broke away simultaneously.

Mildred limped forward until it was evident each step was torture. Finally she sobbed, sank to the ground and buried her face in her hands.

Clyde ran on. It would take an act of God now to stop

him. He reached the truck at twelve minutes before midnight.

For a long time neither Lottie nor Butcher moved. Neither spoke. Butcher had turned the audio off as soon as Clyde reached the truck, and now there were the usual after-game recaps, the congratulations, the helicopter liftouts of the other contestants.

Butcher sighed. "One of the better shows," he said. He was hoarse.

"Yeah. About the best yet."

"Yeah." He sighed again and stood up. "Honey, don't bother with all this junk now. I'm going to take a shower, and then I'll help you clean up, okay?"

"It's not that bad," she said. "I'll be done by the time you're finished. Want a sandwich, doughnut?"

"I don't think so. Be right out." He left. When he came back, shaved, clean, his wet hair brushed down smoothly, the room was neat again, the dishes washed and put away.

"Let's go to bed, honey," he said, and put his arm lightly about her shoulders. "You look beat."

"I am." She slipped her arm about his waist. "We both lost."

"Yeah, I know. Next week."

She nodded. Next week. It was the best money they ever spent, she thought, undressing. Best thing they ever bought, even if it would take them fifteen years to pay it off. She yawned and slipped into bed. They held hands as they drifted off to sleep.

STROBOSCOPIC

Alastair Reynolds

Alastair Reynolds is a frequent contributor to Interzone, *and has also sold to* Asimov's Science Fiction, Spectrum SF, *and elsewhere. His first novel,* Revelation Space, *was widely hailed as one of the major SF books of the year; it was quickly followed by* Chasm City, Redemption Ark, Absolution Gap, *and* Century Rain, *all big books that were big sellers as well, establishing Reynolds as one of the best and most popular new SF writers to enter the field in many years. His other books include a novella collection,* Diamond Dogs, Turquoise Days. *His most recent book is a new novel,* Pushing Ice. *Coming up are two new collections,* Galactic North *and* Zima Blue and Other Stories. *A professional scientist with a PhD in astronomy, he comes from Wales, but lives in the Netherlands, where he works for the European Space Agency.*

Here's a taut, inventive, and fast-paced story that speculates that the newish realm of computer game design will eventually merge with the field of daredevil exhibitions of the jump-over-a-canyon-on-a-rocket sled sort, to produce a sport where everything can change in the blink of an eye—sometimes with fatal results.

"OPEN THE BOX."

I wasn't making a suggestion. Just in case the tone of my voice didn't make that clear, I backed up my words with an antique but functional blunderbuss; something won in a gaming tournament half a lifetime earlier. We stood in the airlock of my yacht, currently orbiting Venus: me, my wife, and two employees of Icehammer Games.

Between us was a gray box the size of a child's coffin.

"After all this time," said the closest man, his face hidden behind a mirrored gold visor on a rococo white helmet. "Still don't trust us?"

"First rule of complex systems," I said. "You can't tell friends from enemies."

"Thanks for the vote of confidence, Nozomi."

But even as he spoke, White knelt down and fiddled with the latches on the lid of the box. It opened with a gasp of air, revealing a mass of translucent protective sheeting wadded around something very cold. After passing the blunderbuss to Risa, I reached in and lifted out the package, feeling its bulk.

"What is it?

"An element of a new game," said the other man, Black. "Something called *Stroboscopic*."

I carried the package to a workbench. "Never heard of it."

"It's hush-hush," Black said. "Company hopes to have it up and running in a few months. Rumor is it's unlike anything else in Tycho."

I pulled back the last layer of wadding.

It was an animal packed in ice; some kind of hard-shelled arthropod; like a cross between a scorpion and a crab—all segmented exoskeletal plates and multijointed limbs terminating in various specialized and nasty-looking appendages. The dark carapace was mottled with patches of dirty white, sparkling with tiny reflections. Elsewhere it shone like polished turtleshell. There were ferocious mouth parts but nothing I recognized as an eye, or any kind of sensory organ at all.

"Looks delicious," I said. "What do I cook it with?"

"You don't eat it, Nozomi. You play it." Black shifted nervously as if wary of how much he could safely disclose. "The game will feature a whole ecology of these things—dozens of other species; all kinds of predator-prey relationships."

"Someone manufactures them?"

"Nah." It was White speaking now. "Icehammer found 'em somewhere outside the system, using the snatcher."

"Might help if I knew where."

"Tough titty. They never told us; we're just one of dozens of teams working on the game."

I couldn't help but laugh. "So you're saying, all I have to go on is one dead animal, which might have come from anywhere in the galaxy?"

"Yeah," White said, his helmet nodding. "Except it isn't dead."

* * *

THE mere fact that I'd seen the creature, of course, meant that I'd have an unfair advantage when it came to playing the game. It meant that I, Nozomi, one of the dozen or so best-known gamers in the system, would be cheating. But I could live with that. Though my initial rise to fame had been driven mainly by skill, it was years since I'd played a game without having already gained an unfair edge over the other competitors.

There were reasons.

I could remember a time in my childhood when the playing of games was not the highest pinnacle of our culture; simply one means by which rich immortals fought boredom. But that was before the IWP commenced the first in a long series of wars against the Halo Ideologues, those scattered communities waging dissent from the system's edge. The Inner Worlds Prefecture had turned steadily more totalitarian, as governments generally do in times of crisis. Stealthily, the games had been pushed toward greater prominence, and shady alliances had been forged between the IWP and the principal gaming houses. The games enthralled the public and diverted their attentions from the Halo wars. And—unlike the arts—they could not be used as vehicles for subversion. For gamers like myself it was a near-utopian state of affairs. We were pampered and courted by the houses and made immensely rich.

But—maybe because we'd been elevated to such loftiness—we also saw what was going on. And turning a blind eye was one of the few things I'd never been good at.

One day, five years ago, I was approached by the same individuals who'd brought the box to my yacht. Although they were officially working for Icehammer, they were also members of an underground movement with cells in all the gaming houses. Its lines of communication stretched out to the Ideologues themselves.

The movement was using the games against the IWP. They'd approach players like myself and offer to disclose material relating to games under development by Icehammer or other houses; material that would give the player an edge over their rivals. The player in turn would siphon a percentage of their profit into the movement.

The creature in the box was merely the latest tip-off.

But I didn't know what to make of it, except that it had been snatched from somewhere in the galaxy. Wormhole manipulation offered instantaneous travel to the stars, but nothing larger than a beachball could make the trip. The snatcher was an automated probe that had retrieved biological specimens from thousands of planets. Icehammer operated its own snatcher, for obtaining material that could be incorporated into products.

This time, it seemed to have brought back a dud.

* * *

"IT just sits there and does nothing," Risa said when the Icehammer employees had left, the thing resting on a chilled pallet in the sick bay.

"What kind of game can they possibly build around it?"

"Last player to die of boredom wins?"

"Possible. Or maybe you throw it? It's heavy enough, as though the damn thing is half-fossilized. Those white patches look like quartz, don't they?"

Maybe the beast wouldn't do *anything* until it was placed into the proper environment—perhaps because it needed olfactory or tactile cues to switch from dormancy.

"Black said the game was based on an ecology?" I said.

"Yeah, but how do you think such a game would work?" Risa said. "An ecology's much too chaotic to build into a game." Before she married me she'd been a prominent games designer for one of the other houses, so she knew what she was talking about. "Do you know how disequilibrate your average ecology is?"

"Not even sure I can pronounce it."

"Ecologies aren't kids's stuff. They're immensely complex—food webs, spectra of hierarchical connectedness. . . . Screw up any one level, and the whole thing can collapse—unless you've evolved the system into some kind of Gaian self-stabilizing regime, which is hard enough when you're not trying to re-create an alien ecology, where there might be all sorts of unexpected emergent phenomena."

"Maybe that's the point, though? A game of dexterity, like balancing spinning plates?"

Risa made the noise that told she was half acknowledging the probable truthfulness of my statement. "They must constrain it in some way. Strip it down to the essentials, and then build in some mechanism whereby players can influence things."

I nodded. I'd been unwilling to probe the creature too deeply until now, perhaps still suspicious of a trap—but I knew that if I didn't, the little arthropod would drive me quietly insane. At the very least, I had to know whether it had anything resembling a brain—and if I got that far, I could begin to guess at the kinds of behavioral routines scripted into its synapses, especially if I could trace pathways to sensory organs. Maybe I was being optimistic, though. The thing didn't even have recognizable eyes, so it was anyone's guess as to how it assembled a mental model of its surroundings. And of course that told me something, though it wasn't particularly useful.

The creature had evolved somewhere dark.

* * *

A MONTH later, Icehammer began a teaser campaign for *Stroboscopic*. The premiere was to take place two months later in Tycho, but a handful of selected players would be invited to an exclusive preview a few weeks earlier, me among them.

I began to warm up to competition fitness.

Even with insider knowledge, no game was ever a walkover, and my contacts in the resistance movement would be disappointed if I didn't turn in a tidy profit. The trouble was I didn't know enough about the game to finesse the required skills; whether they were mental or physical or some combination of the two. Hedging my bets, I played as many different types of games as possible in the time frame, culminating in a race through the atmosphere of Jupiter piloting frail cloudjammers. The game was one that demanded an acute grasp of aerodynamic physics, coupled with sharp reflexes and a willingness to indulge in extreme personal risk.

It was during the last of the races that Angela Valdez misjudged a thermal and collapsed her foil. Valdez had been a friend of mine years ago, and though we'd since fallen into rivalry, we'd never lost our mutual respect. I attended her funeral on Europa with an acute sense of my own mortality. There, I met most of the other gamers in the system, including a youngish man called Zubek whose star was in the ascendant. He and Valdez had been lovers, I knew—just as I'd loved her years before I met Risa.

"I suppose you've heard of *Stroboscopic?*" he asked, sidling up to me after Valdez's ashes had been scattered on Europa's ice.

"Of course."

"I presume you won't be playing, in that case." Zubek

smiled. "I gather the game's going to be more than slightly challenging."

"You think I'm not up to it?"

"Oh, you were good once, Nozomi—nobody'd dispute that." He nodded to the smear of ash on the frost. "But so was Angela. She was good enough to beat the hardest of games—until the day when she wasn't."

I wanted to punch him. What stopped me was the thought that maybe he was right.

* * *

I WAS on my way back from the funeral when White called, using the secure channel to the yacht.

"What have you learnt about the package, Nozomi? I'm curious."

"Not much," I said, nibbling a fingernail. With my other hand I was toying with Risa's dreadlocks, her head resting on my chest. "Other than the fact that the animal responds to light. The mottled patches on its carapace are a matrix of light-sensitive organs; silicon and quartz deposits. Silicon and silicon oxides, doped with a few other metals. I think they work as organic semiconductors, converting light into electrical nerve impulses."

I couldn't see White's face—it was obscured by a golden blur that more or less approximated the visor of his suit—but he tapped a finger against the blur, knowingly. "That's all? A response to light? That's hardly going to give you a winning edge."

"There's nothing simple about it. The light has to reach a certain threshold intensity before there's any activity at all."

"And then it wakes up?"

"No. It moves for a few seconds, like a clockwork toy given a few turns of the key. Then it freezes up again, even if the light level remains constant. It needs a period of darkness before it shows another response to light."

"How long?"

"Seventy seconds, more or less. I think it gets all the

energy it needs during that one burst of light, then goes into hibernation until the next burst. Its chemistry must be optimized so highly that it simply can't process more rapid bursts."

The gold ovoid of his face nodded. "Maybe that ties in with the title of the game," he said. "*Stroboscopic.*"

"You wouldn't care to hazard a guess as to what kind of evolutionary adaptation this might be?"

"I wish there was time for it, Nozomi. But I'm afraid that isn't why I called. There's trouble."

"What sort?" Though I didn't really need to ask.

He paused, looking to one side, as if nervous of being interrupted. "Black's vanished. My guess is the goons got to him. They'll have unpicked his memory by now."

"I'm sorry."

"It may be hazardous for you to risk competition now that you're implicated."

I let the words sink in, then shook my head. "It's too late," I said. "I've already given them my word that I'll be there."

Risa stirred. "Too pigheaded to back down?"

"No," I said. "But on the other hand, I do have a reputation to uphold."

* * *

AS the premiere approached we learned what we could of the creature. It was happier in vacuum than air, although the latter did not seem to harm it provided it was kept cold. Maybe that had something to do with its silicon biochemistry. Silicon had never seemed like a likely rival to carbon as a basis for life, largely because silicon's higher valency denied its compounds the same long-term stability. But under extreme cold, silicon biochemistry might have the edge, or at least be an equally probable pathway for evolution. And with silicon came the possibility of exploiting light itself as an energy source, with no clumsy intermediate molecular machinery like the rhodopsin molecule in the human retina.

But the creature lived in darkness.

I couldn't resolve this paradox. It needed light to energize itself—a flash of intense blue light, shading into the UV—and yet it hadn't evolved an organ as simple as the eye. The eye, I knew, had been invented at least 40 times during the evolution of life on Earth. Nature came up with the eye whenever there was the slightest use for it.

It got stranger.

There was something I called the secondary response—also triggered by exposure to light. Normally, shown a flash every 70-odd seconds, the animal would execute a few seemingly purposeful movements, each burst of locomotion coordinated with the previous one, implying that the creature kept some record of what it had been doing previously. But if we allowed it to settle into a stable pattern of movement bursts, the creature began to show richer behavior. The probability of eliciting the secondary response rose to a maximum midway through the gap between normal bursts, roughly half a minute after the last, before smoothly diminishing. But at its peak, the creature was hypersensitized to any kind of ambient light at all, even if it was well below the threshold energy of the normal flash. If no light appeared during the time of hypersensitivity, nothing happened; the creature simply waited out the remaining half a minute until the next scheduled flash. But if even a few hundred photons fell on its carapace, it would always do the same thing; thrashing its limbs violently for a few seconds, evidently drawing on some final reserve of energy that it saved for just this response.

I didn't have a clue why.

And I wasn't going to get one, either—at least not by studying the creature. One day we'd set it up in the autodoc analysis chamber as usual, and we'd locked it into the burst cycle, working in complete darkness apart from the regular pulses of light every minute and ten seconds. But we forgot to lash the animal down properly. A status light flashed on the autodoc console, signifying some routine health-monitoring function. It wasn't bright at all, but it happened just when the creature was hypersensitized. It thrashed its limbs wildly, making a noise like a box of chopsticks.

And hurled itself from the chamber, falling to the floor.

Even though it was dark, I saw something of its shattering, as it cleaved into a million pieces. It sparkled as it died.

"Oops," Risa said.

* * *

THE premiere soon arrived. Games took place all over the system, but the real epicenter was Tycho. The lunar crater had been domed, pressurized, and infused with a luminous mass of habitats and biomes, all dedicated to the pursuit of pleasure through game. I'd visited the place dozens of times, of course—but even then, I'd experienced only a tiny fraction of what it had to offer. Now all I wanted to do was get in and out—and if *Stroboscopic* was the last game I ever played there, I didn't mind.

"Something's bothering you, Noz," Risa said, as we took a monorail over the Icehammer zone. "Ever since you came back from Valdez's funeral."

"I spoke to Zubek."

"Him?" She laughed. "You've got more talent in your dick."

"He suggested I should consider giving this one a miss."

"He's just trying to rile you. Means you still scare him." Then she leaned toward the window of our private cabin. "There. The Arena."

It was a matt-black geodesic ball about half a kilometer wide, carbuncled by ancillary buildings. Searchlights scissored the air above it, neon letters spelling out the name of the game, running around the ball's circumference.

Stroboscopic.

Thirty years ago the eponymous CEO of Icehammer Games had been a top-class player in his own right—until neutral feedback incinerated most of his higher motor functions. Now Icehammer's frame was cradled within a powered exoskeleton, stenciled with luminous Chinese dragons.

He greeted myself, the players, and assorted hangers-on as we assembled in an atrium adjoining the Arena. After a short preliminary speech a huge screen was unveiled behind him. He stood aside and let the presentation roll.

A drab, wrinkled planet hove into view on the screen, lightly sprinkled with craters; one ice cap poking into view.

"PSR-J2034+454A," Icehammer said. "The decidedly unpoetic name for a planet nearly 500 light-years from here. Utterly airless and barely larger than our moon, it shouldn't really be there at all. Less than ten million years ago its sun reached the end of its nuclear-burning life cycle and went supernova." He clapped his hands together in emphasis; some trick of acoustics magnifying the clap concussively. "Apart from a few comets, nothing else remains. The planet moves in total darkness, even starlight attenuated by the nebula of dust that embeds the system. Even the star it once drew life from has become a corpse."

The star rose above one limb of the planet: a searing point of light, pulsing on and off like a beacon.

"A pulsar," Icehammer said. "A 15-kilometer ball of nuclear matter, sending out an intense beam of light as it rotates, four flashes a second; each no more than 13 hundredths of a second long. The pulsar has a wobble in its rotational axis, however, which means that the beam only crosses our line of sight once every 72 seconds, and then only for a few seconds at a time." Then he showed us how the pulsar beam swept across the surface of the planet, dousing it in intense, flickering light for a few instants, outlining every nuance of the planet's topography in eye-wrenching violet. Followed by utter darkness on the face of the world, for another 72 seconds.

"Now the really astonishing thing," Icehammer said, "is that something evolved to live on the planet, although only on the one face, which it always turns to the star. A whole order of creatures, in fact, their biology tuned to exploit that regular flash of light. Now we believe that life on Earth originated in self-replicating structures in pyritic minerals, or certain kinds of clay. Eventually, this mineralogic life formed the scaffolding for the first form of carbon-based life, which—being more efficient and flexible—quickly usurped its predecessor. But perhaps that genetic takeover never happened here, stymied by the cold and the vacuum and the radiative effects of the star." Now he showed us holo-images of the creatures themselves, rendered in the style of watercolors from a naturalist's fieldbook, annotated in hand-written Latin. Dozens of forms—including several radically different bodyplans and modes of locomotion—but everything was hardshelled and a clear cousin to the animal we'd examined on the yacht. Some of the more obvious predators looked incredibly fearsome. "They do all their living in bursts lasting a dozen seconds, punctuated by nearly a minute of total inactivity. Evidently some selection mechanism determined that a concentrated burst of activity is more useful than long, drawn-out mobility."

Jumping, I thought. You couldn't jump in slow motion. Predators must have been the first creatures to evolve toward the burst strategy—and then grazers had been forced to follow suit.

"We've given them the collective term *Strobelife*—and their planet we've called *Strobeworld*, for obvious reasons." Icehammer rubbed his palms together with a whine of actuating motors. "Which, ladies and gentlemen, brings us rather neatly to the game itself. Shall we continue?"

"Get on with it, you bastard," I murmured. Next to me, Risa squeezed my hand and whispered something calming.

* * *

WE were escorted up a sapphire staircase into a busy room packed with consoles and viewing stands. There was no direct view of the Arena itself, but screens hanging from the ceiling showed angles in various wavebands.

The Arena was a mockup of part of the surface of Strobeworld, simulated with astonishing precision: the correct rocky terrain alleviated only by tufts of colorless vacuum-tolerant "vegetation," gravity that was only a few percent from Strobeworld's own, and a magnetic field that simulated in strength and vector the ambient field at the point on Strobeworld from which the animals had been snatched. The roof of the dome was studded with lamps that would blaze for less than 13 hundredths of a second, once every 72 seconds, precisely mimicking the passage of the star's mercilessly bright beam.

The game itself—Level One, at least—would be played in rounds: single player against single player, or team against team. Each competitor would be allocated a fraction of the thousand-odd individual animals released into the Arena at the start—fifty/fifty in the absence of any handicapping. The sample would include animals from every ecological level, from grazers that fed on the flora, right up to the relatively scarce top predators, of which there were only a dozen basic variants. They had to eat, of course: light could provide their daily energy needs, but they'd still need to consume each other for growth and replication. Each competitor's animals would be labeled with infrared markers, capable of being picked up by Arena cams. It was the competitor's goal to ensure that their population of Strobeworld creatures outperformed the rival's, simply by staying alive longest. Computers would assess the fitness of each population after a round and the winner would be announced.

I watched a few initial heats before my turn.

Most of the animals were sufficiently far from each other—or huddled in herds—that during each movement burst they did little except shuffle around or move slightly more in one direction than another. But the animals that were near each other exhibited more interesting behavior. Prey creatures—small, flat-bodied grazers or midlevel predators—would try and get away from the higher-level predators, which in turn would advance toward the grazers and subordinate predators. But then they'd come to a stop, perfectly motionless, their locations revealed only by the cams, since it was completely dark in the Arena.

Waiting.

It was harder than it looked—the dynamics of the

ecosystem far subtler than I'd expected. Interfering at any level could have wildly unexpected consequences.

Risa would have loved it.

Soon it was my turn. I took my console after nodding briefly at my opponent; a rising player of moderate renown, but no real match for myself, even though neither of us had played *Stroboscopic* before.

We commenced play.

The Arena—initially empty—was populated by Strobelife via robot drones that dashed out from concealed hatches. The Strobelife was in stasis; no light flashes from the dome to trigger the life cycle; as stiff and sculptural as the animal we'd studied in the yacht. My console displayed a schematic overlay of the Arena, with "my" animals designated by marker symbols. The screens showed the same relationships from different angles. Initial placement was pseudo-random; animals placed in lifelike groupings, but with distances between predator and prey, determined by algorithms compiled from real Strobeworld populations.

We were given five minutes to study the grouping and evolve a strategy before the first flash. Thereafter, the flashes would follow at 72-second intervals until the game's conclusion.

The five minutes slammed past before I'd examined less than a dozen possible opening gambits.

For a few flash cycles nothing much happened; too much distance between potential enemies. But after the fifth cycle some of the animals were within striking range of each other. Little local hot spots of carnage began to ensue; animals being dismembered or eaten in episodic bursts.

We began to influence the game. After each movement burst—during the minute or so of near-immobility—we were able to selectively reposition or withdraw our own or our opponent's animals from the Arena, according to a complex shifting value scheme. The immobile animals would be spirited away, or relocated, by the same robots that had placed them initially. When the next flash came, play would continue seamlessly.

All sorts of unanticipated things could happen.

Wipe out one predator and you might think that the animals it was preying on would thrive, or at least not be decimated so rapidly. But what often happened was that a second rival predator—until then contained in number—would invade the now unoccupied niche and become *more successful* than the animal that had been wiped out. If that new predator also pursued the prey animals of the other, then they might actually be worse off.

I began to grasp some of *Stroboscopic's* latent complexity. Maybe it was going to be a challenge after all.

I played and won four rounds out of five. No point deluding myself: at least two of my victories had been sheer luck, or had evolved from dynamics of the ecology that were just too labyrinthine to guess at. But I was impressed, and for the first time in years, I didn't feel as if I'd already exhausted every aspect of a game.

I was enjoying myself.

I waited for the other heats to cycle through, my own name only displaced from the top of the leader board when the last player had completed his series.

Zubek had beaten me.

"Bad luck," he said, in the immediate aftermath, after we'd delivered our sound bites. He slung an arm around my shoulder, matishly. "I'm sorry what I said about you before, Nozomi."

"Would you be apologizing now if I'd won?"

"But you didn't, did you? Put up a good fight, I'll admit. Were you playing to your limit?" Zubek stopped a passing waiter and snatched two drinks from his tray, something fizzy, passing one to me. "Listen, Nozomi. Either way, we won in style and trashed the rest."

"Good. Can I go now? I'd like to speak to my wife." And get the hell away from Tycho, I thought.

"Not so fast. I've got a proposition. Will you hear me out?"

* * *

I LISTENED to what Zubek had to say. Then caught up with Risa a few minutes later and told her what he had outlined.

"You're not serious," she said. "He's playing a game with you, don't you realize?"

"Isn't that the point?"

Risa shook her head exasperatedly. "Angela Valdez is dead. She died a good death, doing what she loved. Nothing the two of you can do now can make the slightest difference."

"Zubek will make the challenge whether I like it or not."

"But you don't have to agree." Her voice was calm but her eyes promised tears. "You know what the rumors said. That the next level was more dangerous than the first."

"That'll make it all the more interesting, then."

But she wasn't really listening to me, perhaps knowing that I'd already made my mind up.

Zubek and I arranged a press conference an hour later, sharing the same podium, microphones radiating out from our faces like the rifles of a firing squad; stroboscopic flashes of cameras prefiguring the game ahead. We explained our proposition: how we'd agreed between ourselves to another game; one that would be dedicated to the memory of Angela Valdez.

But that we'd be playing Level Two.

Icehammer took the podium during the wild applause and cheering that followed our announcement.

"This is extremely unwise," he said, still stiffly clad in his mobility frame. "Level Two is hardly tested yet; there are bound to be bugs in the system. It could be exceedingly dangerous." Then he smiled and a palpable aura of relief swept through the spectators. "On the other hand, my shareholders would never forgive me if I forewent an opportunity for publicity like this."

The cheers rose to a deafening crescendo.

Shortly afterward I was strapped into the console, with neuro-effectors crowning my skull, ready to light up my pain center. The computer overseeing the game would allocate jolts of pain according to the losses suffered by my population of Strobelife. All in the mind, of course. But that wouldn't make the pain any less agonizing, and it wouldn't reduce the chances of my heart simply stopping at the shock of it all.

Zubek leant in and shook my hand.

"For Angela," I said, and then watched as they strapped Zubek in the adjacent console, applying the neuro-effector.

It was hard. It wasn't just the pain. The game was made more difficult by deliberately limiting our overview of the Arena. I no longer saw my population in its entirety—the best I could do was hop my point of view from creature to creature, my visual field offering a simulation of the electrical-field environment sensed by each Strobelife animal; a snapshot only updated during Strobetime. When there was no movement, there was no electrical-field generation. Most of the time I was blind.

Most of the time I was screaming.

Yet somehow—when the computer assessed the fitness of the two populations—I was declared the winner over Zubek.

Lying in the couch, my body quivered, saliva waterfalling from my slack jaw. A moan filled the air, which it took me long moments to realize was my own attempt at vocalization. And then I saw something odd; something that shouldn't have happened at all.

Zubek hauled himself from his couch, not even sweating. He didn't look like a man who'd just been through agony.

An unfamiliar face blocked my view of him. I knew who it was, just from his posture and the cadences of his speech.

"Yes, you're right. Zubek was never wired into the neuro-effector. He was working for us—persuading you to play Level Two."

"White," I slurred. "You, isn't it?"

"The very man. Now how would you like to see your wife alive?"

I reached for his collar, fingers grasping ineffectually at the fabric. "Where's Risa?"

"In our care, I assure you. Now kindly follow me."

He waited while I heaved myself from the enclosure of the couch, my legs threatening to turn to jelly beneath me.

"Oh, dear," White said, wrinkling his nose. "You've emptied your bladder, haven't you?"

"I'll empty your face if you don't shut up."

My nervous system had just about recovered by the time we reached Icehammer's quarters, elsewhere in the building. But my belief system was still in ruins.

White was working for the IWP.

* * *

ICEHAMMER was lounging on a maroon settee, divested of his exoskeletal support system. Just as I was marveling at how pitiable he looked, he jumped up and strode to me, extending a hand.

"Good to meet you, Nozomi."

I nodded at the frame, racked on one wall next to an elaborate suit of armor. "You don't need that thing?"

"Hell, no. Not in years. Good for publicity, though—neural burnout and all that."

"It's a setup, isn't it?"

"How do you think it played?" Icehammer said."

"Black really was working for the movement," I said, aware that I was compromising myself with each word, but also that it didn't matter. "White wasn't. You were in hock to the IWP all along. You were the reason Black vanished."

"Nothing personal Nozomi," White said. "They got to my family, just as we've got to Risa."

Icehammer took over: "She's in our care now, Nozomi—quite unharmed, I assure you. But if you want to see her alive, I advise that you pay meticulous attention to my words." While he talked he brushed a hand over the tabard of the hanging suit of armor, leaving a greasy imprint on the black metal. "You disappointed me. That a man of your talents should be reduced to cheating."

"I didn't do it for myself."

"You don't seriously imagine that the movement could possibly pose a threat to the IWP? Most of its cells have been infiltrated. Face it, man, it was always an empty gesture."

"Then where was the harm?"

Icehammer tried a smile but it looked fake. "Obviously I'm not happy at your exploiting company secrets, even if you were good enough to keep them largely to yourself."

"It's not as if I sold them on."

"No, I'll credit you with discretion, if nothing else. But even if I thought killing you might be justified, there'd be grave difficulties with such a course of action. You're too well known; I can't just make you disappear without attracting a lot of attention. And I can't expose you as a cheat without revealing the degree to which my organization's security was breached. So I'm forced to another option—one that, on reflection, will serve the both of us rather well."

"Which is?"

"I'll let Risa go, provided you agree to play the next level of the game."

I thought about that for a few moments before answering. "That's all? Why the blackmail?"

"Because no one in their right minds would play Level Three if they knew what was involved." Icehammer toyed with the elegantly flared cuff of his bottle-green smoking jacket. "The third level is exponentially more hazardous than the second. Of course, it will eventually draw competitors—but no one would consent to playing it until they'd attained total mastery of the lower levels. We don't expect that to happen for at least a year. You, on the other hand, flushed with success at beating Zubek, will rashly declare your desire to play Level Three. And in the process of doing so you will probably die, or at the very least be severely maimed."

"I thought you said it would serve me well."

"I meant your posthumous reputation." Icehammer raised a finger. "But don't imagine that the game will be rigged, either. It will be completely fair, by the rules."

Feeling sick to my stomach, I still managed a smile. "I'll just have to cheat, then, won't I?"

* * *

A FEW minutes later I stood at the podium again, a full audience before me, and read a short prepared statement. There wasn't much to it, and as I hadn't written a word of it, I can't say that I injected any great enthusiasm into the proceedings.

"I'm retiring," I said, to the hushed silence in the atrium. "This will be my last competition."

Muted cheers. But they quickly died away.

"But I'm not finished yet. Today I played the first two levels of what I believe will be one of the most challenging and successful games in Tycho, for many years to come. I now intend to play the final level."

Cheers followed again—but they were still a little fearful. I didn't blame them. What I was doing was insane.

Icehammer came out—back in his frame again—and made some halfhearted protestations, but the charade was even more theatrical than last time. Nothing could be better for publicity than my failing to complete the level—except possibly my death.

I tried not to think about that part.

"I admire your courage," he said, turning to the audience. "Give it up for Nozomi—he's a brave man!" Then he whispered in my ear: "Maybe we'll auction your body parts."

But I kept on smiling my best shit-eating smile, even as they wheeled in the same suit of armor that I'd seen hanging on Icehammer's wall.

* * *

I WALKED into the Arena, the armor's servo-assisted joints whirring with each step. The suit was heated and pressurized, of course—but the tiny air-circulator was almost silent, and the ease of walking meant that my own exertions were slight.

The Arena was empty of Strobelife now, brightly lit; dusty topsoil like lunar regolith, apart from the patches of flora. I walked to the spot that had been randomly assigned me, designated by a livid red circle.

Icehammer's words still rang in my ears. "You don't even know what happens in Level Three, do you?"

"I'm sure you're going to enjoy telling me."

"Level One is abstracted—the Arena is observed, but it might as well be taking place in a computer. Level Two's a little more visceral, as you're now well aware—but there's still no actual physical risk to the competitor. And, of course, even Level Two could be simulated. You must have asked yourself that question, Nozomi. Why create a real ecology of Strobelife creatures at all, if you're never going to enter it?"

That was when he had drawn my attention to the suit of armor. "You'll wear this. It'll offer protection against the vacuum and the effects of the pulse, but don't delude yourself that the armor itself is much more than cosmetic."

"I'm going into the Arena?"

"Where else? It's the logical progression. Now your viewpoint will be entirely limited to one participant in the game—yourself."

"Get it over with."

"You'll still have the ability to intervene in the ecology, just as before—the commands will be interpreted by your suit and transmitted to the controlling computer. The added complexity, of course, is that you'll have to structure your game around your own survival at each step."

"And if—when—I win?"

"You'll be reunited with Risa, I promise. Free to go. All the rest. You can even sell your story, if you can find anyone who'll believe you."

"Know a good ghostwriter?"

He'd winked at me then. "Enjoy the game, Nozomi. I know I will."

Now I stood on my designated spot and waited.

The lights went out.

I had a sense of rapid subliminal motion all around me. The drones were whisking out and positioning the inert Strobelife creatures in their initial formations. The process lasted a few seconds, performed in total silence. I could move, but only within the confines of the suit, which had now become rigid apart from my fingers.

Unguessable minutes passed.

Then the first stammering pulse came, bright as a nuclear explosion, even with the visor's shielding. My suit lost its rigidity, but for a moment I didn't dare move. On the faceplate's head-up display I could see that I was surrounded by Strobelife creatures, rendered according to their electrical field properties. There were grazers and predators and all the intermediates, and they all seemed to be moving in my direction.

And something was dreadfully wrong. *They were too big*.

I'd never asked myself whether the creature we'd examined on the yacht was an adult. Now I knew it wasn't.

The afterflash of the flash died from my vision, and as the seconds crawled by, the creatures' movements became steadily more sluggish, until only the smallest of them were moving at all.

Then they, too, locked into immobility.

As did my suit, its own motors deactivating until triggered by the next flash.

I tried to hold the scene in my memory, recalling the large predator whose foreclaw might scythe within range of my suit, if he was able to lurch three or four steps closer to me during the next pulse. I'd have to move fast, when it came—and on the pulse after that, I'd have another two to contend with, nearing me on my left flank.

The flash came—intense and eye-hurting.

No shadows; almost everything washed out in the brilliance. Maybe that was why Strobelife had never evolved the eye: it was too bright for contrast, offering no advantage over electrical field sensitivity.

The big predator—a cross among a tank, armadillo, and

lobster—came three steps closer and slammed his foreclaw into a wide arc that grazed my chest. The impact hit me like a bullet.

I fell backward, into the dirt, knowing that I'd broken a rib or two.

The electrical field overlay dwindled to darkness. My suit seized into rigidity.

Think, Noz. Think.

My hand grasped something. I could still move my fingers, if nothing else. The gloves were the only articulated parts of the suit that weren't slaved to the pulse cycle.

I was holding something hard, rocklike. But it wasn't a rock. My fingers traced the line of a carapace; the pielike fluting around the legs. It was a small grazer.

An idea formed in my mind. I thought of what Icehammer had said about the Strobeworld system; how there was nothing apart from the planet, the pulsar, and a few comets.

Sooner or later, one of those comets would crash into the star. It might not happen very often, maybe only once every few years, but when it did it would be very bad indeed: a massive flare of X rays as the comet was shredded by the gravitational field of the pulsar. It would be a pulse of energy far more intense than the normal flash of light; too energetic for the creatures to absorb.

Strobelife must have evolved a protection mechanism.

The onset of a major flare would be signaled by visible light, as the comet began to break up. A tiny glint at first, but harbinger of far worse to come. The creatures would be sensitized to burrow into the topdirt at the first sign of light, which did not come at the expected time. . . .

I'd already seen the reaction in action. It was what had driven the thrashing behavior of our specimen before it dropped to its death on the cabin floor. It had been trying to burrow; to bury itself in topdirt before the storm came.

The Arena wasn't Strobeworld, just a clever facsimile of it—and there was no longer any threat from an X-ray burst. But the evolved reflex would remain, hardwired into every animal in the ecology.

All I had to do was trigger it.

The next flash came, like the brightest, quickest dawn imaginable. Ignoring the pain in my chest, I stood up—still holding the little grazer in my gloved hand.

But how could I trigger it? I'd need a source of light, albeit small, but I'd need to have it go off when I was completely immobile.

There was a way.

The predator lashed at me again, gouging into my leg. I began to topple, but forced myself to stay upright, if nothing else. Another gouge, painful this time, as if the leg armor was almost lost.

The electrical overlay faded again, and my suit froze into immobility. I began to count aloud in my head.

I'd remembered something. It had seemed completely insignificant at the time; a detail so trivial that I was barely conscious of committing it to memory. When the specimen had shattered, it had done so in complete darkness. And yet I'd seen it happen. I'd seen glints of light as it smashed into a million fragments.

And now I understood. The creature's quartz deposits were highly crystalline. And sometimes—when crystals are stressed—they release light; something called piezoluminescene. Not much; only the amount corresponding to the energy levels of electrons trapped deep within lattices—but I didn't need much, either. Not if I waited until the proper time, when the animals would be hypersensitized to that warning glint. I counted to 35, what I judged to be halfway between the flash intervals. And then let my fingers relax.

The grazer dropped in silence toward the floor.

I didn't hear it shatter, not in vaçuum. But in the total darkness in which I was immersed, I couldn't miss the sparkle of light.

I felt the ground rumble all around me. Half a minute later, when the next flash came from the ceiling, I looked around.

I was alone.

No creatures remained, apart from the corpses of those that had already died. Instead, there were a lot of rocky mounds, where even the largest of them had buried themselves under topdirt. Nothing moved, except for a few pathetic avalanches of disturbed dirt. And there they'd wait, I knew—for however long it was evolution had programmed them to sit out the X-ray flare.

Thanks to the specimens on the yacht, I happened to know exactly how long that time was. Slightly more than four and a half hours.

Grinning to myself, knowing that Nozomi had done it again—cheated and made it look like winner's luck—I began to stroll to safety, and to Risa.

SYNTHETIC SERENDIPITY

Vernor Vinge

Born in Waukesha, Wisconsin, Vernor Vinge now lives in San Diego, California, where he is an associate professor of math sciences at San Diego State University. He sold his first story, "Apartness," to New Worlds *in 1965; it immediately attracted a good deal of attention, was picked up for Donald A. Wollheim and Terry Carr's collaborative* World's Best Science Fiction *anthology the following year, and still strikes me as one of the strongest stories of that entire period. Since this impressive debut, he has become a frequent contributor to* Analog; *he has also sold to* Orbit, Far Frontiers, If, Stellar, *and other markets. His novella "True Names," which is famous in internet circles and among computer enthusiasts well outside of the usual limits of the genre was a finalist for both the Nebula and Hugo awards in 1981 and is cited by some as having been the real progenitor of cyberpunk rather than William Gibson's* Neuromancer. *His novel* A Fire Upon the Deep, *one of the most epic and sweeping of modern Space Operas, won him a Hugo Award in 1993; its sequel,* A Deepness in the Sky, *won him another Hugo Award in 2000, and his novella "Fast Times at Fairmont High" won another Hugo in 2003. These days Vinge is regarded as one of the best of the American "hard science" writers, along with people such as Greg Bear and Gregory Benford. His other books include the novels* Tatja Grimm's World, The Witling, The Peace War *and* Marooned in Realtime *(which have been released in an omnibus volume as* Across Realtime*), and the collections* True Names and Other Dangers, Threats and Other Promises, *and* The Collected Stories of Vernor Vinge. *His most recent book is a new novel,* Rainbow's End.

Here's a look at a computer-dominated, high-tech, high-bit-rate future that may be coming along a lot sooner than you think that it could, making members of older generations obsolete and unable to compete in society with the tech-savvy Whiz Kids surrounding them. Even in this wired-up future, though, there'll still be dangerous games to play and boys will still be boys—unfortunately.

YEARS ago, games and movies were for indoors, for couch potatoes and kids with overtrained trigger fingers. Now they were on the outside. They were the world. That was the main reason Miguel Villas liked to walk to school with the Radner twins. Fred and Jerry were a Bad Influence, but they were the best gamers Mike knew in person.

"We got a new scam, Mike," said Fred.

"Yeah," said Jerry, smiling the way he did when something extreme was in the works.

The three followed the usual path along the flood control channel. The trough was dry and gray, winding its way through the canyon behind Las Mesitas subdivision. The hills above them were covered with iceplant and manzanita; ahead, there was a patch of scrub oaks. What do you expect of San Diego north county in early May?

At least in the real world.

The canyon was not a deadzone. Not at all. County Flood Control kept the whole area improved, and the public layer was just as fine as on city streets. As they walked along, Mike gave a shrug and a twitch just so. That was enough cue for his Epiphany wearable. Its overlay imaging shifted into classic manga/animé: The manzanita branches morphed into scaly tentacles. Now the houses that edged the canyon were heavily-timbered, with pennants flying. High ahead was a castle, the home of Grand Duke Hwa Feen—in fact, the local kid who did the most to maintain this belief circle. Mike tricked out the twins in Manga costume, and spikey hair, and classic big-eyed, small-mouthed features.

"Hey, Jerry, look." Mike radiated, and waited for the twins to slide into consensus with his view. He'd been practicing all week to get these visuals.

Fred looked up, accepting the imagery that Mike had conjured.

"That's old stuff, Miguel, my man." He glanced at the castle on the hill. "Besides, Howie Fein is a nitwit."

"Oh." Mike released the vision in an untidy cascade. The real world took back its own, first the sky, then the landscape, then the creatures and costumes. "But you liked it last week." Back when, Mike now remembered, Fred and Jerry had been maneuvering to oust the Grand Duke.

The twins looked at each other. Mike could tell they were silent messaging. "We told you today would be different. We're onto something special." They were partway through the scrub oaks now. From here you could see ocean haze; on a clear day—or if you bought into clear vision—you could see all the way to the ocean. On the south were more subdivisions, and a patch of green that was Fairmont High School. On the north was the most interesting place in Mike Villas' neighborhood:

Pyramid Hill Park dominated the little valley that surrounded it. Once upon a time the hill had been an avocado orchard. You could still see it that way if you used the park's logo view. To the naked eye, there were other kinds of trees. There were also lawns, and real mansions, and a looping structure that flew a parabolic arc hundreds of feet above the top of the hill. That was the longest freefall ride in California.

The twins were grinning at him. Jerry waved at the hill. "How would you like to play *Cretaceous Returns*, but with real feeling?"

Pyramid Hill had free entrances, but they were just for visuals.

"That's too expensive."

"Sure it is. If you pay."

"And, um, don't you have a project to set up before class?" The twins had shop class first thing in the morning.

"That's still in Vancouver," said Jerry.

"But don't worry about us." Fred looked upward, somehow prayerful and smug at the same time. " 'FedEx will provide, and just in time.' "

"Well, okay. Just so we don't get into trouble." Getting into trouble was the major downside of hanging with the Radners.

"Don't worry about it." The three left the edge of the flood channel and climbed a narrow trail along the east edge of Pyramid Hill. This was far from any entrance, but the twins' uncle worked for County Flood Control and they had access to CFC utilities—which just now they shared with Mike. The dirt beneath their feet became faintly translucent. Fifteen feet down, Mike could see graphics representing a ten-inch runoff tunnel. Here and there were pointers to local maintenance records. Jerry and Fred had used the CFC view before and not been caught. Today they blended it with a map of the local nodes. The overlay was faintly violet against the sunlit day, showing comm shadows and active highrate links.

The two stopped at the edge of a clearing. Fred looked at Jerry. "Tsk. Flood Control should be ashamed. There's not a localizer node within thirty feet."

"Yeah, Jer. Almost anything could happen here." Without a complete localizer mesh, nodes could not know precisely where they were. High-rate laser comm could not be established, and low-rate sensor output was smeared across the landscape. The outside world knew only mushy vagueness about this area.

They walked into the clearing. They were deep in comm shade, but from here they had a naked-eye view up the hillside. If they continued that way, Pyramid Hill would start charging them.

The twins were not looking at the Hill. Jerry walked to a small tree and squinted up. "See? They tried to patch the coverage with an airball." He pointed into the branches and pinged. The utility view showed only a faint return, an error message. "It's almost purely net guano at this point."

Mike shrugged. "The gap will be fixed by tonight." Around twilight, when maintenance UAVs flitted like bats around the canyons, popping out nodes here and there.

"Heh. Well, why don't we help the County by patching things right now?" Jerry held up a thumb-sized greenish object. He handed it to Mike.

Three antenna fins sprouted from the top, a typical ad hoc node.

The dead ones were more trouble than bird poop. "You've perv'd this thing?" The node had Breaklns-R-Us written all over it, but perverting networks was harder in real life than in games. "Where did you get the access codes?"

"Uncle Don gets careless." Jerry pointed at the device. "All the permissions are loaded. Unfortunately, the bottleneck node is still alive." He pointed upwards, into the sapling's branches. "You're small enough to climb this, Mike. Just go up and knock down the node."

"Hmm."

"Hey, don't worry. Homeland Security won't notice."

In fact, the Department of Homeland Security would almost certainly notice, at least after the localizer mesh was patched. But just as certainly they wouldn't care. DHS logic was deeply embedded in all hardware. "See All, Know All," was their motto, but what they knew and saw was for their own mission. They were notorious for not sharing with law enforcement. Mike stepped out of the comm shade and took a look at the crime trackers view. The area around Pyramid Hill had its share of arrests, mostly for enhancement drugs . . . but there had been nothing hereabouts for months.

"Okay." Mike came back to the tree and shinnied up to where the branches spread out. The old node was hanging from rotted velcro. He knocked it loose and the twins caused it to have an accident with a rock. Mike scrambled down and hey watched the diagnostics for a moment. Violet mists sharpened into bright spots as the nodes figured out where they and their perv'd sibling were, and coordinated up toward full function. Now point-to-point, laser routing was available; they could see the property labels all along the boundary of Pyramid Hill.

"Ha," said Fred. The twins started uphill, past the property line. "C'mon, Mike. We're marked as county employees. We'll be fine if we don't stay too long."

* * *

PYRAMID Hill had all the latest touchie-feelie effects. These were not just phantoms painted by your contact lenses on the back of your eyeballs. On Pyramid Hill, there were games where you could kick lizard butt and steal raptor eggs—or games with warm furry creatures that danced playfully around, begging to be picked up and cuddled. If you turned off all the game views, you could see other players wandering through the woods in their own worlds. Somehow the Hill kept them from crashing into each other.

In *Cretaceous Returns* the plants were towering gingko trees, with lots of barriers and hidey holes. Mike played the purely visual *Cret Ret* a lot these days, in person with the twins and all over the world with others. It had not been an uplifting experience. He had been "killed and eaten" three times so far this week. It was a tough game, one where you had to contribute or maybe you got eaten. Mike was trying. He had designed a species—quick, small things that didn't attract the fiercest of the critics. The twins had not been impressed, though they had no alternatives of their own.

As he walked through the gingko forest, he kept his eye out for critters with jaws lurking in the lower branches. That's what had gotten him on Monday. On Tuesday it had been some kind of paleo disease.

So far things seemed safe enough, but there was no sign of his own contribution. They had been fast breeding and scalable, so where were the little monsters? Maybe someone had exported them. They might be big in Kazakhstan. He had had success there before. Here today—nada.

Mike stumped across the Hill, a little discouraged, but still uneaten. The twins had taken the form of game-standard velociraptors.

They were having a grand time. Their chicken-sized prey were Pyramid Hill haptics.

The Jerry-raptor looked over its shoulder at Mike. "Where's your critter?"

Mike had not assumed any animal form. "I'm a time traveler," he said. That was a valid type, introduced with the initial game release.

Fred flashed a face full of teeth. "I mean where are the critters you invented last week?"

"I don't know."

"Most likely they got eaten by the critics," said Jerry. The brothers did a joint reptilian chortle. "Give up on making creator points, Miguel. Kick back and use the good stuff." He illustrated with a soccer kick that connected with something running fast across their path. That got some classic points and a few thrilling moments of haptic carnage. Fred joined in and red splattered everywhere.

There was something familiar about this prey. It was young and clever looking . . . a newborn from Mike's own design! And that meant its Mommy would be nearby. Mike said, "You know, I don't think—"

"The Problem Is, None Of You Think Nearly Enough." The sound was like sticking your head inside an old-time boom box. Too late, they saw that the tree trunks behind them grew from yard-long claws.

Mommy. Drool fell in ten-inch blobs from high above.

This was Mike's design scaled to the max.

"Sh—" said Fred. It was his last hiss as a velociraptor. The head and teeth behind the slobber descended from the gingko canopy and swallowed Fred down to the tips of his hind talons. The monster crunched and munched for a moment. The clearing was filled with the sound of splintering bones.

"Ahh!" The monster opened its mouth and vomited horror. It was scarey good. Mike flicker-viewed on reality: Fred was standing in the steaming remains of his raptor. His shirt was pulled out of his pants, and he was drenched in slime—real, smelly slime. The kind you paid money for.

The monster itself was one of Hill's largest robots, tricked out as a member of Mike's new species.

The three of them looked up into its jaws.

"Was that touchie-feelie enough for you?" the creature said, its breath a hot breeze of rotting meat. Fred stepped backwards and almost slipped on the goo.

"The late Fred Radner just lost a cartload of points,"—the monster waved its truck-sized snout at them—"and I'm still hungry. I suggest you move off the Hill with all dispatch."

They backed away, their gaze still caught on all those teeth.

The twins turned and ran. As usual, Mike was an instant behind them.

Something like a big hand grabbed him. "You, I have further business with." The words were a burred roar through clenched fangs. "Sit down."

Jeez. I have the worst luck. Then he remembered that it was Mike Villas who had climbed a tree to perv the Hill entrance logic.

Stupid Mike Villas didn't need bad luck; he was already the perfect chump. And now the twins were out of sight.

But when the "jaws" set him down and he turned around, the monster was still there—not some Pyramid Hill rentacop. Maybe this really was a *Cret Ret* player! He edged sideways, trying to get out from under the pendulous gaze. This was just a game. He could walk away from this four-storey saurian. Of course, that would trash his credit with *Cretaceous Returns,* maybe drench him in smelly goo. And if Big Lizard took things seriously, it might cause him trouble in other games. *Okay*... He sat down with his back against the nearest gingko. So he would be late another day; that couldn't make his school situation any worse.

The saurian settled back, pushing the steaming corpse of Fred Radner's raptor to one side. It brought its head close to the ground, to look at Mike straight on. The eyes and head and color were exactly Mike's design, and this player had the moves to make it truly impressive. He could see from its scars that it had fought in several *Cretaceous* hotspots.

Mike forced a cheerful smile. "So, you like my design?"

It picked at its teeth with eight-inch foreclaws. "I've been worse." It shifted game parameters, bringing up critic-layer details.

This was a heavy player, maybe even a cracker! On the ground between them was a dead and dissected example of Mike's creation. Big Lizard nudged it with a foreclaw. "The skin texture is pure Goldman. Your color scheme is a trivial emergent thing, a generic cliché."

Mike drew his knees in toward his chin. This was the same crap he had to put up with at school. "I borrow from the best."

The saurian's chuckle was a buzzing roar. "That might work with your teachers. They have to eat whatever garbage you feed them—till you graduate and can be dumped on the street. Your design is so-so. There have been some adoptions, mainly because it scales well. But if we're talking real quality, you just don't measure up." The creature flexed its battle scars.

"I can do other things."

"Yes, and if you never deliver, you'll fail with them, too."

That was a point that occupied far too much of Mike Villas' worry time. He glared back at the slitted yellow eyes, and suddenly it occurred to him that—unlike teachers—this guy was not being paid to be nasty. And it was wasting too much time for this to be some humiliating joke. *It actually wants something, from me!* Mike sharpened his glare. "And you have some suggestions, Oh Mighty Virtual Lizard?"

". . . Maybe. I have other projects besides *Cret Ret*. How would you like to take an affiliate status on one of them?"

Except for local games, no one had ever asked Mike to affiliate on anything. His mouth twisted in bogus contempt. "Affiliate? A percent of a percent of . . . what? How far down the value chain are you?"

The saurian shrugged and there was the sound of gingkos swaying to the thump of its shoulders. "My guess is I'm way, way down. On the other hand, this is not a dredge project. I can pay real money for each answer I pipe upwards." The creature named a number; it was enough to play the Hill once a week for a year. A payoff certificate floated in the air between them.

"I get twice that or no deal."

"Done!" said the creature, and somehow Mike was sure it was grinning.

". . . Okay, so what do you want?"

"You go to Fairmont High, right?"

"Yeah."

"It's a strange place, isn't it?" When Mike did not reply, the critter said, "Trust me, it is strange. Most schools don't put Adult Education students in with the children."

"Yeah, Senior High. The old farts don't like it. We don't like it."

"Well, the affiliate task is to snoop around, mainly among the old people. Make friends with them."

Yecch. But Mike glanced at the payoff certificate again. It tested valid. The payoff adjudication was more complicated than he wanted to read, but it was backed by eBay. "Who in particular?"

"So far, my upstream affiliate has only told me its broad interests: Basically, some of these senior citizens used to be bigshots."

"If they were so big, how come they're in our classes now?" It was just the question the kids asked at school.

"Lots of reasons, Miguel. Some of them are just lonely. Some of them are up to their ears in debt, and have to figure out how to make a living in the current economy. And some of them have lost half their marbles and aren't good for much but a strong body and lots of old memories. . . . Ever hear of Pick's Syndrome?"

"Um . . ." Mike googled up the definition: . . . serious social dysfunction. "How do I make friends with someone like that?"

"If you want the money, you figure out a way. Don't worry. There's only one on the list, and he's in remission. Anyway, here are the search criteria." The Big Lizard shipped him a document. Mike browsed through the top layer.

"This covers a lot of ground." Retired politicians, military officers, bioscientists, parents of persons currently in such job categories. "Um, this really could be deep water. We might be setting people up for blackmail."

"Heh. I wondered if you'd notice that."

"I'm not an idiot."

"If it gets too deep, you can always bail."

"I'll take the job. I'll go affiliate with you."

"I wouldn't want you doing anything you feel un—"

"I *said,* I'll *take* the job!"

"Okay! Well then, this should get you started. There's contact information in the document." The creature lumbered to its feet, and its voice came from high above. "Just as well we don't meet on Pyramid Hill again."

"Suits me." Mike made a point of slapping the creature's mighty tail as he walked off down hill.

* * *

THE twins were way ahead of him, standing by the soccer field on the far side of campus. As Mike came up the driveway, he grabbed a viewpoint in the bleachers and gave them a ping. Fred waved back, but his shirt was still too gooey for real comm. Jerry was looking upwards, at the FedEx shipment falling toward his outstretched hands. Just in time, for sure. The twins were popping the mailer open even as they walked indoors.

Unfortunately, Mike's first class was in the far wing. He ran across the lawn, keeping his vision tied to unimproved reality: The buildings were mostly three storeys today. Their gray walls were like playing cards balanced in a rickety array.

Indoors, the choice of view was not entirely his own. Mornings, the school administration required that the Fairmont School News appear all over the interior walls. Three kids at Hoover High had won IBM Fellowships. Applause, applause, even if Hoover was Fairmont's unfairly advantaged rival, a charter school run by the Math Department at SDSU. The three young geniuses would have their college education paid for, right through grad school, even if they never worked at IBM.

Big deal, Mike thought. Somewhere down the line, some percentage of their fortunes would be siphoned sideways into IBM's treasury.

He followed the little green nav arrows with half his attention . . . and abruptly realized he had climbed two flights of stairs. School admin had rearranged everything since yesterday. Of course, they had updated his nav arrows, too. It was a good thing he hadn't been paying attention.

He slipped into his classroom and sat down.

* * *

MS. CHUMLIG had already started.

Search and Analysis was Chumlig's thing. She used to teach a fast-track version of this at Hoover High, but well-documented rumor held that she just couldn't keep up. So the Department of Education had moved her to the same-named course here at Fairmont. Actually, Mike kind of liked her. She was a failure, too.

"There are many different skills," she was saying. "Sometimes it's best to coordinate with lots of other people." The students nodded. Be a coordinator. That's where the fame and money were. But they also knew where Chumlig was going with this. She looked around the classroom, nodding that she knew they knew. "Alas, you all intend to be top agents, don't you?"

"It's what some of us will be." That was one of the Adult Ed students. Ralston Blount was old enough to be Mike's great grandfather. When Blount had a bad day he liked to liven things up by harassing Ms. Chumlig.

The Search and Analysis instructor smiled back. "The pure 'coordinating agent' is a rare type, Professor Blount."

"Some of us must be the administrators."

"Yes." Chumlig looked kind of sad for a moment, like she was figuring out how to pass on bad news. "Administration has changed a lot, Professor Blount."

Ralston Blount shrugged. "Okay. So we have to learn some new tricks."

"Yes." Ms. Chumlig looked out over the class. "That's my point. In this class, we study search and analysis. Searching may seem simple, but the analysis involves understanding results. In the end, you've got to know something about something."

"Meaning all those courses we got C's in, right?" That was a voice from the peanut gallery, probably someone who was physically truant.

Chumlig sighed. "Yes. Don't let those skills die. Use them. Improve on them. You can do it with a special form of pre-analysis that I call 'study.' "

One of the students held up a hand. She was that old.

"Yes, Dr. Xu?"

"I know you're correct. But—" The woman glanced around the room. She looked about Chumlig's age, not nearly as old as Ralston Blount. But there was kind of a frightened look in her eyes. "But some people are just better at this sort of thing than others. I'm not as sharp as I once was. Or maybe others are just sharper. . . . What happens if we try our hardest, and it just isn't good enough?"

Chumlig hesitated. "That's a problem that affects everyone, Dr. Xu. Providence gives each of us our hand to play.

In your case, you've got a new deal and a new start on life." Her look took in the rest of the class. "Some of you think your hand in life is all deuces and treys." There were some really dedicated kids in the front rows. They were wearing, but they had no clothes sense and had never learned ensemble coding. As Chumlig spoke, you could see their fingers tapping, searching on "deuces" and "treys".

"But I have a theory of life," said Chumlig. "and it is straight out of gaming: *There is always an angle*. You, each of you, have some special talents. Find out what makes you different and better. Build on that. And once you do, you'll be able to contribute answers to others and they'll be willing to contribute back to you. In short, synthetic serendipity doesn't just happen. *You* must create it."

She hesitated, staring at invisible class notes, and her voice dropped down from oratory. "So much for the big picture. Today, we'll learn about morphing answer board results. As usual, we're looking to ask the right questions."

* * *

MIGUEL liked to sit by the outer wall, especially when the classroom was on an upper floor. You could feel a regular swaying back and forth, the limit cycle of the walls keeping their balance. It made his mom real nervous. "One second of system failure and everything will fall apart!" she had complained at a PTA meeting. On the other hand, house-of-cards construction was cheap—and it could handle a big earthquake almost as easily as it did the morning breeze.

He leaned away from the wall and listened to Chumlig. That was why the school made you show up in person for most classes; you had to pay a little bit of attention just because you were trapped in a real room with a real instructor. Chumlig's lecture graphics floated in the air above them. She had the class's attention; there was a minimum of insolent graffiti nibbling at the edges of her imaging.

And for a while, Mike paid attention, too. Answer boards could generate solid results, usually for zero cost.

There was no affiliation, just kindred minds batting problems around. But what if you weren't a kindred mind? Say you were on a genetics board. If you didn't know a ribosome from a rippereme, then all the modern interfaces couldn't help you.

So Mike tuned her out and wandered from viewpoint to viewpoint around the room. Some were from students who'd set their viewpoints public. Most were just random cams. He browsed Big Lizard's task document as he paused between hops. In fact, the Lizard was interested in more than just the old farts. Some ordinary students made the list, too. This affiliation tree must be as deep as the California Lottery.

But kids are somebody's children. He started some background checks. Like most students, Mike kept lots of stuff saved on his wearable. He could run a search like this very close to his vest. He didn't route to the outside world except when he could use a site that Chumlig was talking about. She was real good at nailing the mentally truant. But Mike was good at ensemble coding, driving his wearable with little gesture cues and eye-pointer menus. As her gaze passed over him, he nodded brightly and he replayed the last few seconds of her talk.

As for the old students . . . competent retreads would never be here; they'd be rich and famous, the people who owned most of the real world. The ones in Adult Education were the hasbeens. These people trickled into Fairmont all through the semester. The oldfolks' hospitals refused to batch them up for the beginning of classes. They claimed that senior citizens were "socially mature," able to handle the jumble of a midsemester entrance.

Mike went from face to face, matching against public records: Ralston Blount. The guy was a saggy mess. Retread medicine was such a crapshoot. Some things it could cure; others it couldn't. And what worked was different from person to person. Ralston had not been a total winner.

Just now the old guy was squinting in concentration, trying to follow Chumlig's answer board example. He had been with the class most of the semester. Mike couldn't see his med records, but he guessed the guy's mind was mostly okay; he was as sharp as some of the kids in class. And once-upon-a-time he had been important at UCSD.

Once-upon-a-time.

Okay, put him on the "of interest" list. Who else? Doris Nguyen. Former homemaker. Mike eyed the youngish face. She looked almost his mom's age, even though she was forty years older. He searched on the name, shed collisions and obvious myths; the Friends of Privacy piled the lies so deep that sometimes it was hard to find the truth. But Doris Nguyen had no special connections in her past. On the other hand . . . she had a son at Camp Pendleton. Okay, Doris stayed on the list.

Chumlig was still going on about how to morph results into new questions, oblivious to Mike's truancy.

And then there was Xiaowen Xu. PhD physics, PhD electrical engineering. 2005 Winner of Intel's Grove Prize. Dr. Xu sat hunched over, looking at the table in front of her. She was trying to keep up on a *laptop!* Poor lady. But for sure she would have connections.

Politicians, military, scientists . . . and parents or children of such. Yeah. This affiliance could get him into a lot of trouble. Maybe he could climb the affiliate tree a ways, get a hint if Bad Guys were involved. Mike sent out a couple hundred queries, mainly pounding on certificate authorities. Even if the certs were solid, people and programs often used them in stupid ways. Answers came trickling back.

If this weren't Friends of Privacy chaff, there might be some real clues here. He sent out followup queries—and suddenly a message hung in letters of silent flame all across his vision:

Chumlig → Villas: _You've got all day to play games, Miguel! If you won't pay attention here, you can darn well take this course *over.*

Villas → Chumlig: *Sorry. Sorry!*

Most times, Chumlig just asked embarrassing questions; this was the first she'd messaged him with a threat.

And the amazing thing was, she'd done it in a short pause, where everyone else thought she was just reading her notes. Mike eyed her with new respect.

* * *

SHOP class. It was Mike Villas' favorite class, and not just because it was his last of the day. Shop was like a premium game; there were real gadgets to touch and connect. That was the sort of thing you paid money for on Pyramid Hill. And Mr. Williams was no Louise Chumlig. He let you follow your own inclinations, but he never came around afterwards and complained because you hadn't accomplished anything. It was almost impossible not to get an A in Ron Williams' classes; he was wonderfully old-fashioned.

Shop class was also Mike's best opportunity to chat up the old people and the do-not-call privacy freaks. He wandered around the shop class looking like an utter idiot. This affiliance required way too much people skill. Mike had never been any good at diplomacy games.

And now he was schmoozing the oldsters. Trying to.

Ralston Blount just sat staring off into the space above his table. The guy was wearing, but he didn't respond to messages. Mike waited until Williams went off for one of his coffee breaks. Then he sidled over and sat beside Blount. Jeez, the guy might be healthy but he really *looked* old. Mike spent a few moments trying to tune in on the man's perceptions. Mike had noticed that when Blount didn't like a class, he just blew it off. He didn't care about grades. After a few moments, Mike realized that he didn't care about socializing either.

So talk to him! It's just another kind of monster whacking.

Mike morphed a buffoon image onto the guy, and suddenly it wasn't so hard to cold start the encounter. "So, Professor Blount, how do you like shop class?"

Ancient eyes turned to look at him. "I couldn't care less, Mr. Villas."

O-*kay*! Hmm. There was lots about Ralston Blount that

was public record, even some legacy newsgroup correspondence. That was always good for shaking up your parents and other grownups. . . .

But the old man continued talking on his own. "I'm not like some people here. I've never been senile. By rights, my career should be on track with the best of my generation."

"By rights?"

"I was Provost of Eighth College in 2006. I should have been UCSD Chancellor in the years following. Instead I was pushed into academic retirement."

Mike knew all that. "But you never learned to wear."

Blount's eyes narrowed. "I made it a point never to wear. I thought wearing was demeaning, like an executive doing his own typing." He shrugged. "I was wrong. I paid a heavy price for that. But things have changed." His eyes glittered with deliberate iridescence.

"I've taken four semesters of this 'Adult Education.' Now my resumé is out there in the ether."

"You must know a lot of important people."

"Indeed. It's just a matter of time."

"Y-you know, Professor, I may be able to help. No wait—I don't mean by myself. I have an affiliance."

". . . Oh?"

At least he knew what affiliance was. Mike explained Big Lizard's deal. "So there could be some real money in this."

Blount squinted his eyes, trying to parse the certificates. "Money isn't everything, especially in my situation."

"But anybody with these certs is important. Maybe you could get help-in-kind."

"True."

The old man wasn't ready to bite, but he said he'd talk to some of the others on Mike's list. Helping them with their projects counted as a small plus in the affiliance. Maybe the Lizard thought that would flush out more connections.

Meantime, it was getting noisy. Marie Dorsey's team

had designed some kind of crawler. Their prototypes were flopping around everywhere.

They got so close you couldn't really talk out loud.

Villas → Blount: *Can you read me?*

"Of course I can," replied the old man.

So despite Blount's claims of withittude, maybe he couldn't manage silent messaging, not even the finger-tapping most grownups used.

* * *

XIAOWEN Xu just sat at the equipment bench and read from her laptop. It took even more courage to talk to her than Ralston Blount.

She seemed so sad and still. She had the parts list formatted like a hardcopy catalog. "Once I knew about these things," she said. "See that." She pointed at a picture in the museum section. "I designed that chip."

"You're world class, Dr. Xu."

She didn't look up. "That was a long time ago. I retired from Intel in 2005. And during the war, I couldn't even get consulting jobs. My skills have just rusted away."

"Alzheimer's?" He knew she was *much* older than she looked, even older than Ralston Blount.

Xu hesitated, and for a moment Mike was afraid she was really angry. But then she gave a sad little laugh. "No Alzheimer's. You—people nowadays don't know what it was like to be old."

"I do so! I have a great grandpa in Phoenix. G'granma, she does have dementia—you know, a kind they still can't fix. And the others are all dead." Which was about as old as you can get.

Dr. Xu shook her head. "Even in my day, not everyone over eighty was senile. I just got behind in my skills. My girlfriend died. After a while I just didn't care very much. I didn't have the energy to care." She looked at her laptop. "Now, I have the energy I had when I was sixty. Maybe I have the same native intelligence." She slapped the table softly. "But I can't even understand a current tech paper." It looked like she was going to start crying, right in the middle of shop class. Mike scanned around; no one seemed to be watching. He reached out to touch Xu's hand. He didn't have the answer. Ms. Chumlig would say he didn't have the right question.

He thought a moment. "What's your shop project going to be?"

"I don't know." She hesitated. "I don't even understand this parts catalog."

Mike waved at her laptop, but the images sat still as carved stone. "Can I show you what I see?"

"Please."

He saved her display to his vision of the parts list. The view weaved and dived, a bad approximation to what Mike could see when he looked around with his headup view. Nevertheless, Xu leaned forward and nodded as Mike tried to explain the list.

"Wait. Those look like little wings."

"Yeah, there are lots of small fliers. They can be fun."

She gave a wan smile. "They don't look very stable."

Mike had noticed that, but not in the view she could see. *How did she know?* "That's true, but hardly anything is passively stable. I could take care of that, if you want to match a power supply."

She studied the stupid display. "Ah, I see." The power supplies were visible there, along with obvious pointers to interface manuals.

"You really could manage the stability?" Another smile, broader this time. "Okay, let's try."

The wings were just tissue flappers. Mike slid a few dozen onto the table top, and started some simulations using the usual stuff from ReynoldsNumbers-R-Us. Xiaowen Xu alternated between querying her laptop and poking her small fingers into the still tinier wings.

Somehow, with virtually no help from anywhere, she had a power train figured out. In a few more minutes, they had five design possibilities. Mike showed her how to program the fab board so that they could try a couple dozen variations all at once.

They tossed handsful of the tiny contraptions into the air. They swirled around the room—and in seconds, all were on the floor, failing in one way or another.

From the far end of the table, Marie Dorsey and her friends were not impressed. "We're making fliers, too, only ours won't be brain damaged!" Huh? And he'd thought she was making crawlers!

Dr. Xu looked at the Dorsey team's floppers. "I don't think you've got enough power, Miss."

Marie blushed. "I—yeah." Her group was silent, but there was heavy messaging. "Can we use your solution?" She rushed on: "With official credit, of course."

"Sure."

Marie's gadgets were making small hops by the time the class bell rang.

End of class, end of school day. But Xiaowen Xu didn't seem to notice. She and Mike collected their midges and merged improvements.

Three generations later, all their tiny flappers were flying. Xu was smiling from ear to ear.

"So now we put mini-nodes on them," said Mike. "You did pretty well with the power configuration." Without any online computation at all.

"Yeah!" She gave him a strange look. "But you got the stability in less than an hour. It would have taken me days to set up the simulations."

"It's easy with the right tools."

She looked disbelieving.

"Hey, I'm near failing at bonehead math. Look Dr. Xu, if you learn to search and use the right packages, you could do all this." He was beginning to sound like Chumlig. *And this fits with the affiliance!* "I-I could show you. There are all sorts of joint projects we could do!" Maybe she would always be one of those deep resource people, but if she found her place, that would be more than he could ever be.

He wasn't sure if Dr. Xu really understood what he was talking about. But she was smiling. "Okay."

* * *

MIKE was late walking home, but that was okay. Ralston Blount had signed onto the affiliance. He was working with Doris Nguyen on her project. Xiaowen Xu had also signed on. She was living at Rainbow's End rest home, but she had plenty of money. She could buy the best beginner's wearable that Epiphany made.

Big Lizard would be pleased, and maybe some money would come Mike's way.

And maybe that didn't matter so much. He suddenly realized he was whistling as he walked. What did matter . . . was a wonderful surprise. He had coordinated something today. *He* had been the person who helped other people. It was nothing like being a real top agent—but it was something.

The Radner twins were almost home, but they showed up to chat.

"You've been scarce, Mike." They were both grinning. "Hey, we got an A from Williams!"

"For the Vancouver project?"

"Yup. He didn't even check where we got it," said Jerry.

"He didn't even ask us to explain it. *That* would have been a problem!" said Fred.

They walked a bit in companionable silence.

"The hole we put in the Pyramid Hill fence is already repaired."

"No surprise. I don't think we should try that again anytime soon."

"Yeah," Fred said emphatically. His image wavered. The slime was still messing his clothes.

Jerry continued, "And we collected some interesting gossip about Chumlig." The students maintained their own files on faculty. Mostly it was good for laughs. Sometimes it had more practical uses.

"What's that?"

"Okay, this is from Ron Williams. He says he got it firsthand, no possibility of Friends of Privacy lies." That's how most FOP lies were prefaced, but Mike just nodded.

"Ms. Chumlig was never fired from Hoover High. She's moonlighting there. Maybe other places, too."

"Oh. Do the school boards know?" Ms. Chumlig was such a straight arrow, it was hard to imagine she was cheating.

"We don't know. Yet. We can't figure why Hoover would let this happen. You know those IBM Fellows they were bragging about? All three were in Chumlig's classes! But she kinda drifted out of sight when the publicity hit. Our theory is there's some scandal that keeps her from taking credit. . . . Mike?"

Mike had stopped in the middle of the path. He shrugged up his record of this morning, and matched Big Lizard's English usage with Chumlig's.

He looked back at the twins. "Sorry. You . . . surprised me."

"It surprised us, too. Anyway, we figure this could be useful if Jerry and I have serious grade problems in her class."

"Yeah, I guess it could," said Mike, but he wasn't really paying attention anymore. It suddenly occurred to him that there could be something beyond top agents. There could be people who helped others on a time scale of years. Something called teachers.

HOW WE GOT IN TOWN AND OUT AGAIN

Jonathan Lethem

Here's a wry but poignant look at an impoverished future America desperate for almost any kind of entertainment . . . and at the down-and-outers desperate enough to provide it for them . . .

Jonathan Lethem is one of that generation of talented young writers who came along in the '90s and the Oughts to date, and whose reputation spreads far outside the usual genre limits. He has worked at an antiquarian bookstore, written slogans for buttons, and lyrics for several rock bands (including Two Fettered Apes, EDO, Jolley Ramey, and Feet Wet), and is also the creator of the Dr. Sphincter character on MTV. In addition to all these certifiably cool credentials, Lethem has also made sales to magazines as varied as Asimov's Science Fiction *and* The New Yorker, *as well as* Interzone, The Magazine of Fantasy and Science Fiction, *and* McSweeney's Enchanted Chamber of Astonishing Stories. *His first novel,* Gun, With Occasional Music, *won the Locus Award for Best First Novel as well as the Crawford Award for Best Fantasy Novel, and was one of the most talked-about books of the year. His other books include the novels* Amnesia Moon, As She Climbed Across the Table, Girl in Landscape, *and* The Fortress of Solitude, *and two collections of his short fiction,* The Wall of the Sky, the Wall of the Eye *and* Men and Cartoons: Stories. *His novel*

Motherless Brooklyn *won the National Book Critics Circle Award in 2000. His most recent book is a nonfiction collection,* The Disappointment Artist: Essays. *Coming up is a new fiction collection,* How We Got Insipid.

WHEN we first saw somebody near the mall Gloria and I looked around for sticks. We were going to rob them if they were few enough. The mall was about five miles out of the town we were headed for, so nobody would know. But when we got closer Gloria saw their vans and said they were scapers. I didn't know what that was, but she told me.

It was summer. Two days before this Gloria and I had broken out of a pack of people that had food but we couldn't stand their religious chanting anymore. We hadn't eaten since then.

"So what do we do?" I said.

"You let me talk," said Gloria.

"You think we could get into town with them?"

"Better than that," she said. "Just keep quiet."

I dropped the piece of pipe I'd found and we walked in across the parking lot. This mall was long past being good for finding food anymore but the scapers were taking out folding chairs from a store and strapping them on top of their vans. There were four men and one woman.

"Hey," said Gloria.

Two guys were just lugs and they ignored us and kept lugging. The woman was sitting in the front of the van. She was smoking a cigarette.

The other two guys turned. This was Kromer and Fearing, but I didn't know their names yet.

"Beat it," said Kromer. He was a tall squinty guy with a gold tooth. He was kind of worn but the tooth said he'd never lost a fight or slept in a flop. "We're busy," he said.

He was being reasonable. If you weren't in a town you were nowhere. Why talk to someone you met nowhere?

But the other guy smiled at Gloria. He had a thin face

and a little mustache. "Who are you?" he said. He didn't look at me.

"I know what you guys do," Gloria said. "I was in one before."

"Oh?" said the guy, still smiling.

"You're going to need contestants," she said.

"She's a fast one," this guy said to the other guy. "I'm Fearing," he said to Gloria.

"Fearing what?" said Gloria.

"Just Fearing."

"Well, I'm just Gloria."

"That's fine," said Fearing. "This is Tommy Kromer. We run this thing. What's your little friend's name?"

"I can say my own name," I said. "I'm Lewis."

"Are you from the lovely town up ahead?"

"Nope," said Gloria. "We're headed there."

"Getting in exactly how?" said Fearing.

"Anyhow," said Gloria, like it was an answer. "With you, now."

"That's assuming something pretty quick."

"Or we could go and say how you ripped off the last town and they sent us to warn about you," said Gloria.

"Fast," said Fearing again, grinning, and Kromer shook his head. They didn't look too worried.

"You ought to want me along," said Gloria. "I'm an attraction."

"Can't hurt," said Fearing. Kromer shrugged, and said, "Skinny, for an attraction."

"Sure, I'm skinny," she said. "That's why me and Lewis ought to get something to eat."

Fearing stared at her. Kromer was back to the van with the other guys.

"Or if you can't feed us—" started Gloria.

"Hold it, sweetheart. No more threats."

"We need a meal."

"We'll eat something when we get in," Fearing said. "You and Lewis can get a meal if you're both planning to enter."

"Sure," she said. "We're gonna enter—right, Lewis?"

I knew to say right.

* * *

THE town militia came out to meet the vans, of course. But they seemed to know the scapers were coming, and after Fearing talked to them for a couple of minutes they opened up the doors and had a quick look then waved us through. Gloria and I were in the back of a van with a bunch of equipment and one of the lugs, named Ed. Kromer drove. Fearing drove the van with the woman in it. The other lug drove the last one alone.

I'd never gotten into a town in a van before, but I'd only gotten in two times before this anyway. The first time by myself, just by creeping in, the second because Gloria went with a militia guy.

Towns weren't so great anyway. Maybe this would be different.

We drove a few blocks and a guy flagged Fearing down. He came up to the window of the van and they talked, then went back to his car, waving at Kromer on his way. Then we followed him.

"What's that about?" said Gloria.

"Gilmartin's the advance man," said Kromer. "I thought you knew everything."

Gloria didn't talk. I said, "What's an advance man?"

"Gets us a place, and the juice we need," said Kromer. "Softens the town up. Gets people excited."

It was getting dark. I was pretty hungry, but I didn't say anything. Gilmartin's car led us to this big building shaped like a boathouse; only it wasn't near any water. Kromer said it used to be a bowling alley.

The lugs started moving stuff and Kromer made me help. The building was dusty and empty inside, and some of the lights didn't work. Kromer said just to get things inside for now. He drove away one of the vans and came back and we unloaded a bunch of little cots that Gilmartin the advance man had rented, so I had an idea where I was going to be sleeping. Apart from that it was stuff for the contest. Computer cables and plastic spacesuits, and loads of televisions.

Fearing took Gloria and they came back with food, fried chicken and potato salad, and we all ate. I couldn't stop going back for more but nobody said anything. Then I went to sleep on a cot. No one was talking to me. Gloria wasn't sleeping on a cot. I think she was with Fearing.

* * *

GILMARTIN the advance man had really done his work. The town was sniffing around first thing in the morning. Fearing was out talking to them when I woke up. "Registration begins at noon, not a minute sooner," he was saying. "Beat the lines and stick around. We'll be serving coffee. Be warned, only the fit need apply—our doctor will be examining you, and he's never been fooled once. It's Darwinian logic, people. The future is for the strong. The meek will have to inherit the here and now."

Inside, Ed and the other guy were setting up the gear. They had about thirty of those wired-up plastic suits stretched out in the middle of the place, and so tangled up with cable and little wires that they were like husks of fly bodies in a spiderweb.

Under each of the suits was a light metal frame, sort of like a bicycle with a seat but no wheels, but with a headrest too. Around the web they were setting up the televisions in an arc facing the seats. The suits each had a number on the back, and the televisions had numbers on top that matched.

When Gloria turned up she didn't say anything to me but she handed me some donuts and coffee.

"This is just the start," she said, when she saw my eyes get big. "We're in for three squares a day as long as this thing lasts. As long as we last, anyway."

We sat and ate outside where we could listen to Fearing. He went on and on. Some people were lined up like he said. I didn't blame them since Fearing was such a talker. Others listened and just got nervous or excited and went away, but I could tell they were coming back later, at least to watch. When we finished the donuts Fearing came over and told us to get on line too.

"We don't have to," said Gloria.

"Yes, you do," said Fearing.

On line we met Lane. She said she was twenty like Gloria but she looked younger. She could have been sixteen, like me.

"You ever do this before?" asked Gloria.

Lane shook her head. "You?"

"Sure," said Gloria. "You ever been out of this town?"

"A couple of times," said Lane. "When I was a kid. I'd like to now."

"Why?"

"I broke up with my boyfriend."

Gloria stuck out her lip, and said, "But you're scared to leave town, so you're doing this instead."

Lane shrugged.

I liked her, but Gloria didn't.

The doctor turned out to be Gilmartin the advance man. I don't think he was a real doctor, but he listened to my heart. Nobody ever did that before, and it gave me a good feeling.

Registration was a joke, though. It was for show. They asked a lot of questions but they only sent a couple of women and one guy away, Gloria said for being too old. Everyone else was okay, despite how some of them looked pretty hungry, just like me and Gloria. This was a hungry town. Later I figured out that's part of why Fearing and Kromer picked it. You'd think they'd want to go where the money was, but you'd be wrong.

After registration they told us to get lost for the afternoon. Everything started at eight o'clock.

* * *

WE walked around downtown but almost all the shops were closed. All the good stuff was in the shopping center and you had to show a town ID card to get in and me and Gloria didn't have those.

So, like Gloria always says, we killed time since time was what we had.

* * *

THE place looked different. They had spotlights pointed from on top of the vans and Fearing was talking through a microphone. There was a banner up over the doors. I asked Gloria and she said "Scape-Athon." Ed was selling beer out of a cooler and some people were buying, even though he must have just bought it right there in town for half the price he was selling at. It was a hot night. They were selling tickets but they weren't letting anybody in yet. Fearing told us to get inside.

Most of the contestants were there already. Anne, the woman from the van, was there, acting like any other contestant. Lane was there too and we waved at each other. Gilmartin was helping everybody put on the suits. You had to get naked but nobody seemed to mind. Just being contestants made it all right, like we were invisible to each other.

"Can we be next to each other?" I said to Gloria.

"Sure, except it doesn't matter," she said. "We won't be able to see each other inside."

"Inside where?" I said.

"The scapes," she said. "You'll see."

Gloria got me into my suit. It was plastic with wiring everywhere and padding at my knees and wrists and elbows and under my arms and in my crotch. I tried on the mask but it was heavy and I saw nobody else was wearing theirs so I kept it off until I had to. Then Gilmartin tried to help Gloria but she said she could do it herself.

So there we were, standing around half naked and dripping with cable in the big empty lit-up bowling alley, and then suddenly Fearing and his big voice came inside and they let the people in and the lights went down and it all started.

"Thirty-two young souls ready to swim out of this world, into the bright shiny future," went Fearing. "The question is, how far into that future will their bodies take them? New worlds are theirs for the taking—a cornucopia of scapes to boggle and amaze and gratify the senses. These lucky kids will be immersed in an ocean of data overwhelming to their undernourished sensibilities—we've assembled a really brilliant collection of environments for them to explore—and you'll be able to see everything they see, on the monitors in front of you. But can they make it in the fast lane? How long can they ride the wave? Which of them will prove able to outlast the others, and take home the big prize—one thousand dollars? That's what we're here to find out."

Gilmartin and Ed were snapping everybody into their masks and turning all the switches to wire us up and getting us to lie down on the frames. It was comfortable on the bicycle seat with your head on the headrest and a belt around your waist. You could move your arms and legs like you were swimming, the way Fearing said. I didn't mind putting on the mask now because the audience was making me nervous. A lot of them I couldn't see because of the lights, but I could tell they were there, watching.

The mask covered my ears and eyes. Around my chin there was a strip of wire and tape. Inside it was dark and quiet at first except Fearing's voice was still coming into the earphones.

"The rules are simple. Our contestants get a thirty minute rest period every three hours. These kids'll be well fed, don't worry about that. Our doctor will monitor their health. You've heard the horror stories, but we're a class outfit; you'll see no horrors here. The kids earn the quality care we provide one way: continuous, waking engagement with the datastream. We're firm on that. To sleep is to die—you can sleep on your own time, but not ours. One lapse, and you're out of the game—them's the rules."

The earphones started to hum. I wished I could reach out and hold Gloria's hand, but she was too far away.

"They'll have no help from the floor judges, or one another, in locating the perceptual riches of cyberspace. Some will discover the keys that open the doors to a thousand worlds, others will bog down in the antechamber to the future. Anyone caught coaching during rest periods will be disqualified—no warnings, no second chances."

Then Fearing's voice dropped out, and the scapes started.

* * *

I WAS in a hallway. The walls were full of drawers, like a big cabinet that went on forever. The drawers had writing on them that I ignored. First I couldn't move except my head, then I figured out how to walk, and just did that for a while. But I never got anywhere. It felt like I was walking in a giant circle, up the wall, across the ceiling, and then back down the other wall.

So I pulled open a drawer. It only looked big enough to hold some pencils or whatever but when I pulled it opened like a door and I went through.

"Welcome to Intense Personals," said a voice. There were just some colors to look at. The door closed behind me. "You must be eighteen years of age or older to use this service. To avoid any charges, please exit now."

I didn't exit because I didn't know how. The space with colors was kind of small except it didn't have any edges. But it felt small.

"This is the main menu. Please reach out and make one of the following selections: women seeking men, men seeking women, women seeking women, men seeking men, or alternatives."

Each of them was a block of words in the air. I reached up and touched the first one.

"After each selection touch *one* to play the recording again, *two* to record a message for this person, or *three* to advance to the next selection. You may touch three at any time to advance to the next selection, or four to return to the main menu."

Then a woman came into the colored space with me. She was dressed up and wearing lipstick.

"Hi, my name is Kate," she said. She stared like she was looking through my head at something behind me, and poked at her hair while she talked. "I live in San Francisco. I work in the financial district, as a personnel manager, but my real love is the arts, currently painting and writing—

"How did you get into San Francisco?" I said.

"—just bought a new pair of hiking boots and I'm hoping to tackle Mount Tam this weekend," she said, ignoring me.

"I never met anyone from there," I said.

"—looking for a man who's not intimidated by intelligence," she went on. "It's important that you like what you do, like where you are. I also want someone who's confident enough that I can express my vulnerability. You should be a good listener—"

I touched three. I can read numbers.

Another woman came in, just like that. This one was as young as Gloria, but kind of soft-looking.

"I continue to ask myself why in the *heck* I'm doing this personals thing," she said, sighing. "But I know the reason—I want to date. I'm new to the San Francisco area. I like to go to the theater, but I'm really open-minded. I was born and raised in Chicago, so I think I'm a little more east coast than west. I'm fast-talking and cynical. I guess I'm getting a little cynical about these ads; the sky has yet to part; lightning has yet to strike—"

I got rid of her, now that I knew how.

"—I have my own garden and landscape business—"

"—someone who's fun, not nerdy—"

"—I'm tender, I'm sensuous—"

I started to wonder how long ago these women were from. I didn't like the way they were making me feel, sort of guilty and bullied at the same time. I didn't think I could make any of them happy the way they were hoping but I didn't think I was going to get a chance to try, anyway.

It took pretty long for me to get back out into the hallway. From then on I paid more attention to how I got into things.

The next drawer I got into was just about the opposite. All space and no people. I was driving an airplane over almost the whole world, as far as I could tell. There was a row of dials and switches under the windows but it didn't mean anything to me. First I was in the mountains and I crashed a lot, and that was dull because a voice would lecture me before I could start again, and I had to wait. But then I got to the desert and I kept it up without crashing much. I just learned to say "no" whenever the voice suggested something different like "engage target" or "evasive action." I wanted to fly a while, that's all. The desert looked good from up there, even though I'd been walking around in deserts too often.

Except that I had to pee I could have done that forever. Fearing's voice broke in, though, and said it was time for the first rest period.

* * *

"—STILL fresh and eager after their first plunge into the wonders of the future," Fearing was saying to the people in the seats. The place was only half full. "Already this world seems drab by comparison. Yet, consider the irony, that as their questing minds grow accustomed to these splendors, their bodies will begin to rebel—"

Gloria showed me how to unsnap the cables so I could walk out of the middle of all that stuff still wearing the suit, leaving the mask behind. Everybody lined up for the bathroom. Then we went to the big hall in the back where they had the cots, but nobody went to sleep or anything. I guessed we'd all want to next time, but right now I was too excited and so was everybody else. Fearing just kept talking like us taking a break was as much a part of the show as anything else.

"Splendors, hah," said Gloria. "Bunch of secondhand cyberjunk."

"I was in a plane," I started.

"Shut up," said Gloria. "We're not supposed to talk about it. Only, if you find something you like, remember where it is."

I hadn't done that, but I wasn't worried.

"Drink some water," she said. "And get some food."

They were going around with sandwiches and I got a couple, one for Gloria. But she didn't seem to want to talk.

Gilmartin the fake doctor was making a big deal of going around checking everybody even though it was only the first break. I figured that the whole point of taking care of us so hard was to remind the people in the seats that they might see somebody get hurt.

Ed was giving out apples from a bag. I took one and went over and sat on Lane's cot. She looked nice in her suit.

"My boyfriend's here," she said.

"You're back together?"

"I mean ex-. I'm pretending I didn't see him."

"Where?"

"He's sitting right in front of my monitor." She tipped her head to point.

I didn't say anything but I wished I had somebody watching me from the audience.

* * *

WHEN I went back the first thing I got into was a library of books. Every one you took off the shelf turned into a show, with charts and pictures, but when I figured out that it was all business stuff about how to manage your money, I got bored.

Then I went into a dungeon. It started with a wizard growing me up from a bug. We were in his workshop, which was all full of jars and cobwebs. He had a face like a melted candle and he talked as much as Fearing. There were bats flying around.

"You must resume the quest of Kroyd," he said to me, and started touching me with his stick. I could see my arms and legs, but they weren't wearing the scaper suit. They were covered with muscles. When the wizard touched me I got a sword and a shield. "These are your companions, Rip and Batter," said the wizard. "They will obey you and protect you. You must never betray them for any other. That was Kroyd's mistake."

"Okay," I said.

The wizard sent me into the dungeon and Rip and Batter talked to me. They told me what to do. They sounded a lot like the wizard.

We met a Wormlion. That's what Rip and Batter called it. It had a head full of worms with little faces and Rip and Batter said to kill it, which wasn't hard. The head exploded and all the worms started running away into the stones of the floor like water.

Then we met a woman in sexy clothes who was holding a sword and shield too. Hers were loaded with jewels and looked a lot nicer than Rip and Batter. This was Kroyd's mistake, anyone could see that. Only I figured Kroyd wasn't here and I was, and so maybe his mistake was one I wanted to make too.

Rip and Batter started screaming when I traded with the woman, and then she put them on and we fought. When she killed me I was back in the doorway to the wizard's room, where I first ran in, bug-sized. This time I went the other way, back to the drawers.

Which is when I met the snowman.

I was looking around in a drawer that didn't seem to have anything in it. Everything was just black. Then I saw a little blinking list of numbers in the corner, touched the numbers. None of them did anything except one.

It was still black but there were five pictures of a snowman. He was three balls of white, more like plastic than snow. His eyes were just o's and his mouth didn't move right when he talked. His arms were sticks but they bent like rubber. There were two pictures of him small and far away, one from underneath like he was on a hill and one that showed the top of his head, like he was in a hole. Then there was a big one of just his head, and a big one of his whole body. The last one was of him looking in through a window, only you couldn't see the window, just the way it cut off part of the snowman.

"What's your name?" he said.

"Lewis."

"I'm Mr. Sneeze." His head and arms moved in all five pictures when he talked. His eyes got big and small.

"What's this place you're in?"

"It's no place," said Mr. Sneeze. "Just a garbage file."

"Why do you live in a garbage file?"

"Copyright lawyers," said Mr. Sneeze. "I made them nervous." He sounded happy no matter what he was saying.

"Nervous about what?"

"I was in a Christmas special for interactive television. But at the last minute somebody from the legal department thought I looked too much like a snowman on a video game called *Mud Flinger*. It was too late to redesign me so they just cut me out and dumped me in this file."

"Can't you go somewhere else?"

"I don't have too much mobility." He jumped and twirled upside down and landed in the same place, five times at once. The one without a body spun too.

"Do you miss the show?"

"I just hope they're doing well. Everybody has been working so hard."

I didn't want to tell him it was probably a long time ago.

"What are you doing here, Lewis?" said Mr. Sneeze.

"I'm in a scape-athon."

"What's that?"

I told him about Gloria and Fearing and Kromer, and about the contest. I think he liked that he was on television again.

* * *

THERE weren't too many people left in the seats. Fearing was talking to them about what was going to happen tomorrow when they came back. Kromer and Ed got us all in the back. I looked over at Lane's cot. She was already asleep. Her boyfriend was gone from the chair out front.

I lay down on the cot beside Gloria. "I'm tired now," I said.

"So sleep a little," she said, and put her arm over me. But I could hear Fearing outside talking about a "Sexathon" and I asked Gloria what it was.

"That's tomorrow night," she said. "Don't worry about it now."

Gloria wasn't going to sleep, just looking around.

* * *

I FOUND the SmartHouse Showroom. It was a house with a voice inside. At first I was looking around to see who the voice was but then I figured out it was the house.

"Answer the phone!" it said. The phone was ringing.

I picked up the phone, and the lights in the room changed to a desk light on the table with the phone. The music in the room turned off.

"How's that for responsiveness?"

"Fine," I said. I hung up the phone. There was a television in the room, and it turned on. It was a picture of food. "See that?"

"The food, you mean?" I said.

"That's the contents of your refrigerator!" it said. "The packages with the blue halo will go bad in the next twenty-four hours. The package with the black halo has already expired! Would you like me to dispose of it for you?"

"Sure."

"Now look out the windows!"

I looked. There were mountains outside.

"Imagine waking up in the Alps every morning!"

"I—"

"And when you're ready for work, your car is already warm in the garage!"

The windows switched from the mountains to a picture of a car in a garage.

"And your voicemail tells callers that you're not home when it senses the car is gone from the garage!"

I wondered if there was somewhere I could get if I went down to drive the car. But they were trying to sell me this house, so probably not.

"And the television notifies you when the book you're reading is available this week as a movie!"

The television switched to a movie, the window curtains closed, and the light by the phone went off.

"I can't read," I said.

"All the more important, then, isn't it?" said the house.

"What about the bedroom?" I said. I was thinking about sleep.

"Here you go!" A door opened and I went in. The bedroom had another television. But the bed wasn't right. It had a scribble of electronic stuff over it.

"What's wrong with the bed?"

"Somebody defaced it," said the house. "Pity."

I knew it must have been Fearing or Kromer who wrecked the bed because they didn't want anyone getting that comfortable and falling asleep and out of the contest. At least not yet.

"Sorry!" said the house. "Let me show you the work center!"

* * *

NEXT rest I got right into Gloria's cot and curled up and she curled around me. It was real early in the morning and nobody was watching the show now and Fearing wasn't talking. I think he was off taking a nap of his own.

Kromer woke us up. "He always have to sleep with you, like a baby?"

Gloria said, "Leave him alone. He can sleep where he wants."

"I can't figure," said Kromer. "Is he your boyfriend or your kid brother?"

"Neither," said Gloria. "What do you care?"

"Okay," said Kromer. "We've got a job for him to do tomorrow, though."

"What job?" said Gloria. They talked like I wasn't there.

"We need a hacker boy for a little sideshow we put on," said Kromer. "He's it."

"He's never been in a scape before," said Gloria. "He's no hacker."

"He's the nearest we've got. We'll walk him through it."

"I'll do it," I said.

"Okay, but then leave him out of the Sexathon," said Gloria.

Kromer smiled. "You're protecting him? Sorry. Everybody plays in the Sexathon, sweetheart. That's bread and butter. The customers don't let us break the rules." He pointed out to the rigs. "You'd better get out there."

I knew Kromer thought I didn't know about Gloria and Fearing, or other things. I wanted to tell him I wasn't so innocent, but I didn't think Gloria would like it, so I kept quiet.

* * *

I WENT to talk to Mr. Sneeze. I remembered where he was from the first time.

"What's a Sexathon?" I said.

"I don't know, Lewis."

"I've never had sex," I said.

"Me neither," said Mr. Sneeze.

"Everybody always thinks I do with Gloria just because we go around together. But we're just friends."

"That's fine," said Mr. Sneeze. "It's okay to be friends."

"I'd like to be Lane's boyfriend," I said.

* * *

NEXT break Gloria slept while Gilmartin and Kromer told me about the act. A drawer would be marked for me to go into, and there would be a lot of numbers and letters but I just had to keep pressing "1-2-3" no matter what. It was supposed to be a security archive, they said. The people watching would think I was breaking codes but it was just for show. Then something else would happen but they wouldn't say what, just that I should keep quiet and let Fearing talk. So I knew they were going to pull me out of my mask. I didn't know if I should tell Gloria.

Fearing was up again welcoming some people back in. I

couldn't believe anybody wanted to start watching first thing in the morning but Fearing was saying "the gritty determination to survive that epitomizes the frontier spirit that once made a country called America great" and "young bodies writhing in agonized congress with the future" and that sounded like a lot of fun, I guess.

A woman from the town had quit already. Not Lane though.

* * *

A GOOD quiet place to go was Mars. It was like the airplane, all space and no people, but better since there was no voice telling you to engage targets, and you never crashed.

* * *

I WENT to the drawer they told me about. Fearing's voice in my ear told me it was time. The place was a storeroom of information like the business library. No people, just files with a lot of blinking lights and complicated words. A voice kept asking me for "security clearance password" but there was always a place for me to touch "1-2-3" and I did. It was kind of a joke, like a wall made out of feathers that falls apart every time you touch it.

I found a bunch of papers with writing. Some of the words were blacked out and some were bright red and blinking. There was a siren sound. Then I felt hands pulling on me from outside and somebody took off my mask.

There were two guys pulling on me who I had never seen before, and Ed and Kromer were pulling on them. Everybody was screaming at each other but it was kind of fake, because nobody was pulling or yelling very hard. Fearing said, "The feds, the feds!" A bunch of people were crowded around my television screen I guess looking at the papers I'd dug up, but now they were watching the action.

Fearing came over and pulled out a toy gun and so did Kromer, and they were backing the two men away from me. I'm sure the audience could tell it was fake. But they were pretty excited, maybe just from remembering when feds were real.

I got off my frame and looked around. I didn't know what they were going to do with me now that I was out but I didn't care. It was my first chance to see what it was like when the contestants were all in their suits and masks, swimming in the information. None of them knew what was happening, not even Gloria, who was right next to me the whole time. They just kept moving in the scapes. I looked at Lane. She looked good, like she was dancing.

Meanwhile Fearing and Kromer chased those guys out the back. People were craning around to see. Fearing came out and took his microphone and said, "It isn't his fault, folks. Just good hacker instincts for ferreting out corruption from encrypted data. The feds don't want us digging up their trail, but the kid couldn't help it."

Ed and Kromer started snapping me back into my suit. "We chased them off," Fearing said, patting his gun. "We do take care of our own. You can't tell who's going to come sniffing around, can you? For his protection and ours we're going to have to delete that file, but it goes to show, there's no limit to what a kid with a nose for data's going to root out of cyberspace. We can't throw him out of the contest for doing what comes natural. Give him a big hand, folks."

People clapped and a few threw coins. Ed picked the change up for me, then told me to put on my mask. Meanwhile Gloria and Lane and everybody else just went on through their scapes.

I began to see what Kromer and Fearing were selling. It wasn't any one thing. Some of it was fake and some was real, and some was a mix so you couldn't tell.

The people watching probably didn't know why they wanted to, except it made them forget their screwed-up life for a while to watch the only suckers bigger than themselves—us.

"Meanwhile, the big show goes on," said Fearing. "How long will they last? Who will take the prize?"

* * *

I TOLD Gloria about it at the break. She just shrugged and said to make sure I got my money from Kromer. Fearing was talking to Anne, the woman from the van, and Gloria was staring at them like she wanted them dead.

A guy was lying in his cot talking to himself as if nobody could hear and Gilmartin and Kromer went over and told him he was kicked out. He didn't seem to care.

I went to see Lane but we didn't talk. We sat on her cot and held hands. I didn't know if it meant the same thing to her that it did to me but I liked it.

After the break I went and talked to Mr. Sneeze. He told me the story of the show about Christmas. He said it wasn't about always getting gifts. Sometimes you had to give gifts too.

* * *

THE Sexathon was late at night. They cleared the seats and everyone had to pay again to get back in, because it was a special event. Fearing had built it up all day, talking about how it was for adults only, it would separate the men from the boys, things like that. Also that people would get knocked out of the contest. So we were pretty nervous by the time he told us the rules.

"What would scapes be without virtual sex?" he said. "Our voyagers must now prove themselves in the sensual realm—for the future consists of far more than cold, hard information. It's a place of desire and temptation, and as always, survival belongs to the fittest. The soldiers will now be steered onto the sexual battlescape—the question is, will they meet with the Little Death, or the Big one?"

Gloria wouldn't explain. "Not real death," is all she said.

"The rules again are so simple a child could follow them. In the Sex-Scape environment our contestants will be free to pick from a variety of fantasy partners. We've packed this program with options, there's something for every taste, believe you me. We won't question their selections, but—here's the catch—we will chart the results. Their suits will tell us who does and doesn't attain sexual orgasm in the next session, and those who don't will be handed their walking papers. The suits don't lie. Find bliss or die, folks, find bliss or die."

"You get it now?" said Gloria to me.

"I guess," I said.

"As ever, audience members are cautioned never to interfere with the contestants during play. Follow their fantasies on the monitors, or watch their youthful bodies strain against exhaustion, seeking to bridge virtual lust and bona-fide physical response. But no touchee."

Kromer was going around, checking the suits. "Who's gonna be in your fantasy, kid?" he said to me. "The snowman?"

I'd forgotten how they could watch me talk to Mr. Sneeze on my television. I turned red.

"Screw you, Kromer," said Gloria.

"Whoever you want, honey," he said, laughing.

* * *

WELL I found my way around their Sex-Scape and I'm not too embarrassed to say I found a girl who reminded me of Lane, except for the way she was trying so hard to be sexy. But she looked like Lane. I didn't have to do much to get the subject around to sex. It was the only thing on her mind. She wanted me to tell her what I wanted to do to her and when I couldn't think of much she suggested things and I just agreed. And when I did that she would move around and sigh as if it were really exciting to talk about even though she was doing the talking. She wanted to touch me but she couldn't really so she took off her clothes and got close to me and touched herself. I touched her too but she didn't really feel like much and it was like my hands were made of wood, which couldn't have felt too nice for her though she acted like it was great.

I touched myself a little too. I tried not to think about the audience. I was a little confused about what was what in the suit and with her breathing in my ear so loud but I got the desired result. That wasn't hard for me.

Then I could go back to the drawers but Kromer had made me embarrassed about visiting Mr. Sneeze so I went to Mars even though I would have liked to talk to him.

* * *

THE audience was all stirred up at the next break. They were sure getting their money's worth now. I got into Gloria's cot. I asked her if she did it with her own hands too.

"You didn't have to do that," she said.

"How else?"

"I just pretended. I don't think they can tell. They just want to see you wiggle around."

Well some of the women from the town hadn't wiggled around enough I guess because Kromer and Ed were taking them out of the contest. A couple of them were crying.

"I wish I hadn't," I said.

"It's the same either way," said Gloria. "Don't feel bad. Probably some other people did it too."

They didn't kick Lane out but I saw she was crying anyway.

Kromer brought a man into the back and said to me, "Get into your own cot, little snowman."

"Let him stay," said Gloria. She wasn't looking at Kromer.

"I've got someone here who wants to meet you," said Kromer to Gloria. "Mr. Warren, this is Gloria."

Mr. Warren shook her hand. He was pretty old. "I've been admiring you," he said. "You're very good."

"Mr. Warren is wondering if you'd let him buy you a drink," said Kromer.

"Thanks, but I need some sleep," said Gloria.

"Perhaps later," said Mr. Warren.

After he left Kromer came back and said, "You shouldn't pass up easy money."

"I don't need it," said Gloria. "I'm going to win your contest, you goddamn pimp."

"Now, Gloria," said Kromer. "You don't want to give the wrong impression."

"Leave me alone."

I noticed now that Anne wasn't around in the rest area and I got the idea that the kind of easy money Gloria didn't want Anne did. I'm not so dumb.

* * *

WORRYING about the Sexathon had stopped me from feeling how tired I was. Right after that I started nodding off in the scapes. I had to keep moving around. After I'd been to a few new things I went to see the snowman again. It was early in the morning and I figured Kromer was probably asleep and there was barely any audience to see what I was doing on my television. So Mr. Sneeze and I talked and that helped me stay awake.

* * *

I WASN'T the only one who was tired after that night. On the next break I saw that a bunch of people had dropped out or been kicked out for sleeping. There were only seventeen left. I couldn't stay awake myself. But I woke up when I heard some yelling over where Lane was.

It was her parents. I guess they heard about the Sexathon, maybe from her boyfriend, who was there too. Lane was sitting crying behind Fearing who was telling her parents to get out of there, and her father just kept saying, "I'm her father! I'm her father!" Her mother was pulling at Fearing but Ed came over and pulled on her.

I started to get up but Gloria grabbed my arm and said, "Stay out of this."

"Lane doesn't want to see that guy," I said.

"Let the townies take care of themselves, Lewis. Let Lane's daddy take her home if he can. Worse could happen to her."

"You just want her out of the contest," I said.

Gloria laughed. "I'm not worried about your girlfriend

outlasting me," she said. "She's about to break no matter what."

So I just watched. Kromer and Ed got Lane's parents and boyfriend pushed out of the rest area, back toward the seats. Fearing was yelling at them, making a scene for the audience. It was all part of the show as far as he was concerned.

Anne from the van was over talking to Lane, who was still crying, but quiet now.

"Do you really think you can win?" I said to Gloria.

"Sure, why not?" she said. "I can last."

"I'm pretty tired." In fact my eyeballs felt like they were full of sand.

"Well if you fall out stick around. You can probably get food out of Kromer for cleaning up or something. I'm going to take these bastards."

"You don't like Fearing anymore," I said.

"I never did," said Gloria.

* * *

THAT afternoon three more people dropped out. Fearing was going on about endurance and I got thinking about how much harder it was to live the way me and Gloria did than it was to be in town and so maybe we had an advantage. Maybe that was why Gloria thought she could win now. But I sure didn't feel it myself. I was so messed up that I couldn't always sleep at the rest periods, just lie there and listen to Fearing or eat their sandwiches until I wanted to vomit.

Kromer and Gilmartin were planning some sideshow but it didn't involve me and I didn't care. I didn't want coins thrown at me. I just wanted to get through.

* * *

IF I built the cities near the water the plague always killed all the people and if I built the cities near the mountains the volcanoes always killed all the people and if I built the cities on the plain the other tribe always came over and killed all the people and I got sick of the whole damn thing.

* * *

"**WHEN** Gloria wins we could live in town for a while," I said. "We could even get jobs if there are any. Then if Lane doesn't want to go back to her parents she could stay with us."

"You could win the contest," said Mr. Sneeze.

"I don't think so," I said. "But Gloria could."

* * *

WHY did Lewis cross Mars? To get to the other side. Ha ha.

* * *

I CAME out for the rest period and Gloria was already yelling and I unhooked my suit and rushed over to see what was the matter. It was so late it was getting light outside and almost nobody was in the place. "She's cheating!" Gloria screamed. She was pounding on Kromer and he was backing up because she was a handful mad. "That bitch is cheating! You let her sleep!" Gloria pointed at Anne from the van. "She's lying there asleep, you're running tapes in her monitor you goddamn cheater!"

Anne sat up in her frame and didn't say anything. She looked confused. "You're a bunch of cheaters!" Gloria kept saying. Kromer got her by the wrists and said "Take it easy, take it easy. You're going scape-crazy, girl."

"Don't tell me I'm crazy!" said Gloria. She twisted away from Kromer and ran to the seats. Mr. Warren was there, watching her with his hat in his hands. I ran after Gloria and said her name but she said, "Leave me alone!" and went over to Mr. Warren. "You saw it, didn't you?" she said.

"I'm sorry?" said Mr. Warren.

"You must have seen it, the way she wasn't moving at all," said Gloria. "Come on, tell these cheaters you saw it. I'll go on that date with you if you tell them."

"I'm sorry, darling. I was looking at you."

Kromer knocked me out of the way and grabbed Gloria from behind. "Listen to me, girl. You're hallucinating. You're scape-happy. We see it all the time." He was talking quiet but hard. "Any more of this and you're out of the show, you understand? Get in the back and lie down now and get some sleep. You need it."

"You bastard," said Gloria.

"Sure, I'm a bastard, but you're seeing things." He held Gloria's wrist and she sagged.

Mr. Warren got up and put his hat on. "I'll see you tomorrow, darling. Don't worry. I'm rooting for you." He went out.

Gloria didn't look at him.

Kromer took Gloria back to the rest area but suddenly I wasn't paying much attention myself. I had been thinking Fearing wasn't taking advantage of the free action by talking about it because there wasn't anyone much in the place to impress at this hour. Then I looked around and I realized there were two people missing and that was Fearing and Lane.

I found Ed and I asked him if Lane had dropped out of the contest and he said no.

* * *

"**MAYBE** there's a way you could find out if Anne is really scaping or if she's a cheat," I said to Mr. Sneeze.

"I don't see how I could," he said. "I can't visit her, she has to visit me. And nobody visits me except you." He hopped and jiggled in his five places. "I'd like it if I could meet Gloria and Lane."

"Let's not talk about Lane," I said.

* * *

WHEN I saw Fearing again I couldn't look at him. He was out talking to the people who came by in the morning, not in the microphone but one at a time, shaking hands and taking compliments like it was him doing the scaping.

There were only eight people left in the contest. Lane was still in it but I didn't care.

I knew if I tried to sleep I would just lie there thinking. So I went to rinse out under my suit, which was getting pretty rank. I hadn't been out of that suit since the contest started. In the bathroom I looked out the little window at the daylight and I thought about how I hadn't been out of that building for five days either, no matter how much I'd gone to Mars and elsewhere.

I went back in and saw Gloria asleep and I thought all of a sudden that I should try to win.

But maybe that was just the idea coming over me that Gloria wasn't going to.

* * *

I DIDN'T notice it right away because I went to other places first. Mr. Sneeze had made me promise I'd always have something new to tell him about so I always opened a few drawers. I went to a tank game but it was boring. Then I found a place called the American History Blood and Wax Museum and I stopped President Lincoln from getting murdered a couple of times. I tried to stop President Kennedy from getting murdered but if I stopped it one way it always happened a different way. I don't know why.

So then I was going to tell Mr. Sneeze about it and that's when I found out. I went into his drawer and touched the right numbers but what I got wasn't the usual five pictures of the snowman. It was pieces of him but chopped up and stretched into thin white strips, around the edge of the black space, like a band of white light.

I said, "Mr. Sneeze?"

There wasn't any voice.

I went out and came back in but it was the same. He couldn't talk. The band of white strips got narrower and wider, like it was trying to move or talk. It looked a bit like a hand waving open and shut. But if he was still there he couldn't talk.

* * *

I WOULD have taken my mask off then anyway, but the heat of my face and my tears forced me to.

I saw Fearing up front talking and I started for him without even getting my suit unclipped, so I tore up a few of my wires. I didn't care, I knew I was out now. I went right out and tackled Fearing from behind. He wasn't so big, anyway. Only his voice was big. I got him down on the floor.

"You killed him," I said, and I punched him as hard as I could, but you know Kromer and Gilmartin were there holding my arms before I could hit him more than once. I just screamed at Fearing, "You killed him, you killed him."

Fearing was smiling at me and wiping his mouth. "Your snowman malfunctioned, kid."

"That's a lie!"

"You were boring us to death with that snowman, you little punk. Give it a rest, for chrissake."

I kept kicking out even though they had me pulled away from him. "I'll kill you!" I said.

"Right," said Fearing. "Throw him out of here."

He never stopped smiling. Everything suited his plans, that was what I hated.

Kromer the big ape and Gilmartin pulled me outside into the sunlight and it was like a knife in my eyes. I couldn't believe how bright it was. They tossed me down in the street and when I got up Kromer punched me, hard.

Then Gloria came outside. I don't know how she found out, if she heard me screaming or if Ed woke her. Anyway she gave Kromer a pretty good punch in the side and said, "Leave him alone!"

Kromer was surprised and he moaned and I got away from him. Gloria punched him again. Then she turned around and gave Gilmartin a kick in the nuts and he went down. I'll always remember in spite of what happened next that she gave those guys a couple they'd be feeling for a day or two.

* * *

THE gang who beat the crap out of us were a mix of the militia and some other guys from the town, including Lane's boyfriend. Pretty funny that he'd take out his frustration on us, but that just shows you how good Fearing had that whole town wrapped around his finger.

* * *

OUTSIDE of town we found an old house that we could hide in and get some sleep. I slept longer than Gloria. When I woke up she was on the front steps rubbing a spoon back and forth on the pavement to make a sharp point, even though I could see it hurt her arm to do it.

"Well, we did get fed for a couple of days," I said.

Gloria didn't say anything.

"Let's go up to San Francisco," I said. "There's a lot of lonely women there."

I was making a joke of course.

Gloria looked at me. "What's that supposed to mean?"

"Just that maybe I can get us in for once."

Gloria didn't laugh, but I knew she would later.

RED SONJA AND LESSINGHAM IN DREAMLAND

Gwyneth Jones

Be careful what you wish for, an old saying warns us, because you just might get it. The same applies to what games you play, as the wry little chiller that follows demonstrates—and who you play with.

One of the most acclaimed British writers of her generation, Gwyneth Jones was a co-winner of the James Tiptree Jr. Memorial Award for work exploring genre issues in science fiction, with her 1991 novel White Queen; *she has also won the Arthur C. Clarke Award for her novel* Bold As Love; *and she has received two World Fantasy Awards—for her story "The Grass Princess" and her collection* Seven Tales and a Fable. *Her other books include the novels* North Wind, Flowerdust, Escape Plans, Divine Endurance, Phoenix Café, Castles Made of Sand, Stone Free, Midnight Lamp, Kairos, Life, Water in the Air, The Influence of Ironwood, The Exchange, Dear Hill, Escape Plans, *and* The Hidden Ones, *as well as more than sixteen young adult novels published under the name Ann Halam. Her too-infrequent short fiction has appeared in* Interzone, Asimov's Science Fiction, Off Limits, *and in other magazines and anthologies, and has been collected in* Identifying the Object: A Collection of Short Stories, *as well as* Seven Tales and a Fable. *She is also the author of the critical study,* Deconstructing the Starships: Science Fiction and Reality. *She lives in Brighton, England, with her husband, her son, and a Burmese cat.*

THE earth walls of the caravanserai rose strangely from the empty plain. She let the black stallion slow his pace. The silence of deep dusk had a taste, like a rich dark fruit; the air was keen. In the distance mountains etched a jagged margin against an indigo sky; snow streaks glinting in the glimmer of the dawning stars. She had never been here before, in life. But as she led her horse through the gap in the high earthen banks she knew what she would see. The camping booths around the walls; the beaten ground stained black by the ashes of countless cooking fires; the wattle-fenced enclosure where travelers' riding beasts mingled indiscriminately with their host's goats and chickens . . . the tumbledown gallery, where sheaves of russet plains-grass sprouted from empty window-spaces. Everything she looked on had the luminous intensity of a place often visited in dreams.

She was a tall woman, dressed for riding in a kilt and harness of supple leather over brief close-fitting linen: a costume that left her sheeny, muscular limbs bare and outlined the taut, proud curves of breast and haunches. Her red hair was bound in a braid as thick as a man's wrist. Her sword was slung on her back, the great brazen hilt standing above her shoulder. Other guests were gathered by an open-air kitchen, in the orange-red of firelight and the smoke of roasting meat. She returned their stares coolly: She was accustomed to attracting attention. But she didn't like what she saw. The host of the caravanserai came scuttling from the group by the fire. His manner was fawning. But his eyes measured, with a thief's sly expertise, the worth of the sword she bore and the quality of Lemiak's harness. Sonja tossed him a few coins and declined to join the company.

She had counted fifteen of them. They were poorly dressed and heavily armed. They were all friends together and their animals—both terror-birds and horses—were too good for any honest travelers' purposes. Sonja had been told that this caravanserai was a safe halt. She judged that this was no longer true. She considered riding out again onto the plain. But wolves and wild terror-birds roamed at night between here and the mountains, at the end of winter. And there were worse dangers; ghosts and demons. Sonja was neither credulous nor superstitious. But in this country no wayfarer willingly spent the black hours alone.

She unharnessed Lemiak and rubbed him down, taking sensual pleasure in the handling of his powerful limbs, in the heat of his glossy hide, and the vigor of his great body. There was firewood ready stacked in the roofless booth. Shouldering a cloth sling for corn and a hank of rope, she went to fetch her own fodder. The corralled beasts shifted in a mass to watch her. The great flightless birds, with their pitiless raptors' eyes, were especially attentive. She felt an equally rapacious attention from the company by the caravanserai kitchen, which amused her. The robbers—as she was sure they were—had all the luck. For her, there wasn't one of the fifteen who rated a second glance.

A man appeared, from the darkness under the ruined gallery. He was tall. The rippled muscle of his chest, left bare by an unlaced leather jerkin, shone red-brown. His black hair fell in glossy curls to his wide shoulders. He met her gaze and smiled, white teeth appearing in the darkness of his beard. "*My name is Ozymandias, king of kings . . . look on my works, ye mighty, and despair. . . .* Do you know those lines?" He pointed to a lump of shapeless stone, one of several that lay about. It bore traces of carving, almost effaced by time. "There was a city here once, with marketplaces, fine buildings, throngs of proud people. Now they are dust, and only the caravanserai remains."

He stood before her, one tanned and sinewy hand resting lightly on the hilt of a dagger in his belt. Like Sonja, he carried his broadsword on his back. Sonja was tall. He topped her by a head: Yet there was nothing brutish in his size. His brow was wide and serene; his eyes were vivid blue; his lips full and imperious, yet delicately modeled, in the rich nest of hair. Somewhere between eyes and lips there lurked a spirit of mockery, as if he found some secret amusement in the perfection of his own beauty and strength.

The man and the woman measured each other.

"You are a scholar," she said.

"Of some sort. And a traveler from an antique land—where the cities are still standing. It seems we are the only strangers here," he added, with a slight nod toward the convivial company. "We might be well advised to become friends for the night."

Sonja never wasted words. She considered his offer and nodded.

They made a fire in the booth Sonja had chosen. Lemiak and the scholar's terror-bird, left loose together in the back of the shelter, did not seem averse to each other's company. The woman and the man ate spiced sausage, skewered and broiled over the red embers, with bread and dried fruit. They drank water, each keeping to their own waterskin. They spoke little, after that first exchange—except to discuss briefly the tactics of their defense, should defense be necessary.

The attack came around midnight. At the first stir of covert movement, Sonja leapt up, sword in hand. She grasped a brand from the dying fire. The man who had been crawling on his hands and knees toward her, bent on sly murder of a sleeping victim, scrabbled to his feet. "Defend yourself," yelled Sonja, who despised to strike an unarmed foe. Instantly he was rushing at her with a heavy sword. A great two-handed stroke would have cleft her to the waist. She parried the blow and caught him between neck and shoulder, almost severing the head from his body. The beasts plunged and screamed at the rush of blood scent. The scholar was grappling with another attacker, choking out the man's life with his bare hands . . . and the booth was full of bodies; their enemies rushing in on every side.

Sonja felt no fear. Stroke followed stroke, in a luxury of blood and effort and fire-shot darkness . . . until the attack was over, as suddenly as it had begun.

The brigands had vanished.

"We killed five," breathed the scholar, "by my count. Three to you, two to me."

She kicked together the remains of their fire and crouched to blow the embers to a blaze. By that light they found five corpses, dragged them and flung them into the open square. The scholar had a cut on his upper arm, which was bleeding freely. Sonja was bruised and battered, but otherwise unhurt. The worst loss was their woodstack, which had been trampled and blood-fouled. They would not be able to keep a watch fire burning.

"Perhaps they won't try again," said the warrior woman. "What can we have that's worth more than five lives?"

He laughed shortly. "I hope you're right."

"We'll take turns to watch."

Standing breathless, every sense alert, they smiled at each other in new-forged comradeship. There was no second attack. At dawn Sonja, rousing from a light doze, sat up and pushed back the heavy masses of her red hair.

"You are very beautiful," said the man, gazing at her.

"So are you," she answered.

The caravanserai was deserted, except for the dead. The brigands' riding animals were gone. The innkeeper and his family had vanished into some bolt-hole in the ruins.

"I am heading for the mountains," he said, as they packed up their gear. "For the pass into Zimiamvia."

"I too."

"Then our way lies together."

He was wearing the same leather jerkin, over knee-length loose breeches of heavy violet silk. Sonja looked at the strips of linen that bound the wound on his upper arm. "When did you tie up that cut?"

"You dressed it for me, for which I thank you."

"When did I do that?"

He shrugged. "Oh, sometime."

Sonja mounted Lemiak, a little frown between her brows. They rode together until dusk. She was not talkative and the man soon accepted her silence. But when night fell, they camped without a fire on the houseless plain; then, as the demons stalked, they were glad of each other's company. Next dawn, the mountains seemed as distant as ever. Again, they met no living creature all day, spoke little to each other, and made the same comfortless camp. There was no moon. The stars were almost bright enough to cast shadow; the cold was intense. Sleep was impossible, but they were not tempted to ride on. Few travelers attempt the passage over the high plains to Zimiamvia. Of those few most turn back, defeated. Some wander among the ruins forever, tearing at their own flesh. Those who survive are the ones who do not defy the terrors of darkness. They crouched shoulder to shoulder, each wrapped in a single blanket, to endure. Evil emanations of the death-steeped plain rose from the soil and bred phantoms. The sweat of fear was cold as ice melt on Sonja's cheeks. Horrors made of nothingness prowled and muttered in her mind.

"How long?" she whispered. "How long do we have to bear this?"

The man's shoulder lifted against hers. "Until we get well, I suppose."

The warrior woman turned to face him, green eyes flashing in appalled outrage.

* * *

"SONJA" discussed this group member's felony with the therapist. Dr. Hamilton—he wanted them to call him Jim, but "Sonja" found this impossible—monitored everything that went on in the virtual environment. But he never appeared there. They only met him in the one-to-one consultations that virtual-therapy buffs called *the meat sessions*.

"He's not supposed to *do* that," she protested from the foam couch in the doctor's office. He was sitting beside her, his notebook on his knee. "He damaged my experience."

Dr. Hamilton nodded. "Okay. Let's take a step back. Leave aside the risk of disease or pregnancy: Because we *can* leave those bogeys aside, forever if you like. Would you agree that sex is essentially an innocent and playful social behavior—something you'd offer to or take from a friend, in an ideal world, as easily as food or drink?"

"Sonja" recalled certain dreams—*meat* dreams, not the computer-assisted kind. She blushed. But the man was a doctor after all. "That's what I do feel," she agreed. "That's why I'm here. I want to get back to the pure pleasure, to get rid of the baggage."

"The sexual experience offered in virtuality therapy is readily available on the nets. You know that. And you could find an agency that would vet your partners for you. You chose to join this group because you need to feel that you're taking *medicine,* so you don't have to feel ashamed. And because you need to feel that you're interacting with people who, like yourself, perceive sex as a problem."

"Doesn't everyone?"

"You and another group member went off into your own private world. That's good. That's what's supposed to happen. Let me tell you, it doesn't always. The software gives you access to a vast multisensual library, all the sexual fantasy ever committed to media. But you and your partner, or partners, have to customize the information and use it to create and maintain what we call the *consensual perceptual plenum.* Success in holding a shared dreamland together is a knack. It depends on something in the neural makeup that no one has yet fully analyzed. Some have it, some don't. You two are really in sync."

"That's exactly what I'm complaining about—"

"You think he's damaging the pocket universe you two built up. But he isn't, not from his character's point of view. It's part Lessingham's thing, to be conscious that he's in a fantasy world."

She started, accusingly. "I don't want to know his name."

"Don't worry, I wouldn't tell you. 'Lessingham' is the name of his virtuality persona. I'm surprised you don't recognize it. He's a character from a series of classic fantasy novels by E. R. Eddison. . . . *In Eddison's glorious cosmos 'Lessingham' is a splendidly endowed English gentleman who visits fantastic realms of ultramasculine adventure as a lucid dreamer: Though an actor in the drama, he is partly conscious of another existence, while the characters around him are more or less explicitly puppets of the dream. . . .*"

He sounded as if he were quoting from a reference book. He probably was: reading from an autocue that had popped up in lenses of those doctorish horn-rims. She knew that the old-fashioned trappings were there to reassure her. She rather despised them: But it was like the virtuality itself. The buttons were pushed, the mechanism responded. She was reassured.

Of course she knew the Eddison stories. She recalled "Lessingham" perfectly: the tall, strong, handsome, cultured millionaire jock who has magic journeys to another world, where he is a tall, strong, handsome, cultured jock in Elizabethan costume, with a big sword. The whole thing was an absolutely typical male power-fantasy, she thought—without rancor. *Fantasy means never having to say you're sorry*. The women in those books, she remembered, were drenched in sex, but they had no part in the action. They stayed at home being princesses, *occasionally* allowing the millionaire jocks to get them into bed. She could understand why "Lessingham" would be interested in "Sonja" . . . for a change.

"You think he goosed you, psychically. What do you expect? You can't dress the way 'Sonja' dresses and hope to be treated like the Queen of May."

Dr. Hamilton was only doing his job. He was supposed to be provocative, so they could react against him. That was his excuse, anyway. . . . On the contrary, she thought. "Sonja" dresses the way she does because she can dress any way she likes. "Sonja" doesn't have to *hope* for respect, and she doesn't have to demand it. She just gets it. "It's dominance display," she said, enjoying the theft of his jargon. "Females do that too, you know. The way 'Sonja' dresses is not an invitation. It's a warning. Or a challenge, to anyone who can measure up."

He laughed, but he sounded irritated. "Frankly, I'm amazed that you two work together. I'd have expected 'Lessingham' to go for an ultrafeminine—"

"I am . . . 'Sonja' *is* ultrafeminine. Isn't a tigress feminine?"

"Well, okay. But I guess you've found out his little weakness. He likes to be a teeny bit in control, even when he's letting his hair down in dreamland."

She remembered the secret mockery lurking in those blue eyes.

"That's the problem. That's exactly what I *don't* want. I don't want either of us to be in control."

"I can't interfere with his persona. So, it's up to you. Do you want to carry on?"

"Something works," she muttered. She was unwilling to admit that there'd been no one else, in the text-interface phase of the group, that she found remotely attractive. It was "Lessingham," or drop out and start again. "I just want him to stop *spoiling things*."

"You can't expect your masturbation fantasies to mesh completely. This is about getting *beyond* solitary sex. Go with it: Where's the harm? One day you'll want to face a sexual partner in the real, and then you'll be well. Meanwhile, you could be passing 'Lessingham' in reception—he comes to his meat sessions around your time—and not know it. That's *safety*, and you never have to breach it. You two have proved that you can sustain an imaginary world together: It's almost like being in love. I could argue that lucid dreaming, being *in* the fantasy world but not *of* it, is the next big step. Think about that."

The clinic room had mirrored walls: more deliberate provocation. How much reality can you take? the reflections asked. But she felt only a vague distaste for the woman she saw, at once hollow-cheeked and bloated, lying in the doctor's foam couch. He was glancing over her records on his notebook screen; which meant the session was almost up.

"Still no overt sexual contact?"

"I'm not read. . . ." She stirred restlessly. "Is it a man or a woman?"

"Ah!" smiled Dr. Hamilton, waving a finger at her. "Naughty, naughty—"

He was the one who'd started taunting her, with his hints that the meat—"Lessingham"—might be near. She hated herself for asking a genuine question. It was her rule to give him no entry to her real thoughts. But Dr. Jim knew everything, without being told: every change in her brain chemistry, every effect on her body: sweaty palms, racing heart, damp underwear. . . . The telltales on his damned autocue left her precious little dignity. *Why do I subject myself to this?* she wondered, disgusted. But in the virtuality she forgot utterly about Dr. Jim. She didn't care who was watching. She had her brazen-hilted sword. She had the piercing intensity of dusk on the high plains, the snowlight on the mountains; the hard, warm silk of her own perfect limbs. She felt a brief complicity with "Lessingham." She had a conviction that Dr. Jim didn't play favorites. He despised all his patients equally. . . . *You get your kicks, doctor. But we have the freedom of dreamland.*

* * *

"**SONJA**" read cards stuck in phone booths and store windows, in the tired little streets outside the building that housed the clinic. *Relaxing massage by clean-shaven young man in Luxurious Surroundings. . . .* You can't expect your fantasies to mesh exactly, the doctor said. But how can it work if two people disagree over something so vital as the difference between control and surrender? Her estranged husband used to say: "Why don't you just do it for me, as a favor. It wouldn't hurt. Like making someone a cup of coffee. . . ." *Offer the steaming cup, turn around and lift my* *skirts, pull down my underwear. I'm ready. He opens his pants and slides it in, while his thumb is round in front rubbing me. . . . I could enjoy that,* thought "Sonja," remembering the blithe abandon of her dreams. *That's the damned shame. If there were no nonsex consequences, I don't know that there's any limit to what I could enjoy. . . . But all her husband had achieved was to make her feel she never wanted to make anyone, man, woman, or child, a cup of coffee ever again. . . .* In luxurious surroundings. *That's what I want. Sex without engagement, pleasure without consequences. It's got to be possible.*

She gazed at the cards, feeling uneasily that she'd have to give up this habit. She used to glance at them sidelong; now she'd pause and linger. She was getting desperate. She was lucky there was medically supervised virtuality sex to be had. She would be helpless prey in the wild world of the nets, and she'd never, ever risk trying one of these meat-numbers. And she had no intention of returning to her husband. Let him make his own coffee. She wouldn't call that getting well. She turned, and caught the eye of a nicely dressed young woman standing next to her. They walked away quickly in opposite directions. *Everybody's having the same dreams. . . .*

* * *

IN the foothills of the mountains, the world became green and sweet. They followed the course of a little river that sometimes plunged far below their path, tumbling in white flurries in a narrow gorge; and sometimes ran beside them, racing smooth and clear over colored pebbles. Flowers clustered on the banks, birds darted in the thickets of wild rose and honeysuckle. They led their riding animals and walked at ease: not speaking much. Sometimes the warrior woman's flank would brush the man's side; or he would lean for a moment, as if by chance, his hand on her shoulder. Then they would move deliberately apart, but they would smile at each other. *Soon. Not yet. . . .*

They must be vigilant. The approaches to fortunate

Zimiamvia were guarded. They could not expect to reach the pass unopposed. And the nights were haunted still. They made camp at a flat bend of the river, where the crags of the defile drew away, and they could see far up and down their valley. To the north, peaks of diamond and indigo reared above them. Their fire of aromatic wood burned brightly, as the white stars began to blossom.

"No one knows about the long-term effects," she said. "It can't be safe. At the least, we're risking irreversible addiction. They warn you about that. I don't want to spend the rest of my life as a cyberspace couch potato."

"Nobody claims it's safe. If it were safe, it wouldn't be so intense."

Their eyes met. "Sonja" 's barbarian simplicity combined surprisingly well with the man's more elaborate furnishing. The *consensual perceptual plenum* was a flawless reality: the sound of the river, the clear silence of the mountain twilight . . . their two perfect bodies. She turned from him to gaze into the sweet-scented flames. The warrior woman's glorious vitality throbbed in her veins. The fire held worlds of its own, liquid furnaces: the sunward surface of Mercury.

"Have you ever been to a place like this in the real?"

He grimaced. "You're kidding. In the real, I'm *not* a magic-wielding millionaire."

Something howled. The blood-stopping cry was repeated. A taint of sickening foulness swept by them. They both shuddered, and drew closer together. "Sonja" knew the scientific explanation for the legendary virtuality-paranoia, the price you paid for the virtual world's super-real, dreamlike richness. It was all down to heightened neurotransmitter levels, a positive-feedback effect, psychic overheating. But the horrors were still horrors.

"The doctor says if we can talk like this, it means we're getting well."

He shook his head. "I'm not sick. It's like you said. Virtuality's addictive and I'm an addict. I'm getting my drug of choice safely, on prescription. That's how I see it."

All this time "Sonja" was in her apartment, lying in a foam couch with a visor over her head. The visor delivered compressed bursts of stimuli to her visual cortex: the other sense perceptions riding piggyback on the visual, triggering a whole complex of neuronal groups; tricking her mind/brain into believing the world of the dream was *out there*. The brain works like a computer. You cannot "see" a hippopotamus until your system has retrieved the "hippopotamus" template from memory, and checked it against the incoming. Where does the "real" exist? In a sense this world was as real as the other. . . . But the thought of "Lessingham" 's unknown body disturbed her. If he was too poor to lease good equipment, he might be lying in the clinic now in a grungy public cubicle . . . cathetered, and so forth: the sordid details.

She had never tried virtual sex. The solitary version had seemed a depressing idea. People said the partnered kind was the perfect *zipless fuck*. He sounded experienced; she was afraid he would be able to tell she was not. But it didn't matter. The virtual-therapy group wasn't like a dating agency. She would never meet him in the real, that was the whole idea. She didn't have to think about that stranger's body. She didn't have to worry about the real "Lessingham" 's opinion of her. She drew herself up in the firelight. It was right, she decided, that Sonja should be a virgin. When the moment came, her surrender would be the more absolute.

In their daytime he stayed in character. It was a tacit trade-off. She would acknowledge the other world at nightfall by the campfire, as long as he didn't mention it the rest of the time. So they traveled on together, Lessingham and Red Sonja, the courtly scholar-knight and the taciturn warrior-maiden, through an exquisite Maytime: exchanging lingering glances, "accidental" touches. . . . And still nothing happened. "Sonja" was aware that "Lessingham," as much as herself, was holding back from the brink. She felt piqued at this. But they were both, she guessed, waiting for the fantasy they had generated to throw up the perfect moment of itself. It ought to. There was no other reason for its existence.

Turning a shoulder of the hillside, they found a sheltered hollow. Two rowan trees in flower grew above the river. In the shadow of their blossom tumbled a little waterfall, so beautiful it was a wonder to behold. The water fell clear from the upper edge of a slab of stone twice a man's height, into a rocky basin. The water in the basin was clear and deep, a-churn with bubbles from the jet plunging from above. The riverbanks were lawns of velvet; over the rocks grew emerald mosses and tiny water flowers.

"I would live here," said Lessingham softly, his hand dropping from his riding bird's bridle. "I would build me a house in this fairy place, and rest my heart here forever."

Sonja loosed the black stallion's rein. The two beasts moved off, feeding each in its own way on the sweet grasses and springtime foliage.

"I would like to bathe in that pool," said the warrior-maiden.

"Why not?" He smiled. "I will stand guard."

She pulled off her leather harness and slowly unbound her hair. It fell in a trembling mass of copper and russet lights, a cloud of glory around the richness of her barely clothed body. Gravely she gazed at her own perfection, mirrored in the homage of his eyes. Lessingham's breath was coming fast. She saw a pulse beat, in the strong beauty of his throat. The pure physical majesty of him caught her breath. . . .

It was their moment. But it still needed something to break this strange spell of reluctance. "*Lady—*" he murmured—

Sonja gasped. "Back-to-back!" she cried. "Quickly, or it is too late!"

Six warriors surrounded them, covered from head to foot in red-and-black armor. They were human in the lower body, but the head of each appeared beaked and fanged, with monstrous faceted eyes, and each bore an extra pair of armored limbs between breastbone and belly. They fell on Sonja and Lessingham without pause or a challenge.

Sonja fought fiercely as always, her blade ringing against the monster armor. But something cogged her fabulous skill. Some power had drained the strength from her splendid limbs. She was disarmed. The clawed creatures held her, a monstrous head stooped over her, choking her with its fetid breath. . . .

When she woke again she was bound against a great boulder, by thongs around her wrists and ankles, tied to hoops of iron driven into the rock. She was naked but for her linen shift; it was in tatters. Lessingham was standing, leaning on his sword. "I drove them off," he said. "At last." He dropped the sword and took his dagger to cut her down.

She lay in his arms. "You are very beautiful," he murmured. She thought he would kiss her. His mouth plunged instead to her breast, biting and sucking at the engorged nipple. She gasped in shock; a fierce pang leapt through her virgin flesh. What did they want with kisses? They were warriors. Sonja could not restrain a moan of pleasure. He had won her. How wonderful to be overwhelmed, to surrender to the raw lust of this godlike animal.

Lessingham set her on her feet.

"Tie me up."

He was proffering a handful of blood-slicked leather thongs.

"What?"

"Tie me to the rock, mount me. It's what I want."

"The evil warriors tied you—?"

"And you come and rescue me." He made an impatient gesture. "Whatever. Trust me. It'll be good for you too." He tugged at his bloodstained silk breeches, releasing a huge, iron-hard erection. "See, they tore my clothes. When you see *that,* you go crazy, you can't resist . . . and I'm at your mercy. Tie me up!"

"Sonja" had heard that 80 percent of the submissive partners in sadomasochist sex are male. But it is still the man who dominates his "dominatrix": who says *tie me tighter, beat me harder, you can stop now. . . .* *Hey,* she thought. *Why all the stage directions, suddenly? What happened to my zipless fuck?* But what the hell. She wasn't going to back out now, having come so far. . . . There was a seamless shift, and Lessingham was bound to the rock. She straddled his cock. He groaned. "*Don't do this to me.*" He thrust upward, into her, moaning. "*You savage, you utter savage, uuunnnh . . .*" Sonja grasped the man's wrists and rode him without mercy. He was right, it was as good this way. His eyes were half-closed. In the glimmer of blue under his lashes, a spirit of mockery trembled. . . . She heard a laugh, and found her hands were no longer gripping Lessingham's wrists. He had broken free from her bonds, he was laughing at her in triumph. He was wrestling her to the ground.

"No!" she cried, genuinely outraged. But he was the stronger.

* * *

IT was night when he was done with her. He rolled away and slept, as far as she could tell, instantly. Her chief thought was that virtual sex didn't entirely *connect.* She remembered now, that was something else people told you, as well as the "zipless fuck." *It's like coming in your sleep,* they said. *It doesn't quite make it.* Maybe there was nothing virtuality could do to orgasm, to match the heightened richness of the rest of the experience. She wondered if he too had felt cheated.

She lay beside her hero, wondering, *Where did I go wrong? Why did he have to treat me that way?* Beside her, "Lessingham" cuddled a fragment of violet silk, torn from his own breeches. He whimpered in his sleep, nuzzling the soft fabric, "*Mama . . .*"

* * *

SHE told Dr. Hamilton that "Lessingham" had raped her.

"And wasn't that what you wanted?"

She lay on the couch in the mirrored office. The doctor

sat beside her with his smart notebook on his knee. The couch collected "Sonja" 's physical responses as if she were an astronaut umbilicaled to ground control; and Dr. Jim read the telltales popping up in his reassuring horn-rims. She remembered the sneaking furtive thing that she had glimpsed in "Lessingham" 's eyes, the moment before he took over their lust scene. How could she explain the difference? "He wasn't playing. In the fantasy, anything's allowed. But *he wasn't playing*. He was outside it, laughing at me."

"I warned you he would want to stay in control."

"But there was no need! I *wanted* him to be in control. Why did he have to steal what I wanted to give him anyway?"

"You have to understand, 'Sonja,' that to many men it's women who seem powerful. You women feel dominated and try to achieve 'equality.' But the men don't perceive the situation like that. They're mortally afraid of you: And anything, just about *anything* they do to keep the upper hand, seems like justified self-defense."

She could have wept with frustration. "I know all that! That's *exactly* what I was trying to get away from. I thought we were supposed to leave the damn baggage behind. I wanted something purely physical. . . . Something innocent."

"Sex is not innocent, 'Sonja.' I know you believe it is, or 'should be.' But it's time you faced the truth. Any interaction with another person involves some kind of jockeying for power, dickering over control. Sex is no exception. Now *that's* basic. You can't escape from it in direct-cortical fantasy. It's in our minds that relationships happen, and the mind, of course, is where virtuality happens too." He sighed, and made an entry in her notes. "I want you to look on this as another step toward coping with the real. You're not sick, 'Sonja.' You're unhappy. Not even unusually so. Most adults are unhappy, to some degree—"

"Or else they're in denial."

Her sarcasm fell flat. "Right. A good place to be, at least some of the time. What we're trying to achieve here—if we're trying to achieve anything at all—is to raise your pain threshold to somewhere near average. I want you to walk away from therapy with lowered expectations: I guess that would be success."

"Great," she said, desolate. "That's just great."

Suddenly he laughed. "Oh, you guys! You are so weird. It's always the same story. *Can't live with you, can't live without you. . . .* You can't go on this way, you know. Its getting ridiculous. You want some real advice, 'Sonja'? Go home. Change your attitudes, and start some hard peace talks with that husband of yours."

"I don't want to change," she said coldly, staring with open distaste at his smooth profile, his soft effeminate hands. Who was he to call her abnormal? "I like my sexuality just the way it is."

Dr. Hamilton returned her look, a glint of human malice breaking through his doctor act. "Listen. I'll tell you something for free." A weird sensation jumped in her crotch. For a moment she had a prick: A hand lifted and cradled the warm weight of her balls. She stifled a yelp of shock. He grinned. "I've been looking for a long time, and I know. *There is no tall, dark man. . . .*"

He returned to her notes. "You say you were 'raped,'" he continued, as if nothing had happened. "Yet you chose to continue the virtual session. Can you explain that?"

She thought of the haunted darkness, the cold air on her naked body; the soreness of her bruises; a rag of flesh used and tossed away. How it had felt to lie there: intensely alive, tasting the dregs, beaten back at the gates of the fortunate land. In dreamland, even betrayal had such rich depth and fascination. And she was free to enjoy, because *it didn't matter.*

"You wouldn't understand."

* * *

OUT in the lobby there were people coming and going. It was lunchtime; the lifts were busy. "Sonja" noticed a round-shouldered geek of a little man making for the entrance to the clinic. She wondered idly if that could be "Lessingham."

She would drop out of the group. The adventure with "Lessingham" was over, and there was no one else for her. She needed to start again. The doctor knew he'd lost a customer; that was why he'd been so open with her today. He certainly guessed, too, that she'd lose no time in signing on somewhere else on the semi-medical fringe. What a fraud all that therapy talk was! He'd never have dared to play the sex-change trick on her, except that he knew she was an addict. She wasn't likely to go accusing him of unprofessional conduct. Oh, he knew it all. But his contempt didn't trouble her.

So, she had joined the inner circle. She could trust Dr. Hamilton's judgment. He had the telltales: He would know. She recognized with a feeling of mild surprise that she had become a statistic, an element in a fashionable social concern: *an epidemic flight into fantasy, inadequate personalities; unable to deal with the reality of normal human sexual relations. . . . But that's crazy,* she thought. *I don't hate men, and I don't believe "Lessingham" hates women. There's nothing psychotic about what we're doing. We're making a consumer choice. Virtual sex is* easier, *that's all. Okay, it's convenience food. It has too much sugar, and a certain blandness. But when a product comes along that is cheaper, easier, and more fun than the original version, of course people are going to buy it.*

The lift was full. She stood, drab bodies packed around her, breathing the stale air. Every face was a mask of dull endurance. She closed her eyes. *The caravanserai walls rose strangely from the empty plain. . . .*

(with apologies to E. R. Eddison)

THE HALFWAY HOUSE AT THE HEART OF DARKNESS

William Browning Spencer

William Browning Spencer was born in Washington, D.C. and now lives in Lexington, Missouri. His first novel, Maybe I'll Call Anna, *was published in 1990 and won a New American Writing Award, and he has subsequently made quite a reputation for himself with quirky, eccentric, eclectic novels that dance on the borderlines between horror, fantasy, and black comedy, novels such as* Resume with Monsters *and* Zod Wallop. *His short work has been collected in* The Return of Count Electric and Other Stories. *His most recent book is a new novel,* Irrational Fears.

In the free-wheeling, pyrotechnic story that follows, he shows us that there are as many ways to be Saved as there are people to be Saved, even from a peculiar addiction such as computer gaming—and that often the most unexpected way is the way that works the best . . .

KEEL wore a ragged shirt with the holo *veed there, simmed that* shimmering on it. She wore it in and out of the virtual. If she was in an interactive virtual, the other players sometimes complained. Amid the dragons and elves and swords of fire, a bramble-haired girl, obviously spiking her virtual with drugs and refusing to tune her shirt to something suitably medieval, could be distracting.

"Fizz off," Keel would say, in response to all complaints.

Keel was difficult. Rich, self-destructive, beautiful, she was twenty years old and already a case study in virtual psychosis.

She had been rehabbed six times. She could have died that time on Makor when she went blank in the desert. She still bore the teeth marks of the land eels that were gnawing on her shoulder when they found her.

A close one. You can't revive the digested.

* * *

NO one had to tell Keel that she was in rehab again. She was staring at a green ocean, huge white clouds overhead, white gulls filling the heated air with their cries.

They gave you these serenity mock-ups when they were bringing you around. They were fairly insipid and several shouts behind the technology. This particular v-run was embarrassing. The ocean wasn't continuous, probably a seven-minute repeat, and the sun's heat was patchy on her face.

The beach was empty. She was propped up in a lounge chair—no doubt her position back in the ward. With concentration, focusing on her spine, she could sense the actual contours of the bed, the satiny feel of the sensor pad.

It was work, this focusing, and she let it go. Always better to flow.

Far to her right, she spied a solitary figure. The figure was moving toward her.

It was, she knew, a wilson. She was familiar with the drill. Don't spook the patient. Approach her slowly after she is sedated and in a quiet setting.

The wilson was a fat man in a white suit (*neo-Victorian, dead silly,* Keel thought). He kept his panama hat from taking flight in the wind by clamping it onto his head with his right hand and leaning forward.

Keel recognized him. She even remembered his name,

but then it was the kind of name you'd remember: Dr. Max Marx.

He had been her counselor, her wilson, the last time she'd crashed. Which meant she was in Addition Resources Limited, which was located just outside of New Vegas.

Dr. Marx looked up, waved, and came on again with new purpose.

A pool of sadness welled in her throat. There was nothing like help, and its pale sister hope, to fill Keel's soul with black water.

* * *

FORTUNATELY, Dr. Max Marx wasn't one of the hearty ones. The hearty ones were the worst. Marx was, in fact, refreshingly gloomy, his thick black beard and eyebrows creating a doomed stoic's countenance.

"Yes," he said, in response to her criticism of the virtual, "this is a very miserable effect. You should see the sand crabs. They are laughable, like toys." He eased himself down on the sand next to her and took his hat off and fanned it in front of his face. "I apologize. It must be very painful, a connoisseur of the vee like you, to endure this."

Keel remembered that Dr. Marx spoke in a manner subject to interpretation. His words always held a potential for sarcasm.

"We are portable," Dr. Marx said. "We are in a mobile unit, and so, alas, we don't have the powerful stationary AdRes equipment at our command. Even so, we could do better. There are better mockups to be had, but we are not prospering these days. Financially, it has been a year of setbacks, and we have had to settle for some second-rate stuff."

"I'm not in a hospital?" Keel asked.

Marx shook his head. "No. No hospital."

Keel frowned. Marx, sensing her confusion, put his hat back on his head and studied her through narrowed eyes. "We are on the run, Keel Benning. You have not been following the news, being otherwise occupied, but companies like your beloved Virtvana have won a major legislative battle. They are now empowered to maintain their customer base aggressively. I believe the wording is 'protecting customer assets against invasive alienation by third-party services.' Virtvana can come and get you."

Keel blinked at Dr. Marx's dark countenance. "You can't seriously think someone would . . . what? . . . kidnap me?"

Dr. Marx shrugged. "Virtvana might. For the precedent. You're a good customer."

"Vee moguls are going to sweat the loss of one spike? That's crazy."

Dr. Marx sighed, stood up, whacked sand from his trousers with his hands. "You noticed then? That's good. Being able to recognize crazy, that is a good sign. It means there is hope for your own sanity."

* * *

HER days were spent at the edge of the second-rate ocean. She longed for something that would silence the Need. She would have settled for a primitive bird-in-flight simulation. Anything. Some corny sex-with-dolphins loop—or something abstract, the color red leaking into blue, enhanced with aural-D.

She would have given ten years of her life for a game of Apes and Angels, Virtvana's most popular package. Apes and Angels wasn't just another smooth metaphysical mix—it was the true religion to its fans. A gamer started out down in the muck on Libido Island, where the senses were indulged with perfect, shimmerless sims. Not bad, Libido Island, and some gamers stayed there a long, long time. But what put Apes and Angels above the best pleasure pops was this: A player could *evolve spiritually*. If you followed the Path, if you were steadfast, you became more compassionate, more aware, at one with the universe . . . all of which was accompanied by feelings of euphoria.

Keel would have settled for a legal rig. Apes and Angels was a chemically enhanced virtual, and the gear that true believers wore was stripped of most safeguards, tuned to a higher reality.

It was one of these hot pads that had landed Keel in Addiction Resources again.

"It's the street stuff that gets you in trouble," Keel said. "I've just got to stay clear of that."

"You said that last time," the wilson said. "You almost died, you know."

Keel felt suddenly hollowed, beaten. "Maybe I want to die," she said.

Dr. Marx shrugged. Several translucent seagulls appeared, hovered over him, and then winked out. "Bah," he muttered. "Bad therapy-v, bad death-wishing clients, bad career choice. Who doesn't want to die? And who doesn't get that wish, sooner or later?"

* * *

ONE day, Dr. Marx said, "You are ready for swimming."

It was morning, full of a phony, golden light. The nights were black and dreamless, nothing, and the days that grew out of them were pale and untaxing. It was an intentionally bland virtual, its sameness designed for healing.

Keel was wearing a one-piece, white bathing suit. Her counselor wore bathing trunks, baggy with thick black vertical stripes; he looked particularly solemn, in an effort, no doubt, to counteract the farcical elements of rotund belly and sticklike legs.

Keel sighed. She knew better than to protest. This was necessary. She took her wilson's proffered hand, and they walked down to the water's edge. The sand changed from white to gray where the water rolled over it, and they stepped forward into the salt-smelling foam.

Her legs felt cold when the water enclosed them. The wetness was now more than virtual. As she leaned forward and kicked, her muscles, taut and frayed, howled.

She knew the machines were exercising her now. Somewhere her real body, emaciated from long neglect, was swimming in a six-foot aquarium whose heavy seas circulated to create a kind of liquid treadmill. Her lungs ached; her shoulders twisted into monstrous knots of pain.

* * *

IN the evening, they would talk, sitting in their chairs and watching the ocean swallow the sun, the clouds turning orange, the sky occasionally spotting badly, some sort of pixel fatigue.

"If human beings are the universe's way of looking at itself," Dr. Marx said, "then virtual reality is the universe's way of *pretending* to look at itself."

"You wilsons are all so down on virtual reality," Keel said. "But maybe it is the natural evolution of perception. I mean, everything we see is a product of the equipment we see it with. Biological, mechanical, whatever."

Dr. Marx snorted. "Bah. The old 'everything-is-virtual' argument. I am ashamed of you, Keel Benning. Something more original, please. We wilsons are down on virtual addiction because everywhere we look we see dead philosophers. We see them and they don't look so good. We smell them, and they stink. That is our perception, our primitive reality."

* * *

THE healing was slow, and the sameness, the boredom, was a hole to be filled with words. Keel talked, again, about the death of her parents and her brother. They had been over this ground the last time she'd been in treatment, but she was here again, and so it was said again.

"I'm rich because they are dead," she said.

It was true, of course, and Dr. Marx merely nodded, staring in front of him. Her father had been a wealthy man, and he and his young wife and Keel's brother, Calder, had died in a freak air-docking accident while vacationing at Keypond Terraforms. A "sole survivor" clause in her father's life insurance policy had left Keel a vast sum.

She had been eleven at the time—and would have died with her family had she not been sulking that day, refusing to leave the hotel suite.

She knew she was not responsible, of course. But it was

not an event you wished to dwell on. You looked, naturally, for powerful distractions.

"It is a good excuse for your addiction," Dr. Marx said. "If you die, maybe God will say, 'I don't blame you.' Or maybe God will say, 'Get real. Life's hard.' I don't know. Addiction is in the present, not the past. It's the addiction itself that leads to more addictive behavior."

Keel had heard all this before. She barely heard it this time. The weariness of the evening was real, brought on by the day's physical exertions. She spoke in a kind of woozy, presleep fog, finding no power in her words, no emotional release.

Of more interest were her counselor's words. He spoke with rare candor, the result, perhaps, of their fugitive status, their isolation.

It was after a long silence that he said, "To tell you the truth, I'm thinking of getting out of the addiction treatment business. I'm sick of being on the losing side."

Keel felt a coldness in her then, which, later, she identified as fear.

He continued: "They are winning. Virtvana, MindSlide, Right to Flight. They've got the sex, the style, the flash. All we wilsons have is a sense of mission, this knowledge that people are dying, and the ones that don't die are being lost to lives of purpose.

"Maybe we're right—sure, we're right—but we can't sell it. In two, three days we'll come to our destination and you'll have to come into Big R and meet your fellow addicts. You won't be impressed. It's a henry-hovel in the Slash. It's not a terrific advertisement for Big R."

Keel felt strange, comforting her wilson. Nonetheless, she reached forward and touched his bare shoulder. "You want to help people. That is a good and noble impulse."

He looked up at her, a curious nakedness in his eyes. "Maybe that is hubris."

"Hubris?"

"Are you not familiar with the word? It means to try to steal the work of the gods."

Keel thought about that in the brief moment between the dimming of the seascape and the nothingness of night. She thought it would be a fine thing to do, to steal the work of the gods.

* * *

DR. MARX checked the perimeter, the security net. All seemed to be in order. The air was heavy with moisture and the cloying odor of mint. This mint scent was the olfactory love song of an insectlike creature that flourished in the tropical belt. The creature looked like an unpleasant mix of spider and wasp. Knowing that the sweet scent came from it, Dr. Marx breathed shallowly and had to fight against an inclination to gag. Interesting, the way knowledge affected one. An odor, pleasant in itself, could induce nausea when its source was identified.

He was too weary to pursue the thought. He returned to the mobile unit, climbed in and locked the door behind him. He walked down the corridor, paused to peer into the room where Keel rested, sedated electrically.

He should not have spoken his doubts. He was weary, depressed, and it was true that he might very well abandon this crumbling profession. But he had no right to be so self-revealing to a client. As long as he was employed, it behooved him to conduct himself in a professional manner.

Keel's head rested quietly on the pillow. Behind her, on the green panels, her heart and lungs created cool, luminous graphics. Physically, she was restored. Emotionally, mentally, spiritually, she might be damaged beyond repair.

He turned away from the window and walked on down the corridor. He walked past his sleeping quarters to the control room. He undressed and lay down on the utilitarian flat and let the neuronet embrace him. He was aware, as always, of guilt and a hangdog sense of betrayal.

The virtual had come on the Highway two weeks ago. He'd already left Addiction Resources with Keel, traveling west into the wilderness of Pit Finitum, away from the treatment center and New Vegas.

Know the enemy. He'd sampled all the vees, played at lowest res with all the safeguards maxed, so that he could talk knowledgeably with his clients. But he'd never heard of this virtual—and it had a special fascination for him. It was called *Halfway House*.

A training vee, not a recreational one, it consisted of a series of step-motivated, instructional virtuals designed to teach the apprentice addictions counselor his trade.

So why this guilt attached to methodically running the course?

What guilt?

That guilt.

Okay. Well . . .

* * *

THE answer was simple enough: Here all interventions came to a good end, all problems were resolved, all clients were healed.

So far he had intervened on a fourteen-year-old boy addicted to Clawhammer Comix, masterfully diagnosed a woman suffering from Leary's syndrome, and led an entire Group of mix-feeders through a nasty withdrawal episode.

He could tell himself he was learning valuable healing techniques.

Or he could tell himself that he was succumbing to the world that killed his clients, the hurt-free world where everything worked out for the best, good triumphed, bad withered and died, rewards came effortlessly—and if that was not enough, the volume could always be turned up.

He had reservations. Adjusting the neuronet, he thought, "I will be careful." It was what his clients always said.

* * *

KEEL watched the insipid ocean, waited. Generally, Dr. Marx arrived soon after the darkness of sleep had fled.

He did not come at all. When the sun was high in the sky, she began to shout for him. That was useless, of course.

She ran into the ocean, but it was a low res ghost and

only filled her with vee-panic. She stumbled back to the beach chair, tried to calm herself with a rational voice: *Someone will come.*

But would they? She was, according to her wilson, in the wilds of Pit Finitum, hundreds of miles to the west of New Vegas, traveling toward a halfway house hidden in some dirty corner of the mining warren known as the Slash.

Darkness came, and the programmed current took her into unconsciousness.

The second day was the same, although she sensed a physical weakness that emanated from Big R. Probably nutrients in one of the IV pockets had been depleted. *I'll die,* she thought. Night snuffed the thought.

A new dawn arrived without Dr. Marx. Was he dead? And if so, was he dead by accident or design? And if by design, whose? Perhaps he had killed himself; perhaps this whole business of Virtvana's persecution was a delusion.

Keel remembered the wilson's despair, felt a sudden conviction that Dr. Marx had fled Addiction Resources without that center's knowledge, a victim of the evangelism/paranoia psychosis that sometimes accompanied counselor burnout.

Keel had survived much in her twenty years. She had donned some deadly v-gear and made it back to Big R intact. True, she had been saved a couple of times, and she probably wasn't what anyone would call psychologically sound, but . . . it would be an ugly irony if it was an addictions rehab, an unhinged wilson, that finally killed her.

Keel hated irony, and it was this disgust that pressed her into action.

She went looking for the plug. She began by focusing on her spine, the patches, the slightly off-body temp of the sensor pad. Had her v-universe been more engrossing, this would have been harder to do, but the ocean was deteriorating daily, the seagulls now no more than scissoring disruptions in the mottled sky.

On the third afternoon of her imposed solitude, she was able to sit upright in Big R. It required all her strength, the double-think of real Big-R motion while in the virtual.

The effect in vee was to momentarily tilt the ocean and cause the sky to leak blue pixels into the sand.

Had her arms been locked, had her body been glove-secured, it would have been wasted effort, of course, but Keel's willing participation in her treatment, her daily exercise regimen, had allowed relaxed physical inhibitors. There had been no reason for Dr. Marx to anticipate Keel's attempting a Big-R disruption.

She certainly didn't want to.

The nausea and terror induced by contrary motion in Big R while simulating a virtual was considerable.

Keel relied on gravity, shifting, leaning to the right. The bed shifted to regain balance.

She screamed, twisted, hurled herself sideways into Big R.

And her world exploded. The ocean raced up the beach, a black tidal wave that screeched and rattled as though some monstrous mechanical beast were being demolished by giant pistons.

Black water engulfed her. She coughed and it filled her lungs. She flayed; her right fist slammed painfully against the side of the container, making it hum.

She clambered out of the exercise vat, placed conveniently next to the bed, stumbled, and sprawled on the floor in naked triumph.

"Hello Big R," she said, tasting blood on her lips.

* * *

DR. MARX had let the system ease him back into Big R. The sessions room dimmed to glittering black, then the light returned. He was back in the bright control room. He removed the neuronet, swung his legs to the side of the flatbed, stretched. It had been a good session. He had learned something about distinguishing (behaviorially) the transitory feedback psychosis called frets from the organic v-disease, Viller's Pathway.

This Halfway House was proving to be a remarkable instructional tool. In retrospect, his fear of its virtual form had been pure superstition. He smiled at his own irrationality.

* * *

HE would have slept that night in ignorance, but he decided to give the perimeter of his makeshift compound a last security check before retiring.

To that effect, he dressed and went outside.

In the flare of the compound lights, the jungle's purple vegetation looked particularly unpleasant, like the swollen limbs of long-drowned corpses. The usual skittering things made a racket. There was nothing in the area inclined to attack a man, but the planet's evolution hadn't stinted on biting and stinging vermin, and . . .

And one of the vermin was missing.

He had, as always, been frugal in his breathing, gathering into his lungs as little of the noxious atmosphere as possible. The cloying mint scent never failed to sicken him.

But the odor was gone.

It had been there earlier in the evening, and now it was gone. He stood in jungle night, in the glare of the compound lights, waiting for his brain to process this piece of information, but his brain told him only that the odor had been there and now it was gone.

Still, some knowledge of what this meant was leaking through, creating a roiling fear.

If you knew what to look for, you could find it. No vee was as detailed as nature.

You only had to find one seam, one faint oscillation in a rock, one incongruent shadow.

It was a first-rate sim, and it would have fooled him. But they had had to work fast, fabricating and downloading it, and no one had noted that a nasty alien-bug filled the Big-R air with its mating fragrance.

* * *

DR. MARX knew he was still in the vee. That meant, of course, that he had not walked outside at all. He was still lying on the flat. And, thanks to his blessed paranoia, there was a button at the base of the flat, two inches from where his left hand naturally lay. Pushing it would disrupt all current and activate a hypodermic containing twenty cc's of hapotile-4. Hapotile-4 could get the attention of the deepest V-diver. The aftereffects were not pleasant, but, for many v-devotees, there wouldn't have been an "after" without hapotile.

Dr. Marx didn't hesitate. He strained for the Big R, traced the line of his arm, moved. It was there; he found it. Pressed.

Nothing.

Then, out of the jungle, a figure came.

* * *

EIGHT feet tall, carved from black steel, the vee soldier bowed at the waist. Then, standing erect, it spoke: "We deactivated your failsafe before you embarked, Doctor."

"Who are you?" He was not intimidated by this military mockup, the boom of its metal voice, the faint whine of its servos. It was a virtual puppet, of course. Its masters were the thing to fear.

"We are concerned citizens," the soldier said. "We have reason to believe that you are preventing a client of ours, a client-in-good-credit, from satisfying her constitutionally sanctioned appetites."

"Keel Benning came to us of her own free will. Ask her and she will tell you as much."

"We will ask her. And that is not what she will say. She will say, for all the world to hear, that her freedom was compromised by so-called caregivers."

"Leave her alone."

The soldier came closer. It looked up at the dark blanket of the sky. "Too late to leave anyone alone, Doctor. Everyone is in the path of progress. One day we will all live in the vee. It is the natural home of gods."

The sky began to glow as the black giant raised its gleaming arms.

"You act largely out of ignorance," the soldier said. "The god-seekers come, and you treat them like aberrations, like madmen burning with sickness. This is because you do not know the virtual yourself. Fearing it, you have confined and studied it. You have refused to taste it, to savor it."

The sky was glowing gold, and figures seemed to move in it, beautiful, winged humanforms.

Virtvana, Marx thought. *Ape and Angels.*

It was his last coherent thought before enlightenment.

"I give you a feast," the soldier roared. And all the denizens of heaven swarmed down, surrounding Dr. Marx with love and compassion and that absolute, impossible distillation of a hundred thousand insights that formed a single, tear-shaped truth: Euphoria.

* * *

KEEL found she could stand. A couple of days of inaction hadn't entirely destroyed the work of all that exercise. Shakily, she navigated the small room. The room had the sanitized, hospital look she'd grown to know and loathe. If this room followed the general scheme, the shelves over the bed should contain . . . They did, and Keel donned one of the gray, disposable client suits.

* * *

SHE found Dr. Marx by the noise he was making, a kind of *huh, huh, huh* delivered in a monotonous chant and punctuated by an occasional *Ah!* The sounds, and the writhing, near-naked body that lay on the table emitting these sounds, suggested to Keel that her doctor, naughty man, might be auditing something sexual on the virtual.

But a closer look showed signs of v-overload epilepsy. Keel had seen it before and knew that one's first inclination, to shut down every incoming signal, was not the way to go. First you shut down any chemical enhances—and, if you happened to have a hospital handy (as she did), you slowed the system more with something like clemadine or hetlin—then, if you were truly fortunate and your spike was epping in a high-tech detox (again, she was so fortunate), you plugged in a regulator, spliced it and started running the signals through that, toning them down.

Keel got to it. As she moved, quickly, confidently, she had time to think that this was something she knew about (a consumer's knowledge, not a tech's, but still, her knowledge was extensive).

* * *

DR. MARX had been freed from the virtual for approximately ten minutes (but was obviously not about to break the surface of Big R), when Keel heard the whine of the security alarm. The front door of the unit was being breached with an Lsaw.

Keel scrambled to the corridor where she'd seen the habitat sweep. She swung the ungainly tool around, falling to one knee as she struggled to unbolt the barrel lock. *Fizzing pocky low-tech grubber.*

The barrel-locking casing clattered to the floor just as the door collapsed.

The man in the doorway held a weapon, which, in retrospect, made Keel feel a little better. Had he been weaponless, she would still have done what she did.

She swept him out the door. The sonic blast scattered him across the cleared area, a tumbling, bloody mass of rags and unraveling flesh, a thigh bone tumbling into smaller bits as it rolled under frayed vegetation.

She was standing in the doorway when an explosion rocked the unit and sent her crashing backward. She crawled down the corridor, still lugging the habitat gun, and fell into the doorway of a cluttered storage room. An alarm continued to shriek somewhere.

The mobile now lay on its side. She fired in front of her. The roof rippled and roared, looked like it might hold, and then flapped away like an unholy, howling v-demon, a vast silver blade that smoothly severed the leafy tops of the jungle's tallest sentinels. Keel plunged into the night, ran to the edge of the unit and peered out into the glare of the compound lights.

The man was crossing the clearing.

She crouched, and he turned, sensing motion. He was trained to fire reflexively but he was too late. The rolling sonic blast from Keel's habitat gun swept man and weapon and weapon's discharge into rolling motes that mixed with rock and sand and vegetation, a stew of organic and inorganic matter for the wind to stir.

Keel waited for others to come but none did.

Finally, she reentered the mobile to retrieve her wilson, dragging him (unconscious) into the scuffed arena of the compound.

Later that night, exhausted, she discovered the aircraft that had brought the two men. She hesitated, then decided to destroy it. It would do her no good; it was not a vehicle she could operate, and its continued existence might bring others.

* * *

THE next morning, Keel's mood improved when she found a pair of boots that almost fit. They were a little tight but, she reasoned, that was probably better than a little loose. They had, according to Dr. Marx, a four-day trek ahead of them.

Dr. Marx was now conscious but fairly insufferable. He could talk about nothing but angels and the Light. A long, hard dose of Apes and Angels had filled him with fuzzy love and an uncomplicated metaphysics in which smiling angels fixed bad stuff and protected all good people (and, it went without saying, all people were good).

Keel had managed to dress Dr. Marx in a suit again, and this restored a professional appearance to the wilson. But, to Keel's dismay, Dr. Marx in virtual-withdrawal was a shameless whiner.

"Please," he would implore. "Please, I am in terrible terrible Neeeeeeed."

He complained that the therapy-v was too weak, that he was sinking into a catatonic state. Later, he would stop entirely, *of course,* but now, please, something stronger . . .

No.

He told her she was heartless, cruel, sadistic, vengeful. She was taking revenge for her own treatment program, although, if she would just recall, he had been the soul of gentleness and solicitude.

"You can't be in virtual and make the journey," Keel said. "I need you to navigate. We will take breaks, but I'm afraid they will be brief. Say goodbye to your mobile."

She destroyed it with the habitat sweep, and they were on their way. It was a limping, difficult progress, for they took much with them: food, emergency camping and sleeping gear, a portable, two-feed v-rig, the virtual black box, and the security image grabs. And Dr. Marx was not a good traveler.

It took six days to get to the Slash, and then Dr. Marx said he wasn't sure just where the halfway house was.

"What?"

"I don't know. I'm disoriented."

"You'll never be a good v-addict," Keel said. "You can't lie."

"I'm not lying!" Dr. Marx snapped, goggle-eyed with feigned innocence.

Keel knew what was going on, of course. He wanted to give her the slip and find a v-hovel where he could swap good feelings with his old angel buddies. Keel knew.

"I'm not letting you out of my sight," she said.

The Slash was a squalid mining town with every vice a disenfranchised population could buy. It had meaner toys than New Vegas, and no semblance of law.

Keel couldn't just ask around for a treatment house. You could get hurt that way.

But luck was with her. She spied the symbol of a triangle inside a circle on the side of what looked like an abandoned office. She watched a man descend a flight of stairs directly beneath the painted triangle. She followed him.

"Where are we going?" Dr. Marx said. He was still a bundle of tics from angel-deprivation.

Keel didn't answer, just dragged him along. Inside, she saw the "Easy Does It" sign and knew everything was going to be okay.

An old man saw her and waved. Incredibly, he knew her, even knew her name. "Keel," he shouted. "I'm delighted to see you."

"It's a small world, Solly."

"It's that. But you get around some too. You cover some ground, you know. I figured ground might be covering you by now."

Keel laughed. "Yeah." She reached out and touched the old man's arm. "I'm looking for a house," she said.

* * *

IN Group they couldn't get over it. Dr. Max Marx was a fizzing *client*. This amazed everyone, but two identical twins, Sere and Shona, were so dazed by this event that they insisted on dogging the wilson's every move. They'd flank him, peering up into his eyes, trying to fathom this mystery by an act of unrelenting scrutiny.

Brake Madders thought it was a narc thing and wanted to hurt Marx.

"No, he's one of us," Keel said.

And so, Keel thought, *am I*.

* * *

WHEN Dr. Max Marx was an old man, one of his favorite occupations was to reminisce. One of his favorite topics was Keel Benning. He gave her credit for saving his life, not only in the jungles of Pit Finitum but during the rocky days that followed when he wanted to flee the halfway house and find, again, virtual nirvana.

She had recognized every denial system and thwarted it with logic. When logic was not enough, she had simply shared his sadness and pain and doubt.

"I've been there," she had said.

* * *

THE young wilsons and addiction activists knew Keel Benning only as the woman who had fought Virtvana and MindSlip and the vast lobby of Right to Flight, the woman who had secured a resounding victory for addicts' rights and challenged the spurious thinking that suggested a drowning person was drowning by choice. She was a hero, but, like many heroes, she was not, to a newer generation, entirely real.

"**I WAS** preoccupied at the time," Dr. Marx would tell young listeners. "I kept making plans to slip out and find some Apes and Angels. You weren't hard pressed then—and you aren't now—to find some mind-flaming vee in the Slash. My thoughts would go that way a lot.

"So I didn't stop and think, 'Here's a woman who's been rehabbed six times; it's not likely she'll stop on the seventh. She's just endured some genuine nasty events, and she's probably feeling the need for some quality downtime.'

"What I saw was a woman who spent every waking moment working on her recovery. And when she wasn't doing mental, spiritual, or physical push-ups, she was helping those around her, all us shaking, vision-hungry, fizz-headed needers.

"I didn't think, 'What the hell is this?' back then. But I thought it later. I thought it when I saw her graduate from medical school.

"When she went back and got a law degree, so she could fight the bastards who wouldn't let her practice addiction medicine properly, I thought it again. That time, I asked her. I asked her what had wrought the change."

Dr. Marx would wait as long as it took for someone to ask, "What did she say?"

"It unsettled me some," he would say, then wait again to be prompted.

They'd prompt.

" 'Helping people,' she'd said. She'd found it was a thing she could do; she had a gift for it. All those no-counts and dead-enders in a halfway house in the Slash. She found she could help them all."

Dr. Marx saw it then, and saw it every time after that, every time he'd seen her speaking on some monolith grid at some rally, some hearing, some whatever. Once he'd seen it, he saw it every time: that glint in her eye, the incorrigible, unsinkable addict.

"People," she had said. "What a rush."

HER OWN PRIVATE SITCOM

Allen Steele

The Reality TV craze has helped to generate the idea that anybody and everybody can be a television star, but as the sly story that follows indicates, it's not always as easy as it looks . . .

Allen Steele made his first sale to Asimov's Science Fiction *magazine in 1988, soon following it up with a long string of other sales to* Asimov's, *as well as to markets such as* The Magazine of Fantasy & Science Fiction *and* Science Fiction Age. *In 1990, he published his critically acclaimed first novel,* Orbital Decay, *which subsequently won the Locus Poll as Best First Novel of the year, and soon Steele was being compared to Golden Age Heinlein by no less an authority than Gregory Benford. His other books include the novels* Clarke County Space, Lunar Descent, Labyrinth of Night. The Weight, The Tranquillity Alternative, A King of Infinite Space, Oceanspace, Chronospace, Coyote, *and* Coyote Rising. *His short work has been gathered in two collections,* Rude Astronauts and Sex and Violence in Zero G. *His most recent book is a new novel in the* Coyote *sequence,* Coyote Frontier. *He won a Hugo Award in 1996 for his novella "The Death of Captain Future," and another Hugo in 1998 for his novella "Where Angels Fear to Tread." Born in Nashville, Tennessee, he has worked for a variety of newspapers and magazines, covering science and business *assignments, and is now a full-time writer living in Whately, Massachusetts with his wife, Linda.*

RAY'S Good Food Diner was located on the outskirts of town near the interstate, across a gravel parking lot from a Union 76 truckstop. The town only had 1,300 residents, so it supported only two restaurants, the other of which was a pizzeria which served up what was universally acknowledged to be the world's most indigestible pizza. This left Ray's Good Food Diner as the only place within fifteen miles where you could get a decent breakfast twenty-four hours a day.

Every Friday morning at about nine o'clock, Bill drove out to Ray's for the weekly meeting of the Old Farts Club. No one remembered who first started calling it that, but it pretty well described the membership: a half-dozen or so men, each and every one of whom qualified for the senior citizen discount, who liked to get together and chew the fat, both literally and figuratively. There weren't any rules, written or unspoken, against women or children attending the meetings, but since no one had ever brought along any family members—their wives didn't care and their kids were all adults now and, for the most part, living away from home—the issue had never really been raised. Which was just as well; in a world where seemingly everything had been made accessible to all ages and both genders, Ray's Good Food Diner was one of the few places left where a handful of white male chauvinists could safely convene without fear of being picketed.

A grumbling row of sixteen-wheelers idled on the other side of the lot when Bill pulled into Ray's. He parked his ten-year-old Ford pick-up in front of the diner and climbed out. The late autumn air was cool and crisp, redolent with the scent of fallen leaves and diesel fumes; he thrust his hands into the pockets of his Elks Club windbreaker as he sauntered past the line of cars. Even without glancing through the windows, he knew which of his friends were here just by recognizing their vehicles: Chet's charcoal-black Cadillac with the NRA sticker in the rear window; Tom's Dodge truck with corn husks in the bed; Garrett's decrepit Volkswagen hatchback with the mismatched driver's side door and the dented rear bumper. John's Volvo wasn't there—Bill remembered that he was in Daytona Beach, visiting his son's family. Ned hadn't arrived yet, either because he had overslept or—more likely, Bill thought sourly—he was too hungover from his latest whiskey binge. Poor Ned.

The small diner was filled with its usual clientele: long-haul truckers chowing down after sleeping over in their vehicles, local farmers taking a mid-morning break from their chores, a couple of longhair students from the nearby state university. He smelled bacon and fried potatoes, heard music from the little two-songs-for-a-quarter juke boxes above the window booths: Jimmy Buffett from the one occupied by a husband-and-wife trucker family, something godawful from the one taken over by the college kids. He unzipped his windbreaker, looked around . . .

"Hey, Bill!"

And there they were, sitting around two Formica-top tables pushed together at the far end of the room: the Old Farts Club in all their glory. Chet, Tom, Garrett . . . the regular gang, waving for him to come over and join them. A chair had been left open for him; if there was a better definition of friendship, Bill had never heard of it.

"I suppose you're wondering why I called you all here today . . ." he began.

"Aw, shut up and sit down." This from Chet, seated at the end of the table.

"We begin bombing in five minutes," added Garrett.

The same opening lines, reiterated again and again over the last—seven? ten? fifteen?—years. Friendship is also the condition when your buddies tolerate your lame jokes long after they've ceased to be funny. Or perhaps it was only a requisite of growing old.

Bill took his seat, looked around. Everyone had a mug

of coffee before him, but there were no plates on the table. Another unspoken rule of the Old Farts Club was that you ate when you were hungry; no one had to wait for the others to arrive. "Thought I was running late," he observed, "but it looks like we all got here at the same time for once."

"Nope. I've been here for a hour." Chet nodded to Tom. "He's been here almost as long as I have."

"Almost an hour," agreed Tom, studying the menu.

"I got here . . ." Garrett checked his watch. "Exactly forty-two minutes ago." Garrett was like that. "We're still waiting to order."

"You mean, we're waiting for someone to ask if we want to order," Chet said.

"Yes, this is true."

Puzzled, Bill glanced over his shoulder, scanned the room. The diner was no more or less busy than it ever was on a Friday morning; at least a third of the booths were vacant, and only a handful of people sat at the lunch counter. "So where's our waitress?" he asked. "Who's working today?"

Three men who had been nursing lukewarm coffee for the last half-hour or more looked at each other. "Joanne," Chet murmured darkly. "But don't bother to call for her. She's in her own private sitcom."

* * *

AS if taking a cue from an unseen director, Joanne suddenly appeared, walking backward through the swinging kitchen door, balancing a serving tray above her left shoulder. "Okay, all right!" she yelled as she turned around, loud enough to be heard over the dueling jukeboxes. "Just everyone hold their horses! I'm coming as fast as I can!"

In all the uncounted years he had been coming to Ray's, all the many times Bill had observed Joanne at work, he had never before seen her shout at her customers. Joanne was born and raised in this town, and started working at Ray's when she graduated from the county high school. The years had been rough on her—a low-paying job, a drunk husband who abandoned her after two years, a teenage son who dropped out of high school and was now seldom home—and long ago she had lost the looks and charm that had made her a one-time prom queen, but she was still, for guys like himself and the rest of the Old Farts, the little girl they had all watched grow up. If there were good ol' boys, then she was a good ol' gal.

Her uncustomary brashness drew his attention; the object hovering above her held it. A miniature helicopter purred about a foot above her head, its spinning rotors forming a translucent halo; as she walked past the lunch counter, it followed her into the dining room. Suspended beneath the rotors was a softball-size spheroid; a tiny, multijointed prong containing a binaural microphone protruded above three camera lenses that swiftly gimbaled back and forth.

"Oh, lordie," he murmured. "Joanne's got herself a flycam."

"Is that what it's called?" Like everyone else at the table, Tom was watching Joanne. "I knew they were called something, but I didn't know what it was."

"I call it a pain in the you-know-what." Garrett picked up his cold coffee, took a sip, made a face. "What she's doing with one here, I have no idea."

Joanne sashayed to a pair of truck drivers sitting in a nearby booth, the flycam keeping pace with her from above. "All right," she announced as she picked the plates off the tray and placed them on the table, "a western omelette with a side order of bacon, two scrambled eggs with sausage, a glass of orange juice and a glass of tomato juice. Will that be all?"

The drivers looked at the plates she had put before them. "Ma'am, I ordered a ham and bacon omelette," one said quietly, "and I think my friend here asked for his eggs over-easy with ham."

"And I didn't ask for tomato juice, either," added the other. "I wanted orange juice, too."

"We-e-e-elll!" Joanne struck a pose, one hand on an

out-thrust hip, the serving tray tucked under her other arm. "I suppose one of us made a mistake, didn't we?"

"Yes, ma'am, I suppose one of us sure did."

Joanne looked over her shoulder. "Ray!" she bellowed in the direction of the kitchen. "You made a mistake!" Then she pivoted on her heel, and raised her arms. "I swear," she loudly proclaimed to no one in particular (except, perhaps, the flycam), "it ain't my fault no one 'round here speaks English!"

Then she flounced away, her hips swinging with overdone suggestivity. The two drivers gaped at her. "I'm not paying for this!" one yelled at her. "This isn't what I ordered!"

Joanne ignored them. She was already advancing on the two college kids sitting in the next booth. They stared at the flycam as it moved into position above their table. "What'll you have, guys?"

One of the students pointed at the drone. "Uhh . . . hey, is that thing live?"

"Taped," she said briskly, dropping her voice for the first time. "Just pretend it's not there." She raised her voice again. "So what'll you have, kids?"

He gawked at the camera, absently combing back his hair with his fingers. The other student nervously looked back at his menu. "I . . . uh . . . can I have . . . ?"

"Son, what were you smoking last night?"

Startled, he looked up at her. "What?"

"Oh, you were smoking what." She beamed down at him. "That's new to me. I'm just a poor country girl."

"Huh? What are you . . . ?"

"Look, dudes, let me rap with you, okay?" She lowered her order pad, bent over the table to look them in the eye. The flycam dropped a few inches closer, its cameras recording everything. "I was your age once, and yeah, I used to get pretty wild . . ." She took a deep breath. "But dope is just a bad trip, y'know what I'm saying? A thing is a terrible mind to . . ."

"Huh?"

"Aw, dammit." She shook her head, glanced up at the flycam for a moment, then returned her attention to the students. "I mean, a mind is a terrible thing to waste, and you've got your whole future ahead of you."

"I . . . what?" Stammering with disbelief, the student glanced between Joanne and the hovering drone. "I . . . hey, lady, I don't use drugs!"

"Neither of us do!" His companion peered up at the flycam. "Hey, we're straight! I swear, We're straight! Geez, we just came in here to get breakfast and . . ."

"Think about it," Joanne said solemnly. "Just . . . think about it."

Then she was off again, heading for another table, the flycam following her like an airborne puppy. "Can we at least get some coffee?" the first student called after her.

"What in the world is that fool girl up to?" Tom murmured.

"Taping another episode of her net show." Chet watched her progress across the dining room. "*Joanne's Place*, something like that . . ."

"But this isn't her place." Tom was bewildered. "It's Ray's. Ray's Diner. What's she doing, some kind of TV show?"

As always, Tom was behind the times. No surprise there; he was still trying to get over Bush losing to Clinton. But Bill recognized the technology; eight years might have gone by since he retired as physics teacher at the local high school, but he still kept subscriptions to popular science magazines.

Flycams were miniature spinoffs of unpiloted military reconnaissance drones. Initially intended to be used for law enforcement, only police departments were able to buy them at first, but it wasn't long before they became inexpensive enough to enter the consumer market, and now they were available at electronics stores for approximately the same price as a high-end camcorder. Early versions were remote-controlled, but later models had the benefit of newer technology. They could be programmed to automatically track someone by his or her body-heat signature and voice pattern and follow them around, during which time they would record everything he or she did and spoke, with the data being transmitted to a nearby datanest. Bill figured that Joanne had probably parked the nest in the kitchen, or perhaps under the lunch counter.

"It's a net show, Tom." Chet watched Joanne perform for another pair of truckers seated at the counter. Now she was playing the coy vixen while she took their orders; she had loosened the top button of her blouse, and she was letting them get an eyeful of pink cleavage as she freshened up their coffee. The drone waited overhead, its mike and lenses catching everything. "She's got that fly-thing following her around while she works, and when she's done at the end of the day, she takes it home and makes it into another episode."

"Like for a TV show, you mean."

"The net." Chet gave him an arch look. "Don't get out much, do you? No one watches TV anymore 'cept old duffers like us."

"Hey, did anyone catch *Miami Vice* last night?" Garrett, always the peacemaker. "They showed the one where Crockett and Tubbs . . ."

"See what I mean?" Chet waggled a finger at Garrett, cutting him off. "We're used to shows about make-believe characters in make-believe stories, but that's not where it's at anymore. Now you can go out, buy one of those things, hook it up to your DVD and your home computer . . ." He snapped his fingers. "You've got your own show."

"My wife really likes that stuff." Garrett had surrendered; no sense in trying to talk about an old cop show in perpetual rerun on a local cable station. "Every night, she sits down in the den and just searches back and forth, looking for the newest shows people have put on."

"On her computer?" Slowly, Tom was beginning to catch on. "You mean, like on . . . whatchamacallit, web sites?"

Bill nodded. "Sort of like that." He didn't add that the

web sites were old tech; no sense in confusing him any further. "The net has all these different nodes, millions of them, and you can rent time there, put in your own program. Anything you want."

"Anything?" Tom's eyes widened. "Like . . . you mean . . . anything you've recorded with one of those . . . ?"

"Yes. Anything."

Yes, anything. Bill had his own desktop system, a decrepit old Mac he had been nursing along for years with mother boards and internal modems bought from online junkyards or cannibalized from CPUs purchased at flea markets. Slow as autumn sap from a maple tree, but it was enough to let him patch into the net if he didn't mind waiting a few extra minutes.

He didn't mind, although there wasn't much worth looking at, really. Too much homemade porn, for one thing; every fool with a flycam seemed to think he was king stud of the universe when he got in bed with his wife or girlfriend, and wanted to share his glory with the world. Only slightly less prevalent were the boatloads of fanatics who sincerely believed that they had stumbled upon vast conspiracies involving crashed UFOs, biblical prophecies, and political assassinations; their flycam caught them standing outside military bases, government offices, or ancient Egyptian ruins, delivering rants fascinating only for the width and depth of their meaninglessness.

Those shows were easy to ignore, yet they were also the ones made by thousands of ordinary people during the course of their daily lives. They modeled their shows after the TV programs of their youth—*Cheers*, *Seinfeld*, and *Major Dad* for the sitcom enthusiasts; *ER*, *Melrose Place*, and *Law & Order* for the would-be dramatists—and tried to live up to Hollywood tradition. Convenience store clerks who fancied themselves as comedians. Night watchmen thinking they were action heros. Bored housewives staging their own soaps. Teenagers solving mysteries in shopping malls. Truck stop waitresses producing sitcoms, starring themselves in the lead role.

Joanne disappeared into the kitchen, pausing for only a moment to carefully hold open the door for the flycam. "There she goes," Chet murmured. "Probably going to check the system, maybe put in a fresh disk, put a fresh battery in the 'cam. When she gets home, she'll look at everything she got today, edit it down, maybe add some music and a laugh track. Then she'll put it on the net. *Joanne's Place,* staring Joanne the wisecracking waitress. Just a poor ol' country girl trying to make it through the day."

He picked up his coffee cup, saw that it was empty, put it back in its saucer. "Jesus H. Christ. And all I wanted was . . ."

The door swung open again and a lean young man in a cook's apron carried out a couple of plates of food. "There's Ray Junior now," Garrett said. "Let's see if we can get him over here." He raised a hand. "Hey! Ray!"

Ray acknowledged him with a nod of his head before he went to the two drivers who had complained about their breakfast. He delivered the re-orders and spent a minute apologizing for the foul-up, then scurried around the room, pouring coffee for other disgruntled patrons. Bill couldn't help but to feel sorry for him. Ray Junior had taken over the diner a little over a year ago when his dad retired and moved to Florida; he had done well to keep the family business going, especially on this part of the interstate where nearly every other truckstop cafe was owned by one restaurant chain or another, but he couldn't afford to lose regular customers.

"Ray, what's going on with Joanne?" Chet asked when Ray finally got to their table. "I've been here nearly a hour now and she hasn't taken our orders."

"I'm really sorry about this." Ray had fetched a cup for Bill and was pouring coffee for everyone. "I'll get her over here as soon as she comes off break."

"She's taking a break." Chet glanced meaningfully at the others. "At least the second one she's had since I've been here."

"I'll get her back here."

"You ought to fire her. She's more concerned with that damn toy of hers than with doing her job."

"Well . . ." Ray Junior absently wiped a rag across the table. "Y'know, Chet, I really can't do that. Joanne's been here for nearly eighteen years. She's like family. And . . ."

He hesitated. "And?" Garrett prompted.

Ray shrugged. "Well, y'know, we've never been able to afford so much as a billboard. All we've ever had was word-of-mouth. Meanwhile we've got competition from all the chain operations down the highway. But this show she's doing . . . well, she always puts the name of the place in the credits . . ."

"So it's free advertising," Bill finished. "You're hoping it'll draw more customers."

Ray nodded. "The ones that get popular . . . y'know, get a lot of hits . . . and, well, y'know, if it gets picked up by one of the major net servers, AOL or someone like that, then it could make us . . ."

"Famous," Chet said. "Famous across the whole country. Soon you'll be taking down the old sign, put up another one." He raised his hands, spread them open as if picturing a brand-new fiberoptic sign. "I can see it now. 'World-Famous Joanne's Place.' Maybe you can even sell T-shirts and bumper stickers."

"You know I'd never do that," Ray Junior said quietly.

Chet scowled. "Naw, I'm sure the notion's never occurred to you."

"Of course you wouldn't," Bill said quickly. "Thanks for the coffee, Ray. Sorry to keep you."

"On the house. Same for breakfast," he added as he moved away from the table. "I'll get her out here to take your orders."

"Hear that?" Tom said as Ray Junior beat a hasty retreat to the kitchen. "Breakfast on the house! Not bad, huh?"

"No," Bill said. "Not bad at all."

* * *

THERE was an uncomfortable silence at the table. "So . . ." Garret said at last. "Anyone seen today's paper?"

That was how the Old Farts usually spent their Friday meetings: discussing what they had read in the paper. Baseball season was over, so now it was time to talk football. Sometimes the subject was politics, and how those damn liberals were destroying the whole country. Or maybe it would be about what was going on in Russia, or the people who were about to go to Mars, or someone famous died last week, and pretty soon it would be close to eleven and it was time for everyone to go home and do whatever it was that country gentlemen do in their golden years. Check the mailbox, feed the dogs and cats, putter around the yard, make plans to have the kids over for Thanksgiving. Take a midafternoon nap and wait for the world to turn upside-down again, and hope that it didn't fall on you when it did.

"S'cuse me." Chet pushed back his chair and stood up. "Need to get something from my car."

"What did you leave?" Tom asked.

"Just some medicine. Don't let no one take my seat." He pulled his denim jacket off the back of his chair and shrugged into it as he walked past the lunch counter and pushed aside the glass door next to the cash register.

Garrett mentioned an awful murder that had occurred a few days ago in the big city a couple of hundred miles away, the one that had made all the newspapers. Pretty soon everyone was talking about it: how it had been committed, who had been arrested, whether they really had done the deed, so forth and so on. Bill glanced over his shoulder; out the window, he saw that the trunk lid of Chet's Cadillac had been raised. He watched Chet slam it shut; he turned and began walking back to the diner.

"Funny place to keep medicine," he murmured.

"Huh?" Tom cupped an ear. "What's that you say?"

"Nothing. Never mind."

Chet came back into the diner, took his seat again. The rest of the guys were still discussing the murder, but he didn't seem to have anything to add; he simply picked up a menu and opened it to the breakfast page. Bill noted that he didn't take off his jacket.

A couple of minutes later, the kitchen door banged open again, and there was Joanne. The flycam prowled overhead, filming her every move, as she imperiously studied the dining room. Act II, Scene II: Joanne returns from break. Cue incidental music, audience applause.

"Hey, Joanne!" Garrett raised a hand. "Could we have a little service here, please?"

She heaved an expansive sigh (the audience chuckles expectantly), then pulled pen and order pad from her apron. "Can't a girl get a break 'round here?" she said (the audience laughs a little louder) as she came over, the flycam obediently following her.

For the first time, Bill noticed how much makeup she was wearing: pancake on the cheeks, rouge around the eyes, red lipstick across the mouth. She was trying to erase her last ten years, at least for the benefit of the camera.

"Seems to me that's all you've been taking lately," Chet replied, not looking up from his menu. "We've been waiting over an hour now."

Joanne dropped her mouth open in histrionic surprise (*wooo*, groans the audience) as she placed her hands on her hips. "We-l-l-l-l-l! I didn't know you were in such a gosh-darn hurry! What's the matter, Chet, you waiting for a social security check?" (More laughter.)

Chet continued to study the menu. "Joanne," he said quietly, "I've been coming here to eat before you were born. I bounced your little fanny on my knee when you were a child, and told Ray Senior that he should give you a job when you got out of school . . ."

"And if it wasn't for you, I could have been working for NASA by now!" (Whistles, foot-stomping applause.).

Chet ignored her. "Every time I've come here, I've put a dollar in your tip glass, even when you've done no more than pour me a cup of coffee. So after all these years, I think I deserve a little common courtesy, don't you think?"

Joanne's face turned scarlet beneath the make-up. This wasn't part of the script. "Well, I don't . . . I don't think I have to . . . I don't have to . . ."

"Joanne," Bill said softly, "just take our orders, please. We're hungry, and we want to eat."

"And turn off that silly thing," Chet added. "I'd like a little privacy, if it's not too much to ask."

Reminded that the camera was on her (the audience coughs, moves restlessly) Joanne sought to recover her poise. "We-l-l-l-l-l, if it's privacy you . . . I mean, if you don't . . . I mean . . . if you don't mind, I'd just as soon . . ."

"Sorry," Chet said, then he reached up and grabbed the flycam.

The drone resisted as his fingers wrapped around its mike boom, its lenses snapping back and forth. Its motor whined as the rotors went to a higher speed, and for a moment it almost seemed alive as it fought against Chet's grasp, then he yanked it down to the table.

Tom's coffee went into his lap and Garrett nearly overturned his chair as they yelled and lurched out of the way. "No! Hey!" Joanne reached for the flycam as Chet turned it over. "Stop! What are you . . . ?"

Chet pushed her aside with one hand, then twisted the drone over on its back. The rotor blades cleaved through a plastic salt shaker and swept the pepper cellar halfway across the room before they snagged against the napkin dispenser.

Bill instinctively pulled his coffee mug out of the way. "Chet, what the hell . . . !"

Then Chet pulled out from beneath his jacket the tire iron he had fetched from his car trunk and brought it down on the flycam. The first blow shattered the camera lens and broke the mike boom, and the second shattered its plastic carapace and ruined a compact mass of microchips, solenoids, and actuators. The third and forth blows were unnecessary; the flycam was already an irreparable mess.

Then he dropped the tire iron on the table and sat down. There was a long silence as everyone in the diner stared at him. Then . . .

Long, spontaneous applause from the live studio audience.

As Joanne stared at the wreckage on the table, Chet picked up his menu and opened it again. "Okay," he said, letting out his breath, "I'll take two scrambled eggs, bacon, home fries, wheat toast, and tomato juice. Please."

Tears glimmered in the corners of Joanne's eyes. "I don't . . . I don't believe you just . . . that was my . . ."

"Show's canceled, Joanne." Ray Junior, standing at the lunch counter behind them, spoke quietly. "Will you just take the man's order?"

Joanne's hands shook a little as she raised her pad and dutifully wrote down Chet's order. Then she went around the table and copied down everyone else's. Tom asked for blueberry pancakes, link sausage, rye toast; Garrett requested a western omelette, no fries or toast, and a large glass of milk.

Bill had lost his appetite; he only asked for a refill of his coffee.

Joanne snuffled a bit as she thanked no one in particular, then she turned away and marched on stiff legs back into the kitchen. No one said anything when Ray Junior came out a moment later with a brush and a plastic garbage sack. He avoided everyone's gaze as he silently whisked away the debris, then he vanished through the swinging doors.

"Well . . ." Tom began.

"Well," echoed Garrett.

Chet said nothing, slipped the tire iron beneath his chair, and picked up his coffee.

"Joanne's a good kid," Garrett added.

"That she is. That she is."

"Leave her a good tip, guys. She deserves it."

"Yeah, she certainly earns her money."

"Hard-working lady."

"Damn straight. That she is."

More silence. Across the room, someone put a quarter in a jukebox. An old Johnny Cash song entered the diner. The door opened, allowing inside a cool autumn breeze; a heavyset driver sat down at the counter, took off his cap, and picked up the lunch menu. A sixteen-wheeler blew its air horn as it rumbled out of the lot, heading for parts unknown.

"So . . . Braves blew it again, didn't they?"

"Yep. That they did." Bill cleared his throat. "Now it's football season."

THE ICHNEUMON AND THE DORMEUSE

Terry Dowling

One of the best-known and most celebrated of Australian writers in any genre, the winner of eleven Ditmar Awards and three Aurealis Awards, Terry Dowling made his first sale in 1982, and has since made an international reputation for himself as a writer of science fiction, dark fantasy, and horror. Primarily a short-story writer, he is the author of the linked collections Rynosseros, Blue Tyson, Twilight Beach, *and* Wormwood, *as well as other collections such as* Antique Futures: The Best of Terry Dowling, The Man Who Lost Red, An Intimate Knowledge of the Night, *and* Blackwater Days. *He has also written the novels* Beckoning Nightframe, His Own, the Star Alphecca, *and* The Ichneumon and the Dormeuse. *As editor, he also produced* The Essential Ellison, *and, with Van Ikin, the anthology* Mortal Fire: Best Australian SF. *Born in Sydney, he now lives in Hunter's Hill, New South Wales, Australia.*

In the tense story that follows, he shows us that there are some games you can never stop playing, whether you want to or not.

THIS time was different. This time on his way past the tombs, Beni turned left, ignored the guard Stones of the nearer mounds and headed down the path through the trees to the wide low tumulus where her tomb was.

He granted that the Stones had him, though nothing showed it. The tumulus was quiet under the hot afternoon sun; the trees, the grass barely stirred; the fields stretched away to meet the sky. The only movement was the heat shimmer on the other tomb mounds and the endless pull of the sentry Stones.

The Nothing Stones were neither stones nor quite filled with nothing, though that was the sense they gave, all sixteen of them, low basaltic pillars two metres high, as wide as his shoulders, as deep as his thigh, standing in the usual henge circle around the foot of the tumulus itself.

Their onyx-black, outward-facing sides were filled with stars, converging points of light, and while Beni would not look into those glossy midnight fields, he knew that if he remained, if they didn't have him already, the darkling, star-ridden massebots would solve his mysteries, totes and sly conditionings and come to snatch him away, pulling, pulling, grabbing at sight and mind, close obsidian in the hot afternoon.

Always assume the Stones have you, Ramirez had said, told him now in memory, the greatest tomb-robber of them all, and Beni did so, leaving it to his autonomic tote systems to sort out. If they had him in a trance loop, he'd probably soon know. He continued through the perimeter henge, leaving the deadly megaliths at his back, and headed down the access ramp to the black gulf of the doorway.

Doorway not door. None of the old tumulus tombs had ever had doors. Beni stood before the quiet, porcelain-smooth, darkened throat in the side of its vast, low hill and called out.

"Dormeuse! Dormeuse! You have a visitor!"

The words echoed against the ceramic, died. There was only stillness, silence again, smooth cool midnight before him, daylight and blazing summer behind.

Beni, tech'd and toted, wearing a flamer he'd been told

he probably wouldn't use, carrying a metre-long touchpole over his back as nearly all tomb-robbers did, just in case, now brought up his wrist display, saw what the optics gave.

Classic plan clear and sure. Free of the Stones too, if he could trust the readings. It was the standard schema confirmed by all the survivors (most of all by Ramirez himself, one of the very few to make it back totally unharmed) as the basic Tastan design: stretch of corridor, peristyle hall, corridor, burial chamber.

Simple. Direct. Two hundred metres, fifteen, another hundred, then the ten-metre circular chamber: the classic Tastan biocromlech. Simple. Linear. Very deadly.

For there would be traps, illusions, sensory and neural tricks. Standing there, Beni ran the latest figures again, unchanged, of course, since the last postings, but you never knew when new data might be collated and added—the town's comp systems were constantly at it. Outright death with bodies recovered still stayed at 12% of annual penalties, selective maiming and stigma—the 'souvenirs,' 14% (but at least you returned), failure to return at all was still 63% (up 2% on last year's average—things did change), failure to enter the tomb but believing so, 11%.

Beni cleared that, studied the simplified plan again—spinal access corridor (axial, porcelain-smooth), vertebrate peristyle (handsomely corbelled, and otherwise featureless but for the fourteen columns, seven to a side, and the intaglio relief on each of the back walls), more corridor, finally the central tholos, the skull chamber: unavoidable analogy and another of Ramirez's terms, just as he had been the one to revive the old names: tholoi, tumuli, henge megaliths, cromlechs, dolmens, going through the old databases, going on about Celts, Myceneans, Etruscans, whoever they were, much older peoples than the Tastans.

Beni flicked random selections, chance plan superimpositions, hoping to trick any tomb override. The defences were clever but they were old.

No change. The classic plan remained. No *apparent* change.

What would Ramirez do now? Beni wondered again, again, again, putting it off, avoiding. And, finding that he was doing so, made himself take the first step, found the others easier, was soon leaving the square of warm daylight far behind. His cap-light struck out ahead, illuminating the corridor, the smooth and off-white walls; his footsteps echoed off the cool ceramic, carrying him into night, into the underworld of the vast low funerary hill.

"Dormeuse?" he called. "You have company, Dormeuse!" Called it over and over, as Ramirez suggested he do.

"Not so loud," a voice finally said, and a host flashed on beside him, a startling mummiform of light, gaining resolution, female distinction. "I'm trying to sleep."

She was lovely, as perfectly formed, idealized, as Ramirez had said she would be, the tall glowing enantios intercept of an auburn-haired woman in middle-age or backtracked to about 45, with an open, pretty if not wholly beautiful face and eyes like blackest glass, but a gentle gaze all the same, with nothing like the cold arrogant manner of intercepts the grim-faced 'souvenired' veterans back in town had told him about.

Beni glanced down at his scanner, glad to see the basic plan confirmed, even if not to be trusted, never to be trusted, and kept on walking. The intercept 'walked' with him, fully formed now, smiling like a curious servant, which is exactly what she was. It was. She.

"Someone has been talking to you," she said. "You're too confident."

"But new to this all the same. I need as much help as I can get."

"I have much more experience. Listen. Turn round now. I'll let you go. Promise."

Beni smiled. Even without the advice he'd been given, he would have found the offer unacceptable, though it actually did happen now and then. Sometimes did. Justified the old saying that even the tombs had a bad day occasionally.

"Don't believe you. Won't do it. Thanks."

The display flickered but held, his reader sorting, sorting, seeking any other valid plan, if only as a split-second glimpse.

"Last chance," she said. "Keep going and I'll have you."

"You probably already do," Beni said, heart pounding, afraid and exhilarated, entranced by the image, forcing himself to talk down at his scanner display, avoiding the eyes. "The Stones'll have me if they don't already."

"Do you know what souvenir I have planned for you?"

"Please, Dormeuse. Do what you must, but enough of these threats."

And sure enough, the intercept changed tack.

"You see no ethical problem with this, do you?"

Beni smiled at the shift, gave the rote answer. "There has never been a time where one age and culture hasn't plundered the remains of another."

"But why? There's no wealth here. Nothing you can use. No gold, jewels or funerary possessions. Forget the rumours. Not enough precious materials in the circuitry and hardware. Certainly nothing accessible to you. No meaningful tech knowledge."

"I know."

"So why? Why do you use the term 'tomb-robbers' if—?"

"I prefer the 'reasonable' to the 'threat' mode, but could you bring on the next phase? I do need to concentrate."

The phantom hovered, seemed to walk. "Such an arrogant young man. Someone has been talking to you. But I'd really like to know."

Arrogant? Beni stared down at the display and considered it. Overconfident perhaps. Optimistic. Determined to be among the best. But hardly arrogant. "What have others said? Ramirez managed it. What did he say?"

"He was courteous but wouldn't talk to me as freely as you seem prepared to. He probably suspected a voice trap, some trance dislocation induced by word pattern, tone and timbre. You don't seem to fear that."

"There were others though, Dormeuse." The maimed ones, he didn't add. Barlow, Deckley, Kylow, Soont, the others, all skilled men and women, all souvenired. "What did they say?"

"Again, not too much," the phantom answered. "Concentration does that, I suppose. And fear. I gather it is some emblematic thing, using the term 'tomb-robber' and all. You're stealing the chance to do it, aren't you? Stealing the privilege. The mystery of another age. Some said it's rites of passage. The tombs are here, they said. Intact. Penetrable yet at the same time impenetrable ultimately. One age scorning another."

"Scorning? They said that?" Beni found it hard to imagine any of those bluff or dour survivors back in town saying that. He was impressed anew. "But, Dormeuse, you're the one who must feel something like that surely. Scorn."

"A sentry profile can't. I'm just a print of my original; my job is to represent my occupant's self. Keep her safe. Or me, depending on how you view architectural psychonics."

"But no body, I'm told. Just the stored personality index."

"Ah, little hunter. I recognize a question when I hear it. One age does plunder another. You, too, would have my secrets. Perhaps that is what you come for, the chance to steal knowledge of my day, get the old sentry intercepts talking. Yet such a risk. Death and injury on the chance of just a little something more about the Tastan past."

A stab of youthful defiance surged up, made Beni want to stay silent then, but, like countless others before him, he did want to know. He had to ask. "Your body is here?"

"Curious and stubborn, like all who come calling. Why should I tell? Perhaps the people of my day did preserve the body as well. Or the head. Who knows? We may have had cryonics long before we could code personality. The others you spoke to said what?"

"Dormeuse, I'm new to this. A lot of the veterans in town won't talk to me. They only sell what they know. I can't afford them."

"But, little one, you're in this far. I know you won't believe me but you're past the Stones. You're very well prepared tech-wise, my systems show. You've accessed a third-level intercept response from me. I frankly didn't expect that. You have to have the advice of others."

Beni felt his heart pounding. Could it be true? In this far! Free of the Stones. Could it?

"Ramirez," he said, deciding she'd probably guessed it already. "One day he stopped on the way past my family's farm. I was in the orchard. I reminded him of a son he'd lost, he said. He told me things about the tombs. About your tomb. He was giving it up at last, he said, going away. But he told me of you, Dormeuse. Of all the tombs yours was the one, he said. He was an eidetic, as you probably guessed. Perfect recall. Helped him with variants in the tomb plans when there were some, but more with the characteristics of the intercepts, their features and mode changes. He drew your likeness for me. Your image's likeness."

"Why, Beni. Don't tell me you're infatuated? In love?"

"It's not that! It's complex. I was without a father. He was without a son. We just talked."

"Oh stop! Stop! Don't tell me. And I became mother and wife! I love it. Midwife to hunters."

Beni clenched his jaws in anger. They walked in silence awhile down the ceramic corridor, him concentrating on his plan readings, glancing up at the passage ahead, glancing back down, up, down, she flowing beside him, a spindle of light with eyes like onyx.

"You said it was complex," she said after a time, coaxing, sounding just contrite enough. Perhaps he had accessed a new mode from her.

"Then I don't know why I'm here. All my life it was

what the best of us did. The tombs were something you couldn't ignore, how's that? I've walked past yours probably a thousand times. More than a thousand over the years. Yesterday I finally decided to try. Today I came out here again."

"Your point, little hunter?"

"Our own culture formed around the leavings of yours, Dormeuse, but yours keeps intruding. Your language has virtually replaced ours. Do you know how insufferable something like that is? Can you imagine how it's become for us? Competing with our past?"

"You're telling me, little one. I'm sure it's happened before. I seem to recall something about the European Renaissance being in effect a rediscovery of the wisdoms of earlier civilizations in Greece and Egypt. Though I believe that was a very positive thing, probably nothing as desperate as this."

Despite her disparaging words, Beni preferred this mode, this kind of directness. Ramirez had told him to push for it, that the host would treat him differently once he accessed it.

"My father died over in 37. Left our orchard one day, just upped and turned tomb-robber, tomb-visitor, whatever term covers it. It's what more and more of us do. Spent all we had on maps, comp and the best sentry tech he could get. I didn't find out till later! A neighbour came over and told me he hadn't come out of 37. I didn't even know he'd gone in, been planning it all those years. So I ask you: why would he do that? Why do any of us?"

"But I'm asking you that, little hunter."

"Don't call me that. I'm Beni."

"Beni. So as well as being in love you're in hate and loss. Potent mixture. Think of it though. I'm five hundred years in your past, yet held accountable, made responsible somehow for a boy losing his father centuries later. And, marvellous paradox, without me, without the loss and envy, it seems your life, all your lives, would be lacking in purpose."

"That's not it."

"Would be meaningless."

"That's not it!" The cry was swallowed in the ebbing, flowing, warm ceramic night. The thief had stopped walking at last, stood grimly silent. The ghost hovered, drifted, spoke.

"Maybe not. But perhaps you fear so. All your people. So you come here and test yourselves, steep yourselves in the mystery, could that be it? Plunder us from time to time. Carry out acts of astonishing vandalism."

"I haven't done that." Beni started walking again, drew the phantom along with him.

"No, Beni. You haven't yet. Thank you."

"Ramirez didn't."

"No. I agree," she said. "A lot don't. You're different to most. Ramirez was, both of you are, that curious blend of romantic and"—she said it very gently—"innocent. After something else."

Doesn't mean I won't though, he almost said, felt he should say it, a young man scared and confused. But didn't. "So what are we after then, Dormeuse?"

"Back to that, are we? Both wanting the same question answered."

"I'm afraid so." He continued walking, watching the scanner.

"All right. I allow you're motivated by the quest, by envy and reprisals against the past, the need both to have the past mysterious yet know it. I allow disenchantment, rites of passage, because it's there, all that. But we're generalizing. It doesn't tell me why you're here, does it? Why Beni is here as an individual."

Because I want to win, he could have said. Be up there among the greatest of them all: Ramirez, Callido, Asparan. But again didn't, feared sounding arrogant, brash, deluded like so many who came here. He *was* after something more. He was.

"You're being gentle with me, Dormeuse, so I'll try to find an answer. A real answer."

"Please do. And my name is Arasty. 'Dormeuse' means 'sleeping woman' in an ancient language. Which is what I am, just as you are ichneumon."

"I'm what?"

"Ichneumon. Another very old word. Means 'hunter' or 'tracker.' A small animal that used to hunt along river banks. Ate the eggs of crocodiles."

"Of what?"

"No matter. Beni and Arasty. We're here now and, yes, I'm being gentle because you are."

"But it's a mode as well. Tactical."

"Yes. It is." The black eyes glittered.

"You could stop me?"

"I'm sure I can." Glittered.

"Yet the fact is you want us here."

"Oh, tell me why."

"Not yet."

"I'm curious. Tell me why."

"I need to concentrate."

For ahead, his cap-light's glow fell on something different at last, caught in strange verticals, made new shadows for his eyes and tech to fathom.

He had reached the peristyle hall.

Beni had expected it to be little more than a widening of the axial corridor, with the seven pillars on either side keeping the passageway's alignment from entranceway to central tholos. But when he entered, he found it went back even deeper behind the smooth featureless columns than his stylized display suggested, just as the corridors were so very much longer than the plan showed. The walls shone with the same vitreous pallor as the corridor, but opposite each other in the centre of each back wall was the circular intaglio motif Ramirez had told him of.

The intercept appeared beside him while he stood exploring one of the grooved mandalas with a finger.

"Know what that is?"

"Ramirez told me. It's a maze. The classic seven-ring design. The archetypal unicursal maze built round a cross and four points. Used by lots of ancient peoples, the Romans, the Cretans and Syrians, the Irish, the medieval Christians—"

"Yes, yes. So what is its significance? Did Ramirez tell you?"

Beni smiled. "A unicursal maze has a single path from the entrance to the centre. It looks complex but is really very direct."

"Why it appealed to the Tastans too."

"I'm sure."

"Beni, I fear you're an optimist."

"What do you mean?"

"You see it as something complex being ultimately very simple. Like your comp reading there."

"So?"

"Why not a simple path made difficult. Look at your comp now."

Beni glanced down, saw with a stab of alarm, panic, sudden terror, a new reading. He keyed randoms, saw only the new double-peristyle configuration.

"This does get interesting," she said. "Oh, by the way, 'ichneumon' also refers to a parasitic, hymenopterous insect that lays its eggs on another's larvae, using it as food for its own young as they hatch. Nice thought, yes? Little hunter." And she vanished.

Beni had been told this would probably happen, the host's hunt-mode surfacing, solicitous, caring, then cold, callous, vindictive, seeking to undermine any sense of hope.

He strode on, left the columned hall, plunged into the next length of corridor, just the tiniest dagger edge of doubt pushing through the confidence Ramirez had given him. What if there were a second peristyle hall? What if the tomb plan actually shifted, shunted him from one course to another, on and on? The mound was large enough.

Ramirez had spoken of it. It was a doubt he could still push aside. The tholos, the skull chamber, would be ahead. Not far.

The yellow cone pushing ahead became brighter, strengthening, whitening, as the host flashed in.

"Can we resume, Beni? You said that we want you here. Tell me why?"

Beni did not look at the intercept. He walked on, glancing at his display, then ahead, corridor, display, repeating that. He might have stayed silent, punished her for the trickery with the plan. But he sensed, just as Ramirez had told him, that it would probably be the worst thing to do. The tomb profiles liked to talk.

"It occurs to me, Arasty, that a sentry program would want visitors to test itself against, that the self whose tomb this is would have designed the tomb so its sentry profile would be exercised, challenged, kept entertained and satisfied. It's what I'd do."

"That's a very smart observation. What made you think of it all of a sudden? Or was it also something—"

"I asked Ramirez about it that day in the orchard. Mentioned it before he did. We talked about what the tombs really were. He told me that your intercept, Dormeuse—Arasty—would appear at various times, run different modes—"

"And walk with you like this?"

"Not necessarily. Some intercepts did, he said. He also told me that whoever could code personalities and structure reality perception would not bother with ancient mortuary forms—corridors, burial chambers and such like—unless they were playing at something, *wanted* to invite plunderers."

"Again, very shrewd. He didn't say much when he was here but I miss this Ramirez. You're both right. We do want you here. We give each other purpose."

Beni watched his display for the slightest flicker, let his

peripheral vision guide him. "We are your future. We let you exist in time."

"Empowering each other. Yes, Beni. I like that. Like the fish and the fisher. Here for each other."

"So let me get on with it, Arasty. You try to stop me. I try to reach the core chamber."

"And what? Put your name up there with Ramirez's. Scrawl it on the watch screen and hurry out again? Did he tell you he did that?"

"I don't believe you."

"Did he tell you what else he did? Everything he did? You said Ramirez drew my face. Did he love me too, do you think? This image from an ancient age?"

Which part to answer? She was distracting him with her intriguing remarks, possibly giving deliberate untruths to unnerve him. "I'm not sure what he felt. Fascination. Determination to see you as the person who made this. Set this up for the future. It makes for a sort of intimacy. Something very powerful."

"Intimacy. I'm flattered. I never expected this sort of—well—kinship across centuries."

But Beni had stopped.

"What is it?" the phantom asked. "Worried that there's no core chamber? No second peristyle?"

"I should have reached it. Show me the plan. The real one."

"You've already seen it. Look."

Again there was the alarm, the panic, terror surging up.

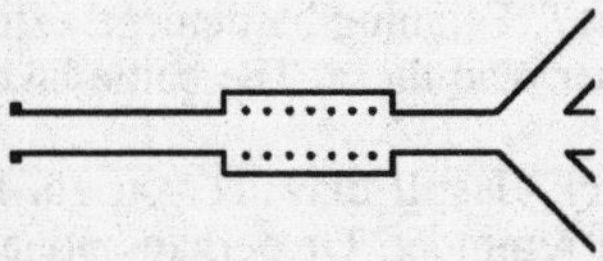

"You continue to make it more interesting."

"It's all I have, like you say. The chance to challenge, be entertained."

Beni needed to talk it through. "One of the few things we learned from you Tastans was sealed comp technology." He touched his scanner. "This can't be tampered with, so you've interfered with my perceptual processes."

He pressed a contact, randomized the grabs, sent surges through both equipment and self. He had practised this, did not flinch from the small electroshocks. The original tomb-plan came and went: single peristyle original, this new triple corridor display, double peristyle, single, double, triple—they flashed and flickered, cycled from one to the other.

It wasn't his vision then—unless it was misinformation at the brain's visual centre.

And when he looked at the phantom's face, saw the smile under the black glass eyes, he understood her simple strategy.

"I can't be sure now can I?"

Again, Ramirez's words were there. Allow that the Stones have you.

Beni sighed as if in frustration and despair, closed his eyes, accessed, believed he accessed, the neural link Ramirez had given him, actually given him, a parting gift surgically implanted in the town clinic, a legacy from surrogate father to surrogate son.

The single peristyle configuration—classic Tastan grab—sat in the light of his mind's eye. He was in the second length of corridor, so close to the chamber. He dared not linger over it in case she suspected. Again he sighed as if in frustration.

"Your decision?" she said.

"Excuse me?" Feigning bafflement, exhaustion, loss of resolve. Let her read those. The battle had been joined in earnest.

"On or back? I still may let you go. Perhaps with a souvenir as a reminder. Or perhaps none, provided you promise to come back and talk to me again. Keep me entertained."

Was that a possibility he dared consider? This intercept—this tomb, to make the distinction—did seem different from all accounts, rhapsodizing, showing whimsy, negotiating, pretending to, taunting like this, first one mode then another, just as Ramirez had told him she would be.

"I'm your little egg-stealer, remember. We continue."

"Hope is always beautiful," she said.

Beni didn't comment, strode on five, ten, twenty metres, surely into the tholos, but would not glance at his display now, nor at her, would not consult his link. He wanted her to court him, whatever came of it. This visit had to matter. But he was in the tholos, the skull chamber, he told himself. Had to be.

Finally she spoke, easily, losing no face by it, perhaps in a new mode, he couldn't tell, though her question suggested it.

"So, little hunter, have you ever wondered why there are only 85 tombs? The Tastan culture lasted seven centuries, at least 35 generations. Why only 85 tombs?"

He didn't understand all her words. Generations. "Tell me."

"Guess."

"No more games."

"Entertainment, remember? There really are only my games here. I'll reward you."

"How?"

"Trust that I will. I'll give you a clue. We were not necessarily royalty. Not rulers."

It did intrigue him. "Another caste in your society?"

"In a sense. Go on."

Beni fought to think, pressured by the changeless, vitreous dark, by the unchanging yellow fan of his lamp showing not the tholos but only more and more corridor, its glow whitened by the added glow of the figure floating, standing beside him, seeming to.

Tholos, maze, wherever he was, the intercept really did seem to want an answer.

"Our culture is five hundred years after yours," he said.

"Good. Yes?"

"But"—he hated saying it—"is debased by comparison. Technologically."

"Such finesse, little hunter."

"You belonged to a scientist caste."

"Wrong."

"A holy order. Priests. Sacerdotes."

"No."

"Criminals being punished."

"Fool!" She said it with incredible fury. The black eyes glittered. "Don't you know any history? What happened to our culture?"

Beni was stunned by her vehemence, the unconcealed contempt. It told him something he did not yet understand.

"You vanished," he said, and then, to show he did know some history, what Ramirez had told him, added: "Like the Mayans. The Anasazi. Your cities were abandoned, allowed to run down; most were reduced to slag by housekeeping programs—"

"So where did we go? Our millions? Our millions, Beni?"

What did she want him to say? And millions. The Tastan millions.

"Into these tombs?" The certainty of it amazed him. "All coded in. Immortal. You're the guardians of your race! Eighty-five repositories but housing millions."

Arasty's expression may have been the result of holistic psychonic printing or just some simulated response selected from a housekeeping menu, but Beni saw what looked like genuine scorn, genuine revulsion. If it were a deception then it was a subtle one, something naked, seeming spontaneous, well beyond the disapproval and impatience it resembled.

What am I missing? Beni asked himself, and with it felt a conviction. She needs me to guess. It really is important that I do. But what did she—it—want him to say? He wanted to shout the question. Didn't dare now. All he could think of was to show humility, self-effacement, and hope for patience.

"Please, Arasty, help me more. This is important." He hoped the compliment, his respectful tone, would do it.

The phantom watched him sidelong with her dark eyes just as a human would, as if in fact a discrete entity deciding, not a defence intercept scanning precedents, selecting options.

"You really have no idea, do you? A great culture, possibly the greatest the world has known, reaches a point where it dismantles itself, gives way to a simpler, let's say impoverished, less sophisticated successor. Why would they do it?"

"I can only think of two answers," he said quickly, honestly. "There was some enemy . . ."

"You could say that." The intercept's eyes flashed with interest. "Or?"

"You gained by it. It had to be progress. Something you saw as better." And he remembered what she'd said—impoverished—and barely dared utter the words. "You became *us!*" Remembered what else she'd said: less sophisticated. "You simplified your culture, someone did, something, some ruling elite maybe, and became us—"

"Yes." There was something like madness in the phantom's darkling bits of eyes, something reckless and fervent, but Beni dared not suggest the tombs housed what remained of the Tastan's dead insane. It was more. It had to be more. But he did not have to stumble over words to form a question. Arasty continued speaking.

"Some ruling elite, yes. An enemy, true, that culled our millions and our cultural heritage. Downgraded us all. To simple, immortal, happy folk like you—"

"Then—"

"Immortal. Happy ichneumon. But able to be maimed, killed by violence. With time to be curious, to ponder, to forget, to indulge. Happy, happy, happy ichneumon!"

"Then you're here—"

"Go on!" Madness spun in the darkness of the eyes.

"To cull us! Prey on us! To give purpose to immortal lives! They planned ahead. Saw we would need—"

"No!" The intercept had halted in blazing fury, actually flickered, flashed off and back again. The face was rigid with a rage and suffering held in such perfect suspension that Beni was faint with the involuntary numbing terror he felt welling up. The eyes, the black false eyes, held him.

"No, little hunter. No. See it our way. To give purpose to *our* thwarted lives. Some kind of revenge for those few among the elite, eighty-five out of all those many, to whom the genetic treatments did *not* bestow immortality. Who had helped cull and simplify, then found themselves without the intended blessing, left to die in the agony of exclusion from that. From you."

Beni saw the extent of the resolve, the old fierce hatred, that she would never let him go. He would never get to tell this story. Never even reach the central chamber. Or know he had.

"These aren't tombs. They're traps," he said, understanding, remembering the other meaning to her name for him, the insect leaving behind its offspring to feed.

"Yes, Beni. Traps to lure immortals curious in their long lives. A way of striking back at time."

And Beni felt the deep-down dread that Ramirez, some kind of Ramirez, tampered with, changed, or no—just allowed to go back unharmed—was acting as a lure out there in the bright summer days, giving hope, keeping the dream alive in others, but part of the trap, knowing or unknowing. Pray Destiny it was unknowing. Such a small shrewd price to pay, letting one or two go free, letting others go back maimed. Let the tombs have a bad day and so keep them coming.

"Be merciful, Dormeuse. Arasty."

"I am, little hunter. With you I truly am. Normally I grant the beautiful lie, tell those I am about to rob of life, light and limb, beauty, eons of youth, of how normally death is what makes lives, cultures, ultimately defines civilization. I remind them that it's right that immortals should reach a point of idle curiosity and need to be challenged, extended, tested. I tell them that whatever their fates individually, those I kill or hurt are helping maintain the tenor of life for all."

"But you're actually culling."

"Avenging. It's simpler."

"Out of envy."

"Bad enough in life. But when it's all there is, all that's left, it fills the largest cup, becomes a vast power. I phrase it so they think they will be spared somehow. That they are different and special. To some I even suggest that their personalities will join mine in the tomb matrix. Then, when there is hope, when vanity and optimism is there in hints and the absolute conviction of ego, then I cripple and kill, then I bring them to the worst of hells, to such terrible insurmountable despair. You I have spared this anguish, Beni."

"Spared me! By telling me the truth?"

"Yes."

"But I can't believe you, can I? Not after what you've just said."

"You really should. Look at your display."

Beni did, saw how simply, elegantly, the tomb's long-dead owner, this printing of her anyway, had expressed his dilemma.

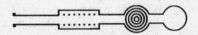

A maze. He was in a maze. He did not know what to say.

Arasty, the ghost of her, smiled. "Well?"

"Never be importunate, I was always told. Never beg."

"I've told you I'm being merciful. I might listen."

"All right. Don't kill me."

"I won't."

"Don't maim me."

"I won't."

"Let me return." As part of the trap, he didn't say, refusing to go so far.

"Earn it."

"I need to think. Concentrate."

"Shall I leave?"

"You'd still be here. You're in the walls."

"True. The tomb."

"The trap."

"The trap, yes. My personality is coded through all this. But it would be easier for you to concentrate."

And the intercept vanished, took away her glow, left only dim yellow lamplight, tunnelling, vitreous, intimate darkness without her darkling eyes.

Beni stopped, pretended to think, triggered his implant, saw again the plan of her tomb picked out in light, saw that he was at the central chamber, the structural heart of what this thwarted, predatory, former woman had become. Out of despair.

"Oh, Dormeuse, Dormeuse," he murmured. "I am so sorry." Imagining how it had to be, the eighty-five labouring over the final secret plan, the hate and loss in their hearts as all the others sailed blissfully on, away, abandoning.

What choice then. What choice now. For them both.

"We can change this," he said, resolved, striding on to his goal, though he did believe he was already there. "We can make a start here. Try to be friends. Let me try to be that, Arasty. At least try to be that."

"Yes," the tomb said, the walls, the night, as he strode on in his cone of yellow light into the endlessness of the hill. "And that is why."

* * *

OUTSIDE the Nothing Stones pull and pull and will forever pull, drawing in the emptiness of infinity, the blackness of eyes made hard, so unforgivingly hard. She is punitive and spiteful and so so determined. It is all she will ever have.

Beni strides on with his young man's dreams—of success, of being different, better than the best, with his

more difficult on the Overland Challenge to the travel pod. Perfect for him and—

"Come on!" Alena said, over the local comm. She was standing thirty feet in front of him, looking back, her face twisted into an angry mask.

"We just lost Nandir."

"I'm going to lose *you* if you don't get moving!"

"Don't you care?"

An inarticulate growl. Then a sigh. They were, after all, all camera, all the time. "Of course I care. But I want to win."

Glenn shook his head. He bounced over to her and tried to take her hand, but she pulled away. "Not now!" she said. Her normally full lips were compressed into a thin line, the soft arcs of her face pulled into something harder and more brutal. The face he used to love. The face he still loved.

She bounded away and he hurried to catch up. She'd made it clear that they were only back together for this one ultimate challenge, bigger than Everest, bigger than freeclimbing Half-Dome, bigger than marathoning the Utah desert, bigger than swimming the English Channel, bigger than their four-year marriage, bigger than anything he could give.

He caught up and tried to give her a smile. She looked ahead grimly. The terrain was getting more rugged. Ahead of them rose part of Ius Chasma, a two-thousand-foot near-vertical wall they would have to freeclimb to reach their transpo pod.

The low gravity was both a blessing and a curse. Glenn was still getting used to what he could do. The squeezesuit and header made him top-heavy, throwing off his balance, but his total weight here was still less than half of what he was used to.

"More human interest, Glenn," the Can blatted at him from his private channel.

He shook his head. They'd been ordering them around since before they left Earth.

"Glenn, we need to see Alena."

He plodded ahead.

"Glenn, we're close to contract breach."

He turned to focus on Alena. The squeezesuit clung to her curves, and the transparent header was designed to show as much of her pretty face as possible. Less attractive now, perhaps, with her hair hanging damp and her mouth set in a hard line.

"More," they said.

Glenn tried running in front of her and feeding the view from one of his rear cameras, but it was too hard to concentrate on the terrain ahead and keep her in frame. Eventually he dropped back to focus on the exaggerated hourglass shape of her suit.

"Good," they said. "Stay there for a while."

"Okay," he said. *Idiots*.

PITCH

"Of course someone is going to die. Probably lots of someones."

Jere Gutierrez nodded solemnly. So maybe the old fuck wasn't just another crank with a stupid dream trying to suck his nuts.

"Death is a legal problem," he said.

"For Neteno?"

Jere didn't answer. He pressed a discreet button and the datanet whispered in his ear. His guest was Evan McMaster, producer of *Endurance*, one of the last reality shows.

So he was real. He was part of the Golden Age.

Jere never prescreened CVs because everyone claimed some kind of connection, whether it was the last great years of Reality, or the almost-mythical Hegemony of the 70s and 80s, when the world was run by television, when audiences sat rapt on their cheap cloth sofas and scarfed microwave dinners in front of the tube, long before the coming of the internet and the rise of Interactives, long before television had been cast into the "Linear, Free-Access" ghetto. Every diapered octogenarian who tottered into his office smelling of piss and death claimed to be part of that great time. They all claimed to know that one compelling idea that would trounce all and return Neteno to some crowning glory, like television of old.

So maybe taking this meeting was not just a complete padre-suckup. Maybe Dad was right, just this once.

"Neteno doesn't do snuff," Jere said.

"What about the new Afghanistan thing? Or the Philippines?"

"That was news."

"What about the Twelve Days in May?"

Jere just looked at him. He waited for the old guy to drop his eyes. And kept waiting.

"Make your pitch," Jere said. "And make it good."

Evan stood up and paced in front of Jere's obsidian desk, backlit by the dim light coming in from the tinted window that overlooked Los Angeles.

"First, let's dispense with the death thing," he said.

"Sponsors don't like it."

"Don't lie. Sponsors love it. They just look properly horrified and give some insignificant percentage of their profits to the survivors and everyone's happy. Your big problem is legal."

"Tell me why we should take the chance."

Evan went back to his pocket projector and remapped the far wall with demographics, charts, multicolored peaks spiking like some impossible landscape. Stuff he had seen before, but this was far out of proportion. And yet it still bore the stamp of 411, Inc. It was good data.

"Three reasons. First, the Chinese."

"The Chinese stopped at the moon."

"Yeah. They said they'd go to Mars, but they're bogged down at the Moon."

"Cost."

"Yeah. Another is NASA. They're dead. Gutted. After the Twelve Days in May, all the money is going to Homeland Security. Everything's being folded into the new

Oversight thing. And the polls show people being OK with the Kevorking of the Mars flights. But underneath it all is a pent-up need to see some great endeavor. It's the Frontier Factor."

"Never heard of it."

"Henry Kase. New pundit. Blames the lack of a Frontier Factor for most of the world's problems. Complete crap, maybe, but it maps well on the audience we're looking at."

"Go on."

"Third, the Rabid Fan. That's real. You know it."

Jere nodded. Everyone dreamed of creating a new Star Trek, still in syndication after all these years, or a new Simpsons. A show that made people dress up, go to conventions, meet in real life, found languages, change dictionaries.

"They'll think this is too game-show," Jere said.

"Yeah. But they'll watch. All the trekkies and scifi nuts and people who dream about getting out, getting away, people who hate their lives for whatever reason, they'll all watch. Look at the numbers."

Jere looked at the projection, peaky and perfect and tantalizing. If they could create something like that . . . he sat silent for a long time, imagining himself at the forefront of a movement.

"There are problems," Jere said finally.

"Of course."

"Death is still one. I can borrow a platoon of lawyers to armor-plate our ass, but the shitstorm that follows may still take us down. Especially if they all kick it. As in Neteno is a goner. Done. Stick a fork in it."

Evan nodded. "I know."

"You're asking me to risk my network? While you sit there, almighty, living off interest from a previous life?"

"I'm prepared to throw in," Evan said.

"How much?"

"Everything."

"It's never everything."

Evan sighed. "I'll sign a personal guarantee."

Jere had the bottom line whispered back to him and whistled. "You need funding like a first-run 'Active for a Free-Access 'Near.'"

"The sponsors will line up."

"Why?"

"Their logo. On Mars. Maybe a featurette. Come on!"

"Sponsors don't like one-shots."

"So tell them this is a series. Tell them we're going to storm the Chinese on the moon!"

It was crazy. It was stupid. And it was, more than likely, impossible. But it was an idea. It was a big idea. And it just might be enough.

"Reality shows are dead," Jere said.

"It's coal. Time to mine it."

Jere nodded. The way things retroed round and round so fast, it was probably comfortably new again. And there were probably millions of people like himself who had caught a glimpse of the last reality shows and remembered them in a fond way.

You've taken big chances, he thought. *Which is why Neteno is a rising star amongst dying losers.*

"We may be able to get some money from NASA," Jere said, finally. *And some money from Dad, since he recommended Evan.*

"You're in?" Evan said.

"How long's the flight?"

"To Mars? Three months. We're going to do it?"

"Then we can definitely get food and bev sponsors. Perfect, too, start on the holidays when everyone's home and be ready for sweeps in Feb."

"We're doing it?"

Jere nodded.

Evan did a little jump and victory dance.

Jere cleared his calendar with a few quick touches and stood up. "Let's go to lunch. I need to know how you intend to pull off this stunt."

Evan's eyes sparkled. "It's Russian tech. You know, the stuff they do, the $250k packages to orbit for a week."

Jere paused at the door. “That’s why I know people will die.”

CRASH

“Pull it out! Come on! Pull!” Sam Ruiz shouted through their local comm. Mike Kinsson and Juelie Peters tugged at the shattered plastic shell. Suddenly the whole side twisted off, and all three ended up in a tangled heap on the dusty ground. Mike Kinsson noticed absently that the Disney and Red Bull and Wal-Mart logos on Juelie’s suit were covered in dust, and reached out to brush them off.

“What are you doing?” Sam said, yanking Juelie to her feet.

“Dust . . .” Mike said, and trailed off. It was stupid anyway. Why should he worry about their sponsors? Why should he worry about anything? They were dead.

Sam’s team had been given the easiest Overland Challenge, nothing more than a fast run over rocky ground, because they had been assigned the toughest rolling and flying part. Soaring over a tiny edge of Valles Marineris was part of their air journey, partly to make it more dramatic and partly to bring back some great images.

But after their brief Overland, they’d bounced up to the scene of a disaster. Their transpo pod had smashed on a huge boulder. Its smooth shape was now twisted into something that more resembled a crushed basketball.

It was supposed to hit and roll, Mike thought. A terrible design, something from last-century NASA that didn’t work then, even with all the redundancy the government could throw at it. Now the Wheel and Kite inside were probably . . .

“Junk,” he said softly, as Sam and Juelie began pulling out bundles of bent and sheared struts and shreds of fabric.

“Are you going to help?” Juelie asked.

Like a robot, Mike went and helped them pull out the contents of the pod. He noticed that the big Timberland and Kia and Cessna logos emblazoned on the outside of the pod had survived intact, and he had to suppress the urge to laugh. Some of the last pieces had been wedged into the rock and wouldn't come out—including the engine that powered the Wheel and Kite.

"Where's the rest of it?" Sam yelled.

"Stuck."

Sam glared at him and crawled inside. When Sam crawled out again, sweat was running down his cheeks and there was a strange, faraway look in his eyes. Mike looked around at the twisted pieces strewn around them and shook his head. Sam saw it and grabbed him.

"What?" he said. "What are you shaking your head for?"

"We're dead," Mike said. "It's over."

"No! We can make something! We can do some hybrid thing, like a wheel." He began rooting through the wreckage, frantic.

"Powered by what?" Mike said softly.

"We can power it! Or we can make skis! Or we can . . ."

Juelie went over to Sam and laid a hand on his shoulder. As soon as he felt her touch, he stopped. He stayed still on his hands and knees, looking down at the rocks and dust, panting.

"Mike's right," Juelie said. "I saw the engine."

Sam stood up. The pale sun reflected off his shiny bronze face. He looked from the wreckage to the horizon and back again. "I don't want to give up!" he said.

"Why?" Juelie said. "We can't win."

Sam looked at her for long moments, as if trying to decipher a strange phrase in an unknown language. Then he slumped. All the tension left him. He sat on a boulder and hugged his knees. Something like a wail escaped him. Under the cloudless alien sky, amidst a red desert unrelieved by water or leaf or lichen, it was a chilling sound.

"What do we do?" he said finally. "How do we get to the Returns?"

"We don't," Mike said, standing carefully away.

Sam just looked up at him.

"Walk overland," Juelie said. "It doesn't matter how long it takes."

"There's not enough food and water," Mike said.

"We'll eat less!"

"We can't cross the Valles Marineris."

"Why not?"

"Mile-high vertical walls."

Juelie was silent for a while. "They'll have to come rescue us," she said finally.

"No," Mike said.

"We've lost," Sam said.

"Wait," Julie said. "What do you mean, 'no'?"

"They can't just come down and get us," Mike told her. "Other than our drops and the return modules, there's no way to get down here and back again."

Julie looked confused.

"They can't rescue us," Mike said. "They don't have the capability."

"Then what do we do?" Sam said. "Sit here and die?"

Mike looked away. Even he knew better than to answer that. Juelie walked over and offered Sam her hand. After a moment, he took it, head hanging low. Mike edged away from the two, not wanting to be part of any coming outburst. Sam had been driven by a single purpose since the start: to win his share of the thirty million dollars. That's what he wanted. Nothing more, nothing less. He hadn't disguised it, hadn't hid it. But now that was taken away. And more.

We knew the risks when we signed, Mike thought, walking farther away. *Or at least I did. I don't know if Sam and Juelie were smart enough to really read through the eighty-page contract. It made them into a grey undefined thing that the legal system could wrangle about for years if the deaths and lawsuits came.*

But I didn't care. All I ever wanted to do was to see another planet. Earth was a dead-end. People pursuing dead-end dreams, interested in nothing more than making money and amusing themselves. Nobody explored. Nobody took chances.

Except for my dreams, I was as bad as everyone else. Too scared to give up my job, to let go of my condo, my 'Actives, my things. Endlessly yearning, but no ability to commit.

And so, this great leap. Finally.

And so, now you die.

Mike tried to make himself feel something, but he couldn't. It was too far away, too remote. They had maybe five days worth of food and water in their packs. Five days, and then a couple of days for the recycling to stop working, or some other suit malfunction.

It's too bad they didn't give the science pack to me, Mike thought. *I would have infinite time to do the experiments.* Or at least many days. But it had gone to the other geek on the Thorens team.

He had wandered a hundred feet or so away from the couple when the voice from the Can blatted in his ear.

"We're aware of your situation," they said.

"So?" he heard Sam ask.

"We're asking the Paul team to divert and rescue," they said. "We think he can carry you in his Wheel. Is your fuel bladder undamaged?"

"Yes!" Juelie said, hope rising in her voice.

"Good. We're transmitting the request to him now."

"Great!" Juelie said. Sam's head still hung, though. "Sam, did you hear that? We're going to be rescued."

"It's a request," Sam said. "Re-quest. Do you think Paul is going to give up his thirty million?"

"Thirty?" she asked

"Yeah. He's the single guy. The nut."

Mike could see Juelie looking up at him for a moment, then down at Sam.

"He might," she said. "He still might."

Sam's laughter echoed in the dying Martian day.

LIES

"Promise them more flights," Evan McMaster said.

"We don't have any," Jere Gutierrez said. The Russians

had looked at their plans, conferred gravely, and named a price that was ten times what their highest projections were. Now they were back in their shabby Moscow hotel, drinking Stoli in a decaying bar that looked like it was last decorated back in the 90s.

"They're bluffing," Evan said.

"What do you mean?"

"They do tourist crap. You don't think they really know how to put together a Mars mission? They never even landed a man on the moon!"

"Yes they did . . ."

"What do they teach you with in school these days? A VCR and a chocolate cake? No Commies on the moon. Just us. 1969."

"The Russians did it, too!" Jere said.

"Nope. Never. Once we did it, they dropped their program and did unmanned probes. Said that sending people was a showboating capitalist move."

"Shit, man, don't scare me."

"You just need to know what we're dealing with," Evan said. "It's a poker game. And they're bluffing."

"If you don't think they can get to Mars, why are we here?"

"I think they can make it to Mars. But it won't be easy. It'll be hard. And they know it."

"So what do we do?" Jere said.

"Bluff right back. Tell them we're going to do this every year. Every three months. Every shittin' week if that's what it takes."

"You're going to lie to the Russian mafia?"

Evan smiled. "No. You are."

"No," Jere said, shivering, remembering too many stories from Dad, the first days of the internet, the way some companies got financed.

"I thought Neteno was the big maverick studio, willing to take any chance."

"We are."

"Then act like it, or I'll take it to Fox."

Jere opened his mouth. Closed it. The rumor had already been spilled. Every network knew about it. And they would probably be interested, if they saw Evan's data.

Evan had him by the nuts.

"How do I do this?" Jere asked. "And live?"

"They're gonna have their setbacks, too, stuff we can put them over a barrel for. Once we've primed the audience, they have to meet our schedule. Or all the advertising for RusSpace goes out the door."

And you think you'll draw them into your web, too, Jere thought. "I wish I had your confidence."

"It's my life, too," Evan said.

Yes, Jere thought. *And you're more visible than I am. I will make sure it is your life. First, you fuck. First.*

"Okay," he said. "We bluff. Now, what's this the lawyers have come up with for the contract?"

"Aha," Evan said. He pulled out a Palm and scrolled through a long document. "Eighty pages of gibberish. They want real signatures in real pen."

"What does it say?"

"You don't want to know," Evan said, eyes still on the screen.

"Give me the gist."

"Has them renounce their US citizenship, become wards of Neteno, hold us harmless, things like that. If they make it back, they may have to live at airports."

"There are always volunteers."

"The lawyers had one other suggestion."

"What's that?"

"Start in the prisons. If they die, public reaction will be less."

"But they'll have less buy-in," Evan said, frowning.

"Yeah, that's a problem. Do you think we can spin it?"

"I'd be happier if most of them were just genpop."

"Maybe a mix," Evan said.

Jere nodded and sipped his drink. There was silence for a time. The sound of an argument deep in the hotel, maybe from the kitchen. Jere let the silence stretch out.

"Why?" Jere said, finally.

"Why what?"

"Why are you doing this? Just the money?"

Evan sighed and looked away, to the cute blonde bartender. For a while, Jere thought he wouldn't answer.

Then Evan looked down at the table and said, "After a while, you get used to it. Not the money. The other shit. Having dinner with George Bush, 'cause you have your hand on the throat of the public. Fucking Mary-Kate Olsen, since you pay more attention to her at one premiere than her husband does all month. Picking up your office phone and asking for anything and getting it, 'cause you're on top, you're on fire. Why else?"

Because you don't want your dad to look at you with that look, that are-you-fucking-stupid look, ever again, Jere thought.

But he just nodded, and they went back to serious drinking. Later, there would be women. Later still would be more negotiation. Endless rounds. Bluff and dare. The real product of Hollywood.

OFFER

The only thing that kept Keith Paul from swatting the tiny cam that dangled in front of him was that he knew that would lose him the thirty million dollars. *Contract breach,* the asswipe PA would say, in that breathy feminine voice of his. All camera, all the time. We can tap in whenever we want.

Yeah, and I hope you get a shot of me taking a great huge shit, Keith thought. Broadcast that to your eight hundred million viewers. Here is Keith Paul, taking a dump on your ratings.

He would be sure to say that when he won. When they pointed the camera at his face, he would tell them exactly what he thought of them. His crowning words, his first major televised fuck-you-all.

And he would win. No doubt about that. Teams were for

pussies. He'd been able to skin the Wheel and string the Kite faster than any team back when they were training. He didn't have arguments with himself, or forget where something went.

No, everything was great. He allowed himself to look up at the light blue sky. Really not that different from Earth. There was only one creepy thing. Nothing moved. It felt old and ancient and unnatural, and the sun looked small and dim. He kept wiping at his header's visor to clear it, but it wasn't cloudy or tinted. That was just the way Mars looked. Because it was farther away from the sun.

"We need to make a request," said the voice of the Can. Not the breathy one, but the cute little girl that the breathy asshole was sleeping with.

"What?" They always had requests. *Look at this, do that, scratch your ass.*

"The Ruiz team's transpo pod had a landing, um, malfunction. They have no transport."

"So?" Tough shit.

"We'd like you to divert your Wheel and collect them."

"I haven't even reached my transpo yet."

"After you get there."

"And you're going to give me extra time for this?"

A pause. "No."

"Then how the hell am I supposed to win?"

Another pause. "They'll die if you don't pick them up."

"So?"

Finally, a new voice, deep and resonant. Frank Sellers, that John Glenn fuck that had rode them out here.

"Keith, we'd really like you to consider this. Even if you don't win the prize money—and you still might—the act of rescue will create its own reward."

"Like, they'll pay me more than thirty million bucks for it?"

"I'm sure our sponsors will be very generous."

"More than thirty million generous?"

Another pause. For a while, Keith thought they'd given

up on him. But Frank started in as he caught the first glimpse of his transpo pod, glittering in the distance.

"Keith, we've got buy-in from several of the sponsors. We can get you a million. Plus other things. Cars . . ."

"No."

"They'll die. That will be on your conscience."

"They can't prosecute me for it." It would be just like them, to dredge up the fact that he was the only former felon, even though he was pardoned, even though it was just a simple carjacking thing, nothing much.

Long pause. "No."

"I think I'll ignore you now."

"Keith . . ."

Keith looked up at the thin sky, as if to try and see the Can spinning overhead. "A million is not thirty. A million and promises is not thirty. Sorry, no can do."

"You may not win."

"I will."

Another pause. This one longer. "We can go two million."

"Did you fail math? Two million is not greater than thirty. Give me an offer more than thirty, and they're saved."

"We . . . probably can't do that."

"I . . . probably can't save them," Keith said, mocking his tone.

Silence. Blissful silence. Long yards passed and the transpo pod swelled in his view. As he reached its smooth, unmarred surface, Frank's voice crackled to life again.

"Even if you win," he said. "People will hate you."

"That's all right," Keith said. "I love myself enough for all of them."

SCIENCE

"I thought they found life on Mars," Jere said.

Evan rolled his eyes heavenward. It was 4:11 AM, and they were screaming down the 5 at triple-digit speeds in

Jere's Porsche. The scrub brush at the side of the road whipped by, ghostly grey streamers disappearing into taillight-red twilight. They were in that no-mans-land between Stockton and Santa Clarita, where the land falls away and you could believe you were the only person in California, at least for a time.

Jere frowned, seeing the look out of the corner of his eye. "What? They didn't? Talk, you fucking know-it-all."

"They still don't know. They're still arguing about it."

"Funny thinking of Mars as a science thing."

Evan shook his head, and then said, "It's too bad we can't do it this year. Do the whole fortieth-anniversary shindig."

"Fortieth anniversary of what?"

"Viking. 1976."

We put shit on Mars way back then? Jere thought. "We're still on for '18?"

"So far."

Silence for a long time. In front of them there was nothing but darkness and stars and the dim outline of mountains. Jere pushed the car to 120, 130, 140. The blur became a haze of motion, almost surreal.

"So what do you think about Berkeley?" Jere said.

"It's crap."

"Why?"

"Like, duh. Berkeley probably can't even design the right experiments package. They're a liberal arts school."

"So we get another school."

"No."

"What?"

"Industry," Evan said. "That's where the money really is. We go to industry."

"Who?"

"Siemens. Or IBM. Someone big, with deep pockets."

Jere nodded. Berkeley had offered them quite a bit of money. With IBM in on a bidding war, how high could the stakes get? This idea was looking better and better all the time.

EXPERIMENTS

Being paired with two beautiful women was, well, distracting, Geoff Smith thought. Their squeezesuits left almost nothing to the imagination, and every time he looked up, his thoughts were shattered by the simple beauty of the feminine form.

And what thoughts they were! Here he was, Geoff Smith, on an alien planet! And he was going to prove there was life on it! He would do what a million scientists back on earth wanted to do! Him, with nothing more than a bachelor's degree in chemistry, would do what all the PhDs told him he couldn't do. He would put Martian life under a microscope for the first time! He would look at it with his own eyes! He would be famous!

Because the big problem was that nobody had ever really looked. They'd tried the Carbon-14 tagging trick on Viking, they'd tried spectrographic analysis, but they'd never just taken a sample of dirt, put it on a microscope slide, and looked at it.

"Damn!" Wende Kirkshoff said. She was hanging from the top curve of their Wheel, holding a strut and looking at it disgustedly. She was a pretty blonde girl with freckles and a pleasant demeanor, but Geoff always thought she was avoiding him.

"What's the matter?" Laci Thorens said. She was on the ground, assembling the engine into a subframe with a grim intensity.

"This strut doesn't have the little fitting on the end," Wende said. "It won't stay in."

"Aren't there spares?"

"Uh, no, I don't think so."

Geoff shook his head and bent back to his work. *Who cared about the prize? With his discovery, he would be so famous that he could name his price.*

He'd set the IBM box in the lee of the transpo pod like the instructions said, digging down like they told him. He was supposed to let it go for a half hour, then take the whole thing with them.

Which was stupid. IBM was doing the same old thing, when all they had to do, really, was give him a bag and a microscope.

So he'd brought his own. Now it was just a matter of getting some dirt, throwing some water on it, putting it on the slide, and looking for wrigglies.

"There aren't any spares," Wende said.

"Shit. Let me see." Laci hopped up to the top of the Wheel.

He fumbled the little vial of water out of the tiny pocket of his squeezesuit. The microscope was already out, sitting perched on top of a medium-sized rock, away from the dust and grit.

How had Viking done it? It had moved a rock, hadn't it? And this new one from IBM was digging down. Probably best to just combine both techniques, Geoff thought, and shoved a medium-sized boulder out of the way.

He dug down into the dust with his fingers, feeling the chill seep through his squeezesuit. At about six inches down, he struck another rock and decided that was enough. The dust was clinging to his transparent header, and the front half of his suit was pink.

He took a pinch of dust from the shallow hole and dropped it onto a glass slide. The water had gone frosty around the top. He dropped a couple of drops on the slide and they froze almost instantly, making something that looked like red ice cream.

Damn, I didn't think of that. There was no way he was going to see something with the microscope through all that gunk.

He sloshed some more water on it and pushed it around with the tip of his finger, trying to get the mixture thin enough to see through. After a couple of tries, he managed to get a thin pink film that looked reasonably transparent.

"Geoff!" Laci said. "We need your help!"

"Can't," he said. "In the middle of an experiment."

"We need your help or we ain't rolling anywhere!"

Geoff slid the slide into the microscope and looked at the watch embedded in his suit. "We have time." And in fact, they did have almost twenty minutes left.

"We have to do it now!" Wende said.

"Wait a minute," Geoff said. Slide in place. Microscope to eye. Nothing but fuzzy grey darkness. Focus. Dark, dark. Sliding into focus. Becoming great boulders.

"Geoff, now!" Laci said.

"Just a few seconds," Geoff said. "Then you can have me." Focus. Ah. Crystal-clear. Scan it over a bit and find a brighter area. There. Ah.

Water crystals. Boulders. Bright light. Nothing else.

Well, of course it wouldn't move. But where was the rounded wall of a bacterium, or the jelly of an amoeba?

"Now," Laci said, and strong hands picked him up. He felt his grip on the microscope slipping. He grabbed it tighter, and it popped from his hands. He was jerked back as he watched it fall, with agonizing slowness, into the dust and grit.

He wrenched out of Laci's grip and scooped up the microscope. It was dusty, but looked okay. He looked through it. The slide was out of position, but he could still see. He reached for the focus knob . . .

The microscope was torn out of his hands. He looked up to see Laci standing in front of him, holding the microscope behind her back.

"Give it back!" he said. "This is important. I'm right . . ."

She punched his header. Hard. He could see the soft transparent plastic actually conform to her fist. It didn't quite touch him, but the kinetic energy of the blow knocked him to the ground.

"Go," she said. "Help Wende. You'll get your toy back when you're done."

"Give it back!"

Laci raised the instrument and made as if to smash it on

a boulder. Geoff lunged forward at her, but she danced away. "No," she said. "Go help. I'll give it back later."

"Laci, this is important!"

"Yeah, and so is surviving. Go help."

Geoff knew when he was beaten. He sighed and joined Wende atop the Wheel, where they quickly discovered another problem: the epoxy they'd provided for quick repairs wasn't setting in the Martian cold.

"What do we do now?" Wende asked.

Geoff stopped looking longingly at the microscope—now sitting on top of their hydrazine engine—and inspected the problem. The strut was one of the main load-bearers that held them suspended under the top of the Wheel.

"What about the Kite?" Geoff said. "Doesn't it share components with this? Maybe it has a strut with the right connector on it."

"What about when we have to fly?"

"We make sure we don't forget the damn thing."

They dug into the bundle of struts and fabric. The components were the same, and many of them were the same length. When Geoff found one with the right connector on the end, he pulled it out and handed it to Wende.

"Just like Ikea," he said.

"They aren't the sponsor!"

"Same idea."

Then he noticed that Laci was frantically tightening the straps that held the little engine in place. "We're late!" she said. "Check the time! Come on come on come on! Let's go!"

Laci started the engine. Near the Wheel, his microscope was still parked on top of a rock.

"Wait!" he said, running to get it.

The Wheel was already moving. "Hurry up!" Laci said.

He grabbed the microscope and ran back, throwing himself up the scaffold toward the perch by the cabin. The landscape sped by. The soft rim of the Wheel bounced over rocks and boulders.

But he had his microscope. Between that and the IBM package, he would surely find something. He would still be famous.

The IBM package!

Oh, shit, no! No no no!

He'd never picked it up.

"Stop! he cried. "You have to go back! I left the IBM package."

Laci gave him a disgusted look. "How could you be that stupid?"

"Go back."

She just looked at him. A slow smile spread on her face. "Sorry," she said.

Geoff looked back at the remains of their transpo pod, but it had already disappeared over a hill. They were moving. And he was lost.

SPONSORS

"It seems like a lot of work for just a show," said the shithead from P&G. He was looking at the model of the Can, sprouting its ring and eleven pods.

God save me from executives who think they're smart, Jere thought. *Send them to the golf course and the cocktail lounge, where the conversational bar is comfortably low.*

They were in the Neteno boardroom, which had been transformed into a neomodern interpretation of a 70s NASA workroom, redone on a much greater scale and budget. A movingink banner was cycling though imagined Marsscapes and the logo for Neteno's *Winning Mars*, and models of the Can, the drop and transpo pods, the Kites and the Wheels and the Returns, hung from the ceiling or were suspended with cheap magnetic trickery.

But there were a lot more people than the P&G guy in today. There was Altria, and J&J, and Foodlink, and a whole bunch of other guys who wanted to have product placed on the show.

So he was playing to an audience when he answered:

"Not really," he said. He pointed at the ring. "Take the ring. It's a standard component of the new RusSpace orbital hotels. And we're saving four module drops by incorporating all the Return pods into a single big softlander. The transpo pods are as simple and reliable as they get, just a big bouncing ball. We're actually using a lot of proven technology for this, just in new ways."

"Probably what they said about the Titanic," P&G shithead said, grinning at the other execs. "Once you drop them on the surface, you have a road course, or something like that?"

"Five courses," Jere said, changing the graphics on the movingink banner. "All of them have three phases of travel: on foot, rolling on a Wheel, and flying in a Kite. We've picked routes that will highlight some spectacular scenery, like parts of the Valles Marineris . . ."

"What?"

"Think Grand Canyon. Times ten."

"Oh."

"And we have a vertical climb of 2000 feet set for one group. We're hoping to get some extreme-sports aficionados in the audience."

"Is that safe?" the P&G guy asked.

"We don't claim infallibility." *And you're not complaining,* Jere thought. *Don't think we don't notice that.*

"Who's signed so far?" shithead asked.

"That's confidential. If you want to buy a prospectus package, we'll discuss that further." *And you aren't saying anything about that, either, are you? Because you know this is the deal of the century.*

"What you don't see is the most important part," Jere said. "The people who will actually make this happen."

"You already have your team picked?"

"No. I just want to show you what the teams might look like. Because I know you have this idea of a bunch of spacesuit-clad guys hopping around on a dead planet. Boring, right? Well, no."

At that moment, Evan McMaster entered the boardroom

through the double doors at the back, accompanied by a trio of young women wearing cosmetic squeezesuits and headers. The suits hugged every one of their curves, making them seem impossibly perfect, unattainable, unreal.

There was a collective gasp from the execs, and Jere smiled. It always worked that way.

"I don't see how it will work." Not the asswipe. Another one. This one from Altria.

"Mars does have a thin atmosphere," Evan said. "We can provide pressurized air through a small backpack only to the face. The pressure required to maintain body integrity is provided by the squeezesuit."

"Showboating," muttered the original P&G geek.

"Which would you rather look at—this, or some old Russian cosmonaut in a wrinkled-up body sock?"

"Your contestants may not look that good."

Evan smiled. "The squeezesuit is of variable thickness. We can make a wide variety of body types look good. And it provides an excellent palette for logo placement."

He snapped his fingers, and logos appeared at strategic spots on the suits. Spots with high visual magnetism, to use the geek phrase. One of the girls spun to reveal a P&G competitor's logo emblazoned over her buttocks.

Oh, they loved it. Jere could see it in their eyes. They were sold. They would talk tough and haggle, but they had them. Just like Panasonic and Canon and Nikon fighting over the imaging rights, Sony and Nokia and Motorola fighting over the comms deal, Red Bull and Gatorade fighting over the energy drink part of it, hell, damn near every single nut and bolt was being fought over.

Go ahead, Jere thought. *Talk. Then shut up and give us your fucking money.*

ASCENT

They were halfway up the sheer face, and the way Alena was climbing, they were going to die. Glenn watched her almost literally fly up the rock, making twenty-foot jumps from handhold to handhold, reaching out and grasping the smallest outcropping and crevice with fluid grace and deceptive ease.

Dangerous ease, he thought. Climbing in the low gravity seemed childishly simple compared to climbing on Earth. Which meant it was easy to take one too many chances.

Alena made one last lunge and scrabbled for grip in a tiny crevice. Her feet skidded and she slid down the face for one terrible instant before catching on another tiny outcropping. Tiny pebbles and sand bounced off Glenn's visor.

"Slow down!" he said.

"We need to keep moving!"

"Alena . . ."

Labored breathing over the comm. "Listen to them!" Alena said. "Laci's team is already rolling, and that psycho guy is, too!"

Glenn cursed. The voices from the Can, when they weren't giving orders, provided a blow-by-blow of what the other teams were doing. To get you doing something stupid.

Glenn pulled himself up nearer to Alena. She resumed climbing, too.

"Let me get nearer," he said. "So we can safety each other."

"We have to keep going."

"The others have more time to roll. We aren't falling behind."

Alena stopped for a moment. "I know, but . . ."

"It's hard not to think it, yeah," Glenn finished for her. He pulled himself even higher. She stayed in place for once.

"We'll make the top before nightfall," he said. "Then we shelter and wait it out. We've got a short roll and a reasonable flight. We still have the best chance of winning, Alena."

Pant, pant. He was close enough to be her failsafe now.

Alena looked back, gave him a thin smile, and pulled herself up again. For a while it was all by the book, then Alena began stretching it a bit, leaping a bit too far, aiming at crevices just a bit too small. With the sun below the cliff, the shadows were deep, purple-black, and the cliff was losing definition in the dying day.

When they reached a deep crevice in the rock, Glenn thought things had begun to get better. But the rock was fragile and crumbly, and rust-red chunks came off easily in his hands. Glenn was about to tell Alena that they should get out of there when she reached up and grabbed an outcropping that broke off in her hand.

From ten feet above Glenn, she began to fall, agonizingly slow. Glenn felt his heart thundering in his chest, and had a momentary vision of the two of them tumbling out of the crevice to fall thousands of feet to the rocks below. He tested his handholds and footholds, and a small cry escaped his lips when he realized they probably wouldn't survive the impact of Alena.

Glenn jumped downward, seeking better purchase. Slip and slide. Nothing more. Down once again. Nope.

Down again, and then Alena piled into him, an amazingly strong shock in the weak gravity. *Mass still works,* Glenn thought, wildly, a moment after he'd lost all contact with the cliff face.

Alena flailed, trying to catch the rock surface as it skidded by. Glenn knew that soon they would be moving too fast to stop, and reached frantically himself. He slowed their fall, but didn't stop it.

Where was the edge of the crevice?

He looked below him. Right here. But there was one outcropping that looked reasonably solid. If he could catch it . . .

He hit hard with his feet and felt a shooting pain go up his right leg. His knees buckled and his feet slid to the side, away from the outcropping, towards destruction.

One last thing. He reached out and caught the outcropping, keeping one hand around Alena's waist. For a moment he thought their momentum was still too great, but he was able to hold on. Alena skidded within feet of the opening.

Glenn didn't dare move. He could hear the harsh rasp of Alena's breathing. Meaning they were both alive. Alive!

Alena looked up at him with something in her eyes that might almost have been gratitude. He looked down at her and smiled. For a brief instant, she smiled back and his heart soared.

They backed out of the crevice and continued on up the cliff face. Glenn's right leg roared with pain, and he knew Alena could see that he was slowing down. But she didn't run away from him. She didn't take chances. She didn't say anything at all until they had reached the top, and the last dying rays of the sun painted them both blood-red.

"I'm sorry," she said softly.

He was about to say something, but the Can blatted in his ear. "What an image! Pan slowly across the sunset."

"Thanks," he said, bitterly, as Alena turned away.

SCHEDULE

"What the hell does Timberland know about making space suits?" Evan said. He threw down the thick ream of printouts and rubbed his face, pulling it into a comic mask of fatigue and frustration.

"They'll pay to do it," Jere said.

"Another prime sponsor." Sarcastically.

"What, like you're suddenly worried about our contestants?"

Evan shrugged and stood up to pace. "RusSpace finally got back to me."

"And?"

"And we're fucked."

For a moment, the word didn't even register with Jere. Then he heard the phrase like a physical blow. "Fucked! What does fucked mean, like they won't do it?"

"No, no."

"They want more money."

"It's 2019 now, not 2018."

No. They couldn't move it out again. GM and Boeing pulled out when the schedule last slid. So now it was Kia and Cessna for the Wheels and the Kites. Good names, yeah, but not blue-chip. Maybe it would boost the ratings, that bit of risk, that added chance . . .

Evan nodded. "Yeah, it's a crap cocktail, all right."

"We can't do this," Jere said. His voice sounded hollow and faraway.

Evan shrugged. "We have to."

"What's the problem this time? They lied again? They fucked up? What?"

"No." A sigh. "It's the testing that's killing us. Five drop modules, five backout pods, five Wheels, five Kites, the big package of Returns, a ship with a fucking centrifuge, for God's sake, goddamn, it's a lot of shit to do!"

"So what do we do?"

"We push. Or we scale it back."

"What? Take it to three teams?"

"No. Scale back the build and the test. Leave out the backout pods, for example."

"What happens if the team can't make it to the Returns?"

A slow smile. "Tough snatch, said the biatch."

"What?"

"Before your time." Another shrug. This one slow, lazy, nonchalant. "If they can't make it to the Returns, they probably can't make it back."

"Will this get us back on track?"

"We could do more."

"What?"

"Skip final test of the Kites and the Wheels. All they are is a bunch of fabric and struts anyway."

"And?"

"Leave the spinner down on the ground."

"How are the contestants supposed to stay in shape?"

"We'll put in a whole lot of Stairmasters. They can exercise. Gets us another sponsor, too."

"And?"

"And that might get us back on track. Or so say our formerly communist friends."

"Will they guarantee it?"

"They aren't guaranteeing anything anymore. But I think it's a lot more likely that we'll make the deadlines if you drop some of the fluff."

Fluff. Yeah, fluff. Just a bunch of safety gear. Nobody will notice.

"We're taking a big chance."

"What's a bigger chance? Going to '19 or making a few changes?"

A few changes. Nothing big. Nothing major. Nothing we won't be crucified for if it comes out.

"Can we do this clean? Can we make it look like we never had plans for the centrifuge, the backout stuff, all that?"

"I'm sure we can arrange something."

Jere let the silence stretch out. Evan was watching him intently. In the dim light of the office, his weathered features could have been the craggy face of a demon.

"Do it," Jere said finally, softly. Hating himself.

REJECTION

Wheeling had been easy back on Earth. The training had been out in the Mojave, nice smooth sand and little rocks that you could bounce over easy, and nice and flat as far as you could see.

But Wheeling was a bitch and a quarter here on Mars. Keith Paul gritted his teeth as he came to another long downhill run, scattered with boulders as big as houses and ravines that could catch the edge of the wheel and fuck him up good. He'd already dug the Wheel out twice, once when he swerved to avoid a slope that would pitch it over and ended up in a ditch, and once when he got to bouncing and bounced over a hill into a ravine.

And man, did it bounce! Whenever it hit a rock. Sometimes a foot, sometimes a couple, sometimes ten or twenty feet in the air.

They probably got some good vid of my terrified mug, Keith thought. That wasn't good. Weakness was never good.

But he was being strong on other things. He was making good time across the desert. He'd been up rolling at the moment dawn's light made the landscape even dimly guessable.

Other idiots are probably picking their way along like grandma in a traffic jam, he thought, and smiled. Because he was going to win.

And he was strong on the offers, too. Everyone had talked to him. Both the PA idjits, the associate director, Frank, everyone. They'd promised him everything but a blow-job and a hot dog, but the money hadn't changed.

Almost on cue, the voice. This time it was Frank.

"We're prepared to make you another offer," Frank said.

"Shoot."

"It's our final offer," Frank said. "And it's a very generous one. By air, you have a good chance of being able to pick up the Ruiz team and take the prize as well. You are currently leading the three remaining teams by a fair margin."

"What's the offer?"

"Three million. Plus all the gifts and benefits we've discussed before."

Keith shook his head.

"Keith?" Frank said.

"Yeah."

"What do you think?"

"I think you're very bad at math." Though the idea was intriguing. With three million, he could live pretty well down in Mexico . . .

No! Stupid! You're a winner. You're in the lead. Three is not thirty.

Frank sighed. "It's our final offer," he said.

"No."

Silence for a time. "Your decision has been noted," Frank said. He didn't sound surprised.

Noted?

"What does that mean?" Keith said. Like, were they going to try to disqualify him or something?

Silence.

"Ass! What the hell does 'noted' mean?"

Silence.

"Fuck you, then!"

Silence. On and on.

Was it possible that he could run this whole thing and not win due to some technicality? No. No. He was a winner. He was going to win.

And if they tried to take that away from him, God help them.

ASTRONAUT

Evan hadn't believed Jere about Russia. Now he did. All it took was a couple of days of traveling into the hinterlands in the awful winter chill, grabbing cold-slick vinyl seats as their drivers deftly slid around potholes on the treacherous black-ice roads, potholes that looked as if they could hide black bears, potholes that looked like they could swallow the car, potholes so big and deep and dark they might have gone straight through to some beautiful tropical beach in Brazil.

Now they were standing under the bulk of the main launcher, all four of them, Evan and John Glenn and even Ron Gutierrez, his ever-smiling dad. Not really John Glenn, of course, but that's what everyone called him. Frank Sellers, another good generic white-boy name. He was a wannabe-astronaut, never really flew anything after his training in the 80s, something about the shuttle blowing up. Now he was training to fly the *Mars Enterprise* (some money from the Roddenberry estate). Frank was one of the concessions they'd won. The Russians could build it, fine, but it had to be an American pilot. The spikes on the preliminary audience surveys were real clear on that fact.

When Frank first came down, he'd referred to the *Enterprise* as the Trash Can, and the name had stuck. The comparison was apt. It was squatty and cylindrical, and it did have a utilitarian functionality, and it was even somewhat battered and dirty-looking.

"How goes it?" Evan said, after they'd made their intros.

"Good, good," Frank said. "We've had some problems with the electrical systems, nothing major, just the usual shakedown crap, and they're worried a bit about the air, but I think . . ."

"The air?" Ron said. "On a journey this long?"

Frank shrugged. "They'll make it work," he said.

"It doesn't seem very confidence-inspiring."

"If you could have seen half the stuff I saw behind the scenes at NASA, you wouldn't worry. These are good guys. They'll figure it out."

"If you say so."

The grand tour was less than impressive. Wires hung from open panels while teams of dirty Russians shot heated phrases back and forth with expressions of deep frustration and anger. There was a steady drip in the cockpit that tick-tick-ticked onto the synthetic material of the acceleration seat. When Ron ran a finger across it and looked up questioningly, Frank just shook his head. "Condensation. Can't help it with so many people in here. They'll flush it before we launch."

When they were back out in the freezing cold again, and well away from Russian ears, Ron turned to Jere and said, "Would you fly in this?"

"Of course," Jere said. Not a bit of hesitation. Not a bit. He knew how to deal with Dad.

The older man looked up and down the ship. "If you need more money . . ."

And be even more in your debt? "No," Jere said.

"You sure?"

I'm sure I don't want to hear you remind me about how you bailed me out again. Jere nodded and turned to Evan. "We're on schedule?"

"Unless Frank tells me different."

"We'll make it," Frank said. "No problemo."

Later, when they were back in the car for another freezing, terrifying ride back to the hotel, Ron spoke again.

"Do you get the feeling that Frank wants this to work a little too much?"

"How's that?" Evan said.

"He's an astronaut. But he never flew."

"So?"

A frown. "So maybe he wants to fly. Really badly."

"Sometimes a little enthusiasm is a good thing," Evan said.

Ron turned to Jere. "What do you think?"

Pretend to consider, then answer. "I think it's good we have someone who loves what he does."

Silence from Ron. Then: "I hope you're right."

PERFORMANCE

Last. Dead last. No denying it now. No excuses. It had taken them way too long to assemble the Wheel that morning, far longer than they had taken back on Earth. Blame it on the cold, or the parts that didn't want to fit together, but facts were facts.

And yet Glenn was strangely happy, oddly content. Just like that one freeclimb in Tibet, when it was clear they were beaten, hanging exhausted from numb fingertips beneath a thin sun rapidly disappearing behind a front of ominous purple-grey clouds. That moment when he realized they weren't going to make it, that they would have to go back down. The stress and the worry suddenly lifted from him. And his great surprise when Alena agreed with him. They scrambled down the rock as the icy rain hit.

They made love back in what passed for a hotel with incredible intensity, golden and yellow sparks flying in a perfect night sky, impossible to describe, infinite and endless in a moment's perfection. They finally collapsed, sated, face to face, sweat cooling to an icy chill in the cold room. He waited until her breathing had slowed, and lengthened, and deepened, then said, very softly, "Marry me."

Alena's eyes opened. In the dark they were like the glassy curve of two crystal spheres, unreadable.

"Yes," she said softly, and closed her eyes again.

Had he imagined it? Had she really heard him? He fell asleep with questions resonating in his mind.

When he woke in the morning, she was already pulling on her gear. Glenn had a moment of sleepy pleasure, watching her slim form, before he remembered his question—and her answer—from the night before.

She looked down at him. The light fell pale and grey on her face. She looked like the ghost of an angel.

"Yes," she said. "I said yes."

"Glenn!" Alena shrieked. "Watch out!"

Glenn jerked back to the present as the Wheel caromed off a boulder and promptly went bouncing across a field. He pulled on his harness and leaned outside of its edge, shortening the bounces on his side and bringing them back on course. They'd been experimenting with a new technique. Each of them leaned out the side of the Wheel, giving a better view of the terrain ahead than through the translucent dust-coated fabric, and allowing them to shift its direction more rapidly by leaning in and out to shift the center of gravity.

"Pay attention!" Alena said.

"I know, I know," Glenn said. "I'm sorry."

"What were you thinking?"

"Tibet," he said.

Silence for a time. "Oh."

"Remember?"

"I remember I don't like losing."

"We're making up time," Glenn said, after a while.

"I know."

"The others may have problems with the Kite."

Alena shot him a puzzled look. "Why are you trying to make me feel better?"

Because I love you, Glenn thought. *That's another thing I never wanted to lose.*

OVERSIGHT

The spooks came in the middle of February sweeps, just three months before launch. Jere and Evan were still trying to convince themselves that making the August sweeps would be better than February, but no matter how you garnished it or rationalized it, there would be less access in the summer. Now some of the sponsors wanted guaranteed access levels or kickbacks.

And now this.

"Mr. Gutierrez?" There were two of them, wearing indistinguishable blue suits. One of them wore a cheap black tie, the other a turtleneck. Their eyes were heavy and dead and immobile, and for once Jere was glad that his father was there with him.

He looked at the ID, not seeing the name. It was one of those new fancy holo things that they were trying to sell to everyone, but this one had a big NASA logo and a discreet little eye next to it. He was also wearing a small gold motion-holo pin that flashed and gleamed as the eye morphed into a world and back again. Underneath the holo were the etched letters: USG OVERSIGHT.

"Yes," Jere said.

Agent #1 turned to his father. "And you, sir?"

"I'm Ron."

"Ron . . ."

"Gutierrez."

"Ah. The father. We didn't know you had a stake in this."

"I'm an investor."

"Ah."

Jere held up a hand. "Would you like a seat? Coffee?"

Agent #1 sat. The other remained standing.

"What's this all about?" Jere asked. "Do you want to buy the program or something?"

"There will be no program."

"What!" Jere and Ron said, at once.

The agent just looked at them. "We can't permit the launch."

"You're going to stop a launch on Russian soil?"

"When the launch could be part of a terrorist attack, yes, I'm sure the Russians will cooperate."

"Terrorist! Where do you get that?"

"What if someone was to take over your launch, and turn it back at the US? How big of a crater could he make if it went down on a city?"

Ron's face was red. "That's . . . idiotic!"

"What do you want?" Jere asked.

"We want to prevent any possible attack on the United States."

Ron nodded, sudden understanding gleaming in his eyes. "China."

"Excuse me?"

"China's bitching about our program, aren't they?"

The agent shrugged. "It is your option to speculate."

"So what do you want?" Jere said. "How do we launch?"

"You don't. However, if you turn the program over to us, and allow us to send qualified observers, we would provide proper acknowledgement of your role in this endeavor."

"We can't do that!" Jere said. "What about our sponsors? They'll come for our heads. Hell, the Russian Mafia will come for our heads, too! We can't just hand this over to you."

"I'm sure we can placate the Russians. And your sponsors."

Jere slumped back in his chair. They could do almost anything they wanted. He could be picked up and whisked away and never seen again. He could have everything taken from him piece by piece, a Job job.

Taking their offer might be the best bet. Of course, he'd have to get Evan in on it, but maybe there was some way to profit from it anyway. When you were talking deep pockets, the government had the deepest pockets of all. Maybe they could spin it . . .

"No fucking way!" Ron said. His face was almost purple. He levered himself up out of his chair and went to tower over the seated agent. The standing one tensed, but didn't move.

Ron poked a finger in his chest. "We're not going to Mars to plant fucking flags!"

"Dad . . ."

"Shut up." Low and deadly.

"Did the fucking pilgrims come to plant fucking flags?" Ron said. "No! They came to get away from bureaucratic fucks like you! You assholes had your chance. How many billions did we give to you shitpoles? What did we get for it? Our lunar rovers in Chinese museums! A bunch of rusting hardware crash-landed on Mars. Thanks. Thanks a lot. Now it's our chance!"

Jere watched his dad, open-mouthed. He was frozen in place.

Agent #2 put his hand on Agent #1's shoulder and whispered something in his ear. Agent #1 nodded and stood up.

"So you refuse to turn over the program?"

"Damn fuckin' right," Ron said.

The two swiveled to look at Jere. "And does he speak for you?"

Jere looked at his father. He looked back steadily, intently. He nodded, just a fraction.

"Get out of here," Jere said.

I hope you're right, Dad, he thought. *Or we're both dead.*

MIRAGE

Leaving the IBM package was one thing, but the slide was inexcusable. Geoff Smith squeezed his eyes shut tight. If only he could turn back the clock! All it would have taken was a glance and a five-second diversion, and everything would have been alright.

Now, his best possible fate was winning a prize. And then having to endure the endless interviews that came after it.

And now, flying over the rugged Martian terrain, it looked like they might actually have a chance. Chatter from the Can: the felon's Kite setup wasn't going smoothly, his lead had evaporated, and every second left him farther behind. The extreme sports geeks had never really been in the running. They'd been slow at everything.

Money, he thought dreamily, opening his eyes, watching the landscape pass below. *Money money money*.

He'd hoped that he could make another slide as Laci and Wende built the Kite, but his water was lost and they didn't let him have the time. And truth was, he didn't really feel like it. He was in a haze, as if losing the slide had taken all the fight out of him.

Of course, he could scope the dust all he wanted when they were back on the Can, but that would be surface dust. What if the dust had to be from a few feet down? Or what if the dust had to be from near the water flows that they had seen from MGS, so many years ago? What if he'd never had a chance at all, and they knew that, and they didn't care? His thoughts whirled like a cyclone, all destructive energy and dark currents.

Wende looked back at him from the pilot's sling and smiled at him. Geoff tried to smile back, but his lips felt frozen in place. After a moment, Wende turned away and gestured at Laci. Laci looked back at him and frowned.

Yes, I know you don't like me, he thought. *You've made that abundantly clear. Now turn back around and be a good copilot.*

Laci was probably thinking how much faster they would be running if he accidentally fell off. He looked up nervously at his tether, but it was solid and unfrayed.

His head swam for a moment, and he shook it. His

vision blurred and doubled as if his head was a giant bell that had just been struck. He gripped his perch tighter and held still. After a moment, it passed. The landscape streamed by beneath him, soothing and hypnotic.

We've always looked down at the surface of Mars and imagined things. First, God of War. Next, an arid desert world where intelligence clung to life with massive feats of engineering. Then the dead and dry thing we knew today.

But it wasn't dead! He knew there was life here.

The landscape had changed again from dunefield to dark rocks, rectilinear and almost artificial in appearance. It reminded him of ancient Mayan ruins. Or was it Egypt? Or Stonehenge?

Details swam and ran and resolved themselves again. The rectilinear lines became sharper and more regular. Now he could see individual stones, etched into fantastic designs by the passage of time.

Etched? By what? He shook his head again, and details leaped out: fantastic whorls and patterns, ancient art of the highest order. It wasn't etched by weather. It was etched by intelligence!

Were those patterns he saw in the sand as well? Did they cover ancient squares where people once gathered? For a blinding instant, he could see the entire city as it had stood towering over the rough Martian surface . . .

"Stop!" he cried. His voice sounded strangely high and strangled.

"What?" Wendy said. "Why?"

"It's them!" Geoff said. "Intelligence! The city below us . . . there's a city below us!"

The two looked down, scanning back and forth with puzzled looks.

"Geoff?" Wende said. "What are you talking about?"

"The city! Look at the stones! They're square! Look at the language on them!"

"Geoff, that isn't funny."

A crackle. The voice of Frank Sellers from the Can. "What do you see?"

"A city," Geoff said. "The remains of a city. Stones! Writing! Decoration!"

"Land," Frank said.

"No way!" Laci said.

"The Roddenberry clause says you have to investigate any overt evidence of life," Frank said. "Sorry."

"But there's nothing below us!" Wende said. "Just a rockfield."

"Land. You have to. Contract breach if you don't."

"Shit!" Laci said. Wende grumbled, but they began to fall from the sky.

"Turn around," Geoff said. "The best part is behind us."

Wende wheeled around and he saw it all, the geometric perfection, the ancient city and all its splendor.

"I still don't see it," Wende said. "Frank, can you review our last imagery?"

"Yep," Frank said. "Continue landing. It'll take me a few minutes."

Wende picked a relatively clear section of sand and for a moment they were all acting as landing gear, running over the sand.

Geoff 's legs felt heavy and weak, and he buckled under the weight of the Kite. Down this close, he could see nothing. Rocks were just rocks. Sand was just sand. There was no great city.

"Geoff? You alright?" That was Wende. Pretty Wende. Nice of her to think about him.

Frank's voice crackled back on. "False alarm," he said. "I don't see anything other than some regular volcanic cracking. That's probably what fooled you, Geoff."

"I'm no fool!" he shouted. He had seen it! He had!

Silence for a time. Finally: "What does Geoff look like? Is he blue?"

"No," Wende said. "But he looks funny. Patchy, splotchy. Oh, shit. Does he have a bug?"

"More likely an oxy malfunction. He may be cranked up too high. Funny, that usually doesn't cause hallucinations, but . . ."

"I saw it!" Geoff cried.

Wende was shrugging out of her harness.

"No," Laci said. "Wende, get back in your harness. We need to fly!"

"It'll only take a minute," Frank said.

"It won't kill him."

"Yes it will. Eventually."

"Then we take the chance."

Wende had stopped shrugging out of her harness, under Laci's hard glare. Frank said nothing. Geoff watched them for a moment, thinking, *I saw it! I did! I really did!* There was a distant babble on the comm and things got very bright.

Then Wende's face bent over him. "I'm not like the other monster," she said. "Let's get him fixed up."

"Good girls," Frank said. "Here, open his panel and look for . . ."

He said it would only take a minute, but it took over ten. When they were all back on board and soaring into the sky, even the Rothman team had passed them.

RETRACTION

NASA came back. This time with two grinning executives and their own camera crew. Following them were fifty thousand people who jammed the Burbank streets in cars and on bikes and on foot, holding banners saying "Free Enterprise!" and "New frontiers, not new Oversight!" and of course, "NASA SUCKS!"

Jere and Evan couldn't help grinning.

Within a day, the video of the NASA/Oversight shakedown had been posted on a thousand message boards and ten thousand blogs. The raw video almost brought the AV IM network to its knees in the US, Japan, France, Russia, and even parts of China. A thousand pundits spouted off about "The New Stalin," "The New Face of Censorship," the fact that the Constitution had long been paved over, the free-enterprise foundation of the country, and the "Taking of the New Frontier."

The New Frontier had struck the core audience like a well-spoken diatribe supporting socialized health care at a meeting of Reformed Republicans. Survivalists polished their weapons and streamed out of the Sierras and Appalachians and half-forgotten Nebraska missile silos to demonstrate. TrekCon 18 turned into a huge caravan that converged on Sacramento, trapping senators in their buildings, demanding the governor secede so that Neteno could go about its business. Eventually, over a million people gathered there, some in overalls and prickly beards and armed with shotguns, some wearing Klingon outfits, some housewives in SUVs, some businessmen who worked in aviation and space and engineering. In three days, two slogans were posted at over ten million websites, plastered on bumper stickers, hung from suction-cups behind windows: *Free Enterprise*, and *Give Us New Frontiers*.

Three days after the video hit the net, Jere received a discreet phone call from a higher-up at NASA/Oversight. Jere made his own counteroffer.

A day after that, he received another phone call, politely accepting the prime sponsorship for the mission, for a price greater than the entire funds they had collected to date. The launch would go forward as planned. Jere and Evan were still the primes. The only difference was that there would be another discreet logo added on the ship and the suits.

Evan looked at Jere as the NASA muckty spouted off about "New Partnership with Business," and how wonderful this opportunity was under the big Neteno sign out in front of the building. The press had built a wall around the crowd with cameras and laptops and transmission equipment. The crowd looked happy, vindicated, relieved. As if they were thinking, *Good, good, we still have the power, we still live in a free country*.

"We are proud to be able to support this effort," the muckty said. "For less than the cost of a single robotic Mars lander, we are sending the first manned mission to Mars. With this mission, we have again leaped ahead of the

Chinese. We see this as a model for future exploration of space: USG Oversight and private industry, working hand-in-hand to accomplish our goals."

Some applause, some boos, some catcalls. But it was done. They were back on track. It even got them their advertising hook: Free Enterprise. That was really catching on in a big way, simmering around the net.

So now it's more than a game, he thought. *It's a demonstration of some of the things that people will need to do to conquer the red planet. Or at least we spin it that way.*

He looked at Evan and his hard, unblinking eyes.

To him, it was still just a game.

A game played hard, winner take all.

DYING

Frank was lying to them again. Mike Kinsson didn't blame him. What was he going to tell them otherwise? *Sorry, you're out of luck, best to just ditch the headers and pop off quick.*

"We're still seeing if we can rig one of the Returns for remote operation," Frank said.

"How much longer?" Juelie whined.

It was the morning of the third day. Later, Mike would go and wander around. Juelie and Sam looked like two teenagers who had just discovered sex, and they were probably happy to have the privacy. He'd already walked over to the nearby cliffs, turning over rocks, hoping beyond hope to see the tell-tale carpet of a lichen. He still remembered the first time his mother and father had taken him to the Griffith Observatory, and they had talked about what life might be like on other planets. Lichens and primitive plants for Mars, they'd said. It had fascinated him in a way that nothing had ever done, before or since.

"We're hoping to have a definitive answer by the end of the day," Frank said.

"What if it takes longer?" Sam said.

"Then we wait."

"We're running out of food!" Juelie said.

"We know. Please conserve your energy."

They both looked at Mike. Mike looked right back at them, thinking, *Like what you were doing wasn't more strenuous than my walk.*

He edged away from them. What would they do when they found out there really wasn't any rescue coming? Maybe it would be best just to wander off, and stay wandered off.

"He's walking away!" Juelie said.

"Mild physical exertion won't hurt," Frank said.

They didn't come after him.

He walked past the cliffs from the day before and came to a place where sand and rocks made a steep slope down into a small valley. Rivulets had been cut in the surface of the slope, some still knife-edged.

He remembered old satellite images. Could he be near a place where water was near the surface? He paused to dig into one of the little channels, but turned up only dry sand and dust and pebbles.

He wandered on. He'd keep walking and see where his feet took him. Until it was time to lie down and turn down the heaters as far as they went. Maybe some real pioneer, fifty years from now, would find his desiccated body and say, *This is the other guy, the one who wandered away from camp.*

It wasn't a pleasant thought.

But it was better than imagining Juelie and Sam, when the real news came down.

LAUNCH

Russian summer was the same as Russian winter, except the black ice had been replaced by mud. And it was an entire caravan this time, reporters and pundits and hangers-on, all loudly complaining about the facilities. They swarmed the tiny town, like ants on a dead cockroach.

Reporters slept in taverns, in houses, in barns, in the street if they had to. NO FOOD signs hung from many of the restaurants and bars.

"Shouldn't they pay us extra for the tourism?" Evan said.

"It won't last," Jere said.

"Sure it will. There are enough bored reporters around here to crank out five thousand local-interest pieces. And people will travel anywhere."

Then it was launch day, and Jere didn't know how to feel. He should be worried. He should be thinking about what would happen if the whole shebang blew up on the ground. If that happened, everyone would howl for blood. They would be crucified. If they were lucky.

All because they didn't get their daily dose of excitement. A-muse-ment, Ron used to call it. Non-thinking. To muse is to think, and to A-muse was not to think. Which is what most people wanted. Give them a roof and food and someone to screw, let them buy a few shiny things from time to time, and all they really cared about was filling the gaping void of their lives. They didn't want to muse. They wanted to A-muse.

And God help the person who promised amusement, but didn't come through.

It was a short ride to the launch site. The crowd outside the gates parted for them as they drove to the official grandstand and made their way to the little box at the top. Ron collapsed in his seat with a grunt. Jere and Evan bookended him. They were sitting on camp chairs that looked like they could have come from a Napoleonic campaign.

"Crunch time," Evan said softly.

"Yes," Ron said.

"Anyone in a betting mood?" He rubbed his hands.

"Shut up," Ron said.

Again, Jere was glad to have the old man. Without Ron, Evan would have woven a web tighter and tighter. Evan still held too many purse strings, and was hiding a lot of money, but they could deal with that later.

Ahead of them, the ship towered over the bleak landscape. Gleaming steel and clouds of vapor, a high-tech pillar aimed at the deep blue sky.

One minute. The few people on the field scampered to cover.

Ten seconds.

Jere held his breath.

The numbers flickered down on the big board.

There was an explosion of light and a mind-numbing roar. The Plexiglas windows of the little booth jittered and shook.

Jere held up a hand to shield his eyes. *It's exploded, it's all over, it's done, I'm done.*

But then the cheering of the crowd roused him. He looked at them in disbelief. What were they cheering for? Were they crazy? Did they actually want to see blood?

Then his father pointed and shouted, "Look!"

The pillar was rising into the sky.

Slowly at first, then faster. It was a hundred feet up. Two hundred. Then as tall as a skyscraper, balancing on a long white tail of flame. The wind battered the grandstand and beat at the throngs, standing hundreds deep. The smell of burnt mud and concrete worked its way into the shelter. Sand and dust and grit pattered against the Plexiglas.

My God, Jere thought, as *Mars Enterprise* rose higher. Its flame no longer touched the Earth. It gathered speed like a jet, shrinking smaller and faster as it rose up and arced out.

Eventually, the roar reduced itself to a shout, then a mild grumbling. *Mars Enterprise* was a bright speck in the sky.

They had done it.

"Congratulations," Ron said.

"For what?" Jere said.

His dad allowed himself a thin grin. "You've done something that no government has ever been able to do."

"But . . . it wasn't . . . it was just a . . ."

Ron held up a hand. "Shh," he said.

HONEYMOON

"Come on!" Alena said. "Come on come on come on!"

The Can had been embargoing the status of the teams for an hour, but Glenn knew they were close. They'd made it from dead last to nearly tied with the Paul guy before the Can shut up.

"What can I do?" he asked.

"I don't know! I was talking to the Kite, not you!"

"I'll think positive thoughts."

"Good for you!"

Glenn smiled. And what could he do, other than stay lashed up under the belly of the Kite for minimum aerodynamic drag? Nothing.

The next one they should make more manual, he thought. *Human-powered Kites and Wheels. None of this motor crap.*

"Look!" Alena pointed.

Glenn strained his eyes. Very far in the distance, he could just catch the glint of metal. "Is that it?"

"Yeah, that's it! Come on come on come on come on!"

Alena looked at him, and he saw the girl who he'd fallen in love with, the woman he'd proposed to. She was smiling, her color high and eyes flashing. It was impossible not to love her when she was winning.

Where was Paul? If the race was as close as he thought, he should be able to see his Kite, bright white against the pale sky. He scanned from left to right, but saw nothing.

Whoever makes it to the Returns, wins. They were automatic. There was no way to race to orbit.

Another look. No Kite. Was it possible that Paul had run into trouble? Could they really be first?

Karma will get you all the time, he thought.

From ahead of them, a bright flare. The Kite rocked as Alena started violently.

"No!" she said. "No no no no no!"

"Paul," Glenn said.

"How much longer?" Alena asked.

"A couple of minutes. But it's . . ."

"Go faster!"

"It only takes three minutes to orbit!"

"I don't care!" Her face was twisted into a mask of anguish.

Glenn fell silent and let the only sound be that of the rushing wind and roaring motor. The Return field grew ahead of them, big enough so they could see the remains of Paul's Kite. He had had a hard landing.

When they landed, Alena scrambled to the nearest Return pod and began the launch prep. But when the prep was still less than halfway done, the voices from the Can came back. This time it was the female PA. She sounded tired.

"We have a winner," she said. "Keith Paul is now back on board the *Mars Enterprise*. To our other teams, thank you for a great competition. Please travel safely on your way back. There's no need to hurry now."

"No!" Alena wailed. She beat on the low bench of the Return pod. Glenn tried to gather her in his arms, but she pushed him away violently. He tumbled out onto the cold sand and lay for a moment, stunned, staring up at the alien sky.

"Glenn?" Glenn shook his head, but said nothing.

"Glenn?" Frightened.

She came out of the pod and knelt atop him, her eyes red from crying. "Glenn!" she said, shaking him.

"What?" he said.

"Glenn, I can't hear you! Are you okay?"

"What?" He reached behind him and felt the suit's radio. It seemed okay. Of course, he could have hit something in his fall . . . He shrugged and gave her the thumb-and-forefinger "OK" sign.

"I heard you hit and a big hiss and I thought you'd broken your header." She was crying even more now, big tears hitting the inside of her header and running down toward her chest.

He pushed his header to hers. "I'm okay," he said.

"I can hear you now."

"Yeah, old trick."

She helped him up. The Return pod gaped open like a mouth.

"Let's go," she said.

"Wait a minute." Glenn looked from the Return pods—all four of them—to the sky, and then toward the east, where the Ruiz team was stranded.

Could they? Would it be possible to fly over to the Ruiz team and pick them up? Would they have enough fuel? Could they refuel?

"Alena," he said. "Do you want to be a real winner?"

She got it. Her eyes got big, and she nodded. She stayed helmet-to-helmet with him as she called the Can.

"Frank," she said. "Let's talk about the Ruiz team."

SHOW

Evan, again with his presentations. In the darkness of Jere's office, animated charts showed realtime Viewing Audience, feedback Ratings, inferred Attentiveness, inferred Buyer Motivation, plotted against Neteno's historicals and an average of other Linear, Free-Access networks.

"We broke the 'Near downtrend," Jere said. "Broke it hard."

"We should have charged more for the advertising," Evan said. "VA times BM is a record for 'Near networks, maybe even interactives."

"We're swimming in money."

"Or we could up the ad rates midcourse. They won't desert now."

"Or we could just do another show."

"Not with the average sequel return at fifty-eight percent," Evan said.

Jere frowned. That was a big hole. Unless they could keep costs down. And maybe they could. All the development was done, after all . . .

"Don't even think it," Evan said.

"What?"

"Doing another show."

"I'm not."

Evan shook his head. "I know that look. That starry-eyed shit that gave us the second *Star Wars* threequel. The one with that irritating droopy bastard, whatever his name was . . ."

Jere shuddered. "I know who you're talking about."

"Point is, this show ain't golden. And we aren't perfect. Leave it now and let them clamor for more."

"Like *Star Trek*."

"Damn right. Don't come back till they're jonesing for it."

Jere nodded. *We're on top,* he thought. *We're the magnet. Let the ideas come to us for a while.*

And let that be enough.

WINNER

"I won, right?" Keith Paul said.

"Yeah," Frank said.

"I'll get the money?"

"Yeah."

"So where are the cameras?"

Frank ripped off his earplug and pushed away from the comm board. He grabbed Keith's shirt with both hands and pulled him close. The momentum took them off the floor, spinning through *Mars Enterprise*'s command center.

"There are no cameras!" Frank yelled. His eyes were wide and bright, quivering with that adrenaline-fueled, amped-up look that guys got when they were ready to take you apart with their bare hands. Keith had seen that look a few times in his life, and he knew one thing: he wanted absolutely no part of it.

"Nobody fucking cares about you!" Frank screamed, shaking Keith like he was made out of tissue. "Everyone's watching the real fucking heroes now! You'll get your goddamned money, just like you wanted, but don't expect anyone to care! Now fuck off! I've got important things to do!"

Frank gave him one last shove, pushing Keith into the bulkhead above. His head clanged on metal and he saw stars.

"Okay, man, okay," Keith said, as Frank drifted slowly back down and took his seat.

"Get out of here," Frank said.

HEROES

"Look at these showboating dickweeds," Evan said.

In the hushed velvet darkness of the live feed room, Evan's words were incredibly loud. Technicians swiveled to look at him, then turned quickly away when they saw Jere and Ron.

They were all looking at the competitive feeds. The slice-and-dice screen showed the story. Fox, Helmers, and the SciFi Channel were all tuned on a crappy little town down in Mexico, where a slim needle was being assembled in a shabby old warehouse. Outside, a makeshift derrick grew from a field of concrete. And some hairy guy wearing a dirty coverall was talking about building a colony ship to send to Mars. He called it *Mayflower II*.

"They timed it," Evan said. "Perfect. They wait till we have the Ruiz team back safe and sound, then they spring this shit."

But it was nothing, Jere thought. Just an incomplete ship. A bunch of nuts talking about open-source technology and crap like that. Who cared?

"They knew the ratings would die the instant everyone was back in the Can," Evan said. "They knew it, and they are fucking taking it!"

"What are the ratings like?" Jere said.

Evan shook his head and clicked on the realtime feed. The downward spike was still small, but he could see it accelerating. As he watched, it clicked down a few pixels more.

"Do we have anyone down in Mexico?" Evan said. "Can we get a line on this colony crap, too?"

"No," Jere said.

"Shit. Shit-shit."

It's just a news story, Jere thought. *One they'll forget as soon as they log off.*

But Ron was watching the competitive feeds, his jaw set hard, his eyes bright and glassy. Intent. Hungry. Excited. Jere knew that look. He shivered.

"Get on camera," Ron said, not looking away from the feeds.

"What?" Evan said.

"Get your butts down to the newsroom and get on camera now!" Ron said, finally looking at them. "Before they all tune out."

"Why?" Jere said.

"Tell them this is what you wanted. *Winning Mars* wasn't just a show. This is what you intended all along."

"But we didn't . . ."

"Yes," Ron said. "You did."

In the blue light of the monitors, Evan's expression of confusion suddenly bloomed into an excited smile.

"Will it work?" Jere said, looking at Ron.

Evan made a disgusted noise. "You probably believed the one about Washington never telling any lies, didn't you?"

In the monitors, another talking head, saying they wanted to launch sometime in the next twenty-four months. Looking scared.

They'll never make it, Jere thought.

They'll fucking die up there.

But if they do . . .

Ron, looking at the slice-and-dice, openly smiling now.

"Come on," Evan said. "Let's go make our legacy."